The Polls of Heaven

by C. Paul Owens

PITTSBURGH, PENNSYLVANIA 15238

The contents of this work including, but not limited to, the accuracy of events, people, and places depicted; opinions expressed; permission to use previously published materials included; and any advice given or actions advocated are solely the responsibility of the author, who assumes all liability for said work and indemnifies the publisher against any claims stemming from publication of the work.

All Rights Reserved
Copyright © 2017 by C. Paul Owens

No part of this book may be reproduced or transmitted, downloaded, distributed, reverse engineered, or stored in or introduced into any information storage and retrieval system, in any form or by any means, including photocopying and recording, whether electronic or mechanical, now known or hereinafter invented without permission in writing from the publisher.

RoseDog Books
585 Alpha Drive, Suite 103
Pittsburgh, PA 15238
Visit our website at *www.rosedogbookstore.com*

ISBN: 978-1-4809-7781-5
eISBN: 978-1-4809-7804-1

The Author dedicates this book to his daughters, Paula Owens and Patricia (Trish) McNeely, for their persistence and encouragement to stay with it. Also thanks to son-in-law Tim McNeely for pushing the communication forward. The words are mine, but the final product was a group effort.

About the Author

A native of Mt. Vernon, KY, he was born May 3, 1924, making him eligible for WWII. He spent three years in the Navy, two of those in the Pacific. He had almost completed his first year at Berea College, being released two weeks early at the request of the draft board, and given credit by the College.

During his time in the Navy, he helped edit various journals and unit information papers. In particular, he worked on a pony daily at Midway (Sand Island), and did radio for the island broadcast KMTH.

Upon Naval discharge, he earned a B.S. in Journalism and later a Master's Degree in Political Science at the University of Kentucky. He was associated with radio stations in Lexington and Lebanon, publishing a newspaper in the latter city. He later moved to Eastern Kentucky to serve as President of a deep mine coal company. After selling his newspaper and mining interests, he came back to Lexington to serve as News Director for the University of Kentucky. Upon retirement, he wrote a novel called Bavarian Rhapsody, which he self-published and promoted, making it virtually unknown.

He has been married to the same woman (Helen) for almost seventy years, and is the father of two daughters, Patricia (Tim) McNeely, and Paula. As a Civil War buff he visited most battlefields and donated several war artifacts along with 2,000 books on Lincoln and the war to a library in Richmond, Ky.

His hobbies also included giving lectures on Abraham Lincoln to Rotary clubs and other groups in Central and Eastern Ky. He was a member of the Rotary Club, the American Legion and the VFW. He directed a couple of plays and assisted in recruiting smaller actors for a Civil War based movie made in KY.

Preface

An early morning, on a mountain glory, its celebrated promise of another good day with its expected cool night left over to sunshine. It was like a bit of Heaven to the country schoolboy, Clint Greene leaned against the rail fence where his brogans had carved a recess in the weeded ground about three feet back of the gravel road on a long ago promising morning just like this one. He had waited for the big brand new and heated school bus which would take him off the mountain to the high school by the river in the valley below.

The narrow worn wagon way called a road cut its way through the wild possum grass that briefly touched his family's apple orchard, his now by Roman common law bequest. The boy, man now, yet too soon on the edge of the aging by the speeded up hour that is time's curse on all life, would cherish always this spot so decreed in a carefree creation moment just for him.

In Heaven's blessing to his home on a Kentucky mountain, there was not a break in Earth's harmony with the sun and its promised seasonal reappearance day after day in the higher hills bowing to the east that his people had appropriated rights to. In the sense of eternity's power the dawn arrived along the mountaintops' edge where it had reigned since man's beginning days on Earth, now home to a pubescent hill lad as his first tread upon the stairway to Heaven from this small planet that the gods had chosen for his temporary home.

The early calm held him tightly. In its welcome as it announced new life to the old and green and the beautiful, it excited the escape of the night to the boy as he turned to face the north toward the Bluegrass of Kentucky. It was an awareness of life in the dream of a mountain boy in made-over hand-me-down overalls from his father.

He'd been lucky. His high schooling came just as the county had brought on the big yellow bus. It replaced the sideboards of a coal truck that the county had hired for the past five years to stop and pick up the country school kids, demanding that they stand crowded in the open air for the ride into town.

Today, little less than a half hour from now, if he stayed on his ground, he'd greet the same old sun of his boyhood .In this enchanted moment, he could take in the light of the lingering moon guarding its earth which in its blessedness revealed a silver glamour among the few fruit trees called an orchard as his dad said it was, but sharing the farm's moment with a couple of pines and a scattering of woods of many another name by the early Scot settlers in these Appalachian backwaters.

By the full moon's light amid the tiny forest's night beds the shadows along and astern of the trees called up the mystique that each man or woman who wished to view Heaven before the end of his time in this world called Earth would know they had looked upon the tents of the universe.

It was the moment of creation and it was the gift of the gods, certainly of his God; he was pleased to know that he still believed. It was the crescendo of a symphony by Tchaikovsky, or perhaps Wagner. It deserved to serve as prelude to the dawn which would come as ever with its promise of beginning again.

A grand show such as this early hour emerged into day, the waning night that was neither day nor night, but both had inspired Maurice Utrillo, French painter of a people and their trophies in towns of art in edifice and easy pathways along mystical misty evenings or dawn roads. (A print of the artist's quiet scene, at day's end, had hung over Clint Greene's family fireplace of his home for as long as the boy could recall.)

Perhaps it was an inspired moment of memory that again called this Twentieth Century boy/man back to the mountain of his youth where he would die amid recollection of what was a better time.

It was after his wife Lily's death and loss of his newspaper that should have been his life's dream fulfillment —- yet became in the separation of both a tortured and banished moment from the small city up north in Ohio which in turn had come laced with wish for escape to a man who had walked in his own pastures down south which had defined for him in memory an abundant life without pain, that it would always be.

Clint's reverie was broken by the suffering bang-clap-bang of an old engine in tugs of hurt that had come out of the darkness to his left. With its twin nightlights the driver of the ancient GM pick-up better announced his approach along the narrow fearful skyway.

Neighbor Gus Angus McNew, as Scottish as they come in deed and shared glad life except for his hard work hands and his color, had learned that Clint Greene would be in need of transportation to the depot downtown for the first leg of his journey to the flat country in the north quite early on this day. A night phone call sealed the promise.

It was a familiar and welcome sound from Clint's boy's life on the mountain; Gus in his ancient machine, at least his third from that many earlier owners, dearly bought to assist in his efforts to feed his family which came with a baneful threat to his race intended to isolate his people to another realm. Since the beginning of time he'd accepted his tentative stature. He had endured the many taunts by his fellow earthlings, creatures under the same God though with nothing more than a different set of manners.

Estrangement from the dominant society in which Gus and his family lived had always been his vaguely tolerated days since the fall of the tower of Babel had scattered its builders and divided their tongues to all edges of the Earth, ever reminding him that all men all women are born to suffer and die, then in death to give account for a life on Earth Tending his four acres and offering his truck as dray service to the townspeople had kept Gus and his family from starvation during Clint's life awareness of life among them.

Before Clint's father died he reminded his son to honor Gus and his family despite threats that were made against them by the greater society. "They may have been brought here as slaves," he said, "but they were sent here to the new land for a greater reason. In your lifetime you quite likely will have become aware of it. They came here, some believe, and I accept it along with the others of a different shading of color, to save the white man, son of the founding fathers, save him from himself. It's good to be here on the same land with men like Gus, Twentieth Century American." Clint thanked his father for saying it.

As they scooted down the hill Gus was talking (above the noise of the engine) how the weather was changing. "It's not like it used to be, when you could depend on it for th' plantin' and then th' harvest. Does all kinds o' crazy things . . . right here's where Buddy Q. Evans went off th' road an' slid all th' way t' th' bottom. Lived, but he's been crippled up ever since."

Clint said: "I'm ever leery of this spot in the road . . . steepest here. If I was still in news, I'd write an editorial, maybe get something like a fence built here."

"Reckon you could? Ever done anything like that before?" asked Gus Angus.

Clint thought for a moment. "Ever once in a while I believed that we in the news business thought we might possibly do just that. William Allen White, a friend of Teddy Roosevelt and other presidents of his tine, wrote an editorial: 'What's the matter with Kansas?' which got lots of action, too, not only in Kansas, but throughout the whole country."

"Several hotshot editors of hungry newspapers have been trying ever since to say the same thing. Seldom if ever I reckon did it work for them."

"I know one publisher who could never understand why it didn't do the same thing for him; came close to going broke, but he won a lot of awards. But no award I ever heard of would put honest food on the table."

Gus said: "I always figured you fellers on newspapers had a lot of power. I'm not an educated man, just heard men say so."

They both were silent for a moment. Clint was searching for a brief response better given by a student of political science in the new era of political correctness that seemed to dictate the actions of most men and women as citizens these days.

Gus helped, still on the same wave length, "Get 'em to do something about a fence for this road before somebody runs off the road and gets killed."

Clint realized that he needed to talk about his recent problems in the news business, taking fair advantage of the brief lull in their conversation that Gus had provided, but the pause awarded Gus a reason to lean into another subject:

"Reckon you heard about two more bodies having turned up, one on each side of the county?" It was in the form of a question.

"The late news last night says the two men died with their throats cut like that first one," he said.

"I haven't heard much about that first feller, not since I came home. We newsmen let too much of that sort of thing pass over us almost routinely, since we are every day dealing with it for our news columns. Forgive me. Go ahead with what you know."

"I can't say anything more about these two last victims," said Gus, "except that the TV news feller said they appeared to be from outside of these mountains, and both of the same sort of people as the first victim, which turned up a few weeks ago. These two fellers were not Caucasian. Yet they might have come from a place like the the Caucasus, though, what I once read 'bout it. They had that kind of complexion; sort of olive, like me. They said that they were not Africans," Gus was quick to add.

They crossed the river and turned right to the city's outer limits, just beyond the depot beside the water tower which soon would be giving up its burden to the passing of the steam engine. The train hadn't arrived.

Gus deposited Clint at the station saying few words more and roared the engine of his old bent truck, turning around in the depot lot to head back up the mountain. "You try an' have a real good day," he said. Clint thanked him, watched the truck disappear into the dark of what was left of an almost moonless night.

Old Gus bore the name of a Scot landowner and owner of slaves who at the end of the practice had given up his indentured-for-life people to the new law that offered them their freedom. He would be surprised that among their descendants were men with a rare knighthood like Gus who apparently loved everybody without even a tinge of bitterness; Clint had to ask himself, just why should he love the white man?

That left Clint in the few minutes before the train to think about one of Gus's queries about any meanness around his friend's part of the country where Clint had lived up in Ohio.

"You better believe it," said Clint. "It's everywhere these days. I never understood what it is that has happened in our blessed country to make people like that. It's enough to bewilder all thinking men and women, but to the point of not enough to cause them active concern."

"Maybe for a little while something as serious or even life threatening like that will occupy the news until something else just as screaming in the headlines comes along."

"So many think that an order of meanness which others endured through what they considered an era of mal-adjustment, will pan out with forgiveness as those people get too fat on it. It's time's blessing that right around the bend comes the good life once more."

"They really haven't given up the old for the new. Everything seems to just get worse, though; people keep getting meaner, and it's affecting more of our people every day," Clint told Gus.

"This change in society that is surely coming, as we right now are ruled by iron fists I reckon because people believe there is nothing they can do about it. So many people decide to join everybody else and conform with the times, maybe just play-acting, like they'd been set free of their sins somehow and could start all over again."

"It used to bother me because they used to talk about us down here," said Gus, "how we hillbillies invented the feud between kin and kith. How we killed one another because it was a deed that we had to do. Reckon it's now all over the country; what happens at the end of days."

"People, as far as I see it, are getting all nervous about it, not about the meanness, but more about God's power to put a hard end to it all an' not do it soon enough. The preachers down here talk more lately about it. And money, I reckon a lack of it by so many lonely and scarit people is the worst thing. They's more people than ever that are so full of meanness because they'll never have it like most everybody else but who just lately say that they enjoy not having it. They protest in rags and false sympathy. Those that do have money won't get to spend all the money they got socked away before th' end o' time, an' that bothers 'em."

Gus talked on, disturbed by the news of the recent killings around the county - more lately he said so than in the old days, and of his own survival back then. Clint was sure that Gus had studied all a man is allowed to know about the future safety of himself and his family. Right now Clint didn't want to hear Gus talk about life and death, even back to his ancestors' time in a limited world, how so many of his tribe in Africa and especially in America, so many, had died with a rope around their necks and a tree limb.

Clint didn't want to think more about it, but it was on his mind where Gus had put it, as he waited for the rude interruption of a civilized roar the train to come in its own way again and the calm of the night to return. Gus had gunned his own old noisy rattletrap of a machine and taken off for the mountains. Soon the dark of night was back, and all was still again. He wished another train passenger would come along to take his mind off all these fears that had begun to trouble him and Gus. He reckoned it was so with about everybody. He met a lot of worried faces on the street these days.

It was now in the dimness of night just before dawn, when it was darkest almost with no moon. Down here in the valley, fog from the river wasn't about to let the moon as it was on most nights in its shining Sunday night best steal scenes and imagination of Heaven like he'd just left back on his mountain. If ever people all over his country needed reminders that real beauty was out there in days of a peaceful past and that they still existed intermittently on much of Earth's wide spread, it was now.

After applying his quest to doing the higher dedicated things to which he thought he had a calling, to Clint it would be many of the better expectations that would return as he charted his next move that came and went during his hibernation in the warmth of his family mountain cabin. Recent nightly laid plans in bed began to fade after three days. He recalled the sweat and Heaven's testing in the midst of such beautiful hopes arriving threatening, he lamented, on the back of a sore horse, with the phrase: "What's the use?"

Yet boyhood dreams demanded that he be about his business; great things he'd do with his life occupied rare times for the hopeful day to come after he left the Corps.

He thought about it as other men, mostly fellow veterans in college on the GI Bill, said much the same thing. He hadn't set goals that would influence his tendency to change course even after land was sighted.

Confusing him were blue skies, lazy days along the riverbanks, mountaintops close to the sky. Every boy and man and girl of wonder and hope should have been accorded a part of the dream of what life and with Mother Nature's resolve was there just for them. So he asked himself: is this really what was intended for me?

To someone who hoped retirement meant an hour or three extra hours for sleep until he met the promises of the new day, our protagonist first felt cheated one recent late night while setting the alarm for four on the clock in the morning . . .

L&N Number Twenty-four of the Lebanon branch had pulled in and now sat at the end of the depot platform as usual boasting like other engines of the line that it was right 'on time.' By now it was four forty-two a.m. The night's cool came in welcome to chase away the heat that lingered through most of the night; the 'desert's blast' would return come full morning.

He hadn't worn a jacket. If he found what he'd hoped for once he hit the big town, he couldn't allow his visit to friends between train and bus by carrying the burden during a stop in Mount Vernon be heavier in longer hours than what he planned was a little while.

To the hill people a little after four in summer is the best hour to arise for another day's work, but it's not railroad time. That would be for another honest hour to these people, until first light, when the arrogant summer heat's promise would begin to embrace the entire valley and the day. The weather to a chosen tiller of the land during the summer's heated raiment and the winter's bite is accommodated, haughty maybe like by a work boss but minded.

Our protagonist: even at that early hour suddenly found that he wasn't the train's only passenger. Squeezing past the conductor to allow them to follow if they could make up their minds were three young women who in a last second of the eleven minutes allowed for a stop for the train's brief water rest came from a big black car that had announced its arrival by a scream of its show-off brakes.

Clint, daydreaming, had lingered long on the platform after Gus left. He hadn't been back home enough days after nearly twenty-five years to recall numerous inherited family characteristics in the three young over-dressed ladies in this hour of sleep-deprivation but otherwise it was a pleasing personal visit of the rainbow as he stepped aside to allow the three ladies to board ahead of him, but they refused to move, and he took advantage of these nice girls and their southern manners.

Except for the batting of three pairs of eyes you were aware that the three young women were clad pretty much like for church. He soon learned that they were friends who enjoyed doing everything together and were going up to Lexington for a day's shopping.

Their chosen route because of his planned detour meant that they would beat him up there. He knew that speculation soon would encourage one or all three girls who'd see some reason to begin a conversation with this man of welcome, older and bruised by life as was apparent, who couldn't be that much older than the oldest of them. He wished he'd selected the longer ride, except for a planned stop with old friends, just short miles along the route beyond to Mount Vernon.

They were fair young ladies and appreciated, of southern delicacy who showed no embarrassment over their faddish attire, or forced high-pitched giggles. All three young ladies/women, still girls and how, right away also reflected an unexpected individuality found in American small towns.

Like his memory of even appreciated awe of such local societal debutantes offered at coming-out parties whom he would have known from their pictures in the paper which gave off the blushing appeal of a finishing school somewhere among the local moneyed classes and were said to have been noticed by the locals his peers he was pleased to have them in his audience even for a brief moment.

He noted that none apparently looked to the others for leadership or as pacesetter for a quite beautiful and comfortable life. To him it was that as individuals each girl possessed a greedy batted eye for herself. They were trying hard to hold onto a girlhood not that long past though overdressed certainly for a hot summer's day, because this was the dress for a tour of the big city.

On the rim of giddiness, a habit apparently of their generation, much younger than him doggone it all the same afforded an older man a younger man's anticipation of pleasure in the short rail voyage. Clint, even as a man longer in years, in comfortable company of young women gushing and batting of eyes, was quite thankful for the blessing.

These ladies would go on to Lexington after they would change trains at Mullins Station down the road apiece. It was his hope to stay on Number 24 and get off at Mt. Vernon and tolerate brags over dinner, (lunch to you city fellers, he would say) with an old buddy and his wife.

They were friends primarily in the trade apologetic, yet understanding. They'd left newspaper jobs out of state and returned to their Kentucky roots.

Here they would live out lives looking for the innocence of boyhood and girlhood, to which they once had said goodbye. They recalled college days and newly acquired fancy talk before they went out to save the world.

About mid-afternoon, really closer to a mountain 'evening' (for early night) he'd catch a Big Dog on to Lexington. (That's a Greyhound bus to you guys in the flat country, which is a grass green counterpane right in the center of the state where all the money is) Clint's old jalopy he was afraid wasn't up to making it all the way to Lexington.

The three ladies had taken facing double seats right across from him. The four were the only passengers; he figured they'd want to find out just who he was. For sure since he got on the train back in their town, which a long time ago was his town, also, but it was apparent he was a stranger in their compartments.

He came back after Lily died which he couldn't explain to anyone. He also wanted to make Thomas Wolfe look like a guessing game kind of prophet. Wolfe, like the rest of 'we big writers,' could make a mistake at least now and then.

Wolfe is the novelist from Asheville on the far other side of the mountain who died way too young, in his thirties. It was the world's loss. Among other dictums of long life by Wolfe was: 'you can't go home again.' His work is now in the public domain.

Clint decided to let the other passengers make the first move into anticipated identity and wonder and conversation. Right away one of them did. He didn't hear her name as she gave it but he'd never recall it anyway, and he wasn't going to give away his old man's age by asking her to repeat the question.

He thought how impertinent it would have been just twenty years ago, although he knew one of the young ladies would soon ask what he did and he would have done the same thing. As a former newsman he had to do it so often with an interviewee to nail down the gist of a story.

She had asked: "Who are you?" and he said he was a native of her city. He said, "My name is Clint Greene and I was raised on the mountain behind the town. I just moved back from living up north."

"I've taken over my family's old home place." He told them that he was glad to be home in his cabin above the river and the town.

When one asked if he were married, which he knew would be the next question, he just said 'nope.' He had noted the rings on the left hands of the two older women, but none on the hand of the obviously younger woman, or at least one who still could be called a girl.

Clint knew dang well that the two older ladies were quite tied up with handcuffed or legal, bedfellows: they couldn't hide those third finger left hand diamond rings, each as big as apple cores. A new bachelor in town would just the same set them on fire. The third of the trio, certainly younger, showed less excitement, which pleased him for some reason, or until she would ask to see his driver's license.

This one interested him, even so soon after the death of his wife and the fact that he wasn't yet far from following her to the grave, to a place beside her. He kept reminding himself that he had no right to be more than as an acquaintance and the uncle that he could be, but a man is a man with a leer in suspenders or a wide Texas badge belt and buckles.

Just wait 'til they all get home late by the moon, but they'd phone back before then and mention it incidentally so somebody could do some research about him before they got back to town late, maybe into another day.

Each of them would have a candidate as a house partner for him, even old and ugly as he was. That was after they had learned that he was a renowned newspaper publisher up in Ohio. That last statement wasn't his; he didn't mind the way they understood it, even if they had been told. Man, wait 'til the moment they see the car I drive. The first hint to an American today of a man's status in the world is the size and polish of the automobile sitting out in his driveway...

He asked if they were going up to the city for some shopping. One, apparently the oldest of the bunch, said the other two were but that she was going to check what they had earlier found about her ancestors at the university library, and in some other printed source downtown which he didn't recall and easily forgot to remember. She would spend the whole day here and there and meet the others for dinner.

"All I know is that they came from Ireland," she said, an effort to tell him what she was doing in the archives. Clint wanted to say but he didn't, that everybody these days knew they were Irish, by ancestry by blood by temperament and by a big sense of humor. They sure enjoyed telling about it. Also, they liked to sing of old Ireland.

Clint recalled that Kentucky's old dusty Court House record rooms were filled with Texans, up from that big place in the Southwest settled mostly by Kentuckians before Texas even had birth pains. That meant a first place to seek out those ancestors who went from Kentucky settlement to the 'prairie promise' in time for the Mexican War that would come soon enough.

Her remark made room for him to talk a little in their language and current interests, maybe. He realized that since he had an audience he'd keep right on trying to impress with his newspaperman smarts. Reckon it was part of his birthright. A man of his trade always had to rave on and on, he'd said often half apologetically, because that is exactly what we are in the first place: 'We have to tell all we know about anything, in print or rummage.'

He said, "Likely Scotch-Irish. They settled these mountains early, soon as they heard about the place and learned how to get here. That was after being kicked out of Scotland by King James, forcing them onto lands along the northern coast of Ireland."

Clint wasn't sure the ladies knew King James, he probably was the fellow who had the Bible gather its origin and roots into one volume; a later group brought the Bible into the Twentieth Century.

Clint kept right on trying to sharing his knowledge, trying to impress. .

"James didn't like their brand of Irish either, so it was like killing two birds with one millstone. It looks like the big guys have been doing that sort of thing to the rest of us —- the lesser of us, especially here in Appalachia —- ever since." He was the center of attention by three young and supple, sophisticated mountain women (maybe by right of marriage) and he was bound to enjoy the advantage of his hour on the stage. He tried to look all masculine without throwing out his chest. He thought about how to appear erudite, but he reckoned that 'if you're not there already, it's too late.'

"About a century after King James and his kindness," he said, "the Scotch-Irish people were ready to move again, this time heading for the colonies. Stubborn bunch of hill people, they wanted to live far apart from everybody else.

"They eventually made their way into the mountains, where we are —- they are of the only Scotch-Irish people clan I reckon in the whole world, and they'll let you know about that if you give their girth enough belt." He was pleased he'd used a 'funny phrase.'

"A lot of purists think of no such thing as Scotch-Irish, so they call them Scots-Irish. Scotch is a whisky, they say. Bosh. When we meet again, we'll talk about all this. You have to start somewhere in your search, so we might as well go all the way back to James and his cousin, the first Elizabeth.

"They both had the pleasure of cutting off people's heads. It was either Good Queen Liz, or her daddy, the eighth Henry, who ordered 'off with his head' to one of my people of blood, pardon the pun, back there in our glorious history.

"My train is going ahead, and here's where you meet a new engineer. You ladies try not to spend all your money in one place."

He left them smiling and probably confused as heck, but not 'til he'd made silly eye contact with the unwed, and he'd noted an interest among the blues. He'd never recall their names. It was a small town and the whole conversation would be all over the place by the time he got home; by now, it had gotten into the chronicles of the southern metropolis that he called home.

(Please note, for an untold purpose of this foreword to our story, we have changed the railroad's timetable. Number Twenty-four didn't move to another track, but went right on toward Louisville. Also, by the time it got to Mt. Vernon, it was called the breakfast train.) We won't say how the three ladies got to Lexington.)

At noon it would be back, going south or southeast, now called the dinner train. Then it was the supper train; later, the midnight train, the midnight howler of many a song and railroad story, even a novel. Ask anyone who went through the Great American Depression. Somebody in the family always was catching the midnight train, or they would be singing about it.

These ladies got Clint to thinking of more mountain lore. Our story is strictly fiction, so right soon we switch from first person to 'you all.' Very little of the story is in defense of the men and women of Appalachia; like we've spent most of our life doing just that. They need no defense, a friend would say, "just more ammunition."

Clint said that mountain residents have been maligned, slandered by good people who wanted to show that they are of a different status, even a higher or separate breed. If he were doing the writing, he'd say that 'we hope to touch the hem of the garment.' Clint departed in grins from the company of three pretty young women; he recalled a romantic musical history from his youth.

It was during his momentary fascination with a younger, and the 'sexiest,' he would call her, of one of the former seatmates on the train that the encounter would be recalled and prized yet regretted in memory.

The musical ran through his aging brain during the rest of the day. Her face was wrapped in a tune that was a Tin Pan Alley version from a Symphony by Tchaikovsky, of Tsarist Russia's cultural period in that nation's history.

The composer's Symphony No. One became 'Tonight We Love,' and oh how Clint liked to recall it in the image of a young, and yes, quite supple classmate whom he wanted to impress, by any means and any motive; so he'd kept singing it to her.

Clint tried to forget the tune with a little of 'Old Dan Tucker,' but it didn't work. He had undressed her in his mind —- the later young woman —- then slapped his face hard, like swatting mosquitoes the warning bugs to remind him of a ghetto themed book right off the street he had once read and had forgotten when such a thing for him might have been played with. It was a time when as a boy he knew for sure that he was gifted with a scare of women.

We hope you will get to know the actors —- the people of the book —- as among your neighbors no matter where you live in the U.S. Don't be alarmed and quit on us because we will deign to sneak in a little moonshine and mountain laurel hoping you won't notice.

It is pretty much the story of a small mountain town, and whether historic Camelot was as alive as the WPA of a later century, that it really existed —- in a lost valley or as an island found only at the changing face of the setting sun which set each blue sky day behind it, upon a western English hilltop or along a windy seacoast, as it could be in the imagination of people outside the Kentucky hills.

Speculators have placed the (mythical?) land of Camelot in many places. What some were looking for in the latter part of the Twentieth Century was the hope, which was the dream that many believed they would find in one of America's smaller towns or cities, certainly in a valley like in eastern Kentucky. It was where they would not be afraid, would have neighbors who cared for each other, where the Lord intended that they be.

The town, where many of the events of our brief narrative have taken place, does exist, well, almost. It is where the dream often enough does alight; perhaps it still may be found if the dreamer would allow us to enter her dreams just a wee bit or share the road.

Our town, drawn from a river or frontiersman or patriot by name, which name is never revealed, is deep in the highlands, down in a part of Kentucky and the upper south; it has its very own 'mountain' (a preference of the big town escapees, beyond the hills. Yes, we moved it west a few miles). Townsfolk live on a river, which runs alongside Main Street at the foot of the mountain (yes, the next choice. Dream one or Dream two, which is their own River Shannon to a vast number of Americans).

Its recently paved highways, which appear excessive to the reader (why, who would want to leave?), are taken by young ladies as an open road to far and near shops and music, summoning them to Lexington in the north and Knoxville beyond the state line in the south.

Despite the outside lure of a stage career or even shuttered invitation, schools go right on preparing students for Harvard, as best they know how. At Harvard or State, their students know they will go on to sit in the seats of the mighty, at the same time moms and dads hope they will come right back home again. No jobs are here to satisfy an ambition or talent, so they migrate to the Land of Nod.

When time and other disasters close down their jobs and offices and they are nearing retirement years, or even before, so many know the price of a bus ticket 'back home.' They think of their growing up years, of jobs in big towns attracted by such as might be found in Lexington or Cincinnati which once required booking a Pullman by rail to take away coal and timber.

In their belief, after scoring a share in America's progress that if such advantages were transported to the hills it would be a 'step up to Heaven.' Bigger towns can be reached after supper, home before bedtime.

Please be forgiving as you read. You won't find mass rapes since we didn't. About the only 'sex' is largely buried in the banter of men relaxing over cans of imported beer on the back porch, or in a 'jenny barn' (road house in Texas and Kentucky) as the men recall it, which means you will expect talk of all sorts of big bed adventure.

In fact, beer talk is often all you will find in other media, so we won't be unhappy if you put down this book and go for clandestine refreshment and the fun you envy in big boys acting like school boys.

We have conspired (yes, as plotting together) to give you this story of three one-time warriors who barely knew one another, until in a common cause, perhaps on a bachelor's lonesome day, when they came together to fight the most important battle of their lives; these among (the few?): the coming battle with nature is one more fear placed upon today's American men and women.

They see the warnings at dawn each day on the horizon or conclude from their meeting of sad faces on Main Street that they've heard about it (the end of the world?). They will not become satisfied until the fist of red warning that appears on the horizon as seen by men and women after uneasy sleep, and that radiates traces of blood, goes silent.

One of these three men survived the Great American Depression and Hollywood's glory which to him was a rare Sunday picture show treat before his Marine Corps tour in World War Two; a second voted with his peers in the streets of Chicago for love and justice and an acceptable society; the third was born under the red star flag of Communist Russia, but eventually saw more of the world and great battle in three armies than most men of his time who lived to tell about it.

The latter had escaped one of Russia's bloodlettings to help the others form OMEN, or Old Men to save Earth's Neighborhoods. The three would be affected by what was going on out there. Their motive was more than self-survival —- it was an epical moment seen in the nature of a heroic poem.

Man, born of dust, a dash of vapor, a nucleus of cells and muscle fiber, on Earth has been master of all he surveyed, ever hopeful for a greater part of his share of Earth's largess.

Yet this man is aware that he is only a pinprick in time. Is this his destiny? If that is true, then it means that man and his kin have a place in the grand scheme. Above all, too few of all Earth's creatures, thinking man and his tribe have for centuries believed that they were created in the image of God. That is, until just recently, when so many have begun to believe that even God is a myth foisted on man by whomever in a way to control him.

Man has begun to verify that Mother Earth just might be in her death throes. Literati over at the university recalled a one-time poet from ages past who'd warned that it would be so soon with his world.

Boys at leisure down at the poolroom as well as the mass of the country's democrats (that's lower case) and a beekeeper on Third Street will not admit that turmoil exists outside the secure rim of the Bible's Promised Land, which they believe they've discovered. They want more evidence, for certain, that they have been gripped by the hands of the gods.

It's not far from Mullins Station where the tracks have been divided for another rail destination on to Lexington. Our man Clint was just about to Mt. Vernon. He was surprised he hadn't spent the time as a host of lost days but briefly now in memory only today he is going through the encounter once more with the three women in his mind's struggle with that earlier day in his life. If he'd become enamored with a beautiful young woman where he'd have no rights; he'd ask for Lily's and the Lord's forgiveness.

It was the roar of the train's wheels that lulled him into a near forgotten time when nothing was worth as much as the gold and frankincense of his first days of excitement around girls. He could stay by the passing train's window gazing at the panoramic countryside of woods and fields of grain and the silvery reflections of the creek's movement over the rocks.

He hoped he'd neither think of her again, at least not like that. He breathed like a man again, proud of how he had disposed of those invaded and forbidden moments from that place of evil, where his mother told him bad boys went when they died.

The train had stopped and the conductor came through telling him where he was.

Over breakfast, with his friends at Mt. Vernon after leaving the morning train, Clint said: "This is a heck of a time to be shut out of the newspaper business. As much as I believe in the younger Clint Greene, a time when newspapers could contribute a great big chunk of optimism to the reading public, I still feel it is possible to have a big piece of that one-time historic influence."

He could see an appreciated glint of agreement in the eyes of his hosts. They were listening, but their unspoken agreement with Clint was not surprising.

"I know I'm walking along someone else's beat when I say it but I find newspaper crusaders disturbed by the deluge of boys and girls who don't seem to have the same feel for the game as well as love of country and all that rot that you and I had."

He turned to the feminine side of the local newspaper.

"Max —- that's a funny name for a girl. I apologize to you —- has this guy that you married persuaded you that the best life is to be found in the hinterland? Have you been assigned the women's clubs that seem to thrive in towns like this, perhaps to ease a little of the boredom a woman might have encountered since you came aboard?" Not pausing for comment, he went on, "I've found that everywhere I have been, somebody is in a club of 'bird watching.' I reckon we all don't have enough to do."

"In Caesar's army, if the men appeared restless why the commander would call his aides together and re-organize. Really, I too want to organize people into something like a club that might look to ways to save us from oblivion, in fact from ourselves. That's one thing I wanted to talk to you all about."

"I know that in the end it will be you women who will save us, we men, as always. That's why I hoped you'd go out to breakfast with us, hear what I have to say, give you something to think about; do your best to encourage others to do the same. We shore to heck need you. And anybody else you might know, to be aware of a change in the ecology."

"I have a feeling that you write most of the editorials I read in your partner's family newspaper. Old lazybones here would never admit it. He's too busy polishing all the many trophies you won for him. That's my sermon for the day; then, no more, enough chit-chat."

"Now that I'm home, I'll visit more often. I did all the talking this time; had a lot to unload. Now I must be going."

His friends, newspaper folk like himself, didn't have far to go to make him feel at home. He recalled Sinclair Lewis, who often visited the local newspaper office when he came to town; his hosts and a lot of other people knew that the author's news experience was nigh onto nil, but it had been enough to be accepted by them and recognize him as one of their own. Despite public recognition and good reviews of their books, most writers Clint knew were a lonesome lot; reckon it's because they've been deep into another world, he said.

It wasn't far down the hill to the bus station. He shook hands with his hosts.

The Big Dog was just pulling in. He was the only new passenger; with a slight toss of his head and a wink through the window, it was a silent goodbye.

A hope before seating but now a disappointment he'd be once more amid young beautiful women; they'd want to know who he was. He'd tell them as he smiled, with a gentleman's manner and without affectation but with face of his mountain ancestors as best as he could call them to his mind.

A soldier, who was leaving the bus as Clint was getting on, carried a ditty bag and a full store bag of ten cent store gifts wrapped in pretty paper, likely for the kids at home. The vacated seat joined the others into a ship of empties that bothered him.

The train trips he'd taken across his country, coast to coast four times during the war, were a treat he could tell his grandchildren about. In all four adventures he'd had no place to sleep, sitting up and dreaming of his bed back home when he could draw up his legs beneath him creating a warmth he'd known he might not ever enjoy again.

He was thankful for his friends his people across the green wild girth of his mountain his own corner of his country. Many or most country boys like himself had never flown in an airplane, and likely never would. Most had never been to the big town, except the few who got away to work in wartime industries or as servicemen on liberty in a foreign port.

Come long weekends and vacations, so many as defense workers would head back home for short visits. He laughed to himself. In those pre-war years here they would come, about all wearing silk purple shirts that set them apart. They'd managed to find a used car some place, ones they now could afford. After the war was over and they had to get back to the mountains, the cars were rusting out in the yard.

That's the men in purple shirts. Clint recalled how the girls and women (as a rule, to provide another phrase of the times) wore long dresses that were inches below their knees, to church, to town and to funerals. Slacks as a part of their apparel in the Thirties were pretty much identified with city girls. These country girls coming in out of the cold would lift their dresses in the back as far up as their waists, or their navels, let us say, and would back up to the fire, a big stove in the front rooms of their small houses or in the country stores, to allow the heat to get to their bodies.

Now this is an odd thing; when TV came in they managed to buy into the other lives' phenomena. They would climb a hill even higher than their homes where they would string their antenna wires. They could repair their own TVs, fix their old cars and trucks until they no longer could afford the parts. They began to talk of profit in their own purebred cattle and were aware of the boasts of Wall Street, hire trucks to carry their sweat and blood to market. Amidst all the fancy doodads which would pile up as the children grew up, as they outgrew the play pretties the best their world had to offer, they had their proud community buildings which on Sundays even as abbreviated for all time were their churches which were first log edifices seen from afar at the head of every hollow. Now in clapboard painted white up and through all the mountains, they held onto their churches despite what those city fellers said were useless because God was dead.

You'd see them on Sunday crowding onto log benches. Songs handed down by their elders went back a hundred years. Outlanders came to record the songs. Clint recalled that the churches in every hollow in the hills each had at least two preachers, unpaid, except by a few bushels of apples, pats of butter, maybe sacks of potatoes; they paid doctors the same way, if an ailment got to the point of going to the county seat to find one. Preaching was a lot of gesticulating, shouting. As a faithful people, you'd find the Lord sitting in their midst.

Their wakes for the deceased meant an all-night vigil of quiet respect, people awake in chairs around the coffin. Soon they'd break out in song or prayer.

Music has always been a big thing in their lives. Clint recalled that his grandfather, who lived far back in the hills but on the 'busy' road to town, owned about every musical instrument known to the times on the frontier.

He had no musical abilities, but as often as many who lived a piece down the road, neighbors, reached his house which was a half-way point to town and where they planned to spend the night with grandma and grandpa, then about any instrument they could play would come out. They so paid for their night's bed, their keep.

The place would rock, pleasing Clint's grandparents. His grandfather didn't have an exceptional musical ear, but kept the instruments for his guests who could with their music 'pay for their supper,' he would say.

Mountain music, still alive and well to this day, has found a place in the local music appreciation repertoire as in much of the music-starved nation.

The approaching daylight brought in scenes of his America, his thoughts by a bus window. He was on another bus with mostly other warriors who were as excited as he was, he could tell. Nothing hindered his never to be forgotten memory of getting home from the war —- nothing; he expected no surprises, no change in his people.

He was on a bus all the way down from the lakes, or for most of the way. It was far into the night when he'd changed buses and part of the remaining night was spent on the bus station bench watching other people on the go. He could better appreciate the magic that took over his imagination of what he wanted his country to be, as he'd pictured it from his childhood.

It was soul enhancing like before, to ride along in the dark, with the purr of the engine beneath him. Out on the greater stage: handheld lights guided a farmer's morning chores which emerged through the trees, across the fields meaning people, pleased as planters at peace, safe with their families. Where he'd been and what he'd done, he knew for the first time, was worth it all. He felt Heaven blessed because his country had needed him during the war; he was proud.

Clint, like most of his tribe —- red-blooded, proud of where he'd lived all his boy's life as a free being from Heaven in the Kentucky hills, yet he had a yen to join other free roamers of the world; like the hoboes he'd seen from the riverside of the town as the freight train went through. He was killing time as just any lonely little squirt until the picture show opened up on Saturday afternoon. At home now he'd heard of the GI Bill and knew that if he'd thought of it he'd sure do what the big lot of his buddies said they would be doing, that is, going to college.

He was a lone rider out west trying to forget the years he rode in fight with Sherman or Jeb Stuart, or Chesty Puller, or Terrible Terry Allen. The last two were from his war, the others just as bent on saving the Union or new South in its transfer from the manners of a civilization born in the old country but with a field philosophy based on the cheap labor brought in from Africa.

His part in war was over and done. He thought that for him, it all was wrapped up.

He was on the long road back to the place he'd come from, not caring where he'd go next, except out there was the open range, which was to be took.

Coming home was the same fight he had after the Great Depression and a dream of reconstruction of a dream, which would come for sure after he'd tamed that loud roar in his burning inner other self. His spirit or his soul, restless, prodding him for something he didn't know what.

At a far-off moment he knew was coming but wasn't interested in, like a visit to outer space his people had been wishing for, now had promise of reality. It was enough to be fearful of an uneasy star, to a mankind that had heard the explosion of a big bomb that had ended their war.

Alarmists would soon fear the climate change and a heck of a lot more that could bring down the price of real estate, which like about everything else these days was other-owned. It's time to think of something more possible, he thought.

It was a first day home after the war:

Safely at home, he thanked the not long ago wish he'd fulfilled the day he'd moved back to the cabin on the mountain. Clint Greene breathed deeply that day. This was his heritage, in a dry place but with damp memories of where he'd been. He found a dry corner in his cabin on the hill following his first morning after a hard rain, a place to stash his pack.

Chapter One

Clint's hillside cabin was built to avoid becoming an island in a creek that after a rain had no trees or roots to stop the water as it roared down the hill to what later became a town's Main Street, to roar through wildly in sheets. That's what his mother would have called it. It also was his first morning downtown and here was the same recollection of it coming with the same bother to the residents.

The rain stopped briefly, but the wind did not. He welcomed the flapping open wave of a street awning, a gift by the storekeeper which was more than a safe haven, only seconds before disappointment was stilled by the rain again. It would soon become one more deluge, not the way in the jungle he'd been in when he was on the edge of getting used to it.

Smiling people of the town already were enjoying the kindness of the storekeeper, the awning which was a refuge by way of Clarence the hardware man. Ah, what a relief it is from the already sweltering July day another woman said, adding that heat was left from the day before; one other woman said, "comes now the rain to help us oh what a blessing."

Clarence, the shelter's donor, stood smiling at Clint's elbow, rattling metal things in the wide red pocket of the builder's apron he wore as the badge of a hardware man.

A woman still holding onto an open umbrella uneasily wasn't alone as she joined in a shivering spectacle beneath the noisy street awning which still danced with the wind, even in the rain. She said aloud for nobody in particular that she remembered that 'big one' last year; all were then talking about the furious action from the sky of that day, except that wet-faced man over there who was not bothered by the wind and rain or the townspeople at his elbow.

Clarence and a town citizen then began talking about that sudden downpour like last year's invading heavy raindrops; Fourth of July; sure day to remember, raining almost as hard as this one for a full half hour. Residents would recall this one and that one as one deluge, even if a year apart.

Clint, at the moment, after walking inside the store, was the only customer. The rest of the day, he knew, would be stifling, near oppressive. The heat from that deep concrete would see to it. Physics, though, would take the blame.

Clint and Clarence began talking as old friends just inside the wide open door to the street, partly beneath the awning that reached out to the curb and over the sidewalk, which Clarence said had been designed for "just this sort of thing."

Citizens and a few strangers, possibly drummers, by chance and retreat, talked about the change in the weather and hints of raw vengeance by the elements. They knew from recent experience that it would go on all day. The wet skies meant a contrast to the past; the coming visit to the town by a popular democrat had their interest. The shelter seeking folks beneath the awning knew they were among friends and they knew what others thought.

Clint was a one-time newsman whose 'beat' had been the itinerary of the politicians when they came to the city. It had been a regular visit for them in his two newspaper towns of the past.

Clint was quite pleased that out there dodging the rain were voices of an informed and fearless, satisfied America.

Any talk people-to-people and of politics would have been of thankful interest to the one-time editor; nobody from Clint's typewriter days surely was more used to and grateful, as sensitive to politics and politicians than a newspaper man, which was in gratitude to the times (lower case).

In his thoughts, though, it was his reader interest that determined what was what. A politician to a newspaperman came with what newsmen called 'good copy.' The amazing thing to Clint was that many of his thoughts were in newspaper copy.

As he was on his way to town, Clint thought of his old friend Clarence at the store, pleased he had remembered that he needed some number eight nails.

At the moment, with the sun at its zenith, he would have sworn that not a rain cloud was anywhere. Just the same he was glad to see the out of nowhere downpour because Mother Nature as he had realized had reminded him that he was getting mighty thirsty.

He'd just learned that Clarence's oldest boy, Cecil, had won an appointment to West Point. A bed bid had been re-opened when its first young applicant had asked to be released and the vacancy for Clarence's boy became available, but he had to report in two days. At this very hour the son was at his dad's and mom's house boning up on his math before he was to board the train at Huntington at seven fifteen o'clock of the following day. The entire hardware family would arise at four to drive him to Huntington for goodbye.

"I'm glad for you and him both," he said to Clarence. Looking to the street, Clint saw an old friend enter the drug store, where he knew that other professional folk of the town would be visiting a coffee hour. Clint had generally looked for the practice in towns he'd visited for whatever reason.

"I'd like to get over there, but I sure don't want to get this shirt I just ironed get wrinkled up after drying out from all this rain, I left my jacket and cap in the car, thinking I'd beat the rain," Clint said.

Clarence said he understood all that bachelor practice since his wife had been ill the year before and he'd learned right away how to batch it. He didn't say so to Clint but he was aware that Clint's wife had died not many months before, and Clint had come home maybe for good to his mom and dad's former home on the mountain. Clarence said he knew that they both had died during the war. "We were all sorry to hear it," he said.

Clarence changed to brighter talk, which is still necessary to small town life, to point to a stand of umbrellas near the door next to the lawn care display. After a few seconds' bewilderment, Clint saw the umbrellas and wasn't at all surprised as he thought how pleased he was to be home in a place where the good will of people for others was so evident, even expected. Clarence had always even as a boy growing up in the town did well by his people.

At the seed-weed display's edge Clint saw a dozen umbrellas in a ceramic stand that was made tight by its overstuffed cargo; every color of a Paris Street café scene as painted by Renoir waited invitingly, grinning up at Clint in his hour of desperation.

"I'm surprised nobody out there has been in for a needed umbrella," Clarence said.

"Take one you like and don't feel you have to return it. I learned a long time ago that people never return a borrowed umbrella".

"I buy them real cheap by the dozen and stuff them in that big urn for my customers. Since they don't cost much I don't lose much; I try to take good care of my customers, my friends." Clarence smiled as Clint grabbed a colorful shade from the pack. It was a chute a man would select. Clarence said borrowers brought other umbrellas to the stand. "On their way home after work they realized that they wouldn't need them any longer that day."

Clarence also had a box of assorted nails for customers who needed just one or a dozen, "gratis." The box was near the cash register along with a saucer of pennies with a note that stated: 'for help with your sales tax.'

Clint thanked him as he looked over his shoulder and sprinted across the street, unaware that the rain provided disturbed visibility to drivers. Many of the people beneath the awning had moved on, tired he reckoned that the rain would never stop. Some held open wet newspaper sheets over their heads. The strangers perhaps had never heard of Clarence and his kindness, likely because since the war a lot of new people began to settle and would now live in apartments or multiple housing since land had became scarce.

At the drug store's open door he handed the umbrella to a young woman shivering beneath its awning, maybe trying to decide midst the rain just how to get going on her way to somewhere fast. She obviously was frantic, evident by anxiety on her already wet face, which reflected probably frustration apparently of a recent hire.

The woman, whom he didn't know since he was new, again, in his hometown as perhaps it was the same with this woman. She thanked him even though she didn't appear surprised. She immediately headed up the street toward one of the town's three banks, which were sort of clustered like in their own financial center.

Clint figured she was an employee of one of the banks. He remembered that he'd forgotten his number eight nails, now sitting on Clarence's hardware counter. When the rain let up, he expected the storekeeper would cross the street to deliver the package to him.

Another figure was exiting the drug store and Clint gazed deeply into the man's face as the fellow looked out on the wet sidewalk and street. He carried his own umbrella, or one borrowed from the store. The man's tightly tied prominent necktie over a white shirt labeled him as a professional. Clint didn't recognize him but said howdy, not trusting his eyes and because there was that distant memory of an old school pal maybe, as he tried to recall him from his own days growing up back in his home town. The man turned left after crossing the street, his face now hidden in the chute's folds. This poor fellow, Clint thought, would be concerned for the rest of the morning about how the spattered rain from the sidewalk had ruined his diligently applied shoeshine.

Before, in his growing up years, Clint would say he knew every face in the county. Since the war, he was not long in recognizing that everybody, so many strange to him, was going every which way like in a hurry, fellow townsmen he'd known back then among them. Others had left town by the barrels full. As many came in as left, though,

He was to learn that the post-war street was made up mainly by managers of the new chain stores and way too many lawyers, at least three new doctors, each looking for the ideal place to alight. The GI Bill was doing its job; the sponsors in Congress said it pleased them by taking a mass of boys and girls off the farms making moms and dads proud they had a professional in the family. Clint knew he'd meet a lot of the new bunch inside the drug store.

As he entered Doc's old place, he surveyed the scene with a good feeling that he was home again. The soda fountain was just inside the door to his left; every stool held a body. He would say they were the old cola crowd, but with new faces. The sex division was about the same, somehow different, knees touching, hands at work where once forbidden in public places. The movies still dictated their talk, the leers; half-closed eyes that said 'yes.' They were pleased that they drank at the fountain of youth. It would always be so.

Upon returning to a familiar bar stool at the drug store fountain, they felt a yearning for the earlier days when anyone of the old crowd who might show up with the same yen. They were of a generation that came along in time to be called 'boomers,' children of returning warriors, and the younger children of the boomers.

The usual shelves of salves, pills and hair tonics were on the right, and beyond all this from wall to wall were tables; each chair taken by a man or woman with a coffee cup in hand or resting next to a muffin plate on the table. The back wall café where the people were crowded was a brag and idea of the pharmacist who saw to the town's social needs, and to emphasize the service part of his business, Doc's prescription counter.

The café was a family pride, and Doc would brag about it. Called Doc, he was like his father a pharmacist, who had earned his place in society on the battlefield as a medic in the first war. The island for coffee in his small town kept him in touch with the world.

Each table, at least a dozen maybe without counting and the front bar also served the community by providing its teenagers a way to vie for floor jobs and getting the moneyed folk better acquainted with their courtesy and educated ways.

Clint's friend, seated in perhaps the last chair to be occupied, which could have belonged to the woman who had just left, or maybe the faceless man he'd met at the door, stood up as he saw Clint.

"Well, well, well, if it isn't the bard of ye old Big River High," and to the man at his left, said: "You're leaving, Russ, me lad, get up and make way for Clint Greene." "This man is just home from the news wars up in Ohio; our town's better citizen who had to leave to give away his talent." Russ rose, held the chair for Clint, stuck out his hand and headed for the door, like he'd gotten a hurried call from his wife.

"Howdy, Frank," said Clint. "You still foreclosing on widows and orphans and the poor and downtrodden; it's been what, twenty or what years?"

Frank said: "At least a lifetime and you look as smart in the face even strong of body as you appeared the last time you and just me . . . well, got drunk together."

"You know I don't drink. This old yard bird such as what you see, is still running from the bad guys, and still faking it to make a living, Frank; and as like in the old days still dodging a lot of bullets, I reckon like always, here I am and I reckon the Lord intends to let me go right on living forever and ever . . . heard you reeling in estate and your middle spreading from counting out sugar plums at the bank."

"Still there . . . anybody here you don't know?"

Clint began shaking a few hands. "Oliver here I know; still farming, Oliver? Heard you got rich like Frank here. By the way, I saw your boy the other day. I asked him about you; said you were at your best." "Said you did," said Oliver.

A few at the other tables waved. They mostly all turned around to recognize maybe verify as much as they'd heard of him, now back among them in his old (?) age. At the far end of the cluster of chairs, men and women at coffee around tables set up for four people, a coffee member with hand in his pocket stood partly lazing at the pharmacy's back counter.

The man appeared comfortable, coffee cup in hand, but he was talking in a formal sort of way. Clint said: "What's going on, Frank? Looks like the coffee boys done let things get out of hand. Is this a regular seminar, or a wake maybe?"

"That's our local professor from the college and boy prophet from Yankee country trying to make some sense of today's headlines for us hillbillies."

"Seems a scientist done (sic) found some evidence to support a theory that the Earth is dying. He's tryin' t' make us dumb hillbillies down here believe it and support it."

"He says the Earth is becoming warmer because of the fire and brimstone from cars and coal consumption and that such is filling up the atmosphere with undue haste from automobile emissions and God knows what else."

"Is he for it or is he against it?" Clint asked.

"Well, I reckon you'd say that he's downright agin it," said Frank. "He's a grad of one of those up east colleges where they're agin everything they think a conservative might be for. They can't even talk unless a Harvard man tells them what. Then they repeat their authority and become as one in their thinking."

"The prof shows up here where he knows he'll have an audience —- one besides the classroom. We are wholly captive down here, too. Sometimes he will take advantage of our ignorance. We know his smarts and act like we believe every word of it."

To his left, Clint watched as a one-time school mate, fellow named Curt who had been quietly standing, saw a vacant chair. He was a country boy with shyness on his face. He signaled the right pretty smiling waitress, a pharmacist girl. The server already had a coffee cup in hand and was heading his way.

Across and above the crowd a tall fellow with big hands and a professional mark of printer's ink just beneath his right eye was seriously into a question for the speaker. Clint right away knew about the ink spot, hardest thing in the world to get out.

Clint was hoping to meet the man later, knew him from across the street and town talk, not surprised to learn that the man had been for a long time, and still was, a working Jake Leg printer like himself, the local news editor, a vine worker identical in life to Clint's own. Clint hoped that he would become a printer's news ink friend.

You're about to meet, briefly —- so far it was just himself -- another possibly by faith founder of OMEN; in depth talk about OMEN and more about its concerned citizens, which will come later in the script. Until then, Americanized and comfortably present by fate herself as your small town coffee and beer addicts —- three men who would emerge still sound of body and mind from the century's blood wars.

They would suggest after they had formed this new lobbying club that OMEN should aim its welcome arms out to the usually ignored players at the pool hall, the vast new breed of cross country truck drivers certainly the saloon or cafe habitués —- in most times —- a vast herd of overlooked citizens' bank, law office and store counter clerks, butchers clothiers and fitters, pie makers, cow punchers and other men of the road, drummers, the service people. Those are the patriots who hold the Earth together.

Storied men and women, honored by professional politicians, highly respected, now of a newly-born tradition, were the fount to carry live coals or embers for the fires of trade, men and women who were said by many in the press to be the real policy makers of the world, though they knew better.

They are the people who would go wherever men gather to talk of women, women in talk to think of men; in the usual run of small town life. He'd begun to observe a recent change in his country's political life: men and women especially the latter who were now adding a new color to his country's politics and elective office. Men of ambitious public livelihood would ignore them at personal risk.

Today's speaker ('up at college prof') was enjoying the attention. He said: "One surprising breach in the status quo has led us into an economic implosion. Fallout from time's collapsing infrastructure that began in the late war-diseased West soon will not find a single people untouched by the wailing and gnashing of teeth."

"As a consequence I'd say the Earth will soon witness the big change as both the sea and the landscape become a wasteland, a monument to our selfishness and overindulgence," he continued. "It's been proved that the burning of coals of Appalachia and oil from the wells of Texas and Arabia together are the cause of melting snowcaps, even the snows of the twin peaks of Tanzania and Kenya in the heart of Africa." (Kibo and Kilimanjaro; though he did not elucidate.)

When he cited little known far-flung geographical sites studied mostly by educated folk from the bigger schools, monopolized by the elite of his own college, he paused and looked around. When he recalled that, "It was like gas fumes from hell that were necessary to kill off th' wicked o' th' Bible towns," one in his audience nodded to a neighbor, "Them educated people would never admit that it was said to be the work of the Lord, not at all, He's sayin' that, tryin' t' win over us good church folk." It was one other rebuttal over a coffee cup.

"That done it; I knew sin was back of it all th' time," said Clint's seat neighbor on his right, across from Frank..

Prof was about to sit down; most hoped amid sighs, loudly and rudely, by long practice, prompted him to raise his voice, pointing at nothing, stabbing at a wisp. He said he hoped that the local coal country would forgive:

"When I drove into town on the first day of my tenure as one of your teachers, I was appalled to see what you had done or allowed to be done to your mountains. To get to the coal you destroyed the magnificent footprints Mother Nature left there generations, no, several lifetimes ago. You cut off her hair down to her shoulders."

"You first permanently took away her beauty. This was followed by the waste, overburden from the dig which you kicked over the mountain's side to take away her life-sustaining streams, which also destroyed homes of the people who lived on her sides and in the valleys."

"Time will forget and forgive but no time soon or maybe never for what we have done to our Earth, not only in this town this coal field but throughout the world. Let me amend that to 'right here,' because so much more needs to be forgiven. That's really all I have to say about it, before somebody comes at me with a gun."

A scene from Clint's boyhood home on the side of town hill kept creeping into his attention. He as part of the day's ritual had been to look over the mountains and beyond, aware that in the far array all was the same, until the peaks disappeared in the mist. They indeed were not the same blessing he knew as a boy, hiding he knew the poverty beneath the wispy clouds, the big denial of safety given by the enveloping trees and cliffs; far too many of his people were victims of their former somewhat protected isolation were below, and without refuge,

In scribbled logs kept by the angels, he had been told in his youth that the warning words were on the record. "In time there will be a great upheaval, as it was a dozen or more a thousand years ago when the coal deposits beneath the hills were being formed from the trees and growth during Earth's Eden season."

Clint was beginning to doubt that he would be alive at the passing at last of society's traditional ways. He quit a long time ago his optimistic days of looking for a society that appreciated, really was thankful for what the gods had given to the people. That was when he became convinced that "I alone could not save the world," and began to weep for his home there. Some days it was all beauty, then the Earth was under a wide and dark cloud; some day the creek will quit its flow and the sun will lose its place in the sky as it now becomes brighter upon every new day in its return of springtime.

He wasn't thinking this yesterday or even earlier today. He left his chair expecting to return for more talk after walking Frank to the door. He said that after each talk given by a speaker to the Rotary Club in his Ohio town, members would walk to the front and shake the hand of the guest.

People in most mountain towns apparently don't do that, taking too much of life as it has always been, just as people elsewhere methinks are becoming immune to all that's going on with their Earth.

He'd said to Frank: "I noticed that no courtesy was shown to the prof after his little speech, which was not at all surprising because they'd all heard every word of it before since the threats to their way of life was writ large in papers across the country. What gives?"

Frank said they'd had the prof down to talk about something happening all over, at the time. "Generally,' Frank said, "he is better received."

"Many local residents have sort of gotten used to him. They appreciate having him. They like his Yankee accent, a big facet reminding of Jack Kennedy."

"Having a Harvard man in their midst was something not everyone would boast about. Prof wasn't a Harvard man; he went to a nearby smaller school though it's the same philosophy. Everybody's burg, all over New England, is home to a little college."

"That's why the community college, a recent invention by the University of Kentucky, has been sought after around here as a 'business,' since the war. That is why they have to be educated to appreciate education."

"We've been fortunate in having that little college in our town. You can tell it in the Community Chest boast around here. Many of these early colleges —- about all of them for just two years of study, were set up by people of organized religion; most of the teachers were hill missionaries of a sort."

"What bothers me is the fact that churches lately have so many irons in the fire they'll drop their 'colleges,' one by one, let them stand on their own. We couldn't support our college if we didn't have outside help —- but you know all this. A big bother is that many of these little religious colleges are being assumed by the state, and the politicians manage to purge the thoughts of what's considered evil that lead to doing nothing about the ills of our people."

Coffee men as they passed Clint's chair to the outside, a few offering 'so-longs' promised later to get together. Clint apologized to Frank at the door for not calling on him earlier and said he was going back inside.

As Clint came by the register to get his check on the return to his seat, the girl gave him a package. "Feels heavy; Clarence brought it in several minutes ago," said the girl. "What do you think is in the package?" asked Clint. She was a little baffled: "A love letter and a heavy gift to your girl friend? A pair of roller skates, maybe? "

"Right," he answered. He winked at her, an old man's right. "Hold onto it. I'll be back in a minute or two."

Clint realized he needed to hit the streets soon, to get his errands done. He was eager for the next coffee break, hoped to talk about the gas shortage and the over-portside prices. A younger woman from a back table stuck out her tongue as she passed. He looked toward the front of the store again, to see if new arrivals might be wet. The rain he reckoned had quit. He decided to linger for a few more minutes. Yay, Prof had to return to work. A red-faced citizen was pontificating (big word, Clint thought, but I reckon it was exactly what the man was doing).

It was here at the town coffee hour among the few known (always it seemed a half dozen soreheads or the more arrogant among them than they were entitled to) thinkers determined to learn what happened to the Eden of their fathers.

A few ventured to get the floor. Another big talker had taken over their thinking:

"Evidence is that most citizens are aware of this, yet they seek a stronger hand than theirs to expect how they might escape," he said.

"Listen to your inner voice which assures you that salvation lies in a strong leader. Leadership is the answer. Most people think so," Frank had said.

It was here in a universal setting that the three OMEN men first became aware of the others' in common interest that the idea was forming, in at least few minds, others to follow.

The most arrogant yet tolerated intellectual of the town, Clint learned from the coffee session, was present with a few others who at previous coffee club gatherings had shone perhaps much of the same yet neglected gifts of brain reserve and had provided much or some support. The few smarts earlier had interrupted to offer opinions, which most of the others chose to ignore.

The leader among them began to cite the usual back-ups, recalling an American Nobel novelist in a speech rather than in his books. "It was in Oslo," the intellectual said "that the writer, before the Nobel Prize audience in 1950, said, 'Man will prevail.'"

Hesitating, with mouth full -- chewing a nutty muffin with flair —- the brainy patron added: "His talk was of destiny."

"Whew," whispered one other member, to no one in particular.

"No wonder we call that thing an intellectual. Listen to him carry on so, he's at least in favor of destiny."

One said: "The Earth is playing host to too many people, that's what."

"I can think of no strong man to come tell us what to do. That's what we really have to look for, I agree. We've always found one before when one came right out of the bushes in emergencies."

On this day as on any working weekday, Clint was proud to say: "Ah, my people," which began shortly after dawn. Citizens are down at the drug store, coffee shop or filling station. They are small town folk, or once were in shirt and tie, or plaid, homemade shirts, overalls or dungarees here for coffee if the business kept a hot pot or tea, and a place to sit, trying to be big boys of authority and wit.

By first light they brag, well schooled in politics, taxes, football, round ball, men (and women) and golf at their own country club.

These mountain men and women vie for the best seats at stage center. They entertain whoopee. jump right in with a punch to ribs seeking attention in some awkward way to their wit and humor, and well recall their part in one of America's recent wars, all the way back to WW Two, the big one.

(This is a small upper south town in America, of the Western Hemisphere, of a quite limited count of civilized societies as their country defines civilization —- of newspaper and journal defined developing nations —- of Planet Earth; as far as resident scientists could say in their journals, of the one planet in the universe currently (blessed?) with humans. In the Christian nations of this world it was declared that man was made in an image of God. In the coffee shops of the same nations, beginning doubts were seeping in.)

Before the talk skips to the dire, a club member with the latest joke seizes the opening. Nervous anticipation moves among the others.

In a coffee party such as on this day, a muster of mockery of some minority group is now taboo. In America of a touchy past an insult or alienation intended as jokes were tolerated among non-sensitive souls. They look at Bob here, expecting what is usually forbidden. (As Uncle Billy would say: "He'll shore have hell to pay.")

Fellow named Bob —- that's all, just Bob, always had the latest joke. The big joke was mostly of his own creation, for sure when he runs with friends like today. Just a week ago with his wife and kids, they had come home following a Virginia vacation. He is expected to talk about it. (No last name? It is a quite recent and disorienting custom over America; few men or women, by any civilized reason any longer come with a family name.)

Today's designated jokester said he and his family visited Williamsburg, in Virginia. Yes, that Williamsburg.

"You hear a lot about Thomas Jefferson up there: Jefferson and the Randolph family of that revolutionary bunch who got all stirred up by the flouncing around of George Third and decided to found their own country," Bob continued. No one else on this day could sound as authoritative.

Jokester Bob is expected, unquestioned in his recently acquired knowledge about the founding fathers, knowing all their names and how they went to war with their revolutionary thinking:

"To show their familiarity with young Tom, they referred to him as Red Jefferson, obviously because he at the time had all that red hair. Well, Tom was taken lately with this young woman who not long ago had lost her husband. Tom about the same time had lost his wife. The young woman, whose husband died, left her with his name, Skelton. Her name was now Martha Skelton. As he was squiring her around town and the college campus, the people said: 'Hey, here comes Red 'n' Skelton."

Whether others 'got' the joke, pun it was, the joker always got a good laugh. And, he who laughs at his own jokes, one said a moment later, laughs loudest. Bob was proud as he could be expected, was recorded in the annals of the coffee club as the fellow who got the floor and said something it last, tried to make like it was an original thought.

A caffeine friend said once: "That's what this early hour by democrats (lower case) is about." Jefferson, too, was a democrat.

The coffee men and women got back to a serious moment. Yesterday, or last week at their meeting, Clint was told, the talk was how their own countrymen's rip and tear came to the spoliation of the forests and farms and rivers, by intensive practice.

Right then the farmer in town for coffee with the gentry rose, said, showing off with his best high school elocutionary talent: "The forces of evil are back with vengeance in the Twentieth Century as proclaimed by our tribal seers. They are at it again, messing with our birthright." A fellow opposite said it was the 'loss of morals.'

Every citizen Clint knew around today's coffee meeting tables owned up to his 'good morals,' so, "it's not just us."

In unique interruption, tired of the big talk, a table man interjected, just like a TV end man: "Let's go to the weather, talk about women later."

Clint looked across the heads of the men to two women at a far table who at once showed an interest in the expected man talk, a reason for their being there. They knew for certain that men when no women were around usually talked about women. They looked lonely, Clint decided. A man at his elbow was involved in the quiet of loneliness perhaps for a like reason, aware of Clint's gaze and tried to make up for a general habit of silence and began considering the other side of himself which was a hope for boldness and how to exercise it.

The member wanted to talk about how a time at sea with the army bound for Europe also gave him his chance, convinced that he had something to talk about once he got home. It was how he had felt a near silence of the sea that calm day and in that moment wanted to write a poem about it. The lowered wind gave a new grace to the air above the ship. The dance of the waters around it encouraged the men's thoughts of their war. The sea's peace drowned out fears of their deaths awaiting them as a sure thing.

His memory encouraged a boy's story of a onetime selfish sea urchin, recalling a feeling of peace on the same road across the vast Pacific, to come onto the scene. Eager to emulate salty Navy jive for these country boys once bound for maybe isles like Tahiti and Wahoo, sang, "Take me home instead, mates; take me home."

As seen from a ship's rail, he said the rise and fall of the ship challenged the watery roadway "that reflected by day the blue of the sky and opened the heavens to the stars by night," proving that poets really are born every hour of the day.

The country's landlubbers now in contentment over coffee cups were talking "of how the stars guided the ancient mariners, brave seamen who mapped the waterways that guided them to the land that became my country."

The stars told them which course to pursue as they were bound for the new land; they'd tell their grandkids how they learned of this, so they might find pride. Teenagers in a much later time were told to call them 'flag-wavers.' Climate change talk and an obvious loosening of morals among them had become the latest big scare in talk when as tolerated citizens among them got together with their sons and daughters.

Clint Greene was not alone as he imagined what would be lost in the spread of the new life style, the new beliefs they'd heard about and would have to fight.

There sat Uncle Leo, man of one name whom Clint had just learned about. The young especially chose to stick with just that one name, a custom adopted by their peers.   (We who are with a single name are still men, whatever called), Clint mused. In just minutes to follow he knew he wanted to know more about Uncle Leo. Who? Why now? He said later to Frank.

"There's just something about Leo," said the world traveler. That was Clint, who learned to study most men he met intently while he was with the Marines.

"You couldn't pronounce it even if you once heard a last name for somebody's uncle," said a man who sat near his elbow. Clint was told a little later outside the drug store that Uncle Leo was known as a thinking passive fellow not unlike the stoics of ancient Greece, like an ancient statue on the plain, close-lipped to a hint of a once thriving (desert?) metropolis in the sand, Clint thought, 'odd that most men here today are smart, college educated and they about all took English Lit on the GI Bill,' and he wondered about the origin and current local practice and also suspected that the outlander had his reasons.

(Ozymandias, yes, from Percy Bysshe Shelley's poem by that name; might as well be for what most of them knew about Uncle Leo; Yankees think we hillbillies are crude, uneducated.) As far as the coffee men could surmise, 'uncle' came from a distant desert land or an iced-in city in Tibet.

Clint asked, was Leo a veteran of some forgotten foreign war? In Europe they've always been in a war. The coffee men knew that Leo came to them as a 'foreigner.'

"Has Leo come to bring us hidden secrets of life and death that might save mankind (this here little burg?), from destruction?"

"Was he sent by destiny?" Clint was told that Leo had 'calmed us down,' got us to thinking how we can set it up. "We don't talk of fear. It's been said that men who live in fear first think in panic."

Out there in the vast unknown it is possible that a land of love and peace might still be. Men have been looking for it all through time; they've found no hint of its once being or if it is still alive.

Was it Uncle's heritage? Did he come from an unknown hidden world? Then what? . . . That must be where Leo came from, Clint thought. You might follow a stubbed finger on an Ouija board, since nothing is known of his origin. Clint later, would often attempt to pry answers from Uncle Leo's mocking face —- right now it appeared to be all speculation.

Most at the a.m. gathering had long since accepted the one time soldier (he must have been); just so, harmless but cooperative if that's what they wanted; just another facet of today's American.

Coffee time in this heavenly city of ours in the west can be a fount only of profound thoughts. Allow the brag, the prophets say, the town's street philosophers say. Out of such bluster often will come an idea sent by the gods, to test our ignorance, by birth swagger but sober, in our contribution to coffee table speculation about life, and of course destiny. More often it comes for no reason other than to introduce its keeper speaker as among the learned.

"How many wits among most men and women would believe as they listened for the approach of the horsemen that an answer has always been in the human heart?" That came from the farmer, a church regular and now a coffee clubber.

At last, "Sunday churchmen from the hard benches appear, ringing their bells," said the intellectual; "time they brought in a dead god," he said. "Lordy me," he added, silently and only to himself, realizing that he would be seen as red in face for letting this sudden contradiction get away from him. The others at table knew he didn't believe in God, or he said so. Fellow called Bill since a previous editor bore the name, whose birth name was Oscar, the new local editor, said he was tired of writing warning-type editorials.

He'd suggested that they must save the forests and the former- plowed ground even the air they breathed from the fumes that arose from the bowels of creation which in his time is called civilization. He was tired because nobody cared, Bill said, Oscar said, "You guys I have learned want only good news in your paper. But that's far from life. What is good news? What is bad news?"

Bill (Oscar) was surprised that he'd even spoken up, as was most everyone else. He long since had become inured to unpopular deeper meanings of life he'd been directed to explore in his opinion columns, to be ignored by his subscribers. He felt like he was betraying the code of his profession if he didn't help them think.

Fellow named Bishop —- remember him? He apparently was influenced by what he 'knew' to be oratory at its highest level. He sent in his best and thoughtful question, which he'd chosen carefully. He asked: "Who are we to forego our cars and machines that make life on man's earth at least tolerable? Like indoor plumbing, all-house furnaces, maybe?"

"We can stand a little heat," Oscar laughed.

"We've all been in the kitchen."

Bill (Oscar), pleased he'd redeemed himself, acted as he realized by way of country boy humor that would please the others —- anyway, he thought so, said:

"Coffee hour is for removing the cobwebs of doubt from the night, to rejoice in our ancestors' freedom wars. Today, their children keep freedom's business," Oscar would add.

They mentally slapped their thighs just as Uncle Leo, who since until yesterday had not been a coffee or tea man, weakly pounded the table. Uncle Leo, or just 'Uncle' (again) had no revealed means of support (a legal and editorial term), was believed to live on our taxes, a government pension.

He had no reference to the next item on the agenda since he knew that it always opened Friday's talk before Saturday night's game. It was Leo's unfamiliar voice edged with a far accent that challenged the expected excitement.

Silence flattened itself out across the tables.

Uncle Leo entered what would be his day with a recognized but weak throat-clearing cavalry charge. Encouraged by the respectful silence across the coffee cups, Leo surprisingly had captured the club's interest: they'd been waiting weeks for it, a big event.

"This quirk of nature that you talk about has come as a sign from the heavens that was given to our kind as a warning before, and which we as a usually wise bunch have of course ignored."

"How's that, Uncle? What do you mean . . . 'a warning before'?" The question erupted easily from a seriocomic Main Street crowd: how a respected new citizen (which the town had honored as an expected good citizen) could give an answer to an ancient query by a true unknowing small town bunch like us? Among fellow jokers and skeptics —- the eight-o'clocks —- Leo could have felt a bit insulted; nevertheless, he went on:

"Look at Mars," said Uncle Leo. "That's where we came from, you and me, all of us, after we destroyed the planet which had been our home."

"No wonder we can't find Eden because it was up there, or even before that on some other planet. We had to leave Mars, so a few of us were selected as volunteers mostly to row that space ship (the biblical ark, likely) and to tote that bar. We had ignored a warning by scientists, then as now."

"We sailed to this place that we came to call Earth, which we could see from there, and to colonize this world."

"It's in the folklore of our people —- Earth's people —- in every corner of this planet that we now call home."

"It once was a dominant theme with our new earthlings at least until a few years ago, as we learned from the people of India."

"Our ancestors first landed their ship on Earth -- in India, in its jungle hinterland, today truly a crowded nation of Asian gods and inquiring minds."

"We don't know just how many times it had happened, how many planets we had destroyed just like this one, then had to seek a home out there elsewhere in outer space. Greedy man is a wasteful spoiler wherever he is," Uncle Leo continued.

The downtown coffee post-game quarterbacks were quite much to a man anticipating the club's acceptance of this simple but scary entry to their usual jollity. From an unknown foreign mind now had come an interruption to their previously bothered thoughts by Uncle Leo's recital. This was a shocker sure enough.

"You mean, Uncle," said a man from the back of the room, speaking like a big July Fourth firecracker, gangbuster really, then dropping to a soothing voice like from jars of Vicks Salve, "that we were those little green men who came here from outer space we have been hearing about so much lately? Are you saying that you or your people maybe our people got here before time began and just lately started coming back?"

With its green men bearing comic strip balloons of dialogue that had unexpectedly come into the room from the daily newspaper comic pages something like this deflated balloon created an unusual cup and saucer rattle war and loud haw-haws around the tables; the clubbers looked at Uncle Leo in disbelief, just as you'd expect in this age of educated men and women.

New to the club like Uncle Leo, a generally super quiet man known by his curled ends moustache, the same man who earlier was referred to as the town's intellectual, put down his near-empty cup. He apparently had never heard of the theory from a man who was accepted as everyone's sober friend. Clint noted the man's nervousness as he gripped the cup again. Accepting in unsmiling generosity and holding his voice at a wee distance to protect his slight doubt of words from good ole Uncle Leo, he asked:

"Now, just where did you learn that, Uncle Leo, me lad?" The place was surprisingly quiet except for a gulp or two. A coin dropped on the floor just beyond the door would have landed with a shout.

Uncle Leo didn't hesitate; he said:

"Why the answer's been right in front of us ever since Earth's rocket people sent up the first space explorer, with cameras. Maybe the government knows for sure and isn't about to tell us; can't say that I blame them. But we can't keep a secret for long, even with a good press —- usually."

"We are good citizens most times, so we as a rule won't or we hesitate to question the people who run our government especially when we know that they usually give us only part of the story."

"Most of the visible surface of Mars viewable from as far as our cameras and space ships have shown us give us evidence of being swept by what some say were winds."

"Others contend it was a great rush of waters —- the waters that destroyed all but a chosen few of the inhabitants."

"The waters buried what civilization we had up there. I say water, since it is a sure sign of man's habitation."

Leo hesitated, probably for effect, then added: "The waters must have evaporated into what must have been an overheated atmosphere and on into space, the same thing that hints at what we are now experiencing down here, if you'd maybe call it a atmosphere. Somebody's bound to ask, and certainly I'd have no answer to such a detail."

Questions come, "Like how do we know any of this stuff. If our civilization up there beat the heat, but then saw all the waters evaporate into a heating up of Mars?"

Leo said, "The planet's death throes, er, that is, Mars, are like many of our scientists say will happen to Earth in the future as disturbance of the ecology leads to the death of our forests and vegetation and the fish of the sea and animals which walk upon the earth."

The club's fearful social climbers, as Earth was nearing the Twenty-first century —- hopeful politicians all, reckoned that Uncle Leo had been searching for answers himself much more than everyday plain old reading. Some of his phraseology sure came from the Bible and you can see that, so some truth must be in it.

It was recognition of the Holy Book that diverted their attention from the obtuse to what Uncle was telling them. As expected, they took no time to ponder it. Uncle had no grin on his face, no smirk, but appeared quite sober; his listeners now were ready to stand up and salute.

Uncle said, "Smarter minds than mine are at work out there, even as we who are just beginning to accept such things, see it."

"That's why I believe scientists have reason, certainly a responsibility to alert all of the rest of us before we lose it all."

"I sincerely accept it as what is happening, I tell you, right here on Earth as it very well sure as Heaven and Earth happened on Mars. There's evidence that it occurred just the way I said."

One man broke the nervous silence that had clouded the day of these men of usual wit and raillery. All seemed to be thinking about what Uncle Leo had just said. This man made a lot of sense, likely was the consensus. He said it, though, in what some thought was with tongue in cheek, but it became a fear that they all felt. For once, as the silence crept in, each club member retreated into his own moment.

If that is a truth, let's say from introspection, rolled over Clint's thoughts, then all he knew about the mysteries of life and the hereafter may have to get another think.

"I believe it's time we had a man to man talk with the world about what's happening, about what we of the human race by working together can do about it," one man said.

Somebody said, "Huh? That's when an outside voice told us that we all sound like a bunch of politicians." One coffee clubber emitted something like a wee laugh.

"Oh, dang it, you guys, we got something serious going here."

"Okay, where do we start?" It was a nervous voice from a far table. "We have no leadership any more in this country."

"I can't think of the big kind of leadership we need here or in other parts of the world that we know of —- nowhere, in the government or in our universities, not even in the beer joints or in our barbershops."

"So, mighty Caesar, what 'n 'ell we gonna do to save the future?" One fellow had to say it: "I wonder if Caesar ever saw any o' them flyin' saucers?"

"In the past we just about always had somebody who could do some thinking for most of the rest of us; at least somebody out there to reassure us. But I don't see the likes of him anywhere anymore."

"How about the United Nations?" somebody asked, "where they's bound to be some brains?"

This came from a standing newcomer who didn't have a chance at securing a place at the tables but wanted to get into the graces. He was ignored. He'd come in with his ideas later, just like a lot of other citizens who would hear on the street about all the talk lately at Doc's drug store. That's what Leo feared, wishing that he'd kept his mouth shut but he had to get into the town's graces one way or another.

The leading politician of the moment, like he was hoping to fill in the blanks and sighing with the shrug of resignation at all of the simple talk, had this to say: "Well, we've cut into the shell of the problem and now the nut (for sure that reference got its chuckles from many of them); we all agree that something should be done. What? Well, right away we start looking at the big wide world around us for somebody else out there who can solve it for us. That's no good."

"The nut of us is right." The question came from a far voice. Ah, relief, but not quite, since it was to arouse a go-around of forced laughter. Coffee was being poured and stirred. "Pass that bowl o' sugar there. Just throw me a package."

"Anybody need cream?"

Busy, busy, busy. The cow jumped over the moon.

"Who said that?"

"It was that same old bull."

Clint, now sitting near Uncle Jack (as once called; soon to be Uncle Leo) asked him if where he came from was big business run like it had a powerful corporate board that was represented by a bunch of clowns like this one. Jack said he would not know about things like that since everybody knew just the one boss, likely like Joe Stalin maybe. Jack and Clint looked at each other, both winking with nothing else to say.

The tables held to an unsettled, nervous silence. They all looked to Uncle Leo (Jack), he of the no last name, just as Leo was about to say out loud, hesitated, then went right on and said it, that Stalin ran the biggest clown show he knew about, yet he wasn't allowed to say so. Most coffee men had to wonder what Leo was talking about and why he'd never been noticed before.

"Well, Uncle Leo you shore to kish stirred up th' hornets," said a fellow unidentified, "with that way out spiel o' yourn of a space ship landin' way back on th' other side o' th' world. Do you reckon it's true 'bout th' Garden o' Eden bein' on another planet?" Clint, newly arrived in town, was agitating up to a point of screaming.

After his life's work as a newspaperman up in Ohio, Clint was seated at the edge of action at a table near the front of the café. He tried to hide his sudden amusement at the carryings-on of his re-claimed townsfolk, but he couldn't shut it off.

He was prepared to scoot his chair back and head for the street but at that moment of Leo's landing with his own oral inharmonious chit-chat with these country men and women, residents of a small town in mid-America, he'd be embarrassed. He hesitated, recalling how long he'd been trying to find such men and try to maybe develop friendships for serious talk in the few weeks since he'd come home to his mountain.

The big reason it didn't happen was because he had upon his return to the mountain come down to Main Street generally late in the day after the country boys had gone home. He decided at first that it was his same old town just like it had been way back there, except that now it was upside down like the rest of the country, besides closing most of its stores for everything but for obvious reasons the picture show, just before dark.

He leaned forward, holding his chin in his left hand; resting his elbow on the table's edge. How about this fellow Leo? He would ask the question later to nobody in particular, since Leo was right now at his elbow. He expected serious comment from somewhere. He suspected that the others were hoping for the same thing. Too, after all this time, he, too, was an unknown. The only patron who would recall Clint from his boyhood, his friend Frank, had already left. Somebody help me. Frank would have just might have provided the steed that would have given him the support to ride in on. He was standing now, and alone.

To Clint, it was a compulsive thing. He later would regret it, he knew, as he stood up, pausing briefly, apparent to several in the crowd that he was stuttering into a lecture that he might be unsure about. In the silence accorded an old country boy and an over much sweaty anticipation around the tables he knew that he had to be forceful and he hoped sufficiently at ease; he managed to mumble, haw and hum as he fought for the right words. A houseful of expectant faces was turned to him, about all of them expecting profound words of wisdom and insight.

To a few there that day, this man Clint could be hiding behind that little giggle on his face; they all could see it: it was Miz Mona Lisa's traditionally interpreted an almost smile. Was her little giggle really misinterpreted? Why was he thinking of the girl in the painting even as he, Clint Greene, was sure into what the men and women before him were thinking.

Since he'd just lately returned to the town and too soon to the coffee club, he should not have hoped to get an open arms' reception before venturing onto unfamiliar ground that fools like him would fear to go knocking for a better reception.

What Clint was about to say could be interpreted as part circus, um, say . . . part clowning maybe a little golden praise and more than a bit of old boy strawberry, which to posterity was all of nothing, a great big bowl of . . . bilge water he was certain. Would they know if he were as serious as the Washington Monument in a big wind, say?

A few at table knew that Clint was living in his family's old home place up on the mountain that rose out of the hill-shaded green trees southeast above the river, even as most might not recognize him in town. They knew the hill place had been vacant since the man's mother and father had died some years and some months ago. People of the county didn't like vacant houses.

Still scattered among the tables —- Clint could count them off in his mind later —- the few men and women who might recall the barefoot boy around town in overalls on Saturday maybe Sunday afternoons when he came down to the movie house; among them were the postwar newcomers rich in education provided by the GI Bill.

He went away not long after high school and then the Marines and later enrollment at university, where through the local newspaper they were reminded of his weekly or monthly movements. He was a well liked fellow, it was said (smart one at that), joined the Marines like they knew he would; go and fight right off, after Pearl Harbor.

Clint had come home lately by choice to the county of his birth; no one present could understand why somebody who got away would want to come back to this lonesome, world-and time-forgotten burg squeezed lying hermit-like in the mountains.

"Let 'em bask for awhile in his own sunshine," one lazing drinking mate said back at the ranch the day after Clint had confused them all with what he'd told them, that thing that was really bazaar even to the smarts. "Wacky, I'd say."

It began with what Clint had said at the coffee hour: "Any of you fellers here going to Heaven anytime soon?"

"That looks like our only hope to save this world from what we're doing to it. Since you can't think of anybody who is local or even in the world at large out there, we should go up to Heaven and ask around and hire somebody to be born again and come back to Earth to lead us. I've heard a politician of a same stripe get up on the platform where he could face his inferiors and rave on and on and say the same thing, like we need a somebody from D.C.

"I heard you say that the world's people, wherever they live, in our country or out of it, have no leadership any more. 'Why, they are all up in Heaven,'" you'd also say.

"Think about it. You've got all of history, all of time, to select such a man or woman. Many a big guy or smart woman from history —- someone you recalled from reading about him or her in the Earth's past —- who is frustrated up there from not being active, let's say, in Earth's politics like when they were alive down here."

"A bit far fetched, you say? Yes, of course," as the question jolted the assembled businessmen at the coffee recess. Not a citizen was laughing, yet, but they in raised brows, a birthing smirk told him what they thought as he studied all the puzzled faces. Clint had been sure they'd do so and would howl in just a minute. They were being kind, waiting for the big firecracker to go off.

So far, they were silent; they didn't know whether to haw-haw the question or look closely at it with some respect because of its source, certainly coming from somebody just back from the Land of Beulah (surely). They suspected that in the future the town would be hearing a whole lot more maybe wisdom, maybe more nonsense, from one of their own.

Right then it was the common sigh, as expected, a welcome relief from a great big awakened roundtable about to get out of control: "Not me. I'm not ready to do that, to die any time soon."

"That's what you have to do to get up there, right? I'm just not ready for a big move like that."

One fellow said he knew a man in Indiana who was sure that he was Abraham Lincoln born again; "He was a neighbor to everybody, a politician even when he was a boy. I expected to see him on the street in a tall hat one day shaking hands with everybody."

"Did he want to run for president?" he was asked. Now that was a serious, expected question.

"The preachers are always saying, 'Ye must be born again.' Just what else can they mean?"

"Ah, that's just soul, not body, 'You one o' them there heathens?'"

"You've first got to believe in Heaven."

"Shall we have a big coming home party for this back home person, after he gets here, say either man or woman?"

"Well, first we have to find a volunteer to go up there?"

"Let's draw straws," which was an expected suggestion from a fellow with tongue in cheek and weak fire in his eyes. An old smarty said, "Leave my name out of the hat."

"I got a lot to do before I go anywhere like that."

"Not me neither, I got a wife and kids to feed."

"Not me. No, no, no."

"Hey, Clint, sounds good but a trifle unexpected, like a big dynamite boom down at the quarry. Give us time to think about this thing."

"What we need is somebody to lead us afore they have to wait through most o' life while growing up and living out their whole lives maybe, jus' t' get there."

"Yeah, he or she would come back as a baby, right? We want this here feller right away; like they say in the funny papers, there's no time to go awastin.' What was it ever happened to —- was it Jerry? —- naw, it was this feller Smith, by the drawin' in a panel."

"Don't th' Bible say 'a little child shall lead them?'" This wasn't Clint backing up. It came from someone who was on his side, someone who knew Clint and thought he for sure was speaking with tongue out of place, just hiding back there in his cheek; in just a moment his tongue would jump from his mouth and do a reel dance around the saucers on the coffee cup tables.

The man who was about to take hold of his face to keep it sober, said: "You shore got that right. Learn to lead afore he can even learn t' talk."

Clint knew that about everybody would be getting ready to haw out loud if they could find a way to make a little sport of the thing without giving up the right to believe. Their fear was of just how serious Clint was and reluctant to insult his honor and blaspheme God Almighty sobered the crowd. It wasn't time for Clint to grin with an expected laugh to follow, that big famous laugh everybody was known for.

Clint had paused, giving someone an opportunity to be the first man to shout, slap his thigh and toss a ball if he could talk through a full open mouth into the roar that was sure to come, for sure.

A club member said, hoping for a word that would show how smart he was: "We're talking about reincarnation here."

"Isn't that bringing back one of Heaven's citizens, but one that nobody around here would recognize? Right, Clint?"

"Why, yeah, I'd say it was something like that."

A voice of calm came to the man's rescue: "I'm afraid you guys are talking what we down here have no business getting into. That's blasphemy."

Then, "I agree, this is th' most screwed-up thing I ever heard in all my whole life, and sometimes I think I heard from my home up th' creek about everything under the sun."

"I don't recall th' Bible sayin' anything 'bout that thing called reincarnation. Once you die and get to Heaven's gates, if you do get that far, else-wise I reckon you've had it, your one big chance. Either you took the high road or the wrong fork in the road an' never stopped an' looked back, you never got back no matter how much money you owed."

"Our country's biggest leaders, I'd say, mostly took that road, the wrong one. I wish some of 'em had looked back when they had a chance."

"You're joking, right, Clint? Else you've lost all of your reason."

"Ain't nobody in this here crowd aimin' t' take a first step up th' Jacob's ladder." All, including Clint, were, like, sitting there with big grins on the other side of their faces.

"No it ain't," which was a rebuttal from one of the plowmen, likely among the few real men of faith in the room.

"All things are possible in the eyes of Heaven to those who believe," he said. You could tell that he'd been to church and had a good preacher.

The other plowman said: "Careful, now, we might be on the way to the outhouse.

"You fellers are talking about spiritual leaders. I and my kin submit what makes you think they an' we got all the right answers?"

"Good talking point. I suspect we are on the wrong track here. But let's us change the subject. We are just a bunch of hicks down here, anyway. What kind of influence would any of us have up in Heaven, what with all th' lost souls 'round here already suspect up there?"

One fellow who had been trying finally got the floor long enough to say: "I say we table this thing like Congress and never talk about it again until next Monday at the earliest. Not tomorrow, that's for sure. Maybe next week, no, not then either, not until after the golf tournament is over."

Clint welcomed the invitation that came from a man at the next table. "Come sit down over here, Clint. Tony just left. Got a place waitin' for you here, an empty waitin' here by my side."

"Yeah, old buddy," the man said as Clint sat down, his host punching his new friend. "Tell us what you been doing? Hear tell you some kind o' big newspaperman from afar. How in this old world did a little old mountain boy like yousef get into a work like that?"

Clint's spur to opportunity just came riding out; he'd have sworn minutes ago that what he'd said was a spiel by an idiot. Silly, kidding among the weak-minded like himself. Now, trying to dig himself out of a big three-by-seven foot hole (size of a dug grave, that is) since he didn't know why he'd said it. He was thinking as hard as he could. He was about ready to believe every bit of it, though.

He had to defend it since it came out after his lesser sane self or got it from some far away ghostly prompting. He didn't allow that to happen much if he felt that it was coming. Right now he knew he'd better redeem himself before he left the tables.

He said: "A lot of journalists or a hope-to-be got into this heart breaking business of news because he-they thought it would be a good lazy way to make a living."

"The idea of 'saving the world' has become a cliché within the for instance word and print society, yet there's a lot of truth in it."

"About all hopeful writers in J-school like me back then believed it. Reckon I simply drifted into the newsroom because I liked to write and this was about the only way I could get paid for it. I think I really believed it. All the same, we complained because it was never enough for what we did."

"The newsroom has produced a raft of novelists and successful free lancers. Some of them right good. Excuse me. Let me say they write well." He spelled it out, getting a good laugh from the coffee bunch that pleased him. Ah, relief.

Right then, in an effort perhaps to defend the 'profession,' Oscar, local newsman, piped up: "This feller makes a lot of sense to me. What he says may come from his own faith, but it sounds like he's sincere and believes in the Creator. I say give him a hand."

Clint was studying the faces of the coffee men. Except for a few and the farmer he'd left at the other table, he still expected grins of doubt. Many quiet at table were newcomers, he realized; they had come to town during his absence.

"If I thought about saving the world, I sure as heck never had the feeling that I could do a bit of something about it," he said.

"Let me take that back. There were moments when I thought I could, but the feeling was not to last. In the meantime, to be a better newspaperman it is the study of history, what made the country the nation among nations. That's when you read about or hear about what were called miracles spinning at the loom back through time.

"You think a lot about how you've been blessed with the talent you've been given."

"Way to go, Clint."

"I say, Clint me lad," said the intellectual, "if you got to Heaven or wherever, a bit early, and you recalled the big reason you were hired by us down here as an ambassador, or as a member of the selection committee, let's say, just how would you then go about it?

"And," continued the man with the mustache and too much smarts, "since you have obviously given this piece of philosophy considerable thought, just who might you suggest among so many that you know might be eligible for reincarnation?"

"I can think of a lot of people up to our time, now gone, who'd be capable of doing what you've proposed, but not from Heaven, or perhaps even Buddha, with doctrine of nirvana or wherever, who might be that person, certainly a ghost from the past, eh?"

"I admit," said Clint, "that I've thought of it as a game. I have looked into history, not only that of my country, but for men and women in and out of the pages of history of other nations who came to leadership right out of nowhere when a crisis loomed."

"I asked myself, what if? Remember, we're talking about history, not Heaven. I'd have to say that I've never marked my ballot for any one person, or should I say angel?"

"Now to the crux of the matter, the critical point," said the intellectual. "Just how in the world, or Heaven, if I may say so, can anyone, man or woman mind you, do such a job as you suggested, or at least implied?"

For the purposes of this book, allow Clint Greene, a one-time editorialist, to speak: "The answer can be found in the record of men and women, especially those who gave their sons to the battle. Men in death, or life, are equal under the same Heaven, the same god or God. A few leaders of men and women in history have been so recorded. It's been done often by a determined leader through all of history. You'll find many candidates if you study history; it would be better if you studied your own countrymen first, then you pursue the study of others."

"You asked, how then would I know? I somehow feel that he or she will be waiting for me, or someone like me, especially somebody smarter than me."

"The Gettysburg battlefield especially as Lincoln defined it for history's thousands of Americans who died and those who survived the battle and later millions of others who were not there except in spirit for the next hundred fifty years —- what their country is about. It is a monument to the end of a big facet of a nation's past its lost blood a promise that what was lost and found on time's battlefields will not happen that way again. Some several months later and in just three minutes given at the memorial to the country's dead in the battle of Gettysburg he as the speaker at the cemetery dedication said that the historical tragedy would bring the nation together, that we will continue the union that was formed as a model for the world to follow not many months earlier by men and women of heroic stature. The guy that said it found a place in history as none other we have known, in our reading of it. He is universally honored. If he never did anything else, what he said that day moved on to history's memory, which has recalled his greatness. It is engraved on the face of his memorial.

"All this discussion is simply something to satisfy a quest for a man's self, or his soul, which is why I brought it up. Bang, Bang. Aye and the saints be tolerated by lesser men; all a bit of a fantasy that you and we and your proud kin are aware, in our thoughts designed to encourage our study of what it is that makes men or women great in the eyes of others, and who are suspected by us to be in Heaven."

"There is no reason to believe that these men of courage have taken away the spirit, even if it must be written in stone to forever 'call it spirit' that lives in the annals of their country, and in their heritage. There is no reason to believe or not believe that their spirit died on a field of battle, or elsewhere, or that they had returned to life on Earth many times when summoned by their country." A few Friday coffee folk were still around, smiling.

(Is a smirk the same thing?).

They knew that Clint, the newcomer, talked like Uncle Leo who a few minutes ago had one hand under the weight of his humor. Outside, Clint met Gus on the street.

Clint said to Gus: "I today was an author of the proposition of reincarnation as a solution to our fight in saving the world against climate change and all that s happening out there. I believe in traditional religious teachings of the supernatural. I announce my reserve which gives me a chance to escape a full endorsement. I always say that it is just my opinion built around my religion, nothing more. There are many hurdles to anyone's belief in an afterlife. In one religion we just mentioned it is a big part in the promise of many lives for one person, or individual,"

"You don't have to explain your religion to a Black man. For a lot of centuries we've tried to explain God to our brothers. We go right on maybe revising our religion, our belief in God as we realize nothing much has changed, so we go right on in our prayers," said Gus.

Clint continued: "The fight against evil is followed in the movies, as accepted by the viewing public of a man in a black hat, but more they seek a man known by his swagger and a sure grin, as he looks right in the eye of the range boss's hired challenger. His holstered forty-five reflects the sun from his huge polished holster and outsized badge over his left lung says much about his intent to defend what's right." Clint early became what he easily believed was his talent "as a good judge of men." Clint was looking for a way to talk about life as more than a fight between good and evil. Much of literature and the pulpit, however, are built on a universal theme.

He had met Gus on the street just before the road out to the college left the highway. Clint felt he had to tell Gus what he had said at the coffee meeting and Gus thanked him for what he thought about the encounter.

Chapter Two

As a boy when he was down town he rather enjoyed walking by the larger homes on the town's west side, many of them brick, wondering what they looked like on the inside. The houses were homes to the town's few professional people, a few business people and a few retirees, that is older people who had retired and were said to have money in the bank.

He didn't feel resentful toward them; he knew their kids in high school and at the college where he had begun studies as a student, but none had ever invited him into their homes, not that this bothered him, nor was he ever inclined to ask one of the girls for a date. That's simply the way life is.

"Really, Clint, is that what you thought?" a friend asked one day when he was complaining about how hard it was growing up in his mountain community. "Well, let's say I did have some thoughts on it, fleetingly, but I knew a heck of a lot of country boys who felt it, and deeply. They told me so. Let's leave it at that."

He turned from the brick street onto the short road toward the college. Clint wasn't prepared to get into a chat with the county sheriff he saw just ahead until he knew more about the doodlebug that was bothering him about the murder victim that Gus told him about the night of the ride to the depot. Clint wasn't ready to carry the load of sane conversation with this law man's country boy roughhouse banter. The fat sheriff who now stood facing him would have to be a good friend for that, or likely an old Marine buddy.

Badge and gun both much larger than you'd expect except from a man that you knew could himself be a victim of life on the run. It was far too much swagger for a true law man. Clint wondered what man the badge and the gun were running from. Not the law, because he would say that he was the law, but something else that he wanted to hide. His place within the law was part of the wall he'd built around himself.

"Howdy, Mister Sheriff, made any big arrests lately?" Clint said.

"And a goodly howdy to you, Mister; do I know you?" the big man asked. The sheriff, a good three inches taller than Clint, stooped a bit to look him right in the eye. That's good, Clint thought. He trusts me. He's not hiding something from me now, but still . . . .

"I'm Clint Greene. I was raised up on the mountain right in front of the town. I've been working up in Ohio; now home for good, since I retired."

"Well, now, that's good, you comin' home like that," the sheriff said. "Knowed yore pappy, fine man, yore mammy she was a good woman, too, as a Christian and the Lord would admit to it. Well, I expect you an' me, we'll get along, long's you keep yore nose clean. Stop in an' see me. We'll have a little spit'n chaw t'gether, talk 'bout fishin' maybe like two ol' buddies, Christian buddies, I like to say. My door is open to everybody all th' time, 'cept in th' winter."

He was a few years younger than Clint; after the war and college and the newspaper business, Clint would've allowed the boy to grow up and become sheriff of his county.

A day or two later Clint recalled the invitation and walked into door of the law's quarters. The sheriff had his big feet on the desk, that big forty-five lying next to his boot.

The sheriff was enjoying the breeze from a big fan on the floor next to the window. Air-conditioning was coming in soon and the sheriff would be the first to begin partaking of its blessing. He held out his big hand like any good politician, and said:

"Have a seat, Mister Greene. Welcome to where I live. Could I fix you a cup o' tea? Not coffee. I can get that any place in town. Been a tea drinker ever since I lived with the British after th" war doin' nothin' but cleanin' up landin' fields an' tearin' down barracks. Th' troops gone home long time ago and Hitler was a bad memory. Was too young t' get in an' do any fightin.'" You could see that the sheriff was looking for a way to brag about his role in the big war.

"No thanks," said Clint. "Don't want to take up much of your valuable time. You know I'm an old newspaperman, curious as the town's most nosy old biddy, always looking for some gossip to pass on to my readers, and to satisfy my own curiosity."

"That right? Hey now, what's that got you poised with pencil an' paper to tell about it in that newspaper o' yourn?"

"It's the multiple murders in our county that's getting the people all scared and riled up? All I've heard since the fit hit the shan, just what I've read in the local newspaper."

"Wal now," said the sheriff. "I'd like t' say it's none o' yore business, sir, but th' law and th' constitution they say it is. It has become a dang sore spot with me, an' since I like you an' you bein' a newspaper man an' all, I'll tell you that th' government's got me all tongue-tied an' sore-tailed an' they's nothin' I can do 'bout it, let alone even say anything 'bout it."

"What've you heard; somethin' you know I don't?"

"I thought you could tell me."

Neither man jumped in to go on with the story, since both would rather be doing some positive thinking. At least old print man Clint thought it was positive.

"Wal, Greene," the sheriff said, "right after th' first feller was found with his throat cut I called up th' state police first thing. It wasn't a couple hours here they come, ever dang government agent from D. C. on down; th' whole shebang hit my office an' pulled th' shade an' put a guard on th' door an' started talkin' in whispers to me, lettin' me know I had no business in the matter."

"Sounds to me they might have been bluffing, overstepping an assumed right about what they believed or assumed was their area of authority."

"Me, too, an' I asked 'bout state lines. How'd this feller fit into that definition? Th' first FBI feller said it was part of an international conspiracy an' it was their right an' duty; that's all they said on the matter. Even laughed an' said they'd keep me informed, though. But they never said another serious word to me. Then came more murders like with their throats cut.

That's where it all stopped. No more word and me with my job as sheriff of this here county."

"Mister sheriff," said Clint, laughing all the way down to his sore ankles in a shut demeanor and not showing it because he'd gotten the sheriff to talk about the incident when he had said he had no inclination to do so, "I thank you for being honest with me."

That made the sheriff grin outside the left side of his face.

"I know you will know before I will, so I won't bother you anymore about it, at least not right now," said Clint. "But I sure want to know about an international conspiracy that's concerned this little old town deep in the hills of old Kentucky. Sure looks like our federal government is down deeper into the people's business than we ever thought possible. That sure the dickens bothers me. You'll never know just how much."

Clint was startled the same hot day an hour or two later after a visit to the college campus when an old school friend of a short lifetime long past, while wiping his brow with a wet handkerchief stopped him as he neared the heart of town and said he was glad that Clint came back to his home town and asked where he could buy some firewood.

Families living back in the mountains kept soup in the winter in the big fire pot hanging in the fireplace up to and during the depression and like in pioneer days by selling the firewood left over. Curt recalled their dedication to hard work, the times they lived in.

"You all at your place having a wiener roast like maybe, Curt?" Clint inquired about something that was none of his business.

"Nope, thought I'd just lay in some firewood while business was slow out in the fields and I might get it cheaper."

"I can't help you at all on that little problem, Curt. Last I knew was old man Kirby, the last of the breed. You'll just have to catch him in town when you see him and his wagon. He wouldn't own a phone. I never did see his ad in the local paper. He's a catch as catch can man. Kirby lives over the river by the second bridge if you want to go out there."

Curt thanked him. He walked away still using the wet cloth to wipe sweat off his neck. His shirt was wet through.

That same day out on Rose Avenue a woodcutter who would call himself a friend of Clint's was knocking on doors peddling the last of a load of wood he'd taken to town in his wagon which was pulled by his two storied prize mules.

In years past, the townspeople ordered coal and wood for the following winter in early spring, before housecleaning. The woodsman back then had more business than he could handle.

A handful of former coal miners who had household mines in their backyards once did a good business hauling coal to town to peddle, just like the woodsman who by door-to-door canvassing of the larger homes along Rose and other streets of the neighborhood kept their families alive and warm during hard times.

Since the natural gas pipeline a few years ago came into the county through a deep dug ditch, Kirby's wood customers apologized and the man was about to yield to progress.

Kirby the woodcutter knew the gas wells would give out one day and his old patrons would return, as he waited. He told them so. They told him just to hang in there.

He was a man of solid oak himself, of large stature. The sun and outdoors honored him with a tan leathery face, a squint of a man of the American plains that would make you believe he was like a modern western Indian looking into the dim shadow of his cattle out on the horizon of his ranch. You said that his eyes were there someplace back of the squint.

You'd never take Kirby for a once proud woodcutter. He was more a cattleman, with a cow or two, a steer once in awhile a townsman said of him. Clint only knew Kirby in passing, though. That is all most anybody knew about him because he was a quiet man. Never came to town unless he had to. Clint knew other men from his reading of history and his own people of the mountains like the old west, just like the movies and picture books told you how the men and women who built this country did it in a way that made them strong enough to endure the wide and open plains under a sun close to the Earth and snow and ice that seemed to melt away only after the long days of waiting for spring, which at last began to return.

A different sort of rumor builder or runner-downer who had no reason to be like that, told the coffee family one day that under a sweaty shirt that smelled of the unwashed that Kirby was all over muscle. "I wouldn't want to tangle with him no matter what," he said.

Strong hands arms neck belly all in tune he reckoned from cutting firewood all his life. Clint said that Kirby was of an honorable occupation among working men of the land of a thousand years' or more duration. He was the central character of many fairy tales; the planter-woodcutter was exiting at stage left, except for an encounter with Clint today.

The huge outdoorsman knew that Clint had come home to his mountain and that he'd be a possible customer for his firewood. Clint just hadn't run into him yet. Kirby by every hill measure was all Irishman and full of big brag about it.

He wasn't about to endure that long climb to Clint's place with his 'family,' those two 'fine' mules of his that he said built his fortune. They might go and slip right off the mountain putting him forever out of business. He treated his mules just like a respected citizen shielded his dogs.

"He will (talking about Clint) get mighty tired of trying to cook and heat his place with wood and coal," which to him meant that Clint would need more wood than coal; thinking like that, he figured, was what made him a good businessman.

"I'll also wager he'll either find a place in the valley or move back up into Ohio where he wouldn't have to do much work."

The townsfolk who could see his place on the mountain from under the hill were getting into the guessing game about what Clint intended to do with his life.

"You're probly good n' right, Mr. Kirby. Once you've seen Paree, you won't go back to the farm. If you do nothing else you won't stay long once you've had all these mechanicals around; you won't give 'em up.'

"If I were you I'd hurry Mister Kirby, before he's got chickens in the yard and a cow in the barn. You gotta git. You'd best git up there ere he's settled in. Others will be calling on him, you can bet." It was intended as advice from a businessman.

The woodsman had run into Clint close to downtown on a late summer's day not long after all that stubborn universal talk with the sheriff and more talk in town which was mostly guessing even believing the worst about their town and even the whole country, asking what their country was coming to when they learned about the murders.

The wagon was full of firewood. Kirby introduced his friend on the seat beside him. Clint remembered Kirby from his boyhood of a long time ago, and the introduction was not expected because of Kirby's rasin', although he had offered the helper's name, which Clint rolled over in his memory which came up empty yet told a couple of friends later that the man must have been Hispanic. The man didn't respond to Clint's offer of a handshake. At the time Clint attributed that non-act simply to bad manners.

The stranger had an unusual almost scared look about his eyes, Clint thought. He only grunted after what his boss the woodcutter said about him. Instead he tried to hide his full face, kept it half hidden by lowering his chin like any mountain boy when somebody he didn't know stopped at his family's house for a visit.

In the hill country a visitor to a cabin in the mountains like Clint's family lived in, stopped on the road and called from the gate, "Hello the house," before his daddy shouted back, "Get down and come in, Roscoe. Bring that pretty woman you got there with you." Clint was half grown before he could feel like his dad, as hospitable.

A memory interfered, but he kept on in his study of the man; surely why he couldn't have come from around here. Kirby said it was the first day in town for the man. He said the hired helper had been with him for about six months. "Slept out in the hayloft: even in the winter."

Clint Greene shrugged, visibly. He got no response from the ugly stranger. He could forgive the man as he recalled lots of mountain men and women just like that (and himself, included) and how 'me and most of us used to be especially unkind to a stranger who was too nosy.' He knew it had begun when the revenue people came to the mountains looking for stills and more tax money if there were such a thing as the latter.

Clint suddenly felt uneasy in his stomach. Something is odd here, he thought, the intuitive newspaperman's lifetime in dealing with all sorts of people had begun kicking in. His trained news mind was jumping right out of the printer's type case. It soon would be running around the big press.

With both clinched fists the newsman would call up what was becoming a buried fear, hoping his pride, a journalist's instinct, would be proving itself in just a few moments before the man got away.

Men and women from south of the border, in the new era of the failed Mexican economy, were all around him, most in unskilled jobs. He hadn't any reason to question their dedication and ingenuity —- aware that they'd come here for work, to settle down, as earlier men had come, forced to abandon a home and a difficult lifestyle. But this man was not of their land south of the border; Clint was beginning to be suspicious.

He feared that his suspicions from a long ago boyhood were coming back from the time of the big iron gate he recalled from the first day he saw it and the shivers it sent all through his body, The gate set off a big house of horrors in town like a graveyard in which he and his friends had been told was haunted.

That wasn't totally correct, since he'd often seen both women, the occupants, downtown, and soon knew more about them, and where they lived. That house of theirs behind the big rusting gate still caused all sorts of evil scary talk.

Among the respected members of his gang, who had at first enjoyed the speculation, were young men destined to learn some lessons of life, that among their fellow creatures were that every town should have a big haunted house, even if it was inhabited by odd old people. Two exclusives, two suspicious women, and he never got over his boyhood fear, or suspicions about them.

He was on the verge of deciding that the man was not Hispanic, as his name told him it was possible, suggesting also that he might be, Mongolian? Still, it is possible he could be what Kirby said he was. Or did the man really say? Suddenly, like he was reading Clint's mind, Kirby's farm hand suddenly didn't look away or cover his eyes, but looked straight into Clint's soul, as Clint defined it, deep into his eyes, like a movie Dracula creeping, warning.

Moviegoers had become addicted to the screen's evil characters and the long time in coming acceptance was nourished by a shortage of movie plots during the Great Depression years. Clint said once that the picture show was the greatest American unifier, especially for kids who became wrapped up even in a stale plot by actors who were familiar on black and white screens of lonely times to the thrill seekers on Saturday or Sunday afternoons.

Clint's next stop was the business parlor of an undertaker he knew. The feds would have brought in experts to examine the bodies of the three murdered 'aliens' perhaps watched them be embalmed —- before they were shipped following autopsies so far away to eerie destinations Clint knew he'd never learn about—- and for what government reasons?

"Do you recall any tattoos maybe scars probably from war wounds or any unusual markings on the bodies of any or all three of the murdered men?" Clint asked.

"If I did I wouldn't have said anything about what was evident or almost, not with those two FBI men standing there. They watched every turn of my hand. They brought in their own man to do the autopsies and he did a lot of cutting and corpse scraping," Clint was told, and he believed him.

"How about their clothes, parts of military uniforms maybe? Did they have peculiar haircuts? Their teeth, had they been taken care of, the use of hair tonics or evidence of the use of drugs, any needle marks on their bodies?"

"I couldn't say. Really, I couldn't comment. Afraid to, these boys knew what they were doing and I sure wasn't about to ask any questions."

"Well, were the bodies brought directly here after they were found?"

"That was the coroner's decision. They didn't even wait for the state police."

Clint mentioned the demeanor of a man he recently had met and the essence of evil he'd felt in the presence of the man. "Did you ever maybe feel something like that, Mr. Undertaker?" and to the sheriff: "Something reflecting an evil presence? Let's say it was from an encounter with a gun victim who'd been shot in a gunfight with the law?"

"Can't say that I did; that's an odd question, Clint," said the sheriff. "In this business, dead is dead, and you go right on with the job and I'd say each was just another, er, job. I've encountered a lot of men and women and children, all dead, in my time, and after a while, and you'd better not say so, it becomes quite routine and just another step before the grave."

Clint didn't say so even as he actually felt evil in the man on the farmer's wagon.

It was just another man, alive, and he wondered about him.

He knew that he had no right to think so. Nothing actually to be proud of. He knew the evil hand of Satan was on his shoulder as he talked to one of his cohorts about why he should feel guilty about such thoughts . . . it was like an electric charge which ran through his body and rattled his bones.

He'd known other such men before, but not as so, men you'd never suspect who had seen the fires of hell. The man penetrated his usual calm, gazing at Clint as just a piece of hardened flesh, down deep among the dead, who refused to accept their common lot. Clint's abrupt midnight wakening for too many dark nights followed the wall outlines of a face invading his sleep.

It was weeks before his better self erased the eyes from his bedroom walls. Clint drove the evil face away, not in fury but by good will, as he was to find in affection for his old, his new town.

Today, to get his mind onto another thought, he took an hour to rest in a lounge chair beneath a summer sun by day, giving thanks to the source for another day of sunshine, a night of peace.

In town, business thrived. Customers entered and left the shops through their street doors. The sheriff was on his beat, policing. Shoppers were busy, proudly spending money in their hometown; Pippa Passes.

All was good, even though it was a weekday. Few farmers would be in today, "You'll see, wait until Saturday. That's a farmer's traditional day."

The east end of Main Street was blocked off. Hard hat workmen were stirring a batter of powdered cement, water and sand; they told him they'd be removing every other parking meter and filling the holes with raw concrete.

A pedestrian asked again, "What is going on?" Its parallel parking from now on, said the workman. "Th' mayor said we need an extra lane for traffic. Too many people with cars, I reckon." He added: "The town is in a spurt of progress so that th' next thing to lay out will be a parkin' lot; for sure we'll need it on Saturdays if we can find enough level ground."

Clarence the hardware man used to 'monopolize' the sidewalk in front of his store to display his merchandise; he got complaints to the council. In the spring it was lawn mowers and fertilizer. In winter he carried out sleds and snow shovels and placed them in a line at the front of his store's big display windows.

He said, awkwardly, "The council said the sidewalk was for my customers to walk on. They asked, which do you want, "the whole sidewalk instead of the set-up inside the store?" When they said it was for my 'customers' "that was a neat way of telling me I ought to agree. Just the passing of the old ways, and I can take it or I can leave it, and be fined. They said the old village way of doing things are in the frontier past. "We'll never be a city with a store out on the sidewalk."

Clarence had been blocking the free movement of the citizens until the city told him with the more powerful voice, "Now who has more right to a little part of the sidewalk than do the citizens of this town?"

"Reckon they are right, though. The Constitution levels us out, since those people with money to spend are what built this town."

A poster in the window of the town's only haberdashery screamed in 48-point type the coming of the 'big' Strawberry Festival, noting in much wee type face that Main Street will be blocked off for the annual parade on Saturday.

The Chamber of Commerce folk in tiny print hoped that many floats already under way would be led by the local high school band plus three bands from nearby towns.

Clint knew the leaders of the parade would show a lot of shiny legs by girls with batons of all colors a-twirling, which was a big part of the show for the country boys.

One float would introduce this year's strawberry queen.

Pride, man; pride, that's what it is all about.

Our town raises our share of good-looking corn-fed girls. Clint Greene agreed.

A big farm truck with a load of cattle mooing and bawling today moved right down Main Street toward the stockyards on the other side of the river.

If the price for the livestock didn't come up to a farmer's estimate, he'd load 'em up and take his cattle to a sales yard on the other side of the state -- going right down Main Street once more, confusing shopkeepers and everybody else.

The last time a farmer left town to sell his livestock, too many protests began to be noted by the businessmen. A low offer by the cattle buyers soon was evident at their cash register. The farmers often reminded the businessmen of a certainty, ignoring the fact that they, too, must prepare for the new age which was already here.

Clint would say he loved this town. All-American and a promise fulfilled to the founders of a new country on this side of the Atlantic.

Who would have believed that the perpetrators of an international conspiracy had found it and were bringing it toward the Twenty-First century?

Clint Greene picked up Oscar Bell Blues, that's Bill the editor, at his office one recent noon. They were on their way to lunch at that little cafe just two doors past the drug store, then right around the corner.

Oscar pointed to a building a few steps up the street and said, "I was there yesterday walking around and surveying that place looking for a cross of gold." Clint was startled for a moment, until he recalled the time before the war that he'd done the same thing. He said, "'Et tu, Brute!' I quit thinking about that place a long time ago. That's why I was surprised. Let's eat our lunch and we'll walk around there if you have time."

They'd barely taken their seats in the café than Oscar began to talk about his lately unhappiness with his job and the citizens of the town. "How long, oh Lord, is it before the government and the general run of the long time population will look upon this lost soul as certainly one of their own? No matter who I talk to than I realize that I'm a stranger just stopping for a moment to ask directions."

"Tell me, Clint". . . said (Bill) Oscar, suspecting that a one-time publisher of a country newspaper up in Ohio would recall events that at the time encouraged the brag by natives of their red blood of American primogeniture rights in Clint's new community and back in his home in Kentucky. Oscar wanted to know if townsfolk in either of his towns welcomed the stranger to their midst or if an apparent friendly gesture came from the other side of their smiling faces.

He expected Clint to have been given an education in their ways even if it was of little or no consequence; Clint would have been just a boy when he learned of life and things political of his generation —- let's say, for instance, a lively story of pretty women and their clandestine lovers and fast horses that took a family's bread money.

This is how life in his hill country appeared to him, as defined to outsiders, which had become a hackneyed routine in the past thirty years in print and by hotshot bragamuffins or tatterdemalions who themselves came to the big towns in the north for the first time, most of them in uniforms of the second war. These good old boys he knew on the mountainside as he was growing up pretty much became the way these educated folk viewed a world outside these boys' domain. It was just another bulwark to be overcome by the local Chamber of Commerce.

"Let's take a look for that cross," said Clint, amused by Oscar's eagerness. "I will not laugh at you, since I once was as excited as you are. Later we'll talk about thin-skinned editors, why they appear to have died before their time, how we in the business often expected barbs and knife thrusts in midnight anonymous telephone calls."

On the way to where the cross once was buried in concrete, Oscar said: "I was going through some old dusty files of the newspaper a few days ago and I ran into a story about a dedication along about here somewhere of the golden cross. I walked all around here and I couldn't find any such thing or evidence of it."

Oscar was mumbling something about which was a forgotten big event or dulled memory to the public and for a long time because of childhood non-interest to Clint himself; Clint said for about an hour when he was a boy he did have a little interest in the legend. He was searching his mind's catalogue, and said that it was another local phenomenon and for sure not surprising since this sort of thing happened every day in the mountains.

That was likely why he hadn't thought much of it since Oscar's query came out of nowhere to alert his memory, not unusual for a newspaper editor, ending the sentence that had begun with, "whatever happened to the cross . . . please tell me."

The unusual but nearly forgotten event came across the horizon from a time long ago, not since Clint had run these streets, saying he liked to do so for no reason other than, "to walk the concrete because I liked to get the feel of the city, even a small town, anywhere the people are found, here or in the north or in the south."

He recalled the landmark with a smile of pride from a once-upon-a-time, said, "Used to stand right here on the edge of the sidewalk; got so you never noticed it, 'til it was gone."

Clint grabbed the arm of his friend as a pointer, who was aware of the look of amazement on Clint's face, asking him if he "felt all right?" Clint circled nothing except a memory, now a concern, searching the smooth surface for 'the cross,' at least for the hole in the broken sidewalk that once held all that gold which had become symbolic of an event long ago in the town.

Clint the man now would recall a day right after the war and he was home looking for the boy, which was himself before the war and he had gone away. It wasn't until now that he seriously resumed seeking answers hither and yonder and was told that the Cross of Gold had disappeared long before the war. The subject came up because in memory it was metal, and the country was sending a lot of old cars and other metal to Japan. It's odd, he thought, that his own government would have melted it down to make a part of a tank or gun of some kind.

That new talk and new search was a long time reappearing after the war when people began to follow the newly built super highways built over any existent old country road they could find. Outside workers on the new road showed up down town, spending a lot of money from their fat pay checks. That led to the promise of money, of gold and new paths of promise to riches that would have been taken over by Americans after the Depression and the war in the Twentieth Century. So many citizens were persuaded that they needed to get rich so they might fit into the new society.

At one time the storefront behind the cross was a Masonic lodge; then the Democrat Party came and called it a party headquarters. They moved away for awhile and later came back again. It was once a radio and TV sales outfit which used it as its main office.

Clint was told of its demise by old men of the village what they knew of its origin when he'd talk of it just lately. It bothered him some that no one of a later generation could tell anyone who might have asked what had happened to the cross, as it was with the newer settlers who had to be told that it ever existed. Clint told Oscar to go back to an earlier page of his newspaper and he'd find the possible origin of the story.

"Was it really gold?" asked Oscar.

Clint said, as he recalled it mostly from street talk almost forty years later, that it was erected after the turn of the century in honor of William Jennings Bryan, who had visited the town during his train's whistle stop. Bryan hadn't been expected to appear today, even as the democrats stood hopefully by.

Bryan got off the train to shake a few hands as the engine's tank took on water from the water tower. They'd expected him even as that bunch of democrats were surprised.

It was said by republicans that Bryan just 'happened' on an aide's reminder that it would be politically necessary for him to step off the train as the engine routinely grabbed its necessary water at the river's edge. Bryan's visit came during the presidential campaign of 1908.

Bryan was writ into political history after his famous speech, "You shall not crucify mankind upon a cross of gold," which was a rousing one-liner from the party's convention in 1896. The idea for the cross as a monument jumped again innocently enough right out from the editor's column in Oscar's own newspaper, an ancient sheet which he bought nigh onto a three-quarter century later.

At the time local democrats believed that the cross would be a fitting memorial to the not once but three-time nominee to the U.S. presidency —- and they should commemorate Bryan's short but memorable visit to their humble little metropolis deep in the mountains of Kentucky.

The cross was made of iron by the village smithy. Then it was sent off to a Chicago outfit that applied gold leaf, in a process called gilding. It probably was the gold leaf, or its gilding, that once attracted a thief who nearly broke it off at the street level before he was discovered. It first had been set in concrete (by now it was apparent that the hole later was cemented over). Clint was determined to find the old covered hole now beneath the newer concrete even before he left town for World War II.

The almost theft would have been a painful loss to the democrats. It did leave a 'truth' with townsfolk that it had been purloined. Evil minded men of the world were always out there. Democrats at the time surely more than hinted that it had been a success by the next attempt by a thief.

A kittle while later the party people tried to peddle the unbelievable idea that it simply had been 'retired' and that it would be resurrected for a future campaign or a major political celebration. No good party leader would ever reveal its possible hiding place or the enormity of such an event that would bring it again to life.

Democrats declared that no other city in the country had so honored an outstanding democrat. It would always be there for posterity, the 'cross of gold' line in a speech that had gotten Bryan nearly elected.

Clint said he would track down the truth ("with your help"). The republicans for a gifted time repeatedly led many a reminder when the opportunity arose that the democrats were overwhelmingly represented by a hole in the ground.

Before we leave a once celebrated part of downtown, it should be mentioned that the Jaycees and the American Legion decided at about the same time that the town's face should be washed and the old buildings and attitude of the citizens should be dragged into the new age even if they yelled and moaned of its ill treatment —- out of the nineteenth century and into the arms of the new age.

The bandstand in the city park right downtown was a sentinel, even in hard times, but had been relegated to silent guard duty in a new America. The elements had done its worst to its life and purpose.

Still, it performs as a breath of the past: vine-covered to a gasp of memory looking for a way to serve the weary among a young and bored generation of a (new?) prosperous and fearful new century, however guarding its boy and girl secrets of once on a midnight.

A grove of trees, still alive —- a score of native growth —- was set down for time. Mere saplings then, they had grown to welcome shade of a July day. A fellow could go there and find rest, if they so pleased. Boys and girls with no interest than in each other activities could go there.

An army tank from the second war was on its way to its final rust as it sat largely ignored now on what once was a grassy spot on the courthouse lawn; weeds were bursting into the daylight from a former hiding place along its tracks.

Anti-war folk in other towns were demanding removable of such reminders of their young men marching away to kill kind and kin. "Our children must be taught of peace; this implement of war must go," they called out in a near shout. Even with its guns silenced, it was declared that it represented 'man's inhumanity to man.'

Soon after Clint's return from war the county erected a large crude wooden billboard alongside the courthouse. In forty-eight point hand print, the names and service of all men who were soldiers or sailors from the county were writ large for the public to trace by their fingers those who went to war on orders of their government.

Clint's name was up there. Built entirely of mountain wood, it too would see its dust year in an early memory loss of the greatest event of the century like the elms farther along Main Street that also became victims of a new age because of neglect and the sun the rain and the freeze and the new era of insult and demand for even more parking and pocketbooks of prosperity. The new day also brought new stores and a brand new bank to the downtown court house block which matched other business fronts everywhere.

As the old began to pass and the new came in with annual reminders of later wars, which were left to surviving moms and dads and history; Clint said their loss was not etched in wood, but in the fallen tears that would fertilize the green grass alongside the rusting war memorial at the courthouse —- in a little village that once was visited by one more man with ambition deterred along with thousands of other democrats who lived in the greatest republic the world had ever known.

Aching reminders to a dozen or so citizens of the past and Clint's fondness for it was the only constant to him and citizens who walked by it on their way to a new day's dreary duties, maybe saluting the men who were at last at rest.

"Townsfolk said the ancient façade downtown of the inn was a disgrace like most of its genre in other towns with a past. Its outdated bricked façade made you wonder how the Feds missed it, when tax money was sent to modernize the main streets and byways of other small towns that were passed over as the interstates were laid down after the big war. The politicians said on the city's behalf that we had to get the country moving again."

Funny thing, men, women, whose jobs were on Main Street, said from their own memory that at no time since the Great Depression had the hotel known vacant rooms. They said, though, that the old hotel was 'an eye sore,' whatever that is.

What kept it going, said the word, was an older Social Security permanent guest crowd; they knew of no other such place in town which would make welcome these latest comfortable citizens with little money in their pockets.

Many of the men except in winter could be seen on the wide porch, which was just a step up from the street. Right out front, and there ought to be a plaque, was the same 'exact' spot where a one-time sheriff had left his blood when an assassin's bullet cut off his windpipe.

Clint had heard that the blood spot was still out there. He'd become excited and went straight to the porch to look for it, and he found it. Other places in his town that were also so hallowed, by lawmen mostly, during his boyhood years and way back in the town's history, who suffered from the same vaccinations, about all of them to die right off.

Clint was a wee lad when it happened —- with the first sheriff he knew about. While he was away, one other sheriff made much the same mark on Heaven's gate a few yards down the street. As he thought about it, he recalled telling some of his friends up in Ohio, which then was his temporary home, that he grew to manhood never knowing a sheriff back home who lived out his term.

That was true. He didn't say that one officer died when he tried to beat a train at the railroad tracks. He also recalled the swagger of the man with a big iron on his hip (now that's another cliché, but it was so); he was a man known for his meekness who got elected to the top job in the county. He was no coward, but got shot from the bush. The killer was never found.

He added: "We had a deputy who died from the rain."

This single simple man, after losing his hat during a winter rain as he chased a crook on foot ended his life at home by pneumonia. Clint didn't say in his paper or in talk; he let the Yankees deal with a tangled story about the wilds of Kentucky. They would believe because it was expected.

Clint repeated the story of sheriffs in his county to an Ohio lawman one misty day. That big fellow, who with his boots resting on Clint's desk (the desk was made for boots. The theory was that if they got shot, they died with their boots on).

The man in disbelief enjoyed every shotgun moment of Clint's recollections. His mouth open wide and his bush-covered eyes bulging like two ripened grapes on a dying wild country vine, believed it all mainly because it happened down in Kentucky. Clint knew his Yankee visitor would have taken it in as truth no matter what.

Clint kept it up as he went from Rotary luncheon dates to women's clubs with his recitation about famous Kentucky feuds. Those folks up there couldn't get enough of it, until the day Clint realized he was only feeding deeply-held platitudes from King James' day as told by mountain people, all Clint's neighbors.

Clint was on the sidewalk talking to Uncle Leo settled on the long porch of the hotel with his back to the attached wall of the building next door. Clint thought it was odd that Uncle Leo always sat with his back to the wall every day.

Clint also was aware that Uncle Leo would seldom leave his chair on the hotel's porch during daylight hours except to mingle with others on crowded court days or during mealtime at the city's restaurants or perhaps to visit the bathroom or when he was going to the bank. As well as Clint was aware, Uncle Leo even waited for a crowd to go to coffee hour across the street at the drug store.

"You could expect another killing on election day, not necessarily another sheriff," he said to Leo. "I know one year we had two, one of them just before the polls closed. The consensus after every murder was: 'He had it to do.'" Uncle Leo appeared so interested that Clint thought he must be recording every word in his mind like he was writing a book about it.

The country boy editor realized a day or two after he'd told some mountain stories to a few club people up in Ohio that he'd begun the talk and walk in the lilt of mountain people, which was more like a Texas swagger. The swagger crept in as he recalled following a Saturday western movie he'd seen back when he was an impressionable boy.

Clint and Uncle Leo laughed together the longer Clint got deeper into a story about growing up in the mountains. It was soon after that when this Kentucky news feller was into mountain lore, he (Clint) paused, said it was time the storyteller went back to his job as a reporter like he had first and long dreamed about, and to bury his gunpowder.

"It isn't really Dodge City," Clint said to a young boy the same day he told others that he'd stored his old six gun, in an imagined dresser drawer and Lily uttered a big sigh.

"Have I ever told you about Lily, my wife?" Clint asked his new cousin Leo.

"No, you haven't, but go ahead. I'd like to hear about her," said Leo.

"Well, I will, but later," said Clint. He wanted to ask Leo if he might have once had a wife and what had happened to her. It would be Leo's story, which came out in pieces, so the right thing to do was wait for it.

What he didn't say, not today, was 'Good old practical Lily, the good wife.' She said one day in a 'kitchen fight' that she'd noticed the false swagger that often influenced Clint's personality, "I liked you better when you swaggered."

He never liked her when she was angry. He never liked himself, when he was 'mad.'

After Lily's remark, Clint was forced back to fear of losing her if he kept on yelling at her, unveiling his 'expected mountain meanness.' It was a game he was playing (but not in his paper); he was just showing off, he admitted to himself.

People in the hill country, his 'back home,' kin, friends, wouldn't have liked it either, certainly since the old ways and attitudes surfaced as reminders of their once tortured past. It's still there, a feeling of being betrayed you could call it. "Being a Marine," he said once.

Clint said his fathers going way back had passed on painful experiences from hard times in the old country, on to the new land across the way where an isolated people did what they did because 'they had to.'

Leo said something that startled him. Clint's ears stood out like a side mirror on an automobile: "My people were not a vengeful people; they became so after a drastic change in their nation's leadership that threatened them as a tribe."

"I loved my country, or did so not as much after that great big change at Moscow. I welcomed the opportunity to get out," Leo said. "I told you how I'd spent much time in later years about running away from myself and I was getting quite tired of it. I was not running away, I was running to, and for a reason I knew not what."

"I was leaving the place where I'd made my new home, miles and miles away from here up north here in your country and the folks I worked with told me I must leave and they suggested a place way down in east Tennessee. I was on my journey there with what little I owned in one suitcase and the bus stopped in your town for a fifteen minute rest stop."

"I had a good look at the town as soon as I hit the outskirts —- yeah, you've got outskirts. I got off out stood there on a sun-shiny day and the people smiled at me and said 'howdy' just like I was born here. Everything and everybody about this place said 'welcome home.' I got my suitcase and set it on the bench out front. Something told me to stay."

"A few minutes later the driver closed his door after the rest of the passengers filed out and got aboard and started away. The bus got about a hundred yards down the street. The driver stopped and started backing up, right to where I was standing on the sidewalk and he opened the doors."

"Get in, mister. Sorry about that. Get in, let's go." When I said I was staying, he just smiled, a little awkward, waved, and drove on."

"Best decision I ever made, by Jove, I love this place."

Clint said: "So do I . . . Uncle Leo, I too love this place. Coming back home from the war was the best decision I ever made."

Down the road from Clint's cabin was Gus. Gus had prevailed. He and his kind were all over the U.S. No matter what others might believe about the future, carrying on just like it had been with maybe half the people of the world since they were created as they are, they and Gus knew they would live on yet would suffer; someday they'd walk on golden streets.

Whatever was Uncle Leo's story, it was apparent he had fought in a war or two and probably had seen many others die, likely a great many, perhaps horribly and before their time. Leo had prevailed.

"This small town," he said, "the mountains that rise all the way to the heavens above, people with a real concern for their neighbor and about everyone else is why life was created at the beginning. Don't ever try to take it away from them."

One late summer day, almost dark, shadows came from dark places in town. All was at peace yet with a long memory of constant gunfire and angry men of a once upon a time.   In the mountains, the familiar gun's roar was heard and heeded first by its citizens in its outlying districts because of the deserted downtown that had closed by this time of day. It was nigh onto night, an eerie time for the incident.

Familiar to everyone who knew the Great Depression years, men and women at early bed or at ease over a TV show, life was repeating itself.

Because of taller downtown buildings on their narrow streets, the firing of a weapon —- the bullet later dug from the façade of the building next door to the inn was determined to have come from a pistol of 38-caliber —- its report and its echo traveled along the Avenue to Progress known formerly as Main Street.

Filled supper plates were left on the table as citizens who lived right up to the city limits scurried in the direction of what they believed to be the origin of the sure powder fire of hate from a familiar common Twentieth Century pistol.

Clint at home on the mountain heard the invasion of a town by evil gunfire where this sort of thing belonged to history.

The question by citizens first on the scene was: "Who shot who?" No other reason for powder burns was accepted since it wasn't the Fourth of July; nobody would be getting married this time of day. It wasn't the eve of an election so it must have been something else as big.

The sheriff wasn't the first on the scene, since his home was farther out in the county. He arrived several minutes later, coming upon the growing curious crowd with sirens roaring and all his lights flashing.

A screeching of brakes by the sheriff's official vehicle that parted the crowd almost taking a toll among the citizens who crowded the sidewalk and hotel porch, and blocking the street, which would provide a story just another murder story or attempted murder with its humorous sidebars of speculation would take many months to allay but live on to tease or scare their grandchildren not yet born.

"Somebody done shot Uncle Leo sitting right out front like that every evening while it's still daylight after his supper at the cafe down the street," but you couldn't tell who said it. They sure knew Uncle Leo's schedule, all right.

It seemed everybody was out for the show crowding around looking for what's-his-name as well as for red blood and guts, no matter whose: "Who?" and "Who?" and, "Who?"

You'd expect the sheriff to say something like you all I mean all of you can go home now since you're crowding justice. He likely said it, but nobody moved, not in this town, as red-blooded citizens knew they had a right to the show.

Reason why, the people had a right to be there just like other free Americans; it would energize the drug store coffee hour talk of Main Street habitués for weeks, maybe months to come. Everybody in town knew all that there was to know about the incident by the next morning, anyway.

Clint thought of this lesson in freedom as he watched the faces of the people. No sheriff or an order from the heavens would deny the hill folk of a like day in the memory of their ancestors. Clint was calm. Incidents such as this involving the citizenry and gunfire from the enemy in the tall trees of a far away jungle night had settled its fire on him a numbness of routine in the midst of death despite the source.

As long ago as his boyhood learning time in the hills, had created for him all that was civilized life among active firing pins that had helped him view calmly what surely was a desired trait of a news reporter.

He was thinking of the expectations of the northern press, whose editors had a big inclination to headline the incident since the recent stories of multiple killings in a mountain county had the country's renewed interest. As a stringer for the Association Press, Clint would be getting a lot of phone calls later that night and the next morning.

What he couldn't write or talk about was an apparent universal interest by the local residents in just another mountain shooting, what the northern newspapers would play up in follow-up stories. Whatever he reported would be edited with mention of their recent stories and the tradition of mountaineers with their guns. This bothered him, and he was to wonder again about the ethics of his chosen life's work.

Uncle Leo, whose role as the object of an assassin was known as an outsider to some few. This was a strange posture as seen by most hill people. Clint, late to the scene today, recognized many in the crowd from his boyhood years. There they were, thrilling like the rest of us among the speculators: in particular, he watched a man he'd known since his youth as churlish and clannish attempted in this moment of terror to explain the destiny of men in this new land, killer and intended victim.

These were the people that reporters for northern papers sought to interview during the recent war on poverty. Yankees, who thought of their southern kin as typical mountain folk were hesitant to admit they were born of the same mothers.,people in poverty brought together in another killing incident.

Why should Clint consider his mountain kin, amused, if that's the word, by all the tales of Heaven's largess and the government's food gifts to the poor in the new era, even deny speculation on his coming home in the midst of the convulsion?

It was a time to remember, yet as the region floundered in embarrassment, he and they knew how the northern press would carry the story, just as they would report how the same mountain people looked aside at children in rags who were denied the better things of life during a century of progress.

Even after the sheriff had gone, backing into the thoroughfare with his siren roaring and his lights, blue and red, portraying his authority, the people stayed. They knew they had not gotten the full story.

Uncle Leo until about a month ago could not boast of citizenship. He now could sign his name as a voter, verifying him as full-fledged. Already he was referred to as 'old Leo.' That was before somebody we didn't know tried to kill him. One fellow said, "I was in the middle of 'Gulch Guns.' It was part of the TV show, I thought, until Maggie said it came from outside." The man said it was a bigger show than any he'd seen on the TV.

"Reckon since it was right in front of us. It was to us a new baby, that's why."

He said that his grandpa said it was like 'ever day' in his time. "Now I know just how grandpa thought."

"A former enemy was killed because he had escaped from the battlefield." This was something of "the odd," the man called it, downtown talk that Clint and his buddies from the war had to put up with; it didn't end when they got home.

Clint said it hadn't been a month since some young woman had pinned him against the wall looking this World War II marine right in the eye and asking, "How many human beings did you slaughter, Mr. Greene?"

"The killer is still among us," it was said over a coffee cup or two on many mornings after the big downtown night show. Came an era of suspicion, like little known men and women were watched by neighbors. Others, looking for a gesture, eyes that turned away as they were met on the street; a reaction it was believed was a sure sign of a feeling of guilt.

The sheriff tried to avoid hold a press conference on the jail steps, his office, every time he opened or left for the street. Reporters came from the big towns. The law began to expect a new bunch every day. He combed his hair more for TV, even thought of cultivating a mustache like a Hollywood movie star, changed his shirt every day and tried to sound authoritative before the cameras. One man who knew Clint said: "Sure looks to me like the old-time killing is back like my grandpa, used to talk about."

As for Uncle Leo, he never missed a coffee hour. The curious soon stopped asking him about his enemies, if they ever did hope to find an unknown actor in Uncle Leo's life. On days he'd been asked, Uncle Leo might as well have smiled, nodded, until it was decided to forget trying to get him to talk. He didn't respond to questions about the band-aid across his forehead.

"Reckon its part of Uncle Leo's native-born conduct from when he was a boy, like it was told by my own mama and daddy who said a man had a right to keep all his thoughts behind his speech and problems to pretty much himself and from every stranger who liked to put down the people like of Appalachia or any other people in an isolated area like ours," Clint said to Oscar.

"I believe that Leo was a mountain man in his native country, and they were a whole lot like the mountain people who are us. That's why we can understand him sooner than most people in other parts of the country."

Clint recalled how the coal operators "used to import foreign workers when they ran short of mountain muscle and enthusiasm."

"Boy o' boy when it was found out that some nationalities like to throw their 'better selves' around, against somebody else of a different skin shade, we got a bit of the old outlanders' trouble."

He said that's why you run into Italian-bred and people like them in the stores in town. After them, operators would import Syrians and workers from the Middle East who couldn't speak English. They were eager for work, were fast learners, and raised big families who are mostly still here; used to be, numerous kids who didn't leave for a better education were all over town. Smart, too, would ha' made a big contribution if they had gotten an education.

"This alien mumble act by Uncle Leo has to be Leo's own, giving these boy and girl reporters more reason to be suspicious, never mind about what. He sort of laughed at them, and that angered them mightily; made them more eager to get his story."

He added: "The Sphinx himself, or herself, she's got hair like a woman who could have been a neighbor of Leo's. From his chair against the sidewall of the hotel's porch, Leo by this time has learned much about these Americans who easily could have forgotten the ways of the old country as their immigrated parents died out."

The citizens soon passed his chair on the porch with just a nod and a half wink. "Ah, these Americans; I love 'em, every one, like Tiny Tim used to say in that Dickens story," said Uncle Leo.

Clint didn't forget to talk to Oscar about all that foreign infusion to the mines and local society: "Our people met them and loved them. The new mining workers soon were accepted, as were Blacks before them, all into a hillbilly race," he said.

The first two of these three men who became friends in what was to become like a body of three called a triumvirate in Caesar's time knew very little or nothing about Leo's origin; it was said that Old Uncle was from east of thereabouts, saying it made no difference.

They knew an ancient Asian philosophy guided his thinking; they spent time in their few books at home, then in the public libraries looking for they knew not what. Uncle Leo wouldn't give even friends a slight nod to questions about his background.

"When it's time," said Leo, and that's all he said. They knew he'd been in the military; too many signs kept showing up, recognized by all warriors.

Newsmen were satisfied that he was East European, perhaps an Asian, came from an alien society, yet he spoke in tones and poetry of educated Westerners. His English was so pronounced, so near perfect, except when eager unfriendly young questioners would pursue him in frowns of enmity. The other partners of OMEN laughed when someone he might well have disliked or didn't trust acted stunned.

"He talks just like we hillbillies," they agreed. Since King James exiled their kind from Scotland, mountain men tried but could not or would not stop calling it 'the King's English.' Some in the big press began calling it Elizabethan or the Queen's English.

The twilight affair involving Uncle Leo, said by the papers so well have been an assassination attempt, so well reminded Clint of a murder he witnessed years ago right there on the street in front of the whole town.

It was on a sunny day, not more than forty feet down and across the street, at least thirty years ago. Clint was a boy; it happened right in the middle of the Great Depression.

Clint recalled it in its gruesome entirety from the window of the barbershop on the other side of the street. Prior to that shootout, the sheriff and a guard from the Frankfort State Prison were arguing over who had the power of the law in the sheriff's county. The prison guard had accompanied a resident under his authority to testify in a bank case that wasn't all that unique among court trials rising from bank closings in hard times all over the country. The sheriff told the guard: "You're now in my county, so I'll take charge of this man," meaning the witness.

It's said that the guard drew his pistol first; Clint could not testify to that account since one man at the moment was obscured by the stance of the other.

The sheriff was a popular, respected lawman. It was during another great incident to mark dark pages in the county's history, a difficult crime season running wild like a river in a fit of rampage, of high unemployment, hungry babies, a lot of meanness, the beginning of the alphabet agencies of the Federal government.

No election, no evangelist, no division of wealth during those hard years in Clint's county would divide the people into rivals for whatever was society in those days, like the shooting of a well-liked man of the law on the town's Main Street.

When Clint Greene came home following the big Pacific shootout he was expected, right after the war like all local GI's, to take the road north to Ohio where the jobs were. He might well follow other men from his county up there soon after taking off his uniform.

After college of course and on the GI Bill, he took the highway across the Ohio River and bought a small weekly newspaper with help from his friends and his dad's estate and stayed until 'they' chased him out because 'they' just couldn't stomach his many 'arrogant ways.' Yep, the American way; they didn't come right out and say so, but the implication, the advertising and subscriptions disappearing quite heavily implied a real boycott.

That's a respectable and Christian way to tell of the midnight fire that discommoded him. After a score plus three of four it took to put the fire out, he paid off the last of his indebtedness from the fire and came one more time, he said, back home, after he buried Lily in the cemetery up there, which is what she said once that she wanted. He'd join her up there some day.

His first hours after his return to his cabin home after airing it out following its long-time silence after his dad's death, were to visit the graves of his people. He'd spent the first day cleaning the cemetery next to the small country church quite near the edge of his family farm —- a place where he was taught an informal sort of worship for a man who died by the trigger of a friend. There was much talk at the funeral of a man who was also a friend of his father and mother.

As he touched the names of his father and mother now etched for eternity into the stone, he read the dates of births and years of deaths on the other graves. He surveyed the limited field of grass that was the burial grounds. Flowering shrubs planted by long ago neighbors and their heirs marked the ancient woods and field as sacred; stones facing the near and distant mountains to the east as a final enduring honor to the men and women who came to tame this land of the primeval forests in what once was called the Far West. This was their promised land, just like the one in the Bible.

Only names and statistics of birth and death recorded in a family Bible, stored in a dusty trunk and the government's silent but guarded files boasting the same in fine print was there any proof that they once lived. The older stones were sinking, returning once more to the earth.

Somebody had asked why he'd sought to be a writer. What among his supernal pen nubbins would be invited by someone who actually cared for his country's literature to give him . . . immortality?

He'd answered reluctantly that it mattered to nothing, really nothing at all. It was just a way to make a living. Few, far too few, called them writers; he'd enrolled in the mid-week writers' clubs in the coffee shops to report on his sort of Nirvana.

As he stood alone among the reeds and berry bushes not far from the graves of his ancestors, he recalled curious questions and his too clever response —- that he never for a second believed he would need to share the reason for his vocation with anyone.

The man said he had hoped in his youth to know when the lightning struck, and when had Clint become aware of it —- as a young man in college was the big strike or calling in the sky?

So did he Clint Greene have the same experience? "No, not really," he said.

Ran into an old friend not long ago; he brought us up to date on local thinking since we both left here a thousand years ago, Clint said to Oscar and Leo that he said he believed this country is safe as long as the people can go on talking about what is right, manage to pay the preacher, leave the other fellow's wife alone, and does not envy his neighbor's accumulation of goods and trophies of this world —- let it be.

"We are concerned about the uneasiness that appears of late to be creeping into the daily lives of the American people," Clint had said to nobody in particular across a coffee table.

When he ran into a small group's 'little fears' the other day, three or four lingerers at the filling station, Clint wished he could join their conversation closer to the stove while he waited for new tires for his car; he was only slightly amused by the fears as they reported them.

He would rather listen:

"Remember how they came over the mountains in the picture show, 'The Good Earth;' blocked out the sun like they did, and they ate everything in sight?"

"They were locusts."

"They'll be here, threatening what is left of the live body of us and the crops and the grass and the woods, right after the big drought that is coming as the Earth warms up."

"Have we made room somewhere on the Earth for another hundred million or so bellies to fill? Since we already have an over-populated world, with all of them depending on a fertile breadbasket out west in America, where will they find something to eat?"

"Yeah, how long can we expect to feed our own people? It will kill us all; put it in writing in your little red book, man."

"It's not long 'til th' end o' th' world; some of us alive now will live to see it, then die with it."

"Yeah, th' big corporations have taken over about all the rich plowed ground. From Indiany on; you can bet th' days of food aplenty we can afford will soon be gone.

"What was it the lady in France said, somethin' like, 'Let 'em eat cake,' right?"

"Big earthquake hit the Mississippi River country about where Kentucky, Indiany an' Illinois and Missouri come right together, or come close; caused the river to flow backwards for a long time. Some called it the New Madrid quake, made a new lake that's still there. It's coming back —- that quake.

"An' it'll be bigger than ever."

"When was that?"

"In 1812, I think. I learned about it in school."

"That was two hundred years ago, almost. Probably not to worry since it's been that long. It was west of here in Kentucky where nobody expected it."

"No, in thirty years, scientists say it'll come back. Said quakes are like water. Water never forgets where it has been, not even the little branches."

"Those the same scientists who tell us the dinosaurs were killed when an asteroid hit th' Earth several million or so years ago?"

"Yeah, they say odds are good it'll happen again, too."

"Kill off the dinosaurs? They all got killed, gone after that one."

"Naw, not th' dinos, screwball, those asteroids from way out there comin' in like that big one; in another million years or so? I'll probly be dead by then."

"Left a big round hole in the ground when one hit out west. Arizona, I believe. The hole's still out there, big round, gaping like hungry little birds in the nest waiting for mama bird to bring in th' worm. Tourists come by the thousands to spit in it, that big nest or big hole in the ground."

"An' one o' them asteroids took a big piece of Mexico out when it hit down there. Bet it'll hit one of our sin cities, like maybe th' Lord took out Sodom and Gomorrah."

"We got nothin' t' worry us. No sinnin' 'round here. Not like those cities out in the foreign badlands th' news talks about."

"What we worry about is the atomic bombs buried deep in th' mountains ready to come out when th' president puts pressure on th' red button."

"Th' enemy knows where those bombs are. When that button is pushed he's already launched his missiles. They're heading right to where we are, an' blam, it's all over for us an' for them, too. That's when the world will really come to an end."

"You talked 'bout that asteroid. Jus' a big rock got loose when th' universe was bein' put together. Its twin will come, an' it don't have to be a big 'un neither."

"One little ol' rock again, an' everbody on this world will die. That rock been floatin' around out there all this time, jus' waitin' for th' signal from th' creator to come down right at us."

"Naw, we'll all be gone 'fore that; th' worst scenario is us old men an' th' sea. Th' eatin' fish in the sea are about all gone, too, they's all fished out by those big corporations an' th' canning companies owned by them. Used to, you could say, teach a man t' fish an' you feed him for life. Not true no more."

"You teach him to fish in an empty sea an' he has to go somewhere else t' get food for his family. He comes out lookin' for you, maybe somebody else who just might have some food stored away. Even a good man will kill when he's starving, especially if he's got kids at home in front of empty plates."

"When th' food's gone we'll have food riots especially in big cities where they have to buy all their food. Out here at least we have a place where we can have a garden an' find other food that we can save by cannin' n'dryin'. We can keep bees for all our sweetenin."

"Well, like Sister Scarlett said, 'I'll worry about that after tomorrow.'"

"Don't you remember her standin' out in the field with a little old radish an' sayin' she'd never be hungry again?"

"Yeah, I remember, an' I'll bet she had to do a lot of bed work to get food to eat after Sherman went burnin' an' pillagin' to punish the South for what they did to th' slaves an' kept th' war goin.' Well, this world seen nothin' yet t' compare to what the South was after th' war ended."

"What I worried 'bout is a tsunami like when I was in Hawaii with th' Navy. Big wave comes in from th' ocean, kills ever tree an' food arisin' on those Pacific islands."

"Don't you threat none about the tsunami, think o' yore Cumberland River actin' up over yonder where we buried relatives of yore people an' mine. It can't reach us here longs it's holed up tight in the mountains. You have to be sorry for th' some of us who live down here in the flatlands between the mountains."

"Well, how 'bout Effie's Pond? If that pond ever broke its banks it'd rush right over this town like a bat right outta Hades."

"Haven't you heard? The government came and told old man Hunt to fill it in, that it was a health hazard to man and beast. The actual reason I tell you is that the U.S. engineer corps wanted to get rid of the pond so he'd have to buy all his water for his cattle from the local water company."

"I swan. I didn't know that. Who is the water company, by th' way?"

"Heard tell it was some foreign country in Europe."

"They bought it up with money our government gave to them for foreign aid. We had to help them get back on their feet after th' war."

"Pretty soon we not gonna own nothin', 'cause if it ain't some foreign country that owns the very land where we got a house, it's somebody else. How they bought or got it all through th' courts is a mystery to be solved."

"You're dang right, big corporations bought up all th' land."

Clint knew most of the men and the two women; they didn't recognize him, since the war; that's good. They are mostly keen imitators of the status quo and doing a good job of it. Right now this bunch of land breakers were just shooting the old bull and attempting to outguess the other foot-warmers around the stove.

After his car was released, he turned toward the hills, hurting from what he had seen and heard today, under a breath recalling, "The hills, whence cometh my strength," not at all surprised at the thought.

Lily was a great blessing and he'd have said it to her: "From you cometh my strength. Never a word of complaint from you, just as I've remained faithful to my own secret bother on days I didn't feel up to it in all our life together." With him it was his mountain raisin'. You never knew when a mountain man was really hurting.

They seldom disagreed, he and Lily, except for that place of his mom's and dad's on the mountain, now his. She hadn't stomped the kitchen floor with the heel of her shoe that day four maybe five years before she died when he'd said that after he retired he'd like to go back to his mountain to live.

He recalled the fire in her eyes, more than just a bit of the reticence he never fully sensed was the source of her wrath. Such a beautiful oval face, her ensnaring brown eyes like a teddy bear's but ah so good ol' Lil when she got mad. What a big empathetic heart.

All she'd said was, "No, no Clint no." Every woman to her own brand of tea, and he'd patted her behind and smiled. As the cancer enemy widened in that lithe body, claiming one more victory over its agonizing victim, they carried her to the city cemetery up there in Ohio.

He would never insult the years they had together, never dishonor her wishes by commanding the hearse all the way down to the river of the Cumberland hills instead of the hostile country where she'd grown up and loved the land she'd been as a child. She died in his arms, her eyes open and loving, arms too weak to stroke his face as she often did, usually when he needed it most after a day when another angry mob expected their usual pat on the back from society.

He would have rested for eternity alongside his mom and dad and his kin of several generations. He especially liked the cemetery founders' plan to take in the all-beaming sun, the head stones' facing the distant eastern hills. From the top of that hill he could almost see Heaven. He never had to look far in all his life for the road to that m mysterious place.

He'd told the kids to take him to the grave next to Lily when he died, as he stood by the carriage on the day of her funeral. He hoped he'd shown a sincere enthusiasm for the stripped and broad over-filled cemetery in the north.

He would apologize, too, over the graves of his people of the hilltop on that not long ago day he had visited the green burial ground over the Cumberland River, saying simply, "We will let the living decide where to bury their dead. Really, what difference does it make?"

Lily, good sweet Lily, whom he'd loved from the moment she'd entered his office of the newspaper to place a small ad for her flower and gift shop, which was down the street.

"A red, red rose, my love is," he had said in a stuttering voice as he noted her valued selection among the mention of flowers on the long sheet of paper she'd handed him.

The ad didn't read that way. He saw the amusement in her eyes, widening all over her face as he looked up from the paper and said he'd fix up a nice ad and give it a prominent place in the paper. They both later said the phrase had a romantic ring to it.

If it were acceptable to speak of love with no embarrassment coming from the heart of a former United States Marine, then he reckoned that the world might survive. In the years that followed they'd often laughed when the words 'a red, red rose,' came up, or was in a book one of them held under a night lamp. He felt in painful memory the many nights they sat by a fire in the fireplace, both reading.

Some years later they both were deep into books next to separate lamplight in early evening. Clint suddenly yelled out, more a shriek it was. He had selected a book from the stack of reading matter, 'for quiet retirement hours of the future', kept on a shelf of a table next to his chair. He had chosen a book of poetry; just felt the need for it to end his day which had held much bother for him.

"Well, I'll be danged," he said. "It wasn't old Willie the Shake after all. Here it is; it's Bobby Burns: 'O, my luve (that is Bobby's Scot spelling) is like a red, red rose, that's newly sprung in June ' . . . "what do you know about that? I should have looked it up a long time ago. Bobby Burns, well I be doggone."

He waited for her comment. It never came. He shrugged. He'd expected a something, a little appreciated look, and he didn't get even that.

In the future, when Clint had gone alone to visit his mom and dad or to attend a funeral down south, he'd phoned Lily to talk about his day there and to inform her when he'd be home. He'd said each time: 'Oh my red, red rose . . .' Lily had kept her flower shop through about all of their married life.

Funerals and weddings, and around Easter, those days kept her in business and the sweet smell of the plants didn't come home with her after her work day. If anything, it was the distant smell of manure, said Clint. This somewhat angered her, or at least caused some irritation.

Most of their social life was built mainly around her shop's visitors that Lily had known in the pleasant years during her days in business. Clint noted it once to a print friend, saying "he was grateful for others of his kind, newspapermen for reasons only an editor could tell of isolation, since it was by the code of the profession."

They did not have many mutual friends. "That's the salient ground for our self-imposed isolation," he had said, "why we have no social life, or so little of it."

Besides, he grunted, on many nights he was out on routine news coverage, attending someone else's definition of 'a social life.' That meant the obligatory fundraisers for a big needy bulwark or other. After a few years in the news business, he'd been able to hire a reporter —- later, a social editor —- giving him time at home with Lily.

It was an era for honors, awards for this and other nonsensical reasons, often the tapping of a queen from their own membership; they believed the editor, no mere reporter, should be there to record for posterity the important event and to bring along his camera.

He was expected in the press box if the school had a night-time sporting event within a fifty-mile radius. Sports, and politics especially what was called a rally with an out-of-state big politico, were main interests to the newspaper's readers.

He laughed loudly and for several minutes on a warm day in June when a proud elderly lady of the town's societal exclusives came to his office and with a grand flourish proudly presented him with a press pass to a kiddy corps series of baseball games. She said, as she boasted of herself as the games' biggest sponsor, "Oh, I love those boys."

At dinner that night, as he would recall for another of a score of times the story of the lady's gift, he and Lily and two of their children still at home joined together in chorus for the longest belly laugh of his day.

It was Saturday and you realized it was 'town day' for the hill people because the downtown sidewalks were over-crowded like the day before Christmas. Attempting to edge his way through the gossiping hill people, or to be a bit more kind to his own, accepting their day of non-activity as a way to see relatives and friends like maybe a rare chance between seedtime and harvest to hug and kiss away the isolation of winter, he became blocked by what he believed was a smarty younger woman who refused to let him pass. Oh Lord, he thought, here's another doggoned petition somebody wants me to sign.

"Hello, Clint, is that a way to greet an old sweetheart?"

It wasn't because he didn't expect to run into an old school chum again who first appeared in a dream he'd had of a midnight visitor of a Shakespearean camp follower —- she'd hoped to be cast in one of his plays that he might write he told a friend but never did, as far as we know. He, Clint Greene, had written the play during his high school years, but the class chose not to produce it.

It was a surprise to his forgotten country boy past, in his now revived memory that caused him to lose his speech that was stuck back there with his tonsils, when a young lady of his past accosted him.

He often gulped that way when he was surprised, thinking of out of this world unrelated things like something that was good to eat. He thought of a hundred things, most of it a bunch of nonsense. He'd gulped a lot of words that way that day, when Doris met him on the streets of his town. All he could think of and the smell of it in the oven, was the taste of a cherry cobbler.

He hadn't seen her since he'd been in high school and the war was coming on and he knew he'd be in it and so wasn't about to get involved with a girl, or woman like her who might be on his mind when he was facing an enemy, not get a girl that might want to get married and mess up his chance of missing a part in an event, the biggest opportunity of his life, by being in it.

Just today, he managed to retrieve his voice. "Why, hello . . . Doris, looking as real, as young and sexy in full daylight just like that time at midnight in my innocent boyhood in semi-darkness they'd kissed like he'd learned from the movie stars on the silver screen. We were allowed in old-fashioned passion to perform just like them."

(He was stuttering a lot right there on the street and talking volumes . . . talking.)

"Say . . . Doris . . . you're the last person I'd expect to still be around in this here old burg. I haven't seen you since that time when I was your mother's guest in the kitchen for a glass of milk and the best doggone cherry cobbler I'd ever tasted. I went away to far places way back yonder." He knew he was talking full of silliness trying to think of something to say. He didn't want to admit how pleasantly surprised he'd been.

"Did you hide all that girlhood virginity in those sexy print dresses down here in river city while all the men were away or did you go away yourself for a while?" Clint was again aware that he was talking to the wind, hoping to make sense and get his thinking of sex which was trying to get straight again across his mind, hoping it wouldn't show.

The old country boy had about always bumbled like a honeybee when he tried to talk to a girl or even to older women of much promise, after he was back home in America after his sojourn in far away places, at least until he'd grown to twenty maybe a little more, like forty maybe. All that time with Lily had spoiled him for dealing with other girls (women) when sex (all in his little boy's mind was a forlorn object). He still wasn't sure how to go about a seduction with someone other than his own Lily.

Right now he was grabbing for something clever smart and poetic to say to an old friend, and female at that. All he could say to an 'old sweetheart' (that's what Doris called it) was to me, "it's like 'a red red rose." Dang it, where did that come from?

"Yes, I went away, about the same time you left for the war. Later, after my divorce, I came home. I've been single for seven years now. Have two daughters, one who lives up in Huntington and has two of her own. The other daughter is a freshman away in college. I heard you'd come back home, and all by yourself, too. I just got back myself about the time of your famous proposition at the downtown men's meeting. I was hoping to run into you."

"Yeah, my wife Lily's been dead a couple of years now, I reckon. We'll have to get together soon for . . . uh, coffee. I'll call you. I have a phone now in that little old cabin on the hill. It will be a call in plenty of time so you can wear that blue dress I remember you in. That is, if you still have it."

"I don't remember that blue dress. Funny you should, though. I would say that's the best compliment I've had in a long time."

"At least you didn't say you remembered me as wearing nothing at all, like it has become faddish to put sex into holy handshakes and in everything else these days. It's even on kids' cereal boxes."

Clint wasn't firm about the blue dress. It simply popped up. He wasn't sure of a missed coffee date of long ago, either. She told him of it in table talk some days later.

It was a date that Clint would have enjoyed (making and missed he minded because in those first lonely hours back home, especially with this woman [as a girl] and at least with lots of time to realize by a man who must learn all over again how to court right then any woman).

Since, the wind never spoke of it; he thought it must have been the war's beginning and all the other boys looking forward to getting into uniform.

She said, "Yes, you were getting ready to go into service. I was hurt, but I got over it. A lot of women hurt so much more when they realized that their man might not ever come home."

He wondered what else he'd forgotten from his courting days, and what about Doris? He'd said to a friend who tried 'to fix him up' (twice) that he sure didn't want anybody, man or woman, to mess up his life at this late hour of his on the Earth, which very well could be his last serious association with a woman —- along with the possibility that he didn't have much to give her.

Doris, in fun times in high school, was still graced with some of the pretty she was born with, and as I remember her. I can still taste that cherry cobbler her mama used to make; hmm . . . oh mama, cherry pie, a big offering to the gods it was, with ice cream. I'll ask her if she kept mama's recipe. No I won't. No entanglements.

In a later more sober hour to come, he knew he would never call her even if he half-promised that he would. Did he? Did he really promise her that he would?

He hoped she wouldn't remind him again of a broken cola date (more likely coffee; he was never a cola man), which must have been hinted at often a lifetime ago. Had he never thought of her again? He wasn't sure. At home that night he searched his mom's closet for his high school yearbook with a much younger Doris in a dress, of course, which then was more sexy to a man of any age. The butt butting tight denims girls wear today to tease men as they walk along the avenue can't do what flesh at the knees and ankles and soft skin showing what a woman is made of —- when it concerned men.

As he turned the pages of the old high school album he wondered why he was even doing this thing. He had vowed to end his interest in girls —- (women, that is, at his age) after Lily died, half promising her that he'd never marry again, or even take another woman.

He recalled from reading in a history book that Thomas Jefferson's wife, as she was dying, made him promise never to marry again. And he didn't. In his old age he was to read a lot of books, remember? And to smoke a pipe, drink wine (today, it is beer; wine is for the elite) with friends as they studied and talked and watched the flames of a fire dancing in the fireplace.

Photos in the album from Depression days were all in black and white, black and serious, in favor of hard times, he reckoned. He didn't care for all that color today; it's too intrusive, especially to an old printer like himself.

When pictures were accented only in the black of the times —- as they were in the annuals presenting the familiar all decked out in mystery (today edged in black it means death); he was pleased they didn't come in blue or pink. Magazines have way too much color today, and too many pix are on a single page.

Gently fondling the ancient tome he spent a gratifying hour gazing at the eyes and chins of 'these kids,' trying to recall a connection to each of them.

Some he recalled hated him because he got all 'As.' Upon a few in the book for no reason in particular yet he paid the most mind, lingering for long moments on the smiles of the few budding politicians he recalled as anti-the whole world.

"Maybe it was because in the years before his country got into the war."

Those years leading up to the biggest war in history let them know that fire and brimstone, whatever was brimstone, was out there, waiting for his generation. Smiles genuine were for the camera shots for the annual, however, despite all the approach of the war talk. Time and war hadn't changed the few he'd gotten to know again after coming home.

Now where was Doris of the blue gown? He turned to the book's junior class, bigger than the other separate class sections; perhaps she would've been a year younger than him. Boys those days, he recalled, liked to date younger girls. Nope.

Clint spent the following long moments frozen in time in the picture books before going to bed that night gazing at the faces of his classmates who had left for the war about the same time as he boarded a bus for the same unknown.

Joining the Marines had been his plan ever since he had realized earlier that war was coming by the talk on the street; theatre newsreels, radio, certainly from war correspondents in the daily press; it came to his Saturday movie screens with shattering reality. Smoke and the roar of gunfire over the heads of the innocent who were his own people —- mainly in the Great Britain of his ancestors —- in those early years of the war where and when and how people in the way of the planes and tanks were dying.

He hoped to remember those who had not returned; their faces and his memory of them might have given hurting marks of their approaching death, that way too many were selected to die in the war; he soon realized that this was far far beyond his reason. No. No. Who was he to play God?

Pictures of long forgotten girls from his boyhood didn't jump from the pages in pretty print dresses to remind him of school, or front porches, or of an ice cream sundae and cherry cobblers, or a kiss in the dark, a huddle in a picture show, except . . . in a dark room playing post office.

He tried to think of late swims along the river with girls who wore those kinky brief bathing suits. How did atomic tests influence the styles of the times, like the bikini that came later, not long after the atomic tests on an island of that name?

He recalled the girls who came down from the mountain to school wearing dresses homemade from feed sacks. He was drawn to them, mainly to comfort them. He had no idea how he could save them from the fun-makers who would cause them hurt, embarrassment. because the other kids cruelly pointed to their clothes made from sack cloth. Their name for their attire first was Eden's nothingness.

Clint was mostly known as a sort of fellow alone, a lonesome roving cowboy, and a sort of shy guy a stuttering farm boy from way yonder on the mountain. He came to town in overalls. So many boys his age that he knew boasted of the same old generally respected background, all hill men you didn't mess with.

More than just that once he attended a party in town where they played post office. He would forget the greater details about that first one for a while. When it was a date, he got away with nickel for a coke or bag of popcorn and just a dime each for the movies.

Uncle Leo was fascinated by these American kissing games just as the town was fascinated by Uncle Leo when he first heard about them; you'd reckon it was because he didn't say much of anything. He never spoke of himself when asked. People would just receive a grin; maybe that was it — especially to a stranger in town. The people who tried first to insult him sort of felt insulted themselves.

The citizens were curious about Leo's political and religious views. They'd ask him about his family,try getting something from you because you were known as an only friend of the Russian in town. You'd say you didn't know. You, a friend of Uncle Leo's, a bosom buddy and you don't know his name? You would shrug, answer that it was one of those long foreign names from a small country deep in that monstrous land mass that was Europe and Asia; (perhaps formerly one of the republics?) that joined Russia to come up with the Soviet Union; maybe even one of the Slavic countries, "I don't know."

Nothing helped, so a new avenue must be found even by Clint that you all could surprise him with get him talking about himself which Oscar said was a newsman's right. He agreed, but maybe.

The Post Office would know, but you don't pry into the ways of the Federals, that is, if the mail delivery was still the Feds' job. The sheriff and the resident state troopers would know. Same thing, and that's about it. You gave it a big sigh and a shrug and thought about something else.

Pretty soon it was told that Uncle Leo had been here long enough to stay out of jail and hadn't raped any of the women and always paid his tab at the café next to the theatre with a smile; Citizens accepted him like everybody else in town for all eternity, one of their own fellow democrats like he'd been born here. Clint had hoped that Uncle Leo, now that Clint was home for good, would help make it easy for society's eccentrics to go ahead with a plan he had.

Clint had gotten him out of his chair on the hotel's porch, and Leo agreed to go down the street for a bit . . . of tea, Leo's own quaff, but no crumpets.

On that first day of their budding friendship, Clint and Leo eyed each other over their warmed cups; both managed silly grins or plain amusement on faces that were not defined in any novel as they each pondered the thoughts of the other.

Distrust (now fading)?

Not that exactly; old fishing buddies? Close, after the embarrassing question of genuine friendship like between two men or two women in the America of the latter days of the Twentieth Century had been disposed of and their talk begun to show an appreciation better described as two old fishing buddies or clothing designers together in the new post-war day that came to be warily accepted.

That unexpected suspicion that began in modern clandestine folklore after all that talk of homosexuality maybe seemed to be paramount among men or women friends in conversation as genuine pals who in society's earlier days were not given such thought.

With Leo and Clint, they each would leave open a weakly held door to their once nervously guarded secrets which with Clint and possibly with Leo came with him from the late great war when men of every stripe and paw print were thrown together in squads and platoons.

Each knew the other was searching (yes, searching) for a life purpose that neither could express in words that could be understood by another, nor even perhaps to themselves. Uncle Leo was the most perplexing especially, until they got to know him, to the people of the hills who would say in their own eccentric every day misunderstood ways that this here outlander was an alien in an alien land.

Clint had sought the favor of the hotel porch resident a few weeks after the two had fought for the ball beneath the same net down at the drug store. Clint drew first blood. Leo said, "Sure, let's go down to Emma's for a spot of tea. She'll be expecting me in an hour or so, anyway."

After being seated they studied each other in silence for a few seconds across the table, expecting the other to begin the friendly nonsense, an exercise neither had pretended to know anything about not knowing what to expect. Each in their different backgrounds would be thinking about what he would say as they waited.

Clint after a lifetime as a news interviewer was the first to offer his thoughts that might bring about a similar identity of the separate personalities of the two men. Before him was a recognized expert chess player. Never, in the presence of kings, presidents, barons or basketball coaches or even high-powered CEOs, had news editor Clint felt so intimidated.

Clint knew it was a game between two thinking men.

The pain of a straight-back chair encouraged him to drop a loose elbow on the table. Uncle Leo did not subconsciously imitate him. Nevertheless, Clint began to feel that he had the journalist's advantage.

The old reporter Clint Greene estimated Uncle Leo's height at about two inches shorter than his own Marine Corps ID card had shown him as six feet two. Leo, his opposite, was soldier-straight, probably in his shoulders more broad as in most military men Clint had known.

Leo's face had that same distant Mongol composition as was his speech, at first not distinguished as foreign. The evidence was mostly around his eyes. The healthy youthful face of the man itself especially would interest most Americans.

Like many men of battle that Clint had known, his eyes reflected what they'd seen on bloody ground. Clint stuttered, fearing he was giving away his frustration.

Clint was persuaded that Uncle Leo's gestures, his bearing, especially how he held his dignity as he laughed, nailed a soldier as thoroughly masculine, unafraid. The town's public women would say that he was 'all man.'

By now you were persuaded that you knew Leo better than did most people. His complexion was of an odd color, though Caucasian. Most mountain men that Clint knew would describe it as 'peaches and cream.'

The face was what Clint would call 'preacher's face,' since he had known a couple of preachers who had that same off-scarlet hue to their face. He heard that some called it "a pink face."

Several of the café's early diners (or patrons since this was the fanciest restaurant in town) passed their table. Clint noticed that many appeared surprised that Uncle Leo, the loner, was with another café patron, apparently engaged in friendly fire. They more likely were to greet Leo than himself since he had come home after an almost lifetime away, and they knew Leo as a patron of the hotel sitting outside as they passed.

Clint was puzzled, said, "I dare say Uncle Leo that you are a well-educated man; you were privileged in early life, and you have a cultural background. Your manners were not learned in this here wildcat burg, or in any other refined places in this country, unlike us."

This brought a guffaw from the depths of Uncle Leo's throat, coming as the Voice of God, as someone described Leo's soothing vocal chords to him not many weeks earlier. Depending on his amusement, reaction to an 'insult' by a friend or even praise by an Act by Congress, his voice ran along a scale from the snows of the highest mountain in Tibet down to the cold rivers of Hades.

"I won't offer any more than the fact that yes, I attended university," he said, "Right now I don't choose to talk about it, how fate changed me, this person or presence in another world. I nearly married once, and I loved her; it was in Britain and it was an emotion a bit or somewhat different, just a little from what I had observed of American life, especially their current sexual approach to 'love;' I reckon I was and still am a Victorian to them."

"It may be different from what I once believed as I came to manhood. I tell all this to you because Americans might notice a difference in my manners and that I am not much open about myself when I talk to them, which they might compare to a different sexual calling that beats to a quite different drummer. That's the biggest doglegged thing about most Americans. They seemingly are always looking to see if bow neckties describe sexual orientation. They wouldn't know a real man until they were forced to share a foxhole with him."

"It was a privilege to be taken some years after I left my own country for a propitious moment that came from yon side of the mountain. I'd lived what was a near lifetime in a new profession even if I wasn't born to it, as were all the males of my tribe. We'd all been since birth expected to be soldiers, born to die by the sword."

"You might be surprised if I deigned to tell about serving in two armies, one on the ground of my fathers, the other in the arms of a different command. I won't say in what army. At the moment I have no intention of doing so. Hold it as just another secret." Leo put the cup to his lips as a way of signing off on their little tete a tete, or at least on how the subject had wandered into the military.

They each paid their own part of the check, as if it had been understood. Clint put out his hand and Leo took it in a friendly handshake. He smiled, yet the great mystery remained. Clint looked deep into the man's eyes. He only found a deeper, darker mystery.

Clint would stop for a chat with Uncle Leo, make it a rule in passing the hotel porch stop for a limited moment of good ole boy talk, asking how he was feeling, if some hot shot down from the city had heard of his brutal checkmating and asked to sit across from him, a new challenge to the master.

What the one-time country editor learned about Uncle Leo was not surprisingly what Clint had expected or sought. Come to think about it, his association with good old regular Americans was no different. Underneath I reckon we're all pretty much the same.

Clint knew nothing more than he had learned from his fellow townsmen or from earlier talk with Uncle Leo. Then why would he let this thing of Leo 'bug' him, as it would 'bug' any newspaperman. It had become an obsession, which was not unusual. He would try another tactic. Little of nothing had stopped him before in his pursuit of a news story. This was something he wanted for himself, and his country, for some reason.

Perhaps he wanted it more than for soul satisfaction, like he was training a mean dog, bringing Leo into an Americanized society which would make him a valuable asset to a country which was still looking for its soul even after its two hundred plus years. Yet he was beginning to decide to allow Leo part his own waves, building his own brand of an America after all these years yet as the fellow we'd been looking for all these same years, right now, when I need him now more than ever. That includes the pre-Soviet faith in God before the commies tried to take it away from him.

Clint would be fearful of a newsman who got to Uncle first whatever might be his newshound's intentions. The (Mongol's) story and it would be a really wild one he knew, belonged to him first, then to the country. As he'd told many a reporter; 'go back again,' in his editing years; he'd send the reporter out on a dark night once more, "stay until you get the story."

Uncle Leo had his own reason for not reveling or even sobbing over his past; Clint would honor Uncle's reticence, but he'd research recent and back issues of the little local newspaper for mention of Uncle Leo about the time the mystery man came to his mountain village.

The local library history shelf offered no mention of the last dated Russian pogrom of the Jews, which he believed as belonging to a distant past. He wasn't sure that Uncle Leo might be Jewish; it didn't matter.

A friend said he'd search his computer encyclopedia (in street parlance, the internet), for what neither the friend nor Clint could reasonably explain as 'what for,' even after Clint offered any clue that he could, and still protect Uncle Leo.

It was quite a long shot. So where really to begin?

A couple or three months later, less by a couple weeks, Clint was standing on the street chatting with a friend when he looked up and into the eyes of a store clerk who was placing a poster in the window.

The friend had asked about Clint's grandkids; Clint had been visiting them in Ohio. He was, as usual, caught up in talk of the antics of his four grandkids; he had vowed long ago not to bore people about grandchildren, aware that about all among the human race did so. Besides, being apart from them, there wasn't much he could say.

Both initially ignored the poster and its message. The clerk was grinning, compelling Clint and friend to scan the poster once more, which screamed in huge black letters. The clerk's wide grin came, since he knew of Clint's kinship to Leo. Clint followed the clerk's eyes, not taking in the pompous message (in type an inch high, some two inches; like the circus posters of Clint's boyhood).

Clint returned his attention to the friend. Then here came that movies-born double take from a comic character in 'selected shorts,' which he recalled from his boyhood movie days, registering like the second shot in the dark that he'd have anticipated from his early 'picture show afternoons'.

The message jumped out at him just as the clerk was tossing his head back with a loud laugh that shouted through the glass. He was shaking his head, which said that this was big, as it might affect others. Clint in his shock wasn't kicked onto his back into the street; instead it would be a fist to his chin to return him to reality. He pretended to brush the dust off his shirt from the fall that didn't happen.

The friend was quoting the poster's ten dollar message aloud, aware that Clint had seen the ghost of the pale horse and its rider at full gallop among the stones of a cemetery at midnight. The rider was carrying a sign.

No, it was a poster; Clint eased past the giant type. He leaned closer for the smaller print; the legend was clear in dynamic words. Clint read it through twice more, word after word in the deep guttural voice of Uncle Leo himself.

The poster's message:

Coming to the State Fair
And To the Public for the first Time ever . . .
Leo the Cossack . . .
Direct from the Steppes of Russia . . .
Come see Leo the Cossack.
He can shoot the tail feathers off an eagle
In Full Flight!
From the back of a horse in fast gallop
With rifle, pistol, or weapon of your choice
Every Day.
August 14—August 24
Free with Grounds Admission
In the Stadium
You'll scream with Soul-shearing Delight
At this Awesome
Spectacle!
Not even Buffalo Bill Cody ever
Played Host
To anyone like This . . .
As Leo the Cossack Shows How He Became
The Best Shot In the Whole Wide World!

"Well, I'll be danged," said Clint. "It seems that old dog no longer sleeps, or has at last woken up and has caught its big long tail. An older man on a horse; I can't believe it." For one thing, the message verified Leo as the star of an alien adventure.

"You know this fellow Leo, the Cossack?" the friend from a nearby town asked. You could see that he too was caught up in the old movie screen heroisms.

"You are kidding me? That's our Uncle Leo; it has to be. You see there, he didn't even tell those people at the State Fair his last name: "'Just call me

Leo, the Cossack,'" he'll say. The ripe old son of a gun has re-won his spurs; he comes ropin' an' tyin' into th' big time as an anonymous Buffalo Bill showman. Here he comes as a Cossack, no less, the most fighting, independent warriors of the past hundred years, perhaps two maybe four hundred years."

No wonder he didn't give in to his fellow townsmen who wanted his name. In this world, where you work, a little bit of where you're from, what you drink and what you smoke —- or used to, why that's enough. The kids, who came along as the Boomers after the war believed that was all of it, save for a whole lot more bedroom play.

"Right there is the kids' (definition, maybe), hero, their main screen idol; like I said, they had no last names. No need for it."

"As a one-time Cossack, well, he thought that should have kept him behind a mask forever. You don't see many Cossacks running around loose these days. If there's anybody from the outlander battling past, they would admit they know nothing."

(It took Clint a long time to think that one up. He was waiting for a time to use it in man-to-man talk.)

"History probably would soon be saying that the Cossacks disappeared long ago, especially since the arrival of the Red Scourge.

"I'll stop by the library and see what they have on file that'll tell me what happens to old Cossacks when they die.

"Well, I'll be . . . Leo the Cossack . . . who was it? Yes, Shakespeare who said there are more things in Heaven and Earth than we dreamed of, something similar to that; I'll look it up at the same time."

Clint said goodbye to his friend who was as surprised and interested as he was and sauntered, likely moseyed, a U.S. cowboy's way to say he was as usual not hurried away. And as a horseman would say, "Just who is a Cossack? The guy's English is too perfect, polished until it shines over the footlights like a Shakespearean actor's. It leads me to suspect our Uncle Leo might've been an actor; if he were on stage. Bet he is spilling tea all over his lap, laughing so hard."

"Leo could have said and without boast that he was the last surviving member of Buffalo Bill's Wild West Show. But that big outfit went out of business better'n a hundred years ago, although it's still getting news coverage with men on horseback and a woman who was a crack shot putting all those cowboys to shame." The big black words could even brag (or infer) that Uncle Leo had been a Barnum & Bailey's sharpshooter and be believable.

He was watching the skies for a return of green-tinted little men from way out yonder; anything would be as convincing. "I'll have to go to my mountain and ponder over this little bombshell!" It was Clint's farewell sentence to another rough day at the lathe and pestle. That's not right but ah, today all is possible.

When I consider my own life and that little squeaky voice back there that says you are a writer, but you've always denied that you planned to write a book like many of your fellows of the craft (from) the news business, which they said was their life plan.

Hemingway once claimed to have been first a newspaperman. Sinclair Lewis liked to hang around a newsroom like one of the boys. Clint felt he could not yet swing it. Even if he didn't write the book, he was so taken by the past life of his friend Leo that he may change his mind about real adventure. I've not had much to write home about.

All I have under my own belt are a few years or long months actually fighting the enemy Japanese as a U.S. Marine on some godforsaken island. I've had little more to say than any sorority girl would declare in a letter home to mom and dad.

Published have been so dang many books written about World War II that nobody, not even a publisher, even if the magic words were created by a best-selling author wanted it. They won't go beyond the first paragraph to satisfy a reader.

He believed that an interview with Leo might satisfy a reader as it had awed his own curiosity because of its exotic appeal. Yet, war is war and war is hell in the annals of man on this Earth. He wondered about a love story of a couple living on the wastes of the steppes in a one room slab bedroom with a soil covered roof in the dead of a Russian winter.

He thought of a movie starring Nelson Eddy, adventure actor, in a singing story of warriors on leave, women-hungry troopers hitching their mounts at a café way out there in the badlands, maybe a forest on the lonely steppes -- to Americans, the steppes are a flat, treeless generally war-torn corner of Russia. The soldiers were seeking drink, a fight with anybody in sporty mufti, a night of romance, of course, the boy-girl kind, a ball by music and by candle-light;' through song they told moviegoers that they had a 'rendezvous.'

Clint also recalled an associate in news asking the editor what might have happened to those '30s movies that marked a bit of Russian history. Together they concluded it was because of the Big Red scare. Hollywood played their odd game politically and patriotic and quit producing them and put the theme in a can to re-play at some future friendly hour. So far none have re-appeared.

The more he thought about Uncle Leo's romantic hard-riding past, the greater the challenge to Clint, the one-time newspaperman. I better hurry. Get the Leo story on paper. Both of us are getting old. The same idea would occur to the working writers after Leo's re-birth at the State Fair. The bunch of professional writers, all tried and true wordsmiths far more talented than I, will have a ransacking gleeful ball.

He must hurry to find his friend Leo, get him committed to his story in print. As Clint stands on the edge of time, is he pushed to devote all his life-evaporating hours to an illusion in black and white? Then he had to find a publisher, selling it through 'signings' and radio and other media interviews (with Uncle Leo at his side?). There I go, dreaming again like my years in high school.

Chances are Leo will forbid any public exposure of his early life, so perhaps you do not appear over-eager. It is still as always Leo's prerogative, unless Uncle Leo himself chooses to become a celebrity, in Hollywood, or in politics.

It is very unlikely for a Russian in the U.S. of A. to get an entertainment press they would need. Most Americans would think like the publicists.

He said to himself, 'don't expect to look deeply into an enigmatic Russian way of doing and thinking.' He couldn't let his enthusiasm overcome his better judgment.

Clint knew his press colleagues could not be persuaded to leave it alone, as Leo would wish it. A few might go all the way to the storied Cossack country on the River Don looking for him with an expected American view of the exotic life, which now is public (and in their domain).

Leo would have neither a right nor desire to question their efforts, because Uncle knows he had brought himself into the public scramble. That's what the American press is about.

Of all the by-lines that appeared through his sweating nights during his years as a writer — even as Clint more often would write a story about something of little or no consequence —- he could recall nothing that may have changed anybody's view of their present world or of Heaven or Hell. Every word appearing in red or black on white in his paper with his byline was his. Clint came early to a belief that his name on a news story or editorial meant not a thing. Even if his sweat turned to blood in every exit point of his body, they were his red blood and solely his sweat.

Anybody can write; that is, if you say it on paper as you would shout out aloud at Maggie's Bar on any Saturday night; that's what he once told a journalism prof he knew. The J-Prof was agitated, acted like Clint was insulting his profession, that he (the prof) conceived it as a threat to his hour at the controls.

Clint was on the way to understanding a lot about Leo that even Leo might not be aware of. A man living under the communists trying to survive at any far click of a modern rifle not unlike his own would say nothing out in public or in his home that just might call Moscow's notice to himself if they learned of it.

What kept Leo smiling beneath an Appalachian sky was a cast of children in play and jest several horses' tails down five or six doors of the town's main street. Tagging, shoving, patting; running aimlessly like turkeys in escape of the ax at that Thanksgiving thing, they were the shouting and screaming voices of any country on earth until the reality of adulthood in a country like in his boyhood introduced them to a new era of fear.

From the theatre a short mosey down the street, a coterie of nine or ten birthday party folk stood loosely (in line?) for the matinee, Saturday's shoot-'em-up, as staged in about all American towns today, or then.

They were colorful in dress, maybe even formal, like an older couple bound for a dance or Sunday school picnic but all sporting peaked colorful paper hats held by rubber bands and ribbons: A party, this one for a birthday celebration, a treat for the guests a call for a big playtime, children at play and laughing.

Not long after becoming a citizen, Uncle Leo continued his serious study of American history. He lately had been reading a book on Abraham Lincoln, whom he boasted that he could identify as a blood brother. Like most Americans, Leo said he believed he understood Lincoln quite well. He'd been told that most students of Lincoln believed they were among the better judges of 'that misunderstood man' back when Lincoln as boy in Kentucky and young man in Indiana and Illinois was looking for his soul.

One day, Leo learned from his reading, Lincoln was walking with a friend along a Springfield street. Lincoln suddenly stopped, looked to the taller buildings along his town's Main Street. Above the buildings on the other side of the way came the sound of children at recess, at play. The voices in play and fun were coming from the schoolyard beyond the tall buildings. His friend later would describe Lincoln's face, lighted up like a first day of spring.

Lincoln's 'words' were a lamentation "I never got much time at school, not in a place where we could play and do a little bit of yelling and running about. I've missed it all my life."

"What you are hearing over that way, my good friend, is the sound of democracy. It's the greatest sound of peace you'll ever know."

"I must say", said Leo," that I never was a child. My boyhood was taken from me as it was of most boys and girls my age, though with me it was because I was living under the communists. By age of nine, just like Lincoln, I was in the field chopping and toting wood; I had a crop to see to. When I was of Lincoln's boyhood age, a lethal weapon was put in my hand. Before I'd even reached my fourteenth birthday, I was wearing the uniform as a soldier in the Soviet army."

He told Clint and Oscar the local editor, as the three were drinking beer and dining on grilled hot dogs out on Clint's back porch, that Russian school children were given for study as their heroes from their leaders' choice. Of course the teachers were communists. We didn't have heroes like Lincoln; what we got were men and women as Soviet heroes whom we knew were created in Moscow as communist inventions."

Oscar Blues, third party to the porch convention, had only recently joined Clint and Leo in what was becoming a conspiracy of sorts, three minds united in thinking and exciting objectives. The two editors, in expanding friendship, were waiting for Leo to say who he really was. It has to be a big moment, Clint knew, like maybe in Lincoln's day dream of a formal school that he never knew.

Clint said earlier to Oscar, away from the scene, that he'd tried twice before to get Leo to talk of his past. Mainly Clint wanted to know why Leo the Russian chose to live out the rest of his life in Clint's world. Surely this little town is unlike any old hillbilly park you or anyone else outside his own country might have known. Uncle Leo? He was enjoying their frustration, and he would go on sitting at their game table because his hand held the aces.

Then, right out of the sun, he began. His Cossack teaching was universal, since its traditional plan was put aside and buried by the communists. His people didn't trust the commies from the first, which led to an obsession with secrecy. His mission to America and to a small town beside a mountain stream was fortunate.

He'd been welcomed to an Eden-like place where he could live out his years.

A golden painting of Heaven's blessing was evident, Clint thought. He told how it was with boys and their antics back in their boyhood village.

Too early they all were fighting men in the Red Army, loyal with reservations and their place in the only society they knew —- until the 'new order' proved to be a lie. Leo sighed; you thought he would cry with his head down; you'd think he was preparing to escape their midst. He recalled what he described as 'terrible' years.

Uncle Leo would soon become a name, not today's Leo, but the boy Russian. He had opened the book to his past himself. He wasn't always the man without a country, or without a name. As one name was taken from him, it was necessary to the times that a new one must be found.

In Western Europe, in Britain and finally the U.S., even with a new name, he would never sit with his back unprotected. In late hours of any day he feared the sudden sound of a foot on a loose street brick a bark of a dog aware of something unseen a shadow that had no reason to be there.

The soft rustle of clothing, pants leg against woolen pants somewhere, but quite near whether in full daylight or in the early evening, was an alert. As he'd watched the changing day by a magnificent sunset as viewed mostly in his new American color in the valley of his adopted mountains, he was warmed, although he could not fully give thanks to his God because of a danger unseen.

Nobody should be forced to live in such scene from which he'd fled. Dictates were that he be moved elsewhere. Clint wished that his friend Gus would join his little group.

In his muddy life and in latter days his unhappy native land, which he and much of the rest of the world call Mother Russia, Leo and his countrymen up to today still love their country, despite the fact that they had shown to the West that it had gone mad.

As the western nations strived to understand a leadership of an 'insane' man's life ambition, deadly to a boy in another decade in a newly awakened century, the '30s and '40s, Leo knew that someday an alien army would move against his declared reinvented 'new' country, which he had been sent out as a mere boy to defend.

The conquering Reds' motives were little different from those of at least one other eventual loser: the first Napoleon. Another warped man, by name of Hitler, had harbored a similar ambition in his disturbed and bent aspirations into Leo's century. He would lose his army and ambition in blood largely on Russia's soul.

Leo was aware that his home in the southern river and lake country of his nation had witnessed more spilled blood than any other quarter of Russia. The fierce reputation of his people, the Cossacks, had grown in proportion to the streams of blood they'd once seen sacrificed to the gods of war through Hitler's invaders from the west.

Clint's friend, Oscar's friend, a recently ordained American continued: From the steppes of Russia where he'd fired his gun in anger against his people's enemy, he'd selected the best spot on an American hotel's street porch that would warn and better protect him from an assassin or anyone who might have intent to harm him.

The street light of early evening was between him and the near side. The lamp provided more light to the farther side of the street, however. He seldom was outside as the shadows began to move in. Uncle Leo noticed a sudden darkness but declined to move indoors as his intuition came creeping in.

By day, citizens were not aware of any danger as they walked along in silent agitation by life in general —- unaware of any notion that they were Uncle Leo's best defense against harm, to a man like Leo, the Russian. Leo had learned by war how to detect movement in the night by looking away (askance) from the probable source of an enemy's soft step. A soldier of any country soon learned the how of this little warning.

An experienced assassin would have chosen an escape route in his plan to kill. Leo the next day said he should have been more aware of the whereabouts even suspicious of the slight tread of a possible stalker in the dim light.

Previously, he had routinely retired to his room in an almost hidden corner of the hotel when the day's light had begun to fade, as determined by him, as the hostile evening shadows quickly began to creep along the street.

Today he'd stayed out too long. Seasonal change had not been noted. It was upon his chair in the corner as a warning. The longer days of spring and summer were not at the moment accommodating.

The day's beauty of a part of sun's presence into the night a warning approach of night distracted him from his disciplined caution. He was aware of movement where it shouldn't have been, then the street lamp's reflection on metal, the flash of gunfire.

On June 22, 1941, long-anticipated German troops were in Russia, great armies expecting to live off the land. In early winter, the season's bounty that the communists had not taken of the farmers' stores fell to German foraging parties who began to arrive near Leo's village looking to take the rest of their stores.

Leo (Dimitri) and fellow guardsmen Vladimir, Maxim and Georgi were sent to strategic piles of field refuse and manure to watch for invading German point men (pickets). Dimitri held his weapon at his chest; hopefully he rubbed his hands for blood stimulation. He hoped for some warmth that might be awakened to fight frostbite on a somewhat less than thirty-two degrees day.

So far the foragers had not gotten as far as his village and Dimitri thought about removing his boots and rubbing his feet. He felt fortunate in the leather boots his uncles had bought for him. The best made, they were from his recent academy days, almost not quite sufficient. He'd heard that the German soldiers wore cheap boots in combat, about all issued in summer and in large sizes.

Boots were pulled from the German soldiers' feet in the winter's muck. It was made into slush in a churning by marching troops, heavy rolling trucks and artillery, pulling the boots from the feet of the youthful green soldiers who stumbled unsteadily.

Leo looked for comrade Vladimir. He should have been visible from behind a pile of manure about two hundred yards down the line.

Vladimir was never a friend. On the contrary, he was hostile since they first had known each other and had remained so as they were thrown together in the village guard.

Dimitri figured Vladimir's hostility originated in jealousy. He was aware of it after he came home from the academy where he'd been sent by his uncles.

He was sure the Germans were not near until he heard the gunshot at the same time the bullet passed alongside his head. Blood flooded over his eyes, temporarily blinding him. He felt the wound, satisfied that it was superficial; he was alive. Uncle Leo was become Dimitri, the soldier, and he would live.

A search of the area would not turn up any German foragers. The shooter remained with no identity, just possibly a fellow soldier firing at a ghost. After the evidence was in, he was sure the shot came from Vladimir's hostile trigger.

In America today the long wild chase had ended:

Dimitri was in America where he'd been sent by his army unit and his Cossacks to find the man and to kill him, by then a traitor to his own people. Only a few days ago he'd reasoned that he and his prey again were only a few miles from the other. Just the same, it was the very thing that kept Leo on the move like his target.

The two men —- soon to be three —- of his fellow Americans in OMEN were silent, especially so was Leo, since the others right now including a couple of neighbors, waited with some eagerness and anticipation for him to continue with his story.

As they were talking together the next day, Leo cleared his throat indicating a struggle within himself, the past and apparently with all he intended to say earlier alerted his friends and they waited as his thoughts moved along the flames in the fireplace of Clint's cabin home in the direction they'd anticipated.

It was late the next day and as usual it first was silence; dire concerns had begun to occupy the minds of all three men who had begun to drink together, dine together, and tell lies with knowledge that the others were onto him — little brags that accompanied laugh in their eyes without expectation that they'd be believed. Leo was talking to Clint and now Oscar. They soon would by putting OMEN together.

They talked of how fortunate they'd been to survive until now through a lot of good luck and how great it was to live in a safe place where they could do just what they were doing without fear or bother.

It was time each of the three became aware that they were more than lucky, of good fortune, of good health and blessed by many friends. That was of course Clint Greene's time to say, "What more do you want?"

Leo said, "some days I wake up and wish I hadn't, likely brought on by a bad dream, and I think the whole world is falling into a deep chasm, that the Earth is in its final days and there's nothing any of us can do about it."

"I reckon it's always been like that since the beginning," Clint said.

Leo said: "Maybe I lay too much of the blame for that uneasiness on you and your newspaper friends and of course, the politicians. You smarty guys in the press have begun looking for new ways to scare everybody into buying more papers and setting yourselves up as a band of prognosticators."

"You have encouraged your readers to talk aloud of the final days, as that which so many people believe are upon us. Everybody seems to be looking for the devil bird to arrive upon the hills any day now." Leo now was in a big grin.

"Haven't you honorable men of the press become frustrated because you haven't found news stories with enough loud scream to shake up your readers?"

"Are you guys worried that you won't have the opportunity to make use of that 60-point type you've been holding back all these years?"

"You're right, Uncle Leo," said Oscar Bell Blues; said the local news editor:

"We're waiting for the Second Coming before we use the big stuff. It would be a dull world wouldn't you think if we just printed 'good news stories, red words like in the Bible,' which much of the leadership in this country believes we should. We would all be much happier; especially would it give citizens a chance to make democracy work."

"You have to admit that something is going on out there. Our coffee buddies were joining together for society in loud talk the day all three of us made fools of ourselves by trying to tell them we must change society's ways if we would save the world."

It was time for Clint to lighten the omnipresent soon darkening corners of the day and provide a little humor, do something heroic, smile a little. He said: "I've been hoping for some incentive, some big push to get us going. So let's organize it with our own OMEN.

"I tell you again we have to get Gus over here. His people have suffered fiercely. As a result it's left them with strong belief in Almighty God, even as they watched their prayers go unanswered. It's given them unusual insight into all things in the lives of men."

"What 'n 'ell is that? Say it again." said Oscar.

He continued, "I know we talked about it. I forget, so what's OMEN?"

"That, my friend, is Old Men to save Earth's Neighborhoods. Now that I've given you a name, you birds have to help me find what to do with it," said Clint.

That recent all-American caffeine social meeting had stimulated the bragging joust down at the drug store which the three founders of OMEN each deemed a personal fiasco. This was what occupied the three radical minds at the moment. Too, they wanted to be known as men of vision and not as kooks that they suspected they were in the eyes of the citizens.

(The local editor that day wouldn't admit to anyone else that the talk at the club he had taken part in was a foolish sophomoric knife thrust to his reputation.)

A few moments later Oscar Bell Blues had said so long to the others at the coffee tables. He crossed Main Street against the traffic flow on a gloomy day in the morning sunshine to return to his news office. He was thinking of Clint Greene and others of the town who had suggested that his generation of newsmen ought to put their ideas out where the people could read and talk about them.

Since he was a boy he had wanted to broadcast his ideas that would save the people, especially his generation, from falling into an abyss that so many believed even then was their destiny. Of all the people in the world who might receive his respect, it first would be a fellow journalist like Clint Greene who'd gone up north after the late war and made a name for himself as a small town publisher and service correspondent —- he was aware that Greene had held to his religion, his sanity, a Platonic love of his fellow earthly creatures.

(Of late, on his dark days, Clint would tell him how he had considered escape from his boyhood ideals, leaving it to join the majority, they, men of doubt all the former cynics he'd known, orgy believers in the occult.)

Clint was to talk at length to Oscar about those days. Why Clint had chosen to return to this small Kentucky town was a puzzle.

But the present editor: "I'm Oscar Blues, and I might have harbored a laziness bent in my jerked-up kicked around boyhood and later in my life as a man who incidentally chose membership in their rebellious society of a mid-century era of madness, which not long after kicking the dog made we all wonder by daylight if it had been worth all that we were up to."

"We likely looked at 'the news' then as a shortcut to an expected career. It appeared to be a surrealistic vocation other hopeful writers, daydreamers, might shun when we needed the advice of friends and kin because we knew nothing of the world, and we wanted at the time to be in it."

Oscar was smarter than most. Of that he was certain. He had just gotten a lot of rotten advice. Nevertheless, he was bound to do what he wanted to do; at least most of the time. He said everybody else could paddle their own rowboat and to heck with it.

Despite reams of caution by his family, he had ignored them.

Besides, almost each of them had made of their lives a big mess. So he set out when the opportunity came along to make his way in the world as a journalist. It turned out to be a life of dashed hopes for too many of his generation. He had even more to prove, more than most. That made him different.

Oscar's newest friends in his newest place, in Kentucky —- townspeople he'd learned to know personally, were of liberal bent; after he'd become owner of the local press and preceding the coffee cup episode like the one starring Clint and little-known Uncle Leo. He had been warned to proceed with the short slow wariness of a once kicked dog.

Two new mentors were to be new friends in his new town, where he could anticipate so very few citizens on his side. Oscar Blues soon found what he had expected and hoped for, as a highlands supporter then told him, that mountain boy Clint Greene, his stepbrother newspaperman, and the Russian stranger well could be just what Oscar's venture in a new town needed.

He would never be the good old boy willing to accept regional jabs to his belly or down to Earth's Big Creek politics. That's what he said was pulling him back to the local newspaper office today, before Chicken Little rushed in behind him yelling that the sky was falling in.

He'd told his future wife in his sparking days, whose curiosity was to ask, that he wanted to answer to no one no man other than his readers; he simply was what he was, an unchangeable locally curious American, which was interpreted by friends as stubborn to the end, like the old mule belonging to a farmer named Williams out on the pike. It bothered Oscar that he knew much that he couldn't publish.

He and his rebellious brothers and sisters demonstrated religiously despite warnings from the constabulary and city officials at the Chicago Democrat Party convention, at the Woodstock ecstasy, and on the Kent State day of infamy.

Oscar's generation, by just a few years, had missed the big war in which a Nazi army brought a perverted theory unlike any ever seen before by man. We Americans had done it once and we could do it again, but he didn't regret not being in the fight himself. As a boy too young for war he had watched the

German army roll in a dark night. In history, he had seen little but blood, death and devastation. It was enough to make life-long cynics of us all.

In his hope-to-be-forgotten youth, he had even thought of himself as master of all he surveyed. He challenged the term after joining blood brothers and sisters in a greater calling.

Oscar Blues, guided by the legacy of the greats of his calling screaming from the country's past in black-edged pages of a coterie of newspapers, would he was sure find himself among the greats: men of honor, men of compassion.

Perhaps they were right; he for so long may have been wrong. He wrote of public sin by one, then another official, only to be ignored by his readers. The public, he knew, was patiently waiting for the day when the bad guys out there in the cosmos no longer were victims of a malignant pen wielded in the new savagery by his editorials.

Now, who was he to decide a town's morals? Who among his fellow creatures was guilty of challenging the people's trust? By going their way he'd begun flailing himself for his life's failure: yet he refused to walk in the shoes of anyone he had attacked in his paper.

Oscar often suspected that he'd acted rashly with his angry fingers on the keys of his editorial machine. Yet who sir is the rebel? It was a black day when all but Oscar Blues did not believe the end of the world could be beyond the horizon.

General Robert E. Lee came down the steps of the McLean house. With a dignity that was all that was left of the South, Lee grasped the saddle horn of his mount. He pulled himself above the men to whom he would apologize for 'not having done a better job for them.' Someday this editor called Oscar Blues if not sooner I'll break my press into little bits and scatter the lot of it on Main Street, all the way to the far setting sun.

Oscar for a moment halted in his stroll along Main Street, distracted by a store window display next to his office. He was looking at the glass that reflected the sadness on his face and brow.

"Am I looking for a scapegoat among those many radiant and optimistic kids of the new generation? No, they are so many just like Oscar Blues all over again as I was once in confidence for the future. I envy them. Oh, how I wish I were by age able to start over. But that's not right. If I were there I'd probably go down a different road. No! It would be the same road."

His little old newspaper had gone to press last night, just before dark, so this was the only day of the week that he could think about anything else, like green fields, the gurgling of the creek over the rocks just across the fence from his few acres outside town. It was a little creek, headed for the river. He'd bought the place during his first month in his new town.

He was thinking of the boys in his schoolyard grade school recess a million miles ago. It is over-gilding the lily. He for sure would keep a memory of his boyhood at about that distance from today. Everybody wanted a piece of the boy, now they had the old editor to sass when they disagreed with one of his editorials or his column.

They would phone; more likely though would drop an unsigned note in a no return address envelope in the box, say he had used the wrong modifier in a story he had buried on an inside page. He knew they hadn't read it, but had overheard somebody else's comment on the street as they had passed.

He told a friend: "That's why I began an editorial policy after I bought the paper."

"It was to tell the people when the sky was about to fall in, to suffer what otherwise might be a school of fools." He said to a visitor to his office once, "I suffer fools gladly." Like heck he did. Those barbs cut, hard.

He would tell a journalism student to stay away from a life in the newsroom if she had a thin skin. In fact, he would discourage young persons: "Be sure you know what you want to do with your life. On roads you imagine as level could be rocky."

Editors, writers, big paper columnists had often stopped by his office, usually on their way to somewhere else. It was that courtesy call that newsmen generally looked for among fellows in the print and scream society, no matter how small or how big a visiting newsman or his host had become.

He had arrived at the open door to his Main Street office which he had kept open to the street come the warmer weather of spring. A street person stood limply next to the desk of his number one assistant-interpreter. Ignoring the visitor as well as he could, realizing too late that he'd been seen, he said, "Well, the paper by now has hit everybody's front porch, any complaints?"

Fortunately, he got no response. He walked into his little corner, which was a shoot off the larger front office of the paper. His typewriter, which he hadn't sought to be replaced when others in printer's heaven were lining up to the new computer wasn't right now calling out to be heard, though he'd felt its pleading, a constant ache which just moments ago had sat there eagerly awaiting his return.

Without suffering its demands, the summons he would rather say in sass to the mute machine, he turned and walked in a hurry like he was out to cover the big story. He'd made it through the door and onto the street breathing with a deep sigh the promised warming day when the renewal of life was all around him; Oscar was glad he could leave the door open wide to the rest of the world. On second thought, I'm not at all glad. That just invites the uninvited.

He thought of one thing he had planned to do today. With some reluctance it was back to his wee office. He began to look around for whatever it was he'd forgotten. After he'd shut the door he held the knob tightly until his hand began to hurt.

He sighed with the familiar relief of a sun coming in after the big rainfall of the day as he dropped his hands to his pockets. He wanted to suffer no fools. He thought, I can't go on hiding behind this door every time I don't feel like talking to anyone. Besides, this is my office. I can say to no one what I do in here.

Just lately he'd been apologizing to himself about the need for escape, yet he knew that once married to a printing press there is never a day of forgiveness. That thought made him feel good. At least for the moment he had that feeling of pride I n what he was doing.

He thought, looking around the tiny office, now what did I come back here for? If I'm getting forgetful it's time I got out of the rumble seat. He mumbled to himself, looked around the top of his messy piled-up desk and turned over some papers as he pulled open the middle drawer which he by rote always had locked when he left the office. "Dang, forgot to lock it again. If the town thought this was where I kept its secrets . . .

. . . the whole lot of them would be in here with carving knives." He forgot to look again for what he thought he'd forgotten.

Opening his private door . . . slowly, just . . . he was pleased nobody was waiting with rotten eggs to throw at his ugly face. Now he could leave, again. The front girl was at work; he mumbled, opened the street door, and left.

He could say nobody needed to know where be would be. This was unfair to the girl at her desk; his business was not any more into little lies than great big ones —- especially when you forced others to lie for you. This touched the serious side of his grain. It was against the Oscar Blues purity façade he'd been carefully building into public appreciation during the past twenty years.

Polly, at her desk next to the large front window watched him go. She knew about his secret place. She also knew why he would be going out to his . . . promised land:

Either Oscar wanted to do some undefined thinking, or he wished to be hiding from the fact that he didn't want to do any thinking at all. She thought, if this town just knew what a good man they had in their midst.

Smart woman, that, Oscar mused as he hit the street; hiring her was the best business decision he'd made since he had come to town. She knew what he had in mind an hour even before he uncovered his typewriter. He wouldn't say where he was going primarily so she would not have to lie about where he could be found. He had sinned in her light once more. Besides, you could tell by looking into her eyes that she was protecting the forbidden, which often was his misfortune.

The old editor hoped he could get to his car parked around the corner from the main drag before an encounter that meant a lot of nonsense, which his fellow townsmen would consider their right and would fuss about it.

He thought of Jenny, forty miles north at college. Maybe I'll drive up there for a bit of 'spiritual food,' a term he used often from across the desk with visiting newspaper people.

Jenny was easy to talk to, easy like father to daughter. His wife was generally like that, not always though, when she was living with him before she upped and ran off with some fraud of a bum (if that isn't redundant). She'd given him what she called spiritual food.

The older Jenny, who gave her name to her daughter because it was soundly a verb of her generation, in the beginning had lived up to her birth name, so American, right to the red cent. Daughter Jenny carried her mother's name because her mother believed it gave her a key to immortality. The at home Jenny sensed the exact time that Oscar had need for her empathy. When he'd come knocking at his daughter's door at the dorm, with his face in his lap, she was prepared to listen.

He told her that when he bought the paper he didn't know he'd have to get along with the town's eternal critics and soreheads. This bothered him, and he wasn't at all prepared to accept it. He hadn't realized he was blessed with a so sensitive visible skin —- they raged over piddling little trifles. Why, they'd seek a way to criticize the Prince of Galilee because his garment stirred up dust as its hem dragged as he walked.

What really got to him were the late night telephone calls bounded by what in his belief had become serious threats. He thanked the callers as cheerfully as he could muster by the same rule his mother had taught him:

A sword hanging over him warned to kindly say, 'thank you for calling;' had also taught him patience, to be fearless, unperturbed. He had clinched his fist as a silent retort.

Jenny's mother what a beautiful being she was. Ah yes what a magnificent credit to the species. Once of the same and sane mind with this woman upon a time in his country's history against the time they who would steal and sell the heritage of a nation's promise, she who was loved and who with all his energy his soul and his belief in the heavens sure that she loved him, becoming holy, until that day.

As a king's personal regiment sent against these martyred exiles helped them face the rest of the world, confident even as the tear gas burned their eyes their open skin their questionable resolution in the streets of Chicago along with many other little rebels of an uneasy generation who believed their country had been taken from them.

They went from the unwelcome Chicago streets more committed to battle with the same fixed determination prepared to receive the angels who ruled over them reminding of a promise of a truly new world of love and youth everlasting.

Before that it was Berkeley where they'd found so much deep delight in the cry for 'free speech.' The rest of America could deny yet define even feel all that their cry stood for.

Teach-ins spread across a nation's campus; an inward scream was, "Let the recent past bury its past." Tears real or created were an ointment to their sacred bodies, harking to the orders of their furious peers. Oscar and his woman who with the others had no need to exchange ideas because their minds were a duo like Batman and Robin.

They traveled the south's back roads, welcomed like everywhere all across the north where their brothers ripped up their draft cards. Their sisters and brothers shouted that war was a disgrace and they wept on the shoulders of the founding fathers.

The 'Summer of Love' (caps) that began in San Francisco in 1967 wandered over a nation at rest in backpacks and in the pockets of jeans worn through in threads as a symbol of their battle-cry.

They in nursed hearts signed in blood pledges of protest against the 'rich whose silk pockets they cried held rewards stolen from others' sweat of exploited brows.

Love not war was a cry by day and a refuge by night leading Oscar and his one and only love (unusual, the 'only'), in rebellion to try at making babies by night light to create a family in the image of the shattered world's law now on the way to purity. It was a sweet 'new tradition,' so it was written; he and she walked as one, in common purpose for the new life fitted in swaddling clothes: that was girl two Jenny who'd arrived among them.

Until, lo, the day girl one Jenny his woman left, to go back to where it all began; he'd misread what she had been about and had of late become, but not really. He'd felt, only slightly, far down in his being that it would end this way.

Then Jenny became the girl who had wished to wash away her stay had so wished for a child in her image and in her name: The world was an eternal dawn. So they were Jenny One, Jenny Two, Big Jenny and Baby Jenny. Oscar could not have foreseen a wayward stir in their lives. He would come to know on that bad day that Jenny had been quite capable for the unfortunate choice of the left fork in the road.

He'd come home that bad evening from his own frenzied day at the news office, immediately realizing that she was gone and that he'd never see her again. What really surprised him was her unconcern in love for daughter Jenny. He'd in prayerful haste gone directly to rescue Jenny Two, fearful yet sure she'd be among the other children at the keeper's on the street, panting as he rushed out the door.

His tongue swelled to twice a size as he tried to tell five-year–old Jenny Two about her mother. Two hadn't cried: the stoic little Trojan.

As he'd opened the door he had at once noticed that her papers, which were a large stack of worded stock, were gone. The stack had grown to maybe eight inches in height and included her two unsold novels, poems on which she'd sweated (in her heritage, by her own 'blue blood').

The pile of first thoughts to paper, which she had said she would some day rewrite, he later found. The sum of it, including the two unpublished novels, were in the garbage can out back. It was a newsman's instinct that led him there.

Her clothes, such as they were in disparate up-style and expensive but torn and ripped, were gone. His unsure inventory of what had been hers' assured him that it was complete. The pillow on her side of the bed remained, as it had been when he'd left for the job that morning. The teakettle, which she had bought to use at that exclusive Virginia girls' school from whose campus he had stolen her, was at its place near the stove top.

Jenny Two, for the mostly empty but acceptable years that followed until the grand march of an off-key band led the proud high school grads as they walked past his chair and one of the girls winked the clear eye of delight that said, 'thank you my dear, dear daddy for being such a perfect father' —- had for sure become a calm lady, his own but beautiful like her mother - pure slim chin up full of the same love forever from the youthful Jenny One, as if there had never been reason to be a Jenny Two.

After she'd gone away to that small college in the upper south, which she said was the only thing she ever wanted except for him which was her family —- he slowly became accustomed to the dreaded loneliness and a self-containment once more, ever looking for a way to remember yet not recalling her mother. Jenny through the years hadn't asked much if very little about her mother; a little rebel that clung to him like spilled syrup. By then he was proud the little girl hadn't fully accepted the world as it had forced such a change in her life, but she adapted to it.

Being so far away yet always so near, Jenny never forgot to send regular telephone calls and info letters —- with her love, as he expected would be in every syllable/ He would expect nothing less from his Jenny.

In all his devotion to duty, which he had been identified with in years of memory, recalling all he knew to his readers first as a beat reporter on smaller then larger papers his touch on the typewriter keys had been dedicated in her name. He waited for the hour when the opportunity of ownership of a small rural paper opened up for him.

He was pleased to find the paper a few miles away in eastern Kentucky from Jenny. In less than an hour's drive he could be on her doorstep. In similar time, of which she had so little, she would be sitting across from his newspaper desk or lunch table telling of incidents in life at college.

Together they'd be in the noted little café down town close by his office where he took most of his meals when he didn't feel like cooking supper in the lonely hours at the little house he bought because he could walk most days all the way to his office.

He would not be surprised to hear her admit her interest in a young man she had met which she should have time for in a young woman's life. She talked of 'boys' she knew, but the 'serious one,' a 'promised one,' had so far eluded her. She added that she had other things to do before she would allow something like that to happen.

Jenny, he said, was the daughter any devoted father would consider his own greatest blessing, right next to a woman of love who would have been her mother. Yes, the tear in his eye was for both of them, the eagle and the hawk.

Yet he felt he knew as his mother had felt on that day and said so when her son was off to war during the Korean episode —- that she might never see her son again: That feeling by his mother was translated for him by an aunt, who cared for her while he was gone.

No brothers, no sisters, soon no parents to tell friends how smart she was, even as a little of his mother's cares never were found as he sought her in the eyes of Jenny Two.

He was bothered even as it surfaced in the emphatic nature of his Jenny.

When his hometown paper came by the Saturday post he wasn't surprised to read an item about his place and pseudo heroic deeds in the Army, which his mother had gleaned and enlivened from one or two of his early letters. If this keeps up, he wrote back, I'll come home to a big parade down through the center of the city as shredded newspaper and bricks are tossed from upper story windows.

His life by now was that of a recalled reluctant rebel in the era that followed: too old and creaky for the mass demonstrations among the tired hates that fell upon a weary nation (all that nonsense, he said) for a serious but no nonsense one-time warrior. He wondered too often about how he got into all those protests, adding that it was more for both Jenny's, even then with a deep-seated feeling of love lost between himself Jenny One and his country. He sure had nothing against his society or his country, which most of the time he 'dearly loved' and supported —- (a cliché) he laughed as he said it, but he meant it although he never told Jenny how he really felt.

Besides, in spite of the noise around him, he enjoyed the excitement of his new job.

He sorely walked with a 'troubled mind' as he thought of the country song by that name he had heard as a boy at a homemade musical to which a friend invited him because the friend was to sing on stage that night. Yes, troubled, until he met his lovely Jenny, who could turn his head (the prince) from his inheritance the throne with her at his side. She for sure made him feel like he was on the jewel coveted seat of history.

He had friends now, beginning with two men maybe others who had been born under the morning sun of good feeling, reflecting mysteriously early days of the mist of destiny.

They were three men, and they helped an old editor fulfill his own hour of destiny.

One of the three a man of strength and wisdom who had walked in lightning from the beginning —- after this man had taken his first steps away from his mother's ever fearful, protective eye, of heart and prayer, to fight as a Marine. Like all Irishmen he was descended from kings, yet he wandered through life with a feeling of failure, why he'd gotten almost to middle age without ever having been invited to sit in the seats of the mighty.

And Two, another of the trio was a man of the blood of Asian kings in his veins —- Russian Cossacks too are descended from their investiture of kings; didn't his Cossacks select a mere boy with the blood of a king as a first Tsar of the Russians, whose royal line had lasted more than three hundred years? As a man of history's favor, also, he was content to thank his God that a single honor came to rest in his final hours in a small mountain town in a nation that was chosen for his home that day he left the bus because he was feeling in a mysterious way that here was his destiny. The flowing juices of the River Don ever bound for the sea stormed through this man's body that this was where his God wanted him to be.

Like the honeyed sap of spring, who received military honors for his bravery from the Allied Nations of the second war to make the world safe from a madman and his mighty Red Star war machine who willed the deaths of an entire people whose only desire, with their origin in the deserted steppes of Asia, held a dictum of quietude and love and peace.

And the third man once of an honorable vision whose promise became dimmed early yet not forever by the softness and passion of a woman's body and persuasiveness, for now wilted like that of so many men whom destiny had in its irregular passion had begun to touch awkwardly with manly tears dropped upon him and so many of his kind without apology into history's dust bin?

Here they are, each with memories blessedly dimming; one a widower, another a cuckold and the third a veteran of the weekend pass issued by the Russian Red Army that he might find a masked love in 'hired houses' near his military base, all seated on the hillside porch of Clint's cabin on the side of a mountain above the Cumberland River to dream alone or together.

As bachelors again likely forever, their cussed selves talked of how they'd escaped from what a mountain scarecrow known by them earlier which was defined as 'jail.'

The man had called their situation a 'humble visitation' on a man's life: "The change o' life done hit us, hard." The man of the near hills who owned the cabin personally had accepted his lot as he'd found it. He'd said: "It don't make no difference, none atall. After you're gone," he said, "there ain't no hole in space that can't be filled up, right?"

Aging in brain and deed, now a certified commemorative for all men, the conversation this afternoon inevitably turned to the subject of women.

The Russian said it first, hoping to relieve others on the porch with him from their unwelcome drooping memories. He was aware that they had allowed a sadness to invade their comradeship, pulling each from the present into the past:

"As usual, women are getting the last word. Let's us wake up and get on with saving the world —- both you fellows have told me at least by implication how that was the role that destiny placed on your life and mine." He said, "Such plans which you were forced to consider as boys when society and mama and daddy hoped for, mama especially, are all forgot." The Russian was laughing.

The three had drifted into friendship after long thoughts of that day at the coffee shop when by current noble interest each man had staggered to the street with a feeling of having made a fool of himself.

Clint, the eldest but still aware that all his faculties and facilities were still intact, said: "It may be since I have gotten old and have seen more of the world than I was entitled to, I have never felt so helpless, not for the women in my life but for my country, even for the world because of the up-to-now role of my country in leadership. I've been deep into aching for how I could help her."

"I understand how you feel," said Leo, the once Russian now American. "I can attest to the fact that 'you ain't seen nothin yet' —- that is a line from one of your Broadway plays —- because in my native land I've seen the situation so hell bound, so down deep in hound dog excrement that any man or woman would dig deep into it simply to feel if any warmth was still in it."

Clint took it on:

"You're right," he said. "Yah, I've never seen so many mean people, forced to act above the law to feed their families, or maybe they're just mean for any of a dozen or two other reasons and there's so much stealing in 'high places.' In this land of milk and honey to which the Lord has guided us, we've reaped for our own table but forgotten the hungry; to our own people we toss a little stale bread now and then, hoping the government will find them and relieve us from doing it ourselves."

"Philandering and lying by otherwise so many good men and women has become the definition of a way of life by today's society."

"I've seen way too much of 'man's inhumanity to man.' I've seen growing disrespect of our fellow earthlings, sass of the same God that many of our people have declared dead. What do you say, Oscar?"

Said Oscar: "I don't blame fate for threats of earth-warming and a promise of more but an even greater dose of it, A recent distorted way of life, which you have witnessed as a seemingly bad omen from the future, is the world's fate."

The other writing man recalled the many editorials he'd written, how many news stories he'd printed that carried men's fighting words as reported in his newspaper.

"It's frustrating; heck, it's even worse; it's soul ripping. This wouldn't happen if Benjamin Franklin were still alive, or Thomas Jefferson, maybe."

The third man said he'd been required to read piles of books to attain American citizenship, so much literature about my new nation before I was allowed to take the oath.

"Was this required of your own children?"

"I kept at it because the country's history up to now has been princely, open and so inspiring to a new citizen, it was so much charitable."

"By now I'm well versed in the culture of my new country. I have a greater feel for it than any man save Lincoln who was elected to the presidency."

Oscar said: "I'm of mind we'll not long see a repeat of the biblical punishment like happened to Sodom and Gomorrah. I have the perfect candidate for Lot's wife.

She didn't need it in the many years I knew her; but now I realize that she should be turned into a pillar of salt."

Leo had more to say about his kinship with his new country as compared with his birth land: "I never knew Solzhenitsyn - he's thirty years or so older —- his philosophy made an impression on me. His words spoke to me and to the Russian people, his thoughts came easy in a few paragraphs from his Nobel lecture. He was named Nobel winner for Literature in 1970. He said in his lecture, as reported in the newspapers:"

"The old truths are repeated again; we don't recall that we once lived by it. It is in much Russian literature."

Leo said: "He or someone like him said that the same age-old caveman of greed, violence, envy and mutual hate, which came on into the present, has assumed a respect, class struggle, racial struggle, (and) labor-union struggle —- all tearing our world to pieces."

The other two were astonished that Uncle Leo recalled so much from his fellow Russian. It became Leo's hope as the nugget of his mission. The others believed that what they did today for all the good things would not amount to a farthing.

Oscar said: "So we have OMEN. Where in hell's outhouse do we go from here?"

Clint suggested they go home to sweet dreams of the past. He knew he would forget in sleep much of what they had said about all those good things that they recalled from the past.

From the valley came the roar of a train loaded with coal for the fires of our great cities. The vibration of the rails, of steel on steel, echoed from the valley below long after the train itself had gone on to the pastures of commerce. Then Clint went to sleep.

It was a new day. A light early morning mountain rain danced its playful greeting, a rhythmic tap tap tap across the tin roof of Clint's attic bedroom in his home at his family's cornfield's edge - now dormant —- and now his, high above the river.

As a boy, later as a much older man come home, he had lived in the cabin built by his mom and dad after they were married and hoped to settle in for life. They had been happy here, passed on an eternal optimism given them by their pioneer forebears, and on to him.

Just before daybreak; he could understand why so many Appalachian writers now believed they were compelled to begin their masterpieces by walking their stories and their people through the dew of morning, waiting for the sun as it felt its gentle way among the low hanging limbs of the trees. They were aware that the warmth of the new green of spring in the hills was more than an expected renewal of the Earth because of its promise of life, eternal regeneration of both the land and man.

Especially today when you're just ten and today is Saturday, meaning no school. You can snuggle down in the warm featherbed and its enveloping motherly arms; protected from all that is bad in this world and pretend that the chores will wait. Unless mom calls up and says she's fixed corn cakes and molasses your dad made from squeezing the cane grown right here on the farm. As long as you recall she'd made breakfast on Saturdays and nobody was in a hurry.

Rain on a day in an old place but the same as it forever will be as long as you wish.

Chapter Three

He just felt good and he could not tell why of that, either —- his bed's warmth was soul-soothing as a new-born lamb's bleat or the near silent purr of a house kitten. You are pleased that in an environment made in Heaven since you made it so in your memory, you made it so much more real since in the home place which he brought with him you'd know forever of the eternal promise that you'd keep it always the best with you. It was all that was grand in its simplicity and comfort —- for some reason it felt so different —- today it felt just like that, a new old place but still in the heart of old man Earth.

You stand out on the porch and measure the slow embellishing driblets. The raindrops are so large they capture the morning sun, reflecting the landscape of his hills. They wrestle with the sun, forming nuggets of gold among the silver stream at the rain flowing over the side of the roof and its tilt. You watch contentedly as the vines' leaves fold slightly in prayer as they build a slight hollow a child's china doll's cup much like mom's souvenir cream pitcher, which she bought in Cincinnati.

He had come to accept it as the natural way of things the value of this gift as he had grown to manhood at his family's cabin home on the mountain - as the last of his clan to give it the stroke of Nature's best as she reappears over the land in spring after hiding in the snows of winter, like you feel in the soft fur of an almost new puppy in the house that your dad said you could keep after you found her in the road.

He'd brought puppy food from a brief stop in town toward home after a day visit or frolic. Like his mom and dad, Clint was proud, too, to be such a big part of it all. To his family, like the land of milk and honey that was seen in the clouds that led the children of Israel to their Promised Land.

As his mother had talked of it he told you of her and his own memories of good times and love; the sacrifices you vividly realized she'd made and his father agreed that you might have a world to greet with a smiling face when once you were sent out alone to reap the flowers of his and especially of her bosom. You helped make the ground ready to receive the seed of David your dad and the neighbors called it: the new life pushing through the ground grateful because you helped make it so.

The fields at harvest time with its orange pumpkins, yellow prairie-like flowers that are called bitter-sweet grown on mountain bushes like laurel and sold by the side of the road by his cousins, a bunch of mountaineers; fodder shocks painting a scene dressed for new business advertising in colorful print for next year's calendar declaration of the old season's glory not unlike the ages of man whose memories would be passed on to the birth, expected renewal by Earth for men, women whose time was a promise, on to others through eternity.

Mom's cherry cobblers so tart, the fruit of the gods relished as reward to Caesar's guard as sweet thousands of years later on men's soldierly tongues, picked full ripe from the two trees by the gate at the corner of the yard.

Autumn's tithe of many colors like the cloak of Joseph of old stretching from hill to glen to shield the green vine of the laurel but submitting to the same green leaves the Greeks wove into crowns for sweaty brows of their champions,

The Pythian games, ancient contests of field and hunt at Delphi. —- so little changed along the riverbanks and the sea and woods in the time of Rome, Gaul and Greece.

Over Here, his people had called it Heaven: to others it was a place foretold by the ancients: In the morning you are boy; in full day you would have seen it as duty, in family, and by late day you were looking at it in satisfaction for what you had done and seen in Earth's light of day. In his youth he had watched how his mom had taken the rhododendron and strung it all together with mistletoe and holly to tell their house it was Christmas.

It was a boy's reclaimed feelings from when Mother Nature lived on the mountain. "Betcha I can jump from the highest limb o' that there tree into th' water and never touch bottom, dive into the water like a eagle after a fish an' you can't even hear the water splash."

"Betcha you tryin' t' kill yourself."

"Naw, I can do it. Jus' watch me."

"I think I hear your mama callin' you. Go home." It's all brag, anyway. "Leave. Go on down along the riverside a long way where I can't see you."

In insult, the neighbor boy has no need to suffer as he makes a big fool of himself.

Despite what they say, a boy awake from a dream knows that man will go on living, no matter what the heavens throw at us. This is the way you have to talk; that it is far too soon to destroy what the ages have given us.

Yet, his fatigue dragged him to another scene before he was fully awake. It was noon.

"Come on Marines. Finish your ration; time to go."

"Greene, take the point."

You don't have to recall what happened a half hour later.

You had surprised the enemy and had to fight your way out of your own trap. You didn't like it now and could erase it forever and always from your mind if you wanted to -- you were fighting for that cause the brass was always throwing at you as your duty. Even so was the enemy. That's why he needed to recall it: The one incident that bothered him most; he knew he would have to face it soon since it was the reason for his being here —- his first kill. He recalled all, his first days of asking the reason why.

King David was a soldier before he was king and the people sang songs, ballads they were about David slaying by the ten thousands. And David had to kill a man in face-to-face combat and watch his face his hurt eyes looking up at him before he died. No hate in those eyes —- it was too late for that; the man's eyes alive even as the blood from out of his soldier body turned to acid.

You never had to look at the faces like David did. If there's anything good about that word for war, the killing and your part in it, for what you did, there's no word for it.

("Yeah, you didn't, that time in the jungle; another kill for his company." You had to make a sketch for memory's sake.)

How do you make a picture of a mangled head blood all over as your buddies talked about it? Bodies, but not the anguish you knew following the South Pacific savage forest incident, screaming eyes the nose that wasn't there anymore the tan face gushing out its life, blood red then death and the blood stopped.

The same blood of every battle of brother against brother since it became the lot of man the day after they were ordered to leave the garden.

Somebody's father somebody's son, and the Lord blessed the battle and David the warrior a shepherd a poet, a song of peace in his heart. With a king's crown David laid the Lord's promises on Saul's throne for the people he was called to rule.

"You think you're goin' t' heaven someday, Clint?"

"Yeah, but I hope it's not right away, I got too much sinnin' to do before I'm called up yonder."

"Heaven ain't for sinners."

"Then who's goin' t' go there? We all sinners like that old visitin' preacher said at th' revival a long time ago night. He said we could all go t' heaven; I rightly believed him, then an' ever since th' more I thought about it."

"Flawed man, all around flawed. Jus' a little less than th' angels," the preacher said.

How did that fellow the evangelist know about Heaven like that? How many sins can you get away with before you can still ask for a ticket to Paradise?

Clint reckoned he'd get there all right: sinner and all that he was, so why did he call up the memory of a bad day? Bad memory to be stuck with for th' rest o' your time on Earth.

Not Over Here where you can rid yourself of it. That is the best thing about going down to the Garden of Eden.

Bad day in the jungle heat where the enemy lay silent in a nervous sweat mainly in the tree tops like a buzzard that old vulture sitting up there with a grim smile (what they called it in books he'd read) on his face waiting just for you.

Except the buzzard sitting up there hiding back of the fronds of the jungle tree had a rifle which was for killing men, like yours. He became one with the jungle, the enemy did, watching all of you through eyes like doodle bugs as you came nearer running his hand along his dirty weapon dirty from the sap of jungle trees; eyes people said were slanted, like snake eyes (an enemy must be; he is always defaced in some way, so you won't hurt so much for killing your own kind).

And he's hurting, like you, scared like you —- waiting through a long night legs aching by not moving —- still, he sits. Waiting, Waiting.

He had gotten away from his platoon, too far ahead. Looking over his shoulder through the green fronds, he knew he couldn't be too far away from them.

He couldn't call out —- had he strayed from the others? He felt the soldier's panic, suddenly realizing he was lost, gotten ahead of his men. No time to define panic before the battle that was to come.

He felt the terror, the fear, as it took over all working parts of his body. Was this panic? All over little stinging pin pricks. Caesar's Romans felt the little red bugs running through their veins as they ran their fingers along the sharp edges of their killing blades. Was there blood on the blades from an earlier kill?

He listened for the breathing, sniffing to smell an enemy's sweat, the screaming crack of a fallen tree or a limb on the jungle floor. He was hoping he wouldn't hear a twig break. If he heard it, the enemy would hear it also.

The unforgivable on the walked over woods floor would mean that he or his men had forgotten a sergeant's warning; they'd been careless and now they would have to pay for it.

For a moment an eternity it was nigh onto overwhelming; he fought against a terror running with his blood like a dirge (singing?) through his earthly body. Bug sounds in the tree strange sounds of buzzing flies far off hungry animals. Good and evil sign. Worst thing is not to capture a sound, or perhaps to stifle a cough before a breeze borne odor of rotting trees in a woods pond bowl of still shrill poisonous water nearby. The sergeant said every disease of the jungle was in those waters.

Clint came into a clearing opened up for a small meandering stream at his feet. His instinct caused him to raise his eyes to a slight movement on the other side of the water. The dangerous invitation held by the jungle stream waters of death, thousand diseases sergeant said had been distracting; he knew that it carried dozens maybe a hundred killing jungle rot of organisms. Fear of the creek waters was his distraction to death, the other side.

He was staring right into the face of the enemy, a lone enemy soldier turning his rifle toward him. Death had left the stream and stood almost rigid straight across from him a dozen yards away. Clint acted, and it had to be fast. His own rifle was raised. No time to aim: just fire.

He felt the sting of the bullet through his shirt and warming more so bleeding body, the fiery pain before he passed out. He hadn't time to ask if he were dead, hoping the missile had only grazed his Marine belly. Mama my stomach hurts. He couldn't recall any of it until he was looking through what he thought was a darkened glass.

Faces of his own men came out of the fog the heat created mist of the alien land the jungle above him, faces in the overhanging growth, long drooping fronds of a yet storybook beauty in flesh and sympathy. He felt wet. He thought no he knew it was his own blood.

His whole body ached. He wasn't dead, he now at least was sure of that, unless his men had somehow become angels. He left the hurting in loss of a light in front of his eyes but glad to be aware again, rolling faces in dizziness into sleep one more precious time.

Faces again, new strange faces pasted against a wall out of place. It was a ship's bulkhead bare of anything like home, he knew because of the pipes that ran in and out of metal sheathing like a spider clinging to a tree topside, down from ceiling to floor the deck he was supposed to call it the sailor said to call it all Navy talk and he realized it was part of a ship, Navy ship?

The odor the medicinal smell mingled with Diesel; he heard the throb of engines amid the smell of other bodies disturbing his nostrils. It came near reminding him of the hospital he'd once been in when his father was ill.

On his left the shape of a porthole and in a funny place told him for a moment where he was; a ship with old oily wooden decks —- he felt it suffering and surrounding him, dirty old river boat, rented by his country's Navy until thy could send a little ship to replace it.

Good ol' U S of A Navy ship now. Every part of it meant it had been a private vessel in jungle commerce, right? Rude steamer plying shallow waters before the war something right out of Kipling all over said the word picture. The bulkheads in particular said so by a quick paint job, deck swabbed every hour or so only because he was in sick bay.

"You awake, Corporal?" one of the heads said. A familiar face he knew from somewhere, but not one that belonged among his own men. The man told him what he knew of the story. Clint's story, but he wasn't sure he wanted to hear: Or what the smiling face knew of it after talking to your men. How could he tell the story teller that he really didn't want him to tell it?

His men said, the corpsman said, that a second after the pop they heard which was a brief stuttering sound of rifle fire. The platoon simply parted the bushes to come upon Clint lying on the bank of the jungle creek, blood all over his chest and head. They said they knew for sure he was dead.

"An' you got that son of Tojo dead on the other side of the water. The enemy shot straight through the lower part of his neck. So quick there was no blood. Maybe a peep which would mean he became dead the moment he was hit by your shot,

Funny thing, the men said they heard just one rifle report.

"Figured out both bullets went out screaming at the same time. I expect that's why one of the men called it stuttering: two bullets in the air a hundredth of a second apart. To everybody else it was just one big report dead, as in enemy dead; as called by Clint's Marine fighters in their first major hour of hate 'paying off.'"

"I got 'im, right?"

"You shore did, Corporal."

"If I killed a man, then why do I feel all this pain, this big holy sense of remorse running all the way through me?"

"You're supposed to feel that, especially if it was your first kill."

Fellow called Dave held onto the Japanese soldier's pocket purse, much like the wallet Clint carried in his shirt breast pocket.

Dave, one of the ship's crew, leaned down so he could examine the contents, said, "Look right there." He pointed to a fading from sweat photograph of a woman and three children from among the handful of pictures and papers the enemy soldier carried.

Dave held the photograph close to Clint's face; the wounded man stared at the picture for several minutes. "Just like my family, any family," he said.

My mom and my sister and my brothers, if I had any: like a pose for a picture to be sent to their soldier boy, taken as he pronounced it when they were all children and not long ago either . . . smiles everywhere. "Soldier boy just like us; little more than a teen-age boy too young to go out in the world and slay or be slain," he said.

On a shiny piece of paper, faded in spite of what it was, a man with a family of love back home, taught to kill, raise blood; that was his order.

Like King David in the Bible with his field of dead enemy lying all over, like a bed covering, bodies lying on top of one another on and on to the horizon, a post-battle scene drawn like an artist or as somebody imagined it for a modern age Bible. None of them were showing David's family, with David in the middle staring out of a Bible chapter.

David's eyes killer eyes were fixed right on him, with a modern rifle, another killer soldier he was. The soldier was given a spear, told to kill just like him who with his rifle was ordered to go out and 'git to it.' All he needed to know was where the trigger was and what it was for, how to reload. That's what he was taught in a brief killer camp indoctrination.

Clint said to the men standing around: "Look closely at all those faces. Waiting for their soldier brother probably father, a husband to come home. Why must we do this to each other?" Then he said: "Forgive me, a Japanese man's little family. Forgive me."

One of the men by his bedside crossed himself.

He knew he had been forgiven. Killed, but the slain was from the battle, promises of more just like it to come. For here he was battles forgotten; soon, he knew, he would bury the memory of it for all time.

First, though, he must recall each horrible mini-second. He knew time had forgiven him maybe almost —- until he'd first forgiven himself. Maybe if they had not shone him the picture.

The jungle creek-side event as a big hint became a forecast of more that would come, the sailors on the ship told him. Future victims would only be souls stirring up to be soldiers hardened to death. Clint didn't like the term, but it was what he'd become —- the hardened man of war. David, who would be king, killed his ten thousands.

"What are you going to do when you get out, Clint?"

Like a soldier since man learned he would go into battle, on orders to face men like himself who knew about dying, but talks of life to stay thoughts of death, a rare welcome to moments of silence when the guns quit and they had an hour to think of more to come, to count fingers and toes, he rests up for a next deluge of whistling metal and thinks not much else beyond such almost buried thoughts.

Clint hesitated. "Don't know. Try to find a way to make my living off the land, I reckon. My mom and dad did, for as long as they were raising me. Reckon I can too."

"If you can't you going for a job up north, that's what all you hillbillies do, ain't it?"

"Not if I can help it. I don't feel that it's right to work for the other party, somebody else's profit. Best I do it on my own land, or a small business if I can't, like a printing plant I might have had in mind."

"'Sides, I just can't see myself making a living on all that concrete up in Ohio or over in Detroit. I want my own country green grass under my feet. Right now, even sticky weeds, especially if they are mine, my own sticky weeds."

Yes, even after you have become of age and went up north to where the money jobs are, like all the other warrior boys of your generation and then you have come home as an old man to lie abed and listen to the rain on the roof.

The bit of cool in his bedroom as the sun made an effort to squeeze through the not fully drawn shade underside of itself of the window of his downstairs bedroom his now that once had been the night room of his mom and dad awakened him to the promise of another day on the mountain.

The cool of the morning was enough to invite him to stay under the slight cover.

When he was a boy in his bedroom in the loft his mother would be standing at the foot of the narrow stairway calling that he would be late for school.

Clint let his feet hit the floor; he walked through the living room and joined the porch outside. He could never have felt so good, he thought, allowing his bare feet to catch in the fur of the bearskin rug. For the first time in a long time, ever since he was a boy, he became aware that in his first moments out of bed the worrying pain was gone from his hip, which he'd brought home from a make-up game on the high school football field, a lifetime ago.

The pain wasn't there always, appearing when his night had been stolen from him by an anxiety over nothing that really amounted to the usual world on fire that awaited him the next day. He'd made no effort to conceal the nearly forgotten injury from Marine doctors who verified him for active duty. It'd never distracted him if he remained active in what a Marine does.

In the past the pain would cause a trembling, a shaking, it might be said by the early daylight that briefly demanded that he pay attention to it. He reentered the room and to a closet made for such a day with its coats and sweaters which were so in memory available. Its time he'd called some neighbors to stop by and maybe find wraps fit for further use. He wanted a jacket or sweater just for the morning cool.

He surveyed the ill weather clothing aware that his mother's blue cloak lay on the floor where it had fallen off the hanger. As he reached to claim it, he was surprised that the cloak had hidden in its piled place near the floor a rocking chair he'd made as a possible gift in a YMCA lesson he'd taken years ago so as to improve his wood work. He immediately recalled the lifetime endurance of the chair.

It was the rocker he'd taken for his and Lily's first girl child before her fifth birthday.

Clint held the chair by both its rockers for several minutes wondering how the chair had come to his mom's and dad's home some hundred or so miles southeast from his and Lily's home in Ohio at least a generation ago. He put the chair in its apparently self-chosen place in the closet and returned to the porch. His first girl child, sister to the boys, so loved and so beautiful baby as the happy owner of the chair had died during the several months of the wave of infantile paralysis that came storming through the country not long after.

The chair later sat in the corner nearly hidden between the back wall and next to the room's dresser in the guest room of their home back in Ohio. For a long earlier time it sat in a prominent place in the living room, but Clint not without some protest from Lily, his wife, because she shed a lot of tears every time she walked past it, moved it away without a word from anybody in the family.

He was bothered because of his memory failure, but something was not right in here. He returned to the outside porch, realizing that something was not where the porch furniture should have been. He had not noticed it the first time he was on the porch; the fog had lifted but he still could not see the town below or the woods across the river, because of the mist over the river.

He stood in bewilderment on the porch again for several minutes after his return to it. He could not believe what he was not seeing. He'd missed at a while ago because of an early fog off the river, which often obscured the world including the woods across the valley and the town below. The morning sun after a while usually would burn away the mist. So far it hadn't happened,

The mist had lifted, leaving the scene as Daniel Boone might have known it.

"Hello, neighbor," someone said through the screen at the front door.

The man looking into the house from the outside said his name was Karl and that it looked like he'd come at a good time to answer some of Clint's bewildering questions. It was nothing new to him, Karl said, since he'd seen it happen again and again in the four hundred years he'd been here.

"Who are you who raps at my door to say that the whole world has turned upside down? What's going on?" asked Clint. "Everything's gotten moved around, swallowed up upside and downside making it so awfully hard to figure out and what are you trying to tell me when you say that you've been here four hundred years?"

"I'm your neighbor on the hill behind and above you. You appeared not to realize where you are. Well, I'll tell you; then you can start trying to figure it out. You are in That Place, which you Earth people call Heaven. You live awhile on Earth you die and if you have been good this is where you go. I'm sure you've heard all that from your preachers beginning in kindergarten."

"I died?" said Clint, in the sort of a moment of everyday expectation. "I don't even recall being sick." It was with some deep thoughts, far away thinking and finally acceptance of the facts and Karl's assessment of the new situation that at last convinced him where he was and Karl said it was what he'd slowly learned at church of the new and the old of what he would encounter once he had passed from Earth to his eternal home the promised Here that was his Eternal Home, the Heaven the preachers talked about. It began slowly and perhaps gratefully to enter his mind, a belief you could call it, that fitted into his almost accepted new reality.

"If you are telling me the truth, and I have to believe you mainly because everything that had puzzled me so, means that I must adapt to the new surroundings, new because of the polish and the slight difference that this was my cherished home on the Earth.

"I really loved this old place, and I still do. This is my boyhood home, like they say in the funny papers. I remember saying to a bunch of boys one time when I was free from my few duties around the farm, which later I realized never amounted to much except that I was getting a true education, and that when I died this is where I wanted to spend eternity like some preachers back then called it —- eternity, a word that encompassed everything all that was good about life and all that's beautiful and comfortable in it wherever you are."

"I knew then I reckon that the cabin would be in my Heaven. My mom and dad built it right after they got married and lived in it for the rest of their lives. I wonder where they are. They without any doubt are around here someplace."

Karl said, "Like my drama coach always said, thinking he was using what he thought was a Shakespearean line, 'I will be leaving,' no, he would have said, 'I must depart.'" Karl said shutting the screen door, "you need time to yourself, until you get adjusted."

"Wait, Karl, I don't know anything about this place and all the changes made around the countryside since just this morning. Please come back when you can."

Karl hesitated, asked Clint to look around outside. Clint turned around, said "Well, I'll be dogged, there's the town and the woods over there. What has happened?" he asked.

"Yes, the same old town. You must have forgotten the place. Did you always love the town like you just said, or was there something about it that caused you some grief or maybe a lot of uneasiness?" Karl asked.

Clint continued: "The only thing that bothered me was a bunch of people who lived there and clung together in bitty parties hoping to ignore our bunch who came downtown barefoot and in denim overalls blue no longer but white after a lot of washings in homemade lye soap. The fancy soap did a good job bleaching out the blue. It was so much you would think our 'new' white britches would identify us as waiters at their river yacht club."

"We were proud, all of us knowing that we were defying a tradition of this little old burg itself. We were the way our mamas checked us over before sending us out in the wild. We were generally let's say satisfied that we were as good as anybody else," said Clint.

"I'm detecting something in your explanation that doesn't sound like you mean it. Methinks you are hiding something. Did you hold any grudge against some people in your town?"

Clint said, "All right, Karl, I'll confess, or at least try and get it out of my system. It's now or never. When I was a boy not far from manhood there was this lady in my town who to me as I recall her actually crept around like any old busybody finding fault; she enjoyed following me. She showed up a lot of places that I did. She was full of the old cynical gravy, all sorts of resentment, and she just let go, like her buddies and a few others. Called me all sorts of names, said I was dumb, even stupid; she said I was a dirty farm boy who should not be associating with her children, especially her daughter who was my age and in my class up at school."

"I admit it bothered me a lot. For a long time I tried to avoid her. But she had made her point. It bothered me so much that when I was away from my town, I began to associate her with the bad things about the town itself. I hated her, I really did."

"Not long ago, after I'd forgotten about her, there she was. I met her on the street, this little old lady and she was so kind to me and the more I thought about it I told myself that I'd forgiven her. As you and I have stood here talking about something you couldn't have an interest in hearing about, I realized that I had really not forgiven her. I had to though because the people who run this place said I must."

"Otherwise, I eventually wouldn't be given my resident card. I tell you this because I believed it was my biggest fear over not being admitted, in the end, to Heaven itself. It was a flaw in my character, the preachers called it sin, really; you can why I'm telling you about it just now."

"Is that so? Well, go out on the porch and look down to where the town that wasn't there this morning might be."

"Well what do you know, there it is, the movie house, the school and the college, the bank where my friend Frank works; all right there. I know for sure that I forgave those good folks —- this lady and her friends that we called those uppity people. I realized that once I got away and began to look at the rest of the world's people that they were pretty people, just like me, or I thought I was once and forever."

"Among the so many of the world's people are the ugly, nasty, greedy, hurting and with the same old mean in their heads but they came around to where you actually began to like even trust them. You've helped me know that I forgave them on this day and in this new land, this new and beautiful place."

"Did you forgive all of them?"

"Funny, yesterday or whenever that was, I saw this lady we talked about. She drove by my house in her new Buick, and I recalled for once how she used to be, how she hadn't changed at all. In the next few minutes I began to fell sorry for her in her highness ways."

"So it didn't all happen until just now. I remembered what my mother said, so right then I said to myself that if any of my women had gone through with say probably a man she didn't love, or maybe he beat her or was unkind to her in some other way and I said 'get thee from me Satan whenever they acted toward me in a bad way.'"

"There's the town, Clint. She'll begin to know that you loved her. I'm still talking about the town, maybe the woman too who saw you in your garden yesterday from her new Buick and remembered how much she had missed in not being your friend."

Karl asked something about Clint's association with women since he had intimated that the girls at his school didn't have much to do with his sort. "Did you have a girl friend?

"Let me tell you later about Lily, the woman I loved and married during my Ohio years. Right now because of my shedding of an envious part of my life, I have to talk about Doris, a girl who at the time hadn't come back into my life, but in a way she did."

"I was in town and I wanted to talk to someone. I stopped by the old hotel porch and asked Leo if he had time for coffee, or tea if that was his preference. Leo said that since it was early afternoon he'd had all the caffeine he could take and besides he was waiting for an old chess buddy down from the city, who again had challenged him and that eventually he was going to beat Leo at Leo's famous game."

So Clint went on to the coffee shop and café down the street and around the corner. As soon as he entered the shop there was Doris sitting alone and facing him. No way could he have avoided her, so he sort of sauntered over in his best imitation Texas cowboy fashion and asked if he might join her.

"Please sit down, Clint," she said. "I've been waiting for you."

He passed off the remark without taking time to consider her implication. The conversation with Doris was casual without any hint of reference to a one-time possible evolving relationship beyond the current movies and a book or two since she knew that Clint had always been known as a boy or man who read books.

"Tell me, Clint, did you and I have something going back in our high school days? I know the war coming on, and I know you were busy and then you up and joined the Marines to get into the war," she said. "I know you didn't date any of the girls in high school, or even pay any attention to them. Whatever was it that attracted you to me? I was surprised and delighted. There you were, you and me, and a new world was opening up."

Clint appeared deep in thought. He said: "I think the situation might have been because I felt at the time that here was a girl who had shown some interest in me. Unlike the rest of the girls, especially girls from the town's west end where you and the others lived, here was a girl who didn't see me in red flannel underwear with a long bandanna sticking out of my hip pocket and who ate his French fries with a fork, really, instead of with our fingers. That was one thing about our hillbillies; we had been taught table manners."

Doris laughed, out loud until tears formed on her cheeks.

"Clint, my darling," she actually said it just like that. "I've never heard anything so ridiculous in my whole life." She added, "I must apologize for my red snotty nose friends, at the same time I thank them for turning you over to me. They will never know just how faith and a little kindness and understanding have made such a difference in this old world, and all over a shy even sometimes backward hillbilly boy who felt like he didn't belong."

Clint said to Karl; "Do you think I might have gotten it out of my system and that I'm on my way to being a first class citizen in this Heavenly system?"

"I'm in no position to make a judgment on a thing like this. So, let's us leave it right there for the here and now and thank fate that here we are. Boo and boo and boo."

Before he closed the screen door behind him, Karl said:

"On Earth where you lived you were fortunate in many ways that pleased Heaven."

"Wait just a minute. Tell me if you can, or have a theory on it, why in my mom's and dad's closet I found this rocking chair. How did it get there," said Clint.

He told Karl a little history of the rocker. How it came about from his class in use of his hands to make something practicable to a show-off to his mom and dad, then put to use.

Karl didn't hesitate: "Your daughter died within a few months after she received the chair on her birthday. She brought it with her; it is here in welcome to your new home. She knows you are here. There's the possibility that her mother Lily is with her right now."

"How do you explain she carried the chair after death to This Place?"

"The same chair is right there on Earth where your girl baby left it. One of your other children now has the chair in her home and cherishes it."

"She loves it because it belonged to little sister."

"I sure don't understand. Is it a duplicate?"

"No. it's the chair you made; it's here and it's there. Give yourself some time and you'll come to know This Place."

Clint thought about the chair and everything about the lady hoping to be forgiven; the lady who thought she already had missed so much of the good life as other people in her personal little society maybe did not. She was, let us say, passing on to you who represented what would be the next step in understanding her deprived and vengeful life. You helped her by showing her through your kindness that you had forgiven her.

To Clint, his time way up north with his mom and dad's grandkids often was spent in a distant longing for home and the warm the cool of the cabin home in winter and summer, with its tin roof, the soothing rhythm of life most men would give half their fortunes just to see and luxuriate in with flung abandon and no grief or remorse or no pain for one beautiful year in earthly time, even for just one year.

Back home atop your dad's and your mom's mountain, you found that guitar your dad had before this. It was his number one possession. His only, his father's sole possession you reckoned waiting ready for tuning sitting wrapped up real neat behind the stacked quilts on the shelf of the downstairs closet next to the fireplace.

You tightened the strings as your father did, dusted it off and put it over next to the stacked wood where the cat coming from wherever it had been discovered its paws across the strings returned a pleasant, friendly sound. The music of the instrument was distant, like the gentle cat's feet that made it, soft and welcome as it had touched your sleep on late nights back in your earthly home.

When he thought about it, he also was reminded that there were no cats, or dogs either, in This Place. He hadn't seen any and he learned that all he needed to do was think about them and they were there. The cat loved his dad, purred in contentment as she slept on dad's lap. Too, my orphan dog loved me. I'll think about dad's cat and my own pup later.

Who said there were no cats or no dogs in Heaven? Let them find out for themselves.

Clint could never do with the strings like his father could. He could never sing like his mother could. He couldn't even dance. Hillbilly boy living up there and seldom as he earlier talked about it envying the social scene the kids in the valley created so they could be like the hot shots that they saw on movie screens on Sunday afternoons.

So gifted his father was. He'd retired the instrument to his dad's favorite room yours too now up front where the old man would sit at night or on a snowy day watching the fire the dancing flames. The waving restless wood fire tossed, purred. Flames argued across the logs in the fireplace, hypnotic to the tired and hurting.

Clint recalled neighbor men just like his father watching the flames in an open fire shelter outside, a workday close to a mine mouth or in wood-cutting camp by a sawmill. The men would take their lunch bucket and eat in silence, with their brogans stuck out warming close to the fire.

Often the older man, his dad, would pick up the instrument and carry it to his rocker. He'd sit with his hands guarding the strings until he could make music to accompany the dance of the flames.

If a movie opened downtown at the picture show coming with his predicted scenes it even then became his big interest in life. He knew the worried scenes that would come, but not with his dad, who created poetry with his hands to go with his thoughts, and with his music that was enough of reality even unreality to him.

Music and orange fire licking the inner sky like the flames on the logs danced before the gates of Heaven hoping to open a passage to receive and share the wonder to all Earth's regrettable.

His mother, across the room, would read by the light of a coal oil lamp.

As she had turned a page she would glance toward the silent man wondering about his deep thoughts. The two in mutual solitude would wait for the flames to die. In the hill silence, they walked to their bedroom at a comfortable distance near the room with the fireplace. The fire was banked for the night.

The cat in an incredible discovery didn't know as she walked over the instrument's strings that she made a bit of magic. The distant music was amusing to a lonely mountain family. It was a good earthly memory. He'd carry it to an island of recalled marvels beyond the stars on into eternity. However it was called, perhaps of another dimension where now since he'd become a part of it, his for all time.

Music alive on Earth even from an old dusty guitar whatever its given source would ever be associated with This Place by men and women of music and reckoned that it came from this domain. Like the director of a big city symphony orchestra by talented performers, the maestro maybe a magician reached into his hat for a gift a surprise to an audience; like a newspaper press measuring out time's capsules to be as a stopped clock in the archives for men and women of the future to seek where they once had been how where and when their kind had lived, loved, laughed.

He had earned by right and life and eternity the hill that overlooked the Cumberland River in the green of his part of Kentucky. He could view the silver of the river at any hour of moonlight far below ever flowing to the sea, its green valley of springtime, which had caught and held the gold of the sun on the land and to itself after the dew of morning had flown into a sunbeam. Perhaps only a fog yet a unique signature —- like a Pacific island shore in early morning calm at his feet, only yards away.

He was at rest in the coolness of the cabin porch knowing it would ever be like this; not hoping but knowing his for all time. Clint watched a pair of cardinals, as the bright red male bird flaunted his maleness, his mate flitting and teasing among the upper branches of the tree red on green like on a greeting card, edging near his chair, so near he could have reached out, stroked them both.

A pair of doves lived right at the rim of the porch as he in enchantment had called them up from another time. Doves were birds of peace and love, mating for life. The doves huddled like lovers in all of Earth's ages, balanced on a limb at the porch rail. Even in the winter of white and mirrored Earth, they were out there together; cooing, stroking, sharing, exchanging love motions to teach man and woman how it is possible and rightly so to play at love unashamedly. He had forgotten the birds at first. When he thought of them, there they were.

He'd learned early in This Place of scenes and music of imagination of people of many nations, that when he simply wished, a brief moment would bring a reward. They would come, creatures of the Earth and its forestlands, to where men and women sought to dream. The doves, the cardinals, had pursued Clint to This Place, old to time ever soul-fitting in pairs performing million year-old gigs aware that they were showing off. He would have them, because he understood them. He told them so in whispers that he would always be their friend.

Birds of song of four-legged animals of calico and the tux of children's story books, adopted as real as they had been to Earth's children at bedtime and lazy winter afternoons.

They mimicked men, women in the walk and talk of celluloid meadows.

He'd known few toys as he grew up on the hilltop farm. He'd learned to remedy his loss among children of Earth's playtime. His own playground had been the cabin's back porch, with banisters and spaced boards like for a playhouse, until his age six or seven.

If you'd asked Clint how long he'd been in this New Place, unlike Karl he couldn't tell. All he could say was that he thought he was sitting out on the porch and he'd not recall how or when. It didn't matter. The transition was so sudden and so magnificent at the end of it he'd not want to know the whys, the when.

Yet he could recall all else, even the placement of his mother's furniture inside the cabin, all pleasingly related to Mom's house on the wooded hill, the cabin of his boyhood. It was like he had always been waiting for his Mother's call to supper.

In his evening stroll, which Clint in a state of excitement had discovered people like himself who with hobbies and favorite things from their one-time earthly home; like a waltz and its whirling rhythms and school kids clean with shiny faces in costume for a scene in a play —- in their dance called a musical —- modernized but coming to them from a composer of the century before.

He heard the music before he was upon it, stopping to recall the composer who would be pleased to know the dancers exercised to the music he had written for them.

They danced in wide round convoluted circles, and he was in the center of the current —- a dance known back on Earth for a generation before he'd discovered it.

He was on a wide street now which he first presumed was Vienna, with shops of bread and sausages and piece goods, silk gowns for princesses and fancy collars for young men of fashion. The street was of cobblestone; carriages stylishly appointed by hand straps, leaden embroidery in gold and silver towed by high-stepping teams of the finest Arabians he had ever known, horses rigged out in harnesses gleaming with golden accents, adding in its brand of beauty of enchantment to the evening's excitement.

Couples once old and young but now of an age — of just over thirty years; the new generation wanted it that way, always it would be theirs' —- were at sidewalk tables that told new resident Clint Greene it was not Vienna but the story-book Paris he had seen in picture books as a boy at the library.

Karl turned out to be a good neighbor. You can drop in just any time at a home in The Place and be received like a lifelong friend in expectation of good talk. Karl lived on a shelf with the trees almost on top of Clint's cabin. Karl had walked from his home down to the cabin the day Clint arrived.

Today, Clint was still out, getting the 'feel' of the place. Karl's place he called a chalet. It was his ancestral home. His family had lived near the cliff with a porch which you could see from Clint's front yard. .In the Swiss Alps' picture books, above the open country, were mountains with snow tops that were inviting to painters.

Karl described his home as high above his favorite town probably the only small village for miles around with a residential area before they had a 'Chamber of Commerce' for bragging rights to all the storybook mountain homes of three countries. In today's world, the houses' hosts provide maps to the homes of his nation's poets and storytellers of the past with printed visiting hours, which would be Karl's earthly legacy.

Clint's Cumberland River was to Karl a wide stream flowing swiftly out from the Swiss mountains. Same river it was, sparkling to William Tell (English spelling) as it was to pioneers of Clint's early tribal settlers. In this home along with one of the near seven seas, Karl would never have known Clint's river existed during his life on Earth.

In Clint's family history the habit of an early morning or toward what would be an evening on Earth as they recalled it, their neighbors would come out for a walk, nodding and smiling in a talk of the common language of The Place as the strollers passed their houses today.

Karl had lived mostly in his family home, now in the New Place, for three almost four hundred years, which they both estimated in Earth's time as they sat on Clint's porch and tuned in to the sounds soft and poetic that came from above below and behind them, of people in talk, voices in song, music from instruments universal of many nations of strange origin but instantly familiar.

Or they were at the chalet listening to the far off song on another mountain a yodel by Karl's fellow countrymen as they drove their sheep to the new season's new green growth above their homes always in the early spring. The animals' morning song echoed off a near valley and the mountains. The sheep's bleats he soon knew were an animal's attempt to imitate man sounds.

Small talk had come easily to the two men, exchanging jibes as friends funning in instant laugh's universal common people talk that was automatic, so accepted the moment they'd arrived at This Place.

They soon learned how alike they'd been as country boys. They had played like they owned the world, which they did, usually ran now just because they could —- like boys from ten thousand years before. They wanted to run to where the road or lane or pathway ended at the horizon which never ended like you knew at dusk, imagined as the end of day on Earth but at any hour as you wanted it since there were no real nights at the small college campus with its chimes in the lowlands, just as Karl said it came to his chalet near the white clouds from the neighbor music maker's violin. Karl said the tender melody that to Earth's people was as much imagined as actually heard, surely came to them as the music of Heaven.

Sitting one day back then on Clint's porch above the river, the three friends of OMEN recalled how as boys they'd had a yen to walk in snow where they could feel the icy crunch beneath their feet —- later gratefully rewarded by how it would be to taste snow cream.

Clint recalled how it was to Karl; he said, "Go ahead, let's be boys again." It would be a welcome certainly an unusual treat at This Place, as it would be rewarding to Karl since he'd never tasted snow cream - laughing when told that it was made with snow and diluted with honey or sweet fruit juice and vanilla extract: Karl said "what's that," and Clint never explained. They both recalled and hoped to feel again the cold wind coming off the winter snow (invited) that gave them both a feeling of excitement,

Clint talked of a day Over Here when his walk took him upon the Vikings as they were docking their long ships. By chance Karl said that he'd run into them while strolling rather aimlessly along the narrow beaches beneath the high banks of a fjord, where their country opened up to the sea.

The Vikings said it was Over Here that the sea's cold winds brought winter blasts to Sweden different from any other place on earth. It was from the coves or fjords that history's famous seamen and its conquerors in open narrow boats had sailed without charts and with jubilation to claim discoveries of other people of a different shading of their skin and interesting customs.

By winter they returned to their homes or to the great central hall often preferring to sit out the loneliness by their family home or the hall's fires. It was by firelight that they hoped to entertain Clint as they invited him to their Great Hall where their huge wood fires had left their blackened residue, as well on their bodies.

Shields, swords and hard helmets were set at rest along the walls. In dark halls only of firelight the Vikings played as boys to endless revelry never-ending feasts a long night until the day the new sun summoned them once more to the sea.

Valhalla they called it, a short day and long night, an eternal rest day when hall fires burned high to lighten the darkened warrior faces as they told of exploits in far away places. In their day on Earth's great seven seas Valhalla also was talked of as a place in 'the sky.'

It was where heroes of Vikings' deeds on paths of waters of old seas to new and old lands were welcomed after their deaths —- often called the Hall of Odin to these seafarers.

Clint would lift the heavy iron knocker on the broad wooden door with wide hinges to summon the doorkeeper. He wanted to know more about these iron men of wooden ships.

He would shake hands all round with these strong men who had so broadened man's reach into knowledge of the world in which they had lived and visited. They who had known a world untamed and unspoiled at a time when most men were born believing that the world ended at their horizons.

Sitting out in the sunshine on a rare warm day in winter in their land in the North, a long boat's crew had saluted as he had passed on his way to somewhere else he knew not where - one more exploration, which he hoped for, one more surprising discovery.

He'd wanted to meet these brave men and tell Karl about them as they appeared in his room in midnight reading when he was a boy. They provided him with stories of deeds that boys of later ages found in the movies and on

TV. He would talk about what he had read of their homeland, men he had not known in flesh before in his former cabin on Earth.

Clint gratefully experienced the warm wind to which the Vikings' gods had led them.

He told how they'd given the world first knowledge of the land that had become, and in time, Clint's country. They recalled their discovery of Vinland (Vineland) to him and the heavy purple fruit of the vines of summer so named by Leif Ericsson.

It was on just such a Vinland day, toward an earthly February to March thaw that he recalled hesitating above the body of a living or near-living creature of the wilds in his usual Sunday walk, an excursion along his mountain's graveled road. The still animal's body lay at his feet, partly on the roadway, bloodied in its face and along its neck.

At first he thought it was a small wolf; he'd known such wild woods creatures that sought cold weather refuge in the caves and hollows near his home; they found welcome comfort among the fallen trees in the nearby woods, which was unusual for a large animal, especially wolves and bears, creatures of the cold and wild who feared man and his motives.

His father had warned him to beware when wolves came close to man too near a house where he lives because the ice and snow had made it hard for them to find food.

Remember to lock up the chickens, especially lock in the farm's animals his father had once admonished his growing son. There is always the possibility of rabies which make man and any animal "dangerous to man and beasts of any dimension."

Clint knelt beside the furred creature, seeking a heartbeat in the beautiful black and white -- mostly black -- body. He realized it was a dog and not a coyote likely hit by a careless, or as he hoped surprised driver on the ice and snow slick little-traveled highland road. The body was still warm; he could detect an almost silent beat of life. No blood; he realized the animal could be bleeding internally. He carefully cuddled the animal in his arms to carry home, where he wrapped its near-frozen body in a blanket, gently placing it on the hearth. He didn't find any outer bruises.

He stirred the ashes, soon welcomed a roaring fire in the family all-round room, over-heating even on the winter's day. During the rest of the day and into both nights he left his bed to check on the injured animal. He could not detect any change. He thought about washing the dog's body and spraying on some horse liniment his father kept also might help and he watched hopefully. At about dawn of the second full day, he arose and went straight to the fireplace. He was careful not to disturb the rest of the household.

He gently pulled back the blanket and found the dog's eyes open. He could see the hurt, was aware of the pleading, knowing the animal's faith in this boy who would mollify his suffering. Clint, the dog's new owner attempted to soothe his new friend by running his hand along the soft fur to let him know he was in the home of a friend, a sympathetic and kindred people.

When his mother came into the kitchen, she suggested the new boarder might eat if they would offer soft food. She said they had no simple way to offer milk, but they could try pouring it from a spoon down his throat; he'd seen men toss a pill into an animal's throat.

His mother, with a mush of water and corn meal seasoned with a chunk of bacon poured it onto the animal's tongue as Clint held its mouth open. He later could tell that the animal was grateful as its eyes took on a new color.

In two more days, the dog made an attempt to stand. He fell back on the floor, looking at Clint and his mother and father like he knew he had disappointed them. He was eating better and raised his head to take the food and water from the small dishes pushed close to his body.

When Clint awakened the following day, the newcomer was standing nearer his bed on the couch, but still close enough to the fire.

"The first thing we have to do," his mother said, "is find out where he belongs. If he doesn't live on this ridge, what in the world was he doing way out here?" Good questions. He wished the new family member could find a way to tell them —- also hoping he would not reveal that his home was with someone else.

Inquiries among hillside neighbors, farther along the ridge and into the valley, where they left a crude hand-lettered poster a hopeful word with a store where they often traded; they failed to identify an owner. After a few weeks they decided it was another miracle, rare but often enough to this family, that they in their limited earthly wisdom through mountain superstition couldn't understand, but would accept whatever its outcome. It was like he'd been born here, had come home.

And he was; that dog was a surefire miracle. He took to the family and the household like he'd risen to the moment. He could do about anything but cut kindling for the fire and pile it on the hearth.

The first days he had struggled, crossing the room in a stiff and tortuous animal way, neither looking to Clint nor the others for any help, yet showing off like he could do it all by himself. The liniment his father found in the barn's all around box to cover animal wounds that he suspected were in his muscles, but hidden, had done its job.

Bye and bye the dog so far without a name and certainly sans the law that now would require adoption papers, lost most of his stiffness and would look expectantly at them to let these humans know that he had beat this thing called never.

Clint as a boy learned one more lesson that day: That such an attribute known as courage was not reserved to man alone.

The adoptee taught them all about bravery; Clint called it a universal thing. Until he was a man, perhaps while still more boy than man and the war they knew would be coming soon and he was sent away —- to his generation's war -- he was to learn a lot about courage, recalling where he'd first become aware of it.

His new assignment was a rare test, as he had known it as he watched a rescued dog fighting for its life among strangers.

It came during his many months as a Marine in a jungle war in a tangled wood far and away from home.

The new friend as he recalled him while in the jungles had begun his second life on the mountain. As frisky as a new puppy, he dashed across the porch at chow time with the tattoo of a fast drumbeat. He would wag his tail and look up at you like he was expecting a reward for a job well done. That was at first.

After he'd gotten into the routine of life on the mountain, he did his job just like the other members of the family.

He rested when it was recess time to the others, ate during regular meal hours; by springtime he was going out to find sleep on a porch wide board when came the household bedding hour. His chosen place for a bed out of the rain beneath the preferred porch was to be discovered later. He did what was expected of him without a reminder. Clint wondered if he ought to teach him how to read.

His mother said: "Now if we could teach that animal to do the cooking and to sweep the floor, he'd be worth his weight in gold."

"But he's already worth all of that," Clint said.

"You're right, son. You're more than right."

He would bring in the two cows when it was milking time. The animals would have come in at that time, anyway, but they let the dog member of the family think he'd done it all by himself. He'd bark into retreat any animal that came within view of the house, his house.

The family figured he was a little more or less, about five years old. The dog with no name stayed indoors but come spring he found his own retreat during the cool days under the back porch; there he'd stay most of a hot day. At night it was back to the boards. He could do his job, which was on watch. It was like he was expecting it, and satisfied.

Finally, Clint named him Tom, not for any reason to tell the family about. It was just because he liked the name; it was short and everybody else took to it. His father, who said at first that Tom was a name for a cat but in the end, said, "So Tom it is."

It wasn't long before Clint became aware of how smart Tom really was. Not that he could do tricks, but Tom knew what each member of the family would be doing at any hour (his choice) time of day, and he anticipated it, whether going to the fields or to the store in town or to some school event, that is, if he felt he'd been invited; that dog was just ready to travel, but that's elementary stuff. He'd already be in the wagon before they hitched up for the journey downhill.

Clint realized that Tom was extra smart when he acted like he was listening to everything you said, even nodding slightly; Clint would say, now see here, Tom, and whatever it was, Tom reacted with smarts right off. If he was so commanded, he'd stand —- well, almost —- at attention.

Tom was up to ten maybe eleven years old the day Clint came in and said he would be leaving for the war right away.

"I'm eighteen now, and they'll be coming for me. Might as well go in now, before they draft me into it; this way I might get the outfit I want."

He called Tom over, put his hands on his face, looked him right in the eye, and said, "Tom, I'll be leaving for the Marines in a few days. I don't know when I'll be back.

"I'm leaving you in charge. You take care of the family while I'm gone just like I was here like always."

With that, Tom began whining; he put his head on Clint's lap, turned his face toward Clint, looking deep into his eyes. He buried his face in his paws.

A day in the South Pacific, Clint with his platoon back from the lines where they could get mail and he hadn't thought of Tom for several days, had a letter waiting with his dad's name in the edge, telling how his mother had taken ill and died within two days.

"I am sure she didn't suffer;" his dad's words rang out despite the trace of wetness now dried which were left by his fingerprints of tears.

"She wouldn't tell us if she were. Your mother was like that. I'm sure you knew that. Her concern always was for others; she knew when the ridge people were in pain."

His father added that before we knew she was ill or had come down with something we didn't yet know what, Tom was walking around with the saddest dog face you ever saw.

Tom would shun his food until he was so hungry he'd ease back to his bowl that he to me was a little apologetic about it. He did lots of gazing toward the back door to the porch where your mother was seen the first thing in the morning. He would go over to the door and stand close, his head cocked like he was listening for your mother's voice.

Then he would walk away, but not far. This wasn't right because when he lay wounded just after those first days Tom would always let you know it was time to be fed. Not like now. As spring came he seemed to prefer being outdoors. His dad would take food out to him and push the bowl toward where he lay on the porch.

By mid-day when the sun rose higher with spring, Tom moved slightly to keep the sun on himself. The edge of the porch was a fit as a resting place. Not long after, like all dogs, healthy dogs, Tom never turned down the offer of food, but he didn't appear eager about it and let it sit there before he moved his head over to it.

As he traced his dad's handwriting on the page of tears, he could tell his father was hurting. Clint could feel the sad hands and pain that would be in his dad's eyes, a pause in his writing hand.

Until that first letter with his dad's pen, which came just days ago, a letter to him now of regularity usually arriving with his mom's name in the corner, but both at the top of the page inside, now came another mail call.

It was one more alarm, an immediate worry to Clint as he looked long at his dad's handwriting -- the mail usually came with a mother's pen. To most of his buddies who had both a father and a mother back home —- now it was, "Son, I hate to tell you this so soon after your mother passed away . . ." (The same lead-in to the epistle after the letter that was to declare the death of his mother) . . . Clint knew.

Tom had that same sad look in his eyes like always when somebody in the family became ill or a thing dire, real dire, had happened It was like maybe when the family became worried because they had not heard from Clint for several days. His mother had noticed it, and she mentioned it in one of her letters. Tom must have given them a lot of comfort in his absence.

Clint thought about all the empty homes across the country as millions of their sons were away at war.

A week after they buried his mother, his father had written again, this time to say that Tom, too, had died.

His dad found Tom on the porch when he got up and went out to feed him. Or tried to feed him, all curled up with his head buried under one paw.

"He was old, son. I reckon with you and your mother gone, he didn't have the will. He finally took to me, but his real love was for you, and mama. I buried him in the woods and found a round rock for a headstone." The letter was signed generally as 'Mom, and your father,' but now it came simply as, 'Your Father.'

Clint in this New Place Up Here in reminiscence looked across the porch to where old Tom used to take to his bed or would simply lie quietly in the warm evenings in the summertime when the chores were done and the family was resting before it was time to go inside for the warmth of the house in colder weather and to bed by the fireplace.

"He's up here, all right," Clint said, aloud. He was sure of it. "Right away I'll go looking for him. But I won't even have to do that. They say I can "simply call out his name and then I'll say: Here Tom boy, come in and let's talk about old times." He wondered why Tom had taken so much of his memory Over Here and why he should have recalled those times. Maybe because Clint's time spent with his dog Tom was a best memory.

Later, he told Karl, his friend, that it seemed so many of his good hours back on Earth could be lived again —- if he chose, and of course if only in memory.

"Yes," said Karl.

They agreed that it was what This Place was about, that the good times back there were with the good people he had known, and would live in memory for as long as he wished. Among the best, he said, was with Tom. He said he noticed, like they told around, that there are no animals in Heaven. "But they are," said Karl, "they are here, but only you can see them. They're all around and near, for people who had loved them."

The same might be with the Vikings: why the Vikings? They went out in their open boats not to conquer the world, but they went just the same. Their path of curiosity as Clint read about them on nights abed with a book after the family had retired, had impressed the boy, which led to his gratitude for the Vikings; these sea people who had begun the process of opening up to civilization and a new society a land across the waters. Should I not have seen dogs among the Vikings?

"My dog Tom, if I call him at all, there he'll be, as big as life and a wag of that tail. I'm sure of it, with eyes sparkling like the river at sun-up. He won't be looking at you out of sad eyes anymore, because there's no reason for him to be down."

He would know, Tom would, that Clint's mother and his father were up here also.

And that's maybe where he is now. Just as Clint knew about Tom, he knew his mother and father of earthly time would come if he was ready, or they summoned him. But those things were . . . well, different Over Here. They would be together if that was their wish. I'll see them again as soon as they're ready.

Just as the Vikings had made ready the opening of the old world to the new, old Tom in his own way had prepared his family for This Place.

Another good scene for memory came to him after a passive journey to the war zone without Tom and he had begun to think about his dog more than usual.

Clint's Marine friend Asa, for a short while had a dog, picked him up while on patrol at the side of a creek nearby in the jungle. The two adopted each other right off. He must have belonged to an enemy soldier, maybe even a native.

Asa and his foundling, a dog he had named Bonzai, were a big relationship.

The platoon pretty well took him in, too, but they knew that most of this animal already belonged to Asa, because they had hit it off right from the first day. They said something about the Indian and his dog.

Asa didn't know the breed, a blended dog out of a mixture from unknown parentage, he said, done that for generations, until there he was: a dog's dog.

Asa would talk to him but not in the enemy's verse. As with the rest of the men, Asa hadn't learned any Japanese, only "bonsai." The young Indian, figuring the dog would not know any English, talked to his new friend, maybe in Osage, maybe in some other language.

Talk was in his American Indian tribal language; Creek, partly Osage, he said it was. He had bragged about his mother, whom he said was mostly of the Creek Nation.

Sometimes he used his Creek language —- to the dog —- that the rest of the platoon couldn't understand, but you knew that dog heard him, understood every word, just like it had been with Tom and Clint.

To Clint, it was like Asa's newfound ally had assumed the soul of old Tom, that is, if dogs have souls. This was something else that Clint would think about for a long time, for the rest of his time on the Earth.

He said to Karl: "If dogs are here, then they must have souls. Even in Heaven we don't know everything."

That's when Clint began to think more about old Tom. He figured there was such a thing as dog language. Asa left his own dog at home when he came to the Corps friendship.

It was the same sad moment Clint had felt; Asa's dog, little more than a puppy, was left behind to be taken care of by a boyhood friend.

Asa didn't talk much to his brother Marines, but that dog could sure get him rolling. Asa had to secrete the jungle animal from the officers, who said if the dog up and barked at a wrong time, it would give the enemy a bead on their position. Not much later, Asa for no reason that we knew of was transferred out.

The rest of the guys could never learn the reason for Asa's transfer; they tried to get it out of the headquarters staff, enlisted men there, but even they said they didn't know the ways of their great leaders. It angered them to believe it was because Asa was Indian and their officers wanted him out, for 'purity' reasons. Asa knew more about war and life than any man at command level or even the Corps itself. Clint tried to rationalize the act but as usual he would never understand.

It was just that the orders came down that seven men were being sent to an outside outfit, and the brass wouldn't say who or what or where. They'd warned us in base camp not to cultivate friendships for reasons they didn't tell us but now Clint knew why, that and the possible death of a close friend, but he would try and not think too much about his friend Asa and the odd ways of the Corps or the Navy. Asa had to leave his dog Bonzai behind; somebody else took over, or they tried. Clint recalled shortly after Asa left that he didn't see Asa's friend anymore.

Never knew what happened to Bonzai. Probably went back to the enemy. Clint hoped they'd love, take care of him like Asa did, but the enemy had little food, not enough to share with a dog.

Clint addressed a letter to Asa after the war. They were back home, hoping to recall for him -- or maybe he chose to black it out -- some few lonely moments from out there.

He carried Asa's address in his wallet for years. Even Asa's hometown in Oklahoma disappeared from the map.

Clint's friend Asa an early American he wanted always to remember. His letter came back 'Addressee Unknown.' Clint figured Asa died out there with that other outfit.

That's when Clint said to one of the other men that it sure is strange that God would take the best right off; that was when he decided for himself that unstated purposes lay back of about everything that concerned man on God's Earth. Many other Marines he knew held the same beliefs.

This reasoning was breaking into the religious culture of his people, quiet mountain people who so often moved in strange ways in the eyes of outlanders. To them, God was a neighbor, lived right next door.

Clint recalled a day shortly after the unit's arrival at Oahu's Ewa Marine base on the shore of the Pacific where you could spit in the ocean.

Twenty men in an open bed truck from Ewa Field were on the way to a work detail, a make-do job to keep them busy until time to ship out for battle in the vast southwest or a landing beach that was even nearer. They were all standing in the truck bed, the wind in their faces. He was quiet, solemn as an ancient Biblical prophet.

Asa rested his hands on the cab's top. You tried to imitate him, walk a mile in his moccasins ("GI issue," Clint would say). Asa, whose people were of the land and forest, was the straight tall tan noble statue of America's heartland.

Clint would cast him as uncrowned leader of the Indian nations - reminding of the movies' version of Crazy Horse or Geronimo or Red Cloud or maybe Tecumseh (though not one was either Creek or Osage, Clint recalled).

Another wise, brave youth gone off to war to uphold the promise:

That was the expectation of the Indian people, a fighting Marine in the new century for the new country.

The Corps had a way of making you proud, in uniform and on to civilian life. Up here on the mountain, Clint was king (lower case), at least as far as the gatepost. Builders of his cabin dug into the hard soil; piled up rocks defining land rights making it easier for a next generation. They and their kind turned the soil to feed their families, sang thankfully on a Sunday morning at their little churches no bigger than the garages built later by their heirs, comfortable in their legacy.

Clint, member of a later generation could sit on his porch like always listen to the voices that flowed in song across the hills, over the valley, like now forever, old Irish songs permeating the evening air to best define still moments of all except the birds' song, like the tinkling of waters in the valley below (often handbook reminders of the toys of civilization).

On the family's new ground he could walk to his orchard just across and beyond the house and select apples to give to people in the other nearby houses. These were gifts not in exchange for the cabbages and corn and beans they would leave on his back porch, but because he was a neighbor.

Today he was thinking of Lily, wondered if he'd meet up with the girl he had wed and the woman he cared for, as she did him. All these people of once upon a time he could call to his side just as he knew he could summon old Tom.

He believed he could call Lily's name and she would be there beside him, asking: "What took you so long?" reminding that she had preceded him here.

The stone marker at his grave next to hers' back in the world would say in words chiseled deeply to last through the ages to a forever: "Together for all eternity."

He remembered the promises, and the promises kept.

Across the valley from his recliner on his back porch he saw that big old eagle, and below the scamper of a small animal. Was it a sign that the animal was to be a victim of the eagle? Even up here? A victim to the death: Up Here?

Even in this promised Other Place, where death is a thing of the past? Or was it a photographic memory briefly observed recalled from the hillside porch on an afternoon of relaxation somewhere else maybe up in Ohio back in the world? He had no reason to wonder, since those one-time questions would have become mute.

Then through the still of the day he heard the tenor with a tune he knew, now replete with all the romance now of the Italian wine country, a song of sentiment and sincerity. It was a love song, certainly in Italian as only an Italian could sing it.

He knew that much, this old hillbilly did, knew the language of poetry and song, like from an opera that he and Lily had attended when they lived up in Ohio. He'd gone with her mainly because Lily had always wanted to visit an opera performance. It was in New York, which Lily also wanted to visit, mainly from Clint's talk of it. He'd stopped there with some of his buddies when they'd had a short liberty before they went west to pick up a ship on their way to the South Pacific.

The vocalist grew in his intensity to capture different emotions, spreading the song's melody from the valley in harmony with the mountains and the people who made their home in the highlands of mid-America.

The cloud-borne song touched the Earth boy's Earth-learned definition of romance ever lonely when sung alone but full of the highest of all emotions, appealing to the soul; he felt its call to lovers of all time. Italian phrases, like the French, gave a hidden whisper to its music, a universal meaning in its softened tones, a song for lovers enhanced by the sounds of an instrument not too distant from the guitar Clint had known all his life in the mountains.

A simple thing, love; he knew so little of it. During his life as a boy he spent mostly in long hours of loneliness. Even an old dog like Tom knew about love. Tom had taught him what Tom, like any animal on Earth, knew by instinct. He recalled Saturday afternoons n his town back Earth. His mother allowed him to attend movies in the valley. He knew the cynicism that town kids attached to the never changing plot of the good men chasing the bad guys.

Later, or maybe now, we'll talk more about Karl. Karl was a friend Clint met right away after he had entered the realm of the beyond. Clint never knew the day he'd left Earth and he never knew until later that he'd been chosen among other new other world citizens for a layman's purpose.

Karl liked to hear about the movies but mostly about trains that moved on steel tracks that carried people so far so quickly. He had a bit of skepticism but he accepted the fact that so many miles were covered so conveniently.

Karl was surprised to learn how the people of Western countries had a 'garage' as roomy as their houses, where they kept their automobiles, how the drivers of their carriages obtained fuel that drove their 'cars' a new word to him to what Clint described as a filling station. He didn't smile when he heard that nations went to war over who would control the flow of oil required to operate their machines.

Karl also was amazed at the many wars that engulfed Earth in the twentieth century, how many thousands were killed with no reason by flying machines. These were man-made machines that dropped explosives on the cities and homes in which the workers lived because their religions brought on a war that didn't represent 'the truth,' whatever that might have been.

He asked, "For what purpose?" Clint had no answer.

In a recent bull session on Clint's porch, many residents wanted to talk about how they had conceived Heaven to be as they went about their daily chores back on Earth. They brought up their reading of Dante and how his conceptions of the afterlife had endured through the ages. One or two were influenced by John Milton, and how Satan had led a flock of skeptics across the sky away from Paradise.

The majority of Clint's and Karl's Heaven, the Judeo-Christian was pleased to have generally discovered what teachers of their Bible had taught them in their homes and their churches. Here was their traditional Heaven.

Earthlings from their world's Middle East whose religion was never understood by westerners like Clint and Karl who thought it meant a lot of free sex; they misunderstood thoughts of Heaven; Heaven was what it meant to the widely different residents of Earth as they had been taught by their religious leaders and as it was passed on to them through the generations. There was Heaven with the streets that could be called golden; gardens with all sorts of beautiful foliage, like the Eden of their Bible; like the music, even a universal music of great classical orchestras that were unimaginable to the residents of the many other the different states and nations of the world.

In countries or lands ancient or current, worship took many forms, and much of it based on the idea of the afterlife. They would not challenge any of the other, ancient beliefs.

Clint said the better days of his life on Earth had been spent right where I am sitting, on the porch of the cabin in which I grew up —- but what I've learned so far of what it's about, which means I've only touched the hem of the garment.

A consensus was never to be found, summed up in what each individual had created in his her mind let's say they seconded the ideas as were universal among their countrymen from their former lives, the society and atmosphere in which they were born and lived for most of their lives.

It's odd, Clint thought, that we are still discussing it after life and death, after they won out—- over temptations and the weakness of all who are human.

The neighbors Up Here had left the porch; Clint and Karl were alone.

They faced Earth's river, its flow adapted to the Age of Commercial exploitation.

They'd left; those curious among earlier residents, but not before Clint, by talking to each of them and looking into faces for answers as to why they'd descended upon his cabin.

They'd wondered why he'd brought to This Place an early earthly cabin, like they'd known in old Russia and in early America. One or two also asked about late events among warriors and government in his country.

Mainly though, the older citizens bid him welcome, and learned that he liked to do a little strumming on the guitar, an instrument they'd recognized which they'd seen leaning against the wall. They asked about the authors of the books stacked on the floor.

A light knock on his hillside door roused Clint from his reverie. He was sleepy-eyed, recalling how he had welcomed a Sunday afternoon nap back when. For a brief moment he wondered what he was about. A welcoming party following a bull session on the riverside porch with friend Karl and friends, a few of Heaven's political philosophers, had left him thinking of something else.

At first, he thought Karl was back down to his cabin to tell him something he had forgotten. Karl must have felt it was urgent, something he'd intended to say before Clint ventured out again late in the 'day' to do a little more exploring. The nap, the late pleasant conception of it was not a part of what The Place was about.

(It should be mentioned that no day or night existed here, since there was no sun as such to govern it. The atmosphere always was a lower light similar to a just before dawn or early evening light on Earth; actually it was as a resident or groups might have wished for.)

If he had wanted sunshine at dawn, when the sun was at its best, he would have had it. He had thought: I might try to snatch a nap, a treasured thing he would recall as an earthly pleasure, before the evening ventured in with its skies of filtered gold.

Upon Clint's threshold stood the familiar field messenger all six feet four and almost a military bearing with an official-appearing document in hand and the customary Over Here grin, lighting up a rather otherwise straight face. Beyond his shoulder was Karl, who must have run into the official on the path up the hill. The messenger, a man often a woman, was standing almost at attention which was not necessary in this place, but commanding notice of his or her office; with such customary good manners always sowing seeds of worth and delight, Clint would by now remind.

As Clint accepted the document, which had been removed from a plain pouch with a royal gesture, he looked for earthly-added feather wings, which had adorned all heavenly residents in the printed pictures he knew by turning the pages of books then available to him. Clint opened the roll of parchment, which was much like his high school diploma, but with no ribbon; the messenger's eyes dropped to the document; his face of an unusual patience, since Clint had been taught by his father to take his time as he opened a present under the Yule tree with a sense of hope on his face. Clint said, 'thank you,' before reading aloud:

"To Earth field citizens, specifically of Western Europe, the United States, Canada and former English-speaking freemen:

> ... To Members of Senate Council: Sub-Committee on Ingress and Egress:
>
> "You are requested to attend a special called meeting of your Sub-Committee at a time previously agreed to by your-

self and other members of your charge . . .

. . . At the universally familiar site just outside Senate chambers.

(An hour and day of 'a week' was provided to former Earthlings . . . as reminded.)

Special music, if desired, will be provided."

(Signed) "Scribe Jonathon"

As the messenger departed, still there was his friend Karl.

"Well, I see you got invited down to the square, also," said Karl, Clint's new Swiss friend, as nosy as any reporter he'd k known back in his newspaper days, was wide-eyed.

"Any idea what this is all about?" asked Karl.

"Not a whiff."

"Must be of some urgency," said Karl.

Clint hesitated. Karl recalled something deep in his memory that lent itself to all the formal call down at the big meeting house.

"Urgent whiff or no, from my long ago thinking on this thing I expect it has to do with the reincarnation of somebody important. That means some sort of business from Earth that needs tending to but that couldn't be selective since everybody Over Here is just as important as the next resident."

"And we, all residents I've learned already, possess about equal smarts," said Clint, unsure himself how he would define it. "You must note that it is the 'egress,' which is my sub-committee, that has requested that we attend, by summons yet, aye and now begoud, as my old Scot friend would say."

"Maybe somebody forgot to turn off the stove, or maybe simply forgot to put a coin in the parking meter before they left to come here and wanted to redeem it. I would say the subject of 'egress' itself is what is urgent, since it is a special called meeting."

"I recently talked to the council president about my appointment to the interim chairmanship. Now it appears they've gone and made all the arrangements; this is it."

"I can't think of anything else it might be. When the council president mentioned it, he helped me recall a statement I'd made back there, really an off-hand egotistical bit of nonsense, and said to be prepared sometime soon to 'put my money where my mouth is.'"

Clint knew it was ridiculous to suppose. He knew they'd both hie to, as 'requested,' not by requirement but because they wished to honor Heaven's democratic spirit, and the subcommittee and its reason for being, in place for such occasions. A personal 'justification' reason for the 'special' meeting meant he would stumble explaining how a bunch of people, friends and others, got together every morning just to drink coffee and talk about anything and reasonable things in life's struggle to understand what it all means.

Since its founding no one had ever petitioned the committee for leave to go back to a former world, although some have gone back temporarily on Heaven's assignment.

Clint learned that those who did return, however briefly, might have been anticipated by the pleas of Earth's residents.

"I'd say that the only way we're going to find out is to get on down to the square for a see and hear," said Karl.

As they walked the grassy hillock to the central path, Clint was surprised to hear the familiar soft chords of timeless music, always soul satisfying. He had listened to the then two musicians above the path earlier in the day, probably saluting the messenger whose coming with a document satchel in his hand would have told them that he was on a mission.

The musicians mixed their back home talents to interpret what they had recalled of an earthly masterpiece by one of their nation's composers of an earlier era. Since they were and still are a national treasure, the music their countrymen created was so reckoned by their descendents hereabouts as classical and inspirational. Here were their countrymen, the best of Earth's musicians.

He recalled the last time he'd seen them there were just two, but now they were four. He said, "I thought they were just half a quartet. Now they have a full complement." Karl said, "You are correct or rather you have a good ear. They now have a quartet since they needed to await the arrival of the other half. Not long a wait, even in Earth years."

"They have been patient. Before, as I recall, they were a piano and a violin; now they have been joined by another violin, a viola and a cello, dropping the piano."

"I wonder where it went, the piano, I mean. They're now a string quartet. I prefer them as a piano quartet."

"If it were a Mozart viola quintet, it would feature, as written two centuries ago by the maestro himself, two violins, two violas, and a cello. That's five; I expect they will soon be (famous), even up here, as a quintet," said Karl.

"Now, you old hillbilly, that's the music lesson for today," Karl added. He grinned and looked for several moments toward the Mozart players, listening in rapture as was quite evident on his face, dropping the grin for a more serious tone of voice, but adding just how pleased he was that "the players perform so close to their homes."

He said they could be around for as long as they wish so let's make them welcome. "Now here in the faith of their partners in music, they are," Karl said.

"The first two appeared patient, aware that their countrymen would show up.

"The players here likely passed during World War Two," said Karl.

"Maybe they died in the Holocaust, which I've only recently taught you about. You know about that?" asked Clint.

"But I shouldn't be at all surprised, knowing the pogroms and inquisitions have been in effect for centuries."

"We Earth people have had some bad times," said Karl. "My own century was bad enough, but I would say that your century reached the ultimate in man's inhumanity to man.

"Recently I talked to several people from your century. I expect I know more about it than you realize, even of the origin of your country."

"I've learned a whole lot about your vast experiment in democracy - even as I was interested in your personal recital, or review of its practice."

"What say we soften up a bit and listen to the music?"

Clint ignored the suggestion, said: "We can have the music anytime. For the moment, let's talk about the composers. Mozart was Austrian, right?" asked Clint.

"Yes, but the Germans claimed him, as they later claimed Austria."

"Did they bring all those instruments with them?" inquired Clint, hoping to learn more of the background of the once back home musicians and the music that came in from the older Renaissance. "Are those instruments duplicates?"

"Certainly with the violins, had to be," said Karl, "look over at the carved signatures, under the f-Holes? Those fancy curling slots, on the sides of the bridge. Look to the back of the instrument, beneath the bridge. That is the place to look first for a famous calling card."

"What famous calling card?" It was Clint's turn to pretend ignorance.

"Why Antonio Stradivari, if you really want to know; he was the finest violin maker who ever lived. Now who is pulling whose leg?" said Karl.

"Stradivari was born in the seventeenth century and lived into the middle of the eighteenth, an era that produced so many great composers."

Karl said that reminded him of a story from his boyhood in his native Switzerland. "It is a sad story," he said. "I've warned you now, so do you still want to hear it? It saddens me to the core just to attempt to relay it to others."

As Karl and Clint reluctantly left the impromptu concert, strolling along the path leading to the field square, Karl, in a surprising eagerness, began: "In the village not far from our home on the mountain lived an elderly man and his grandson. The boy's mother had died about three years before, his father years before that."

"The grandfather, of an unknown age, and the grandson, on the edge of manhood about thirteen, were trying to stay alive by tilling a small garden behind their home, which was squeezed between two houses facing the village below. They shared common walls."

"The old man, in his youth talented and with nimble fingers at one time taught music in his home to young men and women, a limited clientele in the village, and to a dwindling few from the countryside, but his health had become so prohibitive that he no longer could pursue his greatly loved and honorable occupation."

"They were poor, but no more so than their fellow villagers who were trying to stay alive in one of the low economic times that often visited the people. The grandfather had in his home a violin, a beautiful instrument which he much prized, perhaps too much in pride considering the poverty of the times. It was because of the lack of food by all that he was able to trade for such an instrument."

"As you've guessed, it was a Stradivarius. He kept it wrapped in heavy cloth atop the wardrobe that dominated the front room of their humble home."

"The grandfather seldom took it from its lofty place in the front room. He did once in the boy's memory and talked about it to his grandson. He said someday the violin would be his upon the death of the grandfather. In the meantime they bought a cheap violin, which had lain in the front window of a store in town. The boy was taught to play, of course by his grandfather. The grandson would look up to the high wardrobe, which corners of the quilt that covered it reassured him that a future as he conceived it held the Stradivarius clear from dust and other threats of damage to the only promise he might ever have in this life. In time, but while the grandson was still just a boy, the old man died."

"As the grandfather lay in state on a wide board in the parlor or front room of their home, the villagers came to view the remains, and in the custom of the times, bearing food that might sustain the boy for a few days."

"It was during the visitation for the dead that the bundle with its precious instrument disappeared. The boy noticed the theft as he closed the door to the last visitor. He was in panic as he ran through the village screaming out his story and inquiring of every face if they had seen anything during their visit to him that might lead them to the thief. The boy ran from face to face with his inquiry. His panic inflamed the people of the village as they tried to recall a stranger in their midst, the culprit."

"Alas, it was not to be so. A few weeks later in despair the boy left the village. His grandfather's home fell into disrepair and was replaced by a small shop common to villages of the time."

"In his old age the boy, now man, returned. No one save an ancient villager here and there could remember him. They did recall the incident, though, and inquired of the man if he had indeed ever recovered the prized instrument."

"They learned of the years of search for the old man's violin, and the thief, by the boy who had become an old man himself in bitterness." He sadly told the villagers: 'It all was of no avail.'"

"Wow," said Clint. "I've heard similar stories all my life, but that is just about the saddest. But why are you telling me all this? It is the story of so many of Earth's residents that we all knew."

"Look over there," said Karl. He pointed to a lone figure by the path. The man was playing a violin, in tune with the quartet across the roadside. It was a soft music divinely inspired that came from the violinist's side of the road.

"Who's he?" inquired Clint.

"That, my friend, is that boy. He has his Stradivarius at last. And it will be his forever."

"But how did he bring it with him?"

"It's like your child's rocking chair. You're just learning about Heaven. It's the same violin, which was sold on Earth again not many years ago, bringing at auction millions of dollars in your currency. Yes, it's the exact violin back there; the same violin that came to the boy over here. You ask with good reason, just how was that possible? Well, it is. Accept it because in Earth's future the owner will hear the soft strains of his famous violin from another room as he is at dinner with guests in another part of the house."

Chapter Four

Stories of the rocking chair and the rare and valuable violin were accepted by Clint Greene among other wonders of This Place and prepared him for others to follow,

Clint asked Karl if he had anything else to add to the story.

Karl said: "The instrument turned up a couple centuries later. We knew in This Place because we have been given the privilege of being told of such things, so many of Earth's secrets. We heard how the Strad, that same violin, came to reveal its history to us. It's heard as it is played in another dimension by its rightful new owner on Earth who came upon it honestly; let me observe that it is the true original violin, now to a new owner in your country, the U.S."

"The boy grew to be an old man when he passed the old sad life for his new home in This Place. He always knew that he would have the violin at last, once he reached Heaven."

"That's him beside the road so very far away from his violin on Earth. The owner on Earth would never be believed if he said to his guests in his home that his violin was being played in Heaven. Now a magic instrument, it was made to do just that."

Karl and Clint were silent as they listened to the Strad's Swiss heir once the owner, standing just a few yards beyond the road, shared the magic with the boy's grandfather.

"Music was everywhere around us during my time," Clint said. "The movies especially attempted to tell a story of the Muse of music and poetry. On the screen a young couple had met and in assuming their romantic destiny were aided by background music, strings of violins punctured by the soft keys of a piano."

"Westerns, as they were called, came as screen portrayals of recent stories from the Indian wars, called by the kids as battles of exciting Saturday afternoon shows of cowboys and Indians. In the chase they yelled to the overloud orchestral stomping of the classics."

A guy up north called his music, 'the best music this side of Heaven.'

Music in the hearts of the people was associated with Heaven.

They stepped aside for a brass band, the players dressed as Clint knew from photos in an album he'd seen at his aunt's home. The bandsmen's uniforms were colorful like their music: traditional heroic fighters of fires in his America of years past.

"Of your time?" asked Karl.

"Well, not exactly," replied Clint. "Before my birth, but near, moving to my country from your country or your neighbors like many of your kinfolk who came to America from perhaps Germany or Austria; scions of a second or third generation in America, like potato famine Irish who went to the U.S. or South Africa."

Clint pointed to the left, toward the horizon:

"Look over there, Karl, at those mountains."

"I recall seeing those before. What do you make of it? "

"To me, they go on for a stretch. I've learned from your world and mine how they dim the farther a mountain goes back to stand behind the other. Painters appreciate that, gives them a chance to form depth, like they are in shading as they go on and on."

"Reminds me a lot of Switzerland," said Karl. "Southlanders thought the Alps were higher than they are, like big stone sculptures pointing right up into the sky, reaching right into Heaven. They are surprised to come in and see the sheep grazing without falling off. Herders in Switzerland are mostly in the high country. Well, I suppose we were all of the high country."

"Must be somebody out there painting the heights. Yes, I see her, a young woman, over to the right, in a wide white hat. That wide brimmed hat must be a badge of artists.

"No one over here would wear a hat like that. It is to protect from sunburn, but there really is no sun, as such."

"It's all pretty and appealing. I'd think to an artist it must be elementary. Nothing but a bunch of hills," said Clint.

"Ah, but it's more than that. Look low where the great mountain rises beyond the long level stretch, next to the ground level water pouring over the rocks of so many colors, of different shapes. The artist is playing with the many tints and hues over there mixed with shades of gray; the water comes out in that stream down below."

Karl's arm was following the direction of the stream as it jumped over challenging rocks as the creek, or the river slowly moving on. "Then it levels off over there," he said. "That's the beauty that painters would look for splashing water, the clouds forming above the deluge."

The young woman picked up her easel and brushes and left.

"Well, I'll be. The mountains, waterfall —- all is gone," said Clint.

Karl said: "It was created just for her personal genre. The mountain wasn't there yesterday, and won't be there tomorrow."

"Reckon that's why I never saw those mountains before," said Clint. Karl appeared amused.

Clint looked onto a flat treeless plain which he knew as a savannah calling to him like from a classical painting; where there were no mountains. The land was yet boasting green grass that to him was a comforting soothing refuge from life's true favors from once earthly bothers. A light wind scooted over the landscape, asking the waving yellow sedge at the edges to get in on the greeting.

Musicians, sculptors, painters, printmakers, dancers, writers scribbling with pen on paper or at outdated typewriter keys, several people with cameras, some of those with old Kodaks (cameras) like his mother fooled with. She did her own developing in a little room once a pantry off the kitchen.

Artists were all around them, apparently pleased with what they alone were creating, painting, gazing often toward the far horizon momentarily as they sought inspiration.

Or they waited for it to pen a poem or the big novel, soul-inspired writing scribbling it seemed to Clint each to himself or herself, with no concern for publishers, editors, critics or art shows.

Actors out there appeared as if on stage, gesturing in ways not called for in a script, as Clint recalled a writing from which they honored life in individual emotion. They were free to recite it their way, moving arms and body, their entire being, for laughs, even for sympathy, performing as the actors' emotions dictated. The scene tossed his recollections far back to a romping stage play in which he appeared, as his graduation day from the Valley High School was upon him.

It was like all of Earth's men and women of the theatre arts were out today, in the cool of a morning like it was back on Earth. Orators, cameramen, scene designers, make-up people, set builders along with painters whatever their one-time earthly skills, appearing from all over the narrow path now widening to show off aprons of many colors, paint blurbs stained by the wet easels the once proudly worn lightly paint dotted outfits.

The farther they walked along the path to the Senate chambers, the greater was the talented mass of performers who in times past were not appreciated.

"I sure don't see any lazy bones out there," said Clint.

"I won't comment on that," said Karl.

They hadn't taken many steps before they were greeted by a huge herd of laughing, running children, a boy and a girl were chasing each other in a turn-about to chase the other.

Clint thought, after he had gotten to an age when he enjoyed a quieter activity, "all that energy should not be wasted on children, certainly on the very young like that."

The boy was maybe six or seven in Earth age, the girl likely a year older. "Where did those kids come from?" asked Clint.

"Up the road a piece, you'll see right soon," answered Karl.

One of the children, excited, yelled: "Hey there, Mister Horsey, gimme a ride; pick me up and let's go gallop like a horsey." The boy said it in a near scream. Clint reached down and gathered up the delicate one-time Earth child, now full of glee and expectation.

Karl said: "What he mean, horsey? You Mister Horsey?"

"He means horse. Yeah, I'm horsey."

"They want to play." Clint raised the boy to his shoulders, holding the boy's knees as he neighed like a horse and raced in circles hoping to stir up dust, but it didn't happen; dust, not in this place.

"Get the girl and let's race," he said.

Clint by now had skidded into laughter at the antics of Karl as he walked on hands and knees with the girl-child on his back. Karl even tried to buck like a horse at a rodeo from Clint's 'Out West.' "If you really want to race, I'll concede," said Karl.

"Don't spoil the party," said Clint.

"I believe we're wasting time," said Karl. "Let's stop this, get on down the road," he repeated. "We're wasting precious time."

That's when Clint said to the Swiss highlander: "Look at Mister Time now. Wasn't it you who said, 'This Place has no time?' You said that Over Here time does not exist? How can you waste what isn't?"

The girl chimed: "Not yet horsey, gitty-up."

Karl fell flat on his stomach. "The race is over. We won, how's that?" The children ran on down the path.

At the top of the rise, Clint stopped and stood still; he felt his body growing weak. He tried to take in the entire scene laid out in an impossible challenge before him. On both sides of the path, children were on swings held aloft by ropes on tree limbs and from steel bars.

They jumped onto slides that he recalled from visits to an amusement park in the north of his country where he had gone to find a job. The war was over and he hoped to get started in newspaper work.

On Earth and again Over Here but not as much as it was (everywhere people and more people). He was tired of long slow lines every place he had been as a newborn citizen (of Earth long lines of men who like himself were out looking for jobs and some sort of decent men's civilian clothing to fit the campus). Once he'd decided to go on to college on the GI Bill, he found life on campus was far different than he had imagined. The veterans were in pieces of uniform; no crazy hats like in movies he recalled from the thirties, every man out to gamble among former warriors for the few women on campus, and afterwards for the best job they could find.

In a nation attempting to re-build as well as define itself he discovered that fellow warriors had been busy in bed. Children were showing up about everywhere. In just a few years they would be taking over the country.

Over there some of the new kids skipped rope. Two or three others joined in the fun or they created their own. Others formed a dance, as if they were performing in a huge movie musical like Clint had seen one cold Sunday afternoon when he was a boy himself. It probably was the only movie he sat through a second time.

The entire scene came alive in the theatre a musical after his chores thinking that he had missed the waving arms and moving legs and bodies like on the stage which were from invented games for a dust-raised schoolyard grassless turf back in time but there was no dust to disturb the scene Over Here. Loose arms legs of the uninhibited at play reminded him of herds of wild horses dashing across the plains in Clint's great American West.

Since the first time he'd seen it, it reminded him of driving on the narrow lanes in his country's highways in traffic. Then as he'd witnessed in his mind a wild lonesome green gray war-broken tree of the wet jungle that surrounded him - scenes from a more quiet less fearful time to allow him an hour in which to allay his fear.

He said aloud to Karl, "All this wildness, the noise reminds me of every road of the automobile age, drivers changing lanes, speeding for an opening, They're asking for a race; bunch of show-offs, reminds me of the narrative poem: 'Charge of the Light Brigade.'"

He recalled from many of his nation's larger cities as he might have viewed from a building high above like water in a stream below trying to get around a barrier such as a tall stone, darting like cattle in a frightened rampage, a stampede —- the picture shows' pent-up animals in a cattle drive escaping like the last time he'd seen it: a scene to last forever, the boys the girls in recess chasing teasing boys, girls, taps of love, vexing, the little pats, girls by boys . . . boys by girls. Overwhelmingly, children thundering shrill screeching lungful voices in a freedom like straight from Heaven passed on to them from the frontier settlers who had discovered El Dorado right where they knew it would be.

Above and beyond the herd, a festive eternal movie set portrayed more thousands of kids milling about eager and restlessly; in their midst was a merry-go-round. He could listen to its dancing circus-like music even through the clamor, coming like a magical ointment to a memory of its treatment for tired muscles of a growing toward puberty farm boy.

Life on Earth was a precious thing to behold mostly taken by each individual with small regret as man and woman recalled it in pain probably as time passed never to be seen again, until today.

Clint wondered if his voice could be heard above squeals and laughter as he asked, in stutters, "Wha wha wher wher what in the name of the road to Bali is all this movement? I sure wouldn't want to try and call the roll on the first day of school with this bunch. Did you know about this, Karl?"

"What this is, now that you've asked, are children of your Earth who were born into poverty and were denied a childhood. Here are the children who never had a Christmas, or what it would be called in different countries of your world."

"They were orphans. They were denied a father. They died in childbirth or if they lived after only a few years they'd become aware that they were alone, not knowing a world without pain. They died in famines or in denial in tents or hovels or under a bridge, and in the wars that were waged against their homes and families from the menace of the skies designed to destroy the innocent you told me about. Raise your arms, be grateful for what you witness here; it is life as first denied at last realized."

Karl continued, "Some were loved. Many more never knew love at all. Most or none ever knew the reason why."

Clint said, "I could stand here all day, thankful every minute for what I see.

"I'm thankful for every dream that was dreamed by these kids and by so many others who might have loved them. I saw far too much cruelty in the world involving people of all ages much of it aimed at our children."

At the time I could never understand why, call it destiny please, that had led them into a life of hurt. They survived without someone holding their hand. Why or who in Heaven had allowed such a thing to exist. At the hour I left Earth it already was becoming onto universal, much worse because there was nothing I could do about it.

"I once said there must be a leveling of a sort out there; kids born to poverty, hunger and suffering would someday dine at the garden table as it was first created in hope for them but it ended in the wild thick growth where the serpent also dwelled.'

"Kids if they had a chance would play in sunshine:, and people who carried evil to children, mostly unheard of before the current society, should be . . . exiled to a fate of loneliness and despair."

"Look at all those grown-ups; they go on and on for miles, spectators at the edge of a kids' amusement park, watching. Do you think they came to recapture their childhood?"

Karl said, "No, I don't. By the way, there's a reason adults all seem to be of an age of thirty-three. Ask a citizen of your particular faith from Earth days. I've been told that the majority of them come here looking for their own children who died as children. They don't have to do it this way. There are reasons for that, too," said Karl.

"You learned that you would have the woman in love you had back on Earth by calling her up. That is so with children?" said Clint.

Karl was prepared to answer quickly: "It is the same with your mother and father.

They were of an earthly love apart from what we see Over Here, different from their days of procreation on Earth. Yet it is the same. Love never changes. It is the single eternal truth that survives through time; certainly it was transferred to the 'Here.'" Karl shrugged. He apparently hadn't made it clear, leaving Clint to figure it out.

Karl went on, "Say like that man over there (he was pointing), they perhaps hope to gather to themselves once again or even for a first time the children they were who never had the privilege of sharing love as they would have wished."

The long-time resident, Clint's friend, continued: "That is simply the way I see it. It is beyond our knowing, Over Here, Earth kinship doesn't enter into it. It's not for us to know, as it was not to be in our earthly thinking, and I accept it."

"That man you pointed out," Clint said, "he looks familiar. I know him. Only this man on Earth had a beard; his imitators numbered in the thousands; as well has he unto today become something of an adopted brother, perhaps a father figure to our people. They loved this man, engraved his image in their parks and government buildings."

"What do you think he is doing over there?" Clint asked, curious from devotion to the man and his country's memory. It was almost a universal thing.

"Of course; he was one of your presidents," said Karl.

Clint, curious, continued: "Yes, he lost two of his sons; one a child of about three; the other died at eleven or twelve. The older boy received much devotion especially during his short illness, from the man and his wife when they had the rare chance to escape their heavy White House and presidential duties."

"His death might even have altered the history of a savage era in which his father's call to duty came during his ordeal of a strife-torn nation in its greatest but tragic years. Coupled with so much bad news from this country's armies in the field; during the hour of great death and tragedy, in which was dictated the Emancipation Proclamation."

Karl said, "I know about that. The man comes here every day, looking for his sons that he knew only as children although he had two other boys who outlived him. He wept for the two youngest, grieving over his loss yet encouraging what became a vast other mark of his greatness. His job as chief magistrate of his country was for the men and women and children of a tomorrow in peace through brotherhood."

"As the leader of his country, he sent great armies of men into war and their deaths in battle. Like you've learned, he could call his sons to him and they would be at his side," said Clint.

"For some odd reason perhaps, he doesn't want to do it that way," said Karl. "I have my own theory, though. The man you see seeks to find his sons among other children on the playground, mixing it up with the other children."

Clint began again: "You said earlier that he was bothered by the fact that he himself had no childhood. You said there were rare times when he might have found other children but a very few as playmates, but even those times would have been limited by his family and duties in the field. He had cousins to play with but mostly they were from afar and he likely saw them only once maybe twice if that often."

"The wilderness of Kentucky, later of Indiana, you said, was at the edge of his world —- then came the day very early in his life when his father put tools in his hands. From that day on, he was expected to be a man," mused Karl.

Clint stared in wonder at a man who watched the kids at play with others among the tall trees. He stood out, a beanstalk of a man but slightly bent. His black cloak appeared out of style, even then, even now. The man leaned forward toward the happy nearer children on the playground, but just with the top half of his body. His hands were clasped behind his back like roller skaters on a city rink that Clint had seen; relaxed but dignified and presidential, together a mark of his historic distinction.

Clint said, "Of all men and women of my country's historic past that I'd expect to see here would be him, among a few others that in my reckoning also deserve honor; I was fortunate to know some few when I was a journalist."

Clint knew he was guilty of judging people during his time on Earth, whether they might be candidates for a seat in Heaven. "The latter question was on the minds of warriors who went with me to the Pacific. As they rested after the day's work or battle was done (or never) they spoke of their fear of death but sincerely knowing or believing they would survive."

You'd told mama or a girl friend that you would be back. They were now only a few paces beyond the roar from the mob behind them, Karl said.

As they continued their walk, Karl said, "Look toward that row of trees and bushes over there. Tell me what you see?"

"I see trees and bushes," said Clint. "No wait, what I see are rooftops and chimneys, a lot of them peeping through and into the top of the trees."

"It must be a town, an old town. It's like a suburb I might have known in the 1930s when I was a lad, before the big war and its go for broke tragic aftermath; that is when the government allowed it to be destroyed in the name of urban renewal," he said. "They came in and leveled it as war-torn Earth's industrial cities of Europe were lo during the late hate."

Karl recalled from his boyhood on Earth, "Even I knew as a farm boy the blessing of talking with my neighbors, even though they didn't live close. It was a day of comparative easy life for a young hilltop boy. It was village life extraordinary with us. They compare to your observations and your memories of a later time."

Clint said, "I recognize what you are about to tell me. These buildings were the homes of rural farm people new to the working class who moved to be near the street scene, and jobs. They founded a new way of life. I had kinfolk who moved there; I visited them."

"They were called the 'blue collar' class. They left their farms when it became hard to make a living; here, though, they would sit on their porches of a warm summer evening, in contentment. This is a factory town, what's left of it."

"Yes," said Karl. "They wished for and got what we see."

"As part of their dream, they might have believed what they had would be Heaven."

"They likely had a church which we don't see, small at first, later enlarged. Just as the church in their home states was the center of social activity, so it became in the city."

Clint, who was pleased by their swapping of a seemingly familiar knowledge of an era, said, "Also, you might say to these new city folks, 'Heaven is a front porch.' Let's go down there, and meet those people."

"It wouldn't be wise. We're a couple of strangers, with too many questions. Like we said, they very well want 'privacy,' as they appreciated neighbors they've always known; they visited, stopped to talk as they were strolling by in early evening. From the sidewalk to the front porch was their best way of communicating," said Karl.

"I expect," said Clint, "many industrial labor unions came of age right there in those houses. Everybody knew the sentiments of everybody else. As it was in the country if a man were to die in the mines or on the railroads, or in any working accident of the machine age, it was the concern of all."

"They'd likely have a little prayer out on the porch. Or it would continue as the wake that began inside in what was called the living room or parlor. As the deceased lay in state, friends and neighbors would fill every chair and corner in the house and out on the porch day and night until the funeral, taking into account the weather."

"In our mining country, where the corporation mines were, housing was built for the miners. People would gather at the country store or in church yards after a funeral or Sunday services on warm mornings, and exchange news."

"In my observation," said Karl, "I've seen how your society evolved from frontier conditions. Europeans I've come to know Over Here say yours was 'a land of beginning again.' I would hope it is still true today."

Karl continued, "You've helped me by talking about TV and radio and telephones. I can see how Earth people began to form a family relationship with the TV screen people. They remind me of Plato's man in a cave viewing shadows on a wall with his back to the outside. Never having known the outside world, the shadows, in illusion, had become his universe."

"I expect many of these folks' illusion gained from TV was the outside city world."

"If you started toward that town over there, no matter how lengthy your stride, the trees and the whole shebang would be an illusion, as far away as when you had started. That's what the residents of a latter age wanted. I expect that's like you viewed your little hillside cabin, on Earth as it is in Heaven."

Clint said: "Well, I reckon many imagine Heaven to be just another name for the Garden; they say so. You'll find versions of it in about any religion or culture throughout history." a place as Heaven as it is 'known' on Earth, as Eden, or the Garden of Eden. I've known writers who attempted to know Eden as fulfillment of man's earthly dreams. Maybe that's why many novelists have created for their characters' aspirations, a road to Eden, or Heaven, where love is."

Clint, former earthly employer of pen and ink, said that often early Americans and their heirs into his century thought of themselves as truly blessed, their fate separate from others. Even as late as what we called World War II, we believed in our 'hopes.'

"Our Heaven was what had made us happy on Earth (within the boundaries of the Ten Commandments). Some grieve for what once was until lately and rent their garments in frustration and shedding of tears as did King David in those dark days before the journey was begun."

Looming was the horizon's scene stealer, a Roman town square with the pillars of a Roman Forum dominating it all the way to land's end..They stood in awe; the Forum, its polished stone (marble? granite?) recalled it as the seat of an empire. Within a few hundred years it would inspire many new governments in western nations to imitation. Its architectural lines remain dominant in many court houses' grandeur to today, reflecting local ambition and pride.

"I expected a huge building for the Senate, maybe like our capitol today," said Clint, for the first time realizing that the meeting of his committee would be on an open ground area, behind the pillars. He also would soon learn that the committee as such was not made up of just a few, but thousands. What if all of them were asking to be recognized at the same time?

As he was briefed upon his appointment along with others of Earth origin he didn't think of it as his charge. Soon after his arrival he learned that he'd been elected as chairman.

He was greeted at what could be called a door by a messenger and ushered to the podium; at that moment the members rose and applauded.

Reflecting faces barely unlike all the others, by choice of the vast number of Earth's diverse races, which also might have defined Earth's continents, the mass was more akin to the population of Nepal and India combined; as their number beyond count overcame his senses, residents by nose count or any other reckoning went on, disappearing into the mist of far away time and place.

It was as if the whole band of Heaven's host was looking expectantly right at him.

To Clint it was enough to send General Robert E. Lee into retreat; what this was all about —- the committee meeting to consider an unusual proposal to their newer existence.

The usher said, "Welcome aboard, Citizen Clint; if you are looking for the gavel, there isn't any. You simply speak out in rounded tones of normal voice. You'll be heard."

The remark from the usher came from a face awash in the universal grin that he found everywhere Up Here. The usher, as it was with the messenger, appeared content —- a performance quite innocent. He was satisfied, though, that he had made a funny. Clint liked the usher's and the messenger's casual way of doing their thing. He thought that could have been a reason that they were chosen to attend This Place and the event in the first place.

"Let my own thinking repeat: Such thoughts are mine; and to myself." said Clint.

"There will be no disorder," said the usher. "Everyone knows the rules; your case, your remarks, when you are ready," he added. "Remarks, huh? My case, what? What is my case?" The hour he'd left Earth was dim in his memory. It must have been; nothing about his departure could be recalled. A breeze left its kindness on his cheek, then moved over Earth to mark the transition to another dimension; that was -- he had learned rather quickly -- what he was reminded about, to call it what?

Really not known universally —- it was the Heaven to his heritage and to his people but with enough difference to each to be among the different versions of it in belief as held by a huge segment of the people of the Earth and perhaps even beyond. They each believed in a hereafter as they were taught about it early in their years, in their learning years, or by conversion to its promises.

Most views and ideas of Heaven, he thought until this moment; he now knew his Heaven was tribal developed, held as dictates of his religion. He wondered how much he'd seen and wondered about when it first came into his own mind.

He hemmed a bit, hawed, as waters of the oceans were rising back on Earth, fed by melting icebergs at Earth's poles. He hoped to recall in his opening remarks his thoughts, and he did, for the expectant faces marking miles of Heaven's turf. He viewed the vast number of faces that continued like forever, beyond the pillars of Rome, in the open air.

"I first want to thank members of this important committee who are here to learn how we can save our Earth your former home from a serious threat of extinction of its people and possibly even the planet itself. I realize that you know what is happening back there, but we are here to ask your help in our attempt to save as much as we can of what it represents."

"Pollution of Earth's atmosphere," he said, "already has caused illness and even death among our people. In parts of our own country it has ruined our crops, and its menace has only begun. The climate change is blamed and its growth is affecting all our people."

"The situation and its solution, we realize, are not pretty. Many of our people have become seriously disturbed. Scientists and others have warned us, yet so far the people do little of nothing because they have not been convinced that nothing about it is real."

"Change and a loosening of morals among the young as well as many older citizens in most societies have said it is a prelude to the decline of society as a whole. Our leaders have warned the people that a first step is recognition that decency is being replaced by obscenity."

"No one trusts anyone else. Crime is rampant, and it's become electric. The temper of the people, said to be a nervous majority, is tolerated to a point already widespread. The situation calls upon us to help them. That is our one purpose here."

"Until a few hours ago, Earth time, I wondered why I was elected to serve you. I am still unsure, but I'm confident that we can find a way to save what is vital to the future of our world. I recall remarks from my latter days as a visitor from Heaven to Earth just like the other residents that I in jest suggested to my colleagues that one from among them join you here with a proposition."

"We were to seek the assembly's suggestions as to how this might be done, that one of you by reincarnation might re-visit Earth. The people believe they have lost leadership and look to the past and now to you."

"My remarks that day should be forgiven, since they were offered in arrogance, pride and in an unguarded moment. I knew nothing of you or This Place. A theory held by Earth's people about reincarnation was only a theory."

"It was a belief among many citizens that acceptance of what religious leaders told them that upon their deaths their souls would be taken up and brought here for eternity.

As a reward for their faith and yours, I would say that it is not mine to know the difference and speculate that any Earth person who is accepted by his fellows would be capable of the (leadership). We've had many like you in Earth's past who have had that persuasive ability, yet could be no better endowed with those powers than anyone else as determined by your fellow residents."

"If I may be forgiven when I allow that this person would have a bit more of his or her human share of 'smarts,' and that he or she on Earth was in the right place at the time when his fellows called upon him. I caution that all these assessments are mine."

"In the event that any are of different mind, I would suggest that if reincarnation is a reality and if some resident of This Place were willing to return to Earth, temporarily of course, that the committee might look closely at his or her 'resume.'"

From the floor came a response. "Would you in your fancy send let's say a farmer, a minister of the gospel or a legislator, perhaps a professor of physics, a scientist or a business person, perhaps a poet —- or choose a once army person who was sent out to make the world safe for democracy?"

Said the chair, "The military possibility is offered since on Earth you came to know the conqueror home from the wars like Caesar to lead his Romans in peace —- a general perhaps who may have displayed a brilliant quality of leadership. You just might consider a military person a warrior who because of past experience might have a poet's gentleness in his soul."

"We welcome all suggestions. If you lived in the Nineteenth Century, you were among poets in America, you knew singers of songs about heroes, in the Twentieth Century songs to the fallen in battle, and say of your native Russia songs of battlefield courage since the country's poets have historically been admired throughout Russian history."

"You once retreated from life to a monastery, to a mountain cave. With pen or reed or quill and ink and papyrus you recalled in poetic language the ancients. You still might call by name a tentmaker whose life was as satisfying as a jug of wine, a loaf of bread and the presence of a maiden of the desert."

From the far corner of the assembly a rumble a subdued voice caused a turning of heads as a self-assumed quiet man stood prepared to offer his suggestions.

The chairman looked into the distance. "Welcome to our first good democrat of the day. With the assembly's agreement for a beginning of the debate, we recognize the citizen in say the twentieth row. Speak, citizen," said Clint.

The speaker now at ease said, "I was a poet. For the information of the heavenly host and for the purpose of this meeting, I speak for the many abused men and women on Earth, whose pleas in the poetry of their age, as is so described only by me as mine, has been lost in the movement of time. From abuse and others by those with power, because of reasons of poverty or for other instances, from societal negligence, by sad and at last recovered souls, has come the best in poetry that is now in appeal to understanding in no other way."

"I urge a second to the poetic voice," a soft voice a soul mate was heard.

The first citizen was still standing even as three others stood and asked to be able to speak, but the chair recognized the first committee person to stand up on the floor, after it was offered. Clint realized that his voice over the other prompted persons before him would be responsible, said, "Let the gentleman continue. I took advantage of his pause."

In the confusion, the man who said that he'd been a poet during his life on Earth, said: "I am confident that others of this assembly are persons who are quite knowledgeable of that place, our one-time home," the citizen said, and from a history in our memory of the many years of keen awareness of what we'd been about through the centuries since we came here.

"With memories of the old, they would be more capable of speaking for the poet than I. yet I thank you for allowing me to speak."

"We're sure that among us are many poets such as Dante Alighieri, a scribe who dared in what Earth's people called the Middle Ages to venture in his poetry to look on the shores of Heaven."

"In this poet's century and in a more populous generation in the world today what he depicted might be seen as blasphemy. With no argument he or she with other writers was a person of courage, an identity not unknown to members of this assembly." He continued:

"Among Earth's sensitive souls who took a measure of death and the gates of This Place are William Shakespeare of England and Emily Dickinson, a poet of your country."

"Mr. Chairman, of a more recent time, yes —- serious poetry and the many writings of persuasion from the heart and soul of a person, with the blood and emotions, a genuine blessing given by the gods, comes naturally to a woman. Among these two I now nominate Miss Emily Dickinson. "

"Poets and writers have inspired us; I wish to be seconded by many on board for a poet for such a task as this; I will add that it is poetry that rings like the strike of an anvil in the orations of statesmen and politicians of ours or any other era."

"The Holy Bible of my religion is a long poem composed by translation of a number of interpreters —- during the reign of King James. Words, Mr. Chairman, can often be as dangerous as the might of the sword. They can be used to bend the will of a people to the purposes of the conqueror, or they can live for many ages because they represent the truth."

"Please accept these, or the one, as only my observations and my nominees."

"Thank you," spoke the chairman. "An excellent appeal, and we appreciate your comments; a poet, whether of profession or spare time pursuit may have been created as a gift to peace, offered by minds of your times, and for our time and immediate needs."

"I would ask if there are others who would speak to any other nomination of a poet to the selection process of a person for the purpose of return to Earth, and we hope, to the leadership as it has been said is the purpose of this assembly."

"Some of you may prefer to wait. We do reserve the right to amend the minutes at a later date as members call on their memory to move them back to their earlier time."

Half a dozen individuals stood up.

"The chair recognizes a citizen in about the ninth row, third from the left."

"Thank you. On Earth I was an American, so I place in nomination the name of one of the great founders of my country. He is a man of many sorts, one who could qualify for his role as a poet-writer-orator among Earth's many nations."

"I nominate Benjamin Franklin. Without his advice, our nation might have been long delayed. Franklin began as a printer. In his paper, 'Poor Richard's Almanac,' and later, 'The Pennsylvania Gazette,' he set the pace for his leadership as a journalist. Our colonial ancestors were influenced by Franklin in his papers to create the country, a nation among nations. He also helped establish freedom of the press in America, which is one of the freedoms listed in the first amendments to our country's Constitution."

"He helped draft the Declaration of Independence. Thomas Jefferson called him 'the greatest man and ornament of the age and of his country for the times.'"

"Mister Chairman, I with pride offer Benjamin Franklin as a leader and wise and a poet, among the greats of his country and in other democratic nations created by man."

The chair thanked the nominator, who stood for several seconds before returning to his seat among his peers —- a man, assuredly, who was a modern arrival to The Place.

Clint called for other comment on 'Benjamin Franklin of the United States.' He said he didn't need a second, since he was positive that Mr. Franklin would be favored in other categories. The chair asked again for others who might fit the request.

A voice came from a row close to the dais: "Mr. Chairman, we must not forget the Russians."

"The chair will recognize certainly any support for a Russian." A former resident of that country was already on the floor, obvious by a distant accent of Mother Russia of czarist time.

"Yes," she said, "their Twentieth Century poets had much to battle, with the Red Russians in power any effort in recognition of an individual within the regime's reach was suppressed in a most horrible way."

The respondent added that she was not a poet but as it was with most Russians she had suffered with writers of the dark night that was the story of the era in her country.

After the first big war of the century and the coming to power of the communists who would replace the czars, their voices for freedom were in jeopardy.

"Would you wish to tell the story or do you intend to allow your poets in their poetry do the talking?" spoke the chair. "You have the floor; the centuries are at your service."

"With remorse, however with some passion, I will not name Count Lev Nikolaevich (their spelling) Tolstoy, who lived into my century and has himself and his mind in an easily different genre today where he might be dealt with more wisely."

"I first will speak in brief to the literature of Fyodor Dostoyevsky, who even before the communists made his voice heard and nearly lost his head along with other body parts before a firing squad. In spite of his pen to paper that aroused the ire of the nation's political theorists, the existing regime after 'a trial' adjusted his 'poetry and novels,' in their sentence to life mainly for criticism of their difference of opinion."

"I really am naming two recent Russian poets; first, I cite Boris Pasternak. The assembly will recall him as the author of 'Dr. Zhivago.'"

"Then, I urge thoughts on just a simple mention of Aleksandr Solzhenitsyn, who spent a great part of his creative years in prison for his criticism of the communist rulers of my country."

"Pasternak, by his or other decision, refused to accept the Nobel Prize in Literature in 1958. His writing told of the creepy feeling among his people that the revolution left on their lives. The regime pretended to stand for a 'bright new day.' Yes, in a 'bright' new day they handed the Russian commonalty the heavier fist of restraint."

"Pasternak's poetry, political and biographical, had in his characters individuals who were envoys to mankind. They were to die under the communists, destined to pay a price for their ideas. Solzhenitsyn's words to pen, in 'The Gulag Archipelago,' were an indictment of Stalin's regime by terrorism. He had a following that led the country to its final days of communism."

The chair interrupted: "Do you think either of the poets might help Earth's people to come awake, by returning their world to reason, away from the grips of the immoralists? Many Earth people often appear bent on destroying civilization. It seems the greedy are too many. Many believed the threat of global warming, and its effects on Earth's people would be only temporary, that their material way of life would go on," the speaker said.

"Yes, otherwise I would not have suggested that we select one of these persons and their philosophies. In poetic fashion, you've brought us the strengths of these two poets. We continue our search for any other nomination of your genre on the floor."

"Please be reminded," said Clint, "that the chair reserves the right, by committee action, to question assessments in other areas, from a time in yours and our own Earth's past. It appears the need was there for generations."

"Russia has ever had a recognized literary history, and it was the communists who brought abusive treatment to the nation's writers, the poets and the written work of men and women of some political powers that have come out of the past."

"If that is the case, you may find as you leave copies of their literature on the table at the rear of the Senate chamber."

Clint as chairman accepted the nominees knowing that he might be ignoring other nominees. He said: "For the sake of the end game, be assured that any further nominations in the poets' category will be heard, as you so choose later in these proceedings if the assembly concurs."

"I see the ayes have it (which, as short and hurried statement), encouraging laughter from the residents. (From a distant row came the call, 'railroader'). I ask that you remind me when it is time to return to the poets' corner."

"Let's swing conversation to the men and women in the military. With the rigid roles in discipline and management, the soldier and seaman have long held a nation's favor as we looked for leadership. In my country we first turned to farmer and soldier General George Washington as our first president; the general was rather more planter than warrior, more persuasive than demanding as would be expected of a fighter."

"His experience, like others in this category, was recognized for his leadership in the Revolutionary War that gave him the people's devotion; respect and honor that was carried over to their choice of him for the presidency. We've had few military people elected to the executive office in my country, the U.S. Historically were Andrew Jackson and Dwight Eisenhower. They were not cited among our greatest as judged by historians of 'their' wars, but for their role in the presidency. They didn't disgrace the office, although there could be an argument over Jackson's relationship with the Indians. We were quite aware that as the voters assessed them, they were men among men and that the country would survive."

"Many of you perhaps believed that as you first supported questionable leadership in your own country you then faced a difficult task of unseating him or her (we cannot recall a woman who had to be ousted by the guns of people as might have been needed in unseating elected leaders who were women)."

From the floor: "All that talk is to the good, Mister Chairman. Let's slow down and get back to business, allowing somebody else do a little of the talking."

"Thanks for the reminder. I also talked way too much when I was a newsman back on Earth," said the 'Mister Chairman'. "That is a weak reminder that most newspapermen fail when away from the typewriter."

He said: "Let's stay on the military for a moment. Do I hear a nomination for a leader in the military as nominee from our little group? Are any among you who've had experience with the military in high posts? Would you offer first nomination? Ah, right down front with the kibitzers I see a hand. Yes, you have the floor."

"Thank you," said the speaker, now standing. "I can't say that I speak from experience as I proffer my 'educated' second-hand knowledge on the subject. My background is what in the press is called an armchair general. I have known battle leaders only from my reading of history of wars in my world."

"I've learned respect for military leaders in their native lands, even those whose storied deeds have lived into the era of my brief visit to Earth; so often I have wished that many of these men and women so worthy of immortality were of my country. I fear I wasn't deeply impressed with most of the 'Who's Who' in my time that we were stuck with. Let me say I am and I was as loyal as the next. My own country wasn't exactly a free nation in comparison to many others who were so blessed."

"We would not have been a 'backward' or third world nation as many in the rest of the world believed us to be if we'd named better leaders when we had the chance. I loved my country, even as I wept for her in my more recent time there."

"Then you've come without realizing it to the fact that leaders do make a difference and you can view men of battle or those with a military background as leaders, or any others as leaders on the planet Earth?" So spoke the chair.

"Yes, I've given this a good deal of thought. Many of you might be surprised that I as a delegate to this enlightened body might choose either Alexander the Great or Julius Caesar. Caesar has been noted by history also as a statesman, and his name has lived for more than two thousand years in

Germany as Kaiser and in Russia as Czar. I mention them since I know they will be spoken for at a later time."

"Caesar fought Rome's wars. Home from his eight-year absence, he had begun to think after he'd received a tremendous welcome home how he'd create a Rome in his own image. He wasn't satisfied with his re-discovery, which was not the democratic society of a bevy of voices that history has given us. It would not recommend him to a world that since has seen so much bloodshed in efforts to set up a government that has a built-in checks and balances guarantee that the voice and advice of the governed may be heard," said the voice.

"In the face of battle Caesar and other leaders of men of his ilk were like a football coach, and each soldier fought for 'the old man,'" said the man on the floor.

"He killed? So did King David," said Clint. "It has ever been so —- for such a man, throughout history."

"As for Alexander the Great," said the nominator," who as conqueror gave subdued nations that he had 'visited' a lasting cultural quest for knowledge and government based on his personal Greek political philosophical understanding; he also left behind bloody fields and orchards. In so doing, he changed the Middle East, though many claim that his legacy faded after his mysterious death, which occurred soon after. He bore many talents for a man born to lead, with a power that helped along the role of man on Earth's own edge of Heaven."

"If the chair may interrupt," said our man Clint, "let us first commend you for your mention of two of history's greatest leaders. You've defined them as my fellow countrymen also set George Washington apart from others in his time and in the two centuries following —- in the history of my country."

"Citizens said of him: 'George Washington, first in war, first in peace, first in the eyes (or hearts) of his countrymen.' This may appear that I'm interrupting your right to the floor, interposing my own comments. Please know that's not the case, and please let's proceed."

He paused, said: "We've heard the names of possible military nominees. These men may not be your first choices for the nomination. That is understood; we welcome your further comments."

Another delegate rose, to be recognized. "I apologize," said the delegate, who had left her seat and now spoke from the aisle. "I don't mean to waste the time of this body. I will speak from my heart, which dictates my choices."

The Polls of Heaven

She continued: "Thank you. In our hour on Earth were military men who were called out of the backfield to lead their countries in a time of uneasy peace, soon to be called the Cold War when carried beyond their borders, as I recall from Earth."

"I would draw your attention to an unusual man who literally came up from the ranks to be war chief of his budding nation's general staff. He survived the war and was named defense minister during his country's victories in their struggling battle for independence. I speak for Moshe Dayan. He soldiered for most of his life, since he was fourteen, serving in British regiments in Palestine ere his call to the Jewish War of Independence. He earned a reputation for his imaginative suggestions to the strategy and application of its tactics against the enemy."

"Dayan was recognized by his peers as the most influential soldier in the state of Israel in its defense against the enemy. His country became the new nation that we know but the leadership accepted a role that was uneasy among older nations of the world. He was cited for his role in helping create the state of Israel, which continues today but under much stress at the beginning of the millennium."

"My second nominee is Robert E. Lee, American general. The former colonies stood as equal but apart as nearly in theory as they had been in their colonialism, but the general chose to lead his native Virginia in the coming brothers' conflict. The country faced a bloody solution, resulting in a strife known in the country's history as the American Civil War.

Lee remains an icon today not only in the South but in a re-united nation and in other nations of the world. The deep respect his men gave him is a reason that would be necessary in the role of leadership that is being sought so diligently on our planet Earth today."

"Are these two men then your choices as nominees for return to Earth in their roles as leaders during the current moral problems and the warming of the Earth that threatens if not the end of life (or at least drastic change) as well as the destruction of an Earth that would be unfitting for life of anyone or thing that currently makes their home there?"

"Yes, Mister Chairman, these are my nominees."

"The chair submits with the assembly's loud voice, the nominations stand without prejudice (that's a legal term that I could never understand, but it must be vital to democratic debate). The chair notes that both the nominees are by historical reference and their presence in the lives of many among you as excellent choices. The chair again thanks you; we will turn in a moment, let's say, to politics?"

"In one account of an afore-mentioned poet's life," added Clint, "a few American newsmen with no need for citation since what they wrote was reported in numerous papers recalled in a lecture the Russian poet gave at Harvard thirty years previously, in which the poet Solzhenitsyn warned that America would soon be in decline because of her 'blindness of superiority.' He said that in America a 'decline of courage' could be 'considered a beginning of the end;' this failing was recalled from ancient times, that nations in fault eventually passed into oblivion. The poet-politician said that the pursuit of happiness through self-gratification and materialism in the west had replaced moral and character development."

Clint continued, "That's enough from the chair, we have a nomination. Let us proceed once again with the business at hand, and less of talk. What do you say, ye guardians of the faith? Shall we continue to separate the poet-politicians from the chaff?"

He said, "We can consider many men in the west who were recognized as statesmen who were politicians as well and left their marks on history. From Great Britain, we invite consideration to Pitt and Disraeli; of recent times; we have Winston Churchill. In America, almost by necessity we begin with George Washington and Thomas Jefferson; later, we have Abraham Lincoln, Theodore Roosevelt and his cousin Franklin. We cannot forget Woodrow Wilson."

"Lyndon Johnson, accidental president, came to high office after the death of John Kennedy, known as the 'emblematic' politician. He was in a hot seat following the popular president, keeper of the people's sentiments at a time when the people had no definition of greatness. Kennedy's term was too short and Johnson was untried."

"Many citizens believe that ending the unpopular Vietnam War would be seen as a call for greatness." The chair for a moment lost its voice as Clint stared at a face in the second row. "Hello, Isaac," he said. "I, uh, thought you were dead," which brought titters and tatters from the floor.

In an attempt to recover from his stunned silence, Clint returned to what had begun to border on just talk. He said: "I apologize to the delegates. I suddenly recognized an old friend from Earth who came here while I was away at my earthly calling which was as a newspaperman in Ohio. I'll talk to you later, friend Isaac."

The chair recovers: "I would like comments from a few or a dozen older members, as well as recent arrivals. Any further nominations before we move on? I ask that guardedly because historians, political scientists and most newsmen back on Earth made their living by speculating on men and women in politics who'd be elected to leadership posts. I sure don't want to lose the interest of this assembly since the subject is boring to so many of you, I am sure."

"Your chairman does not believe that the Creator is ready to give up on his greatest creation: walking, thinking men and women who have proved to have good needed minds."

Clint Greene of Abraham Lincoln's birth state in an uh and ah moment of faltering comments on his as usual one more perfect day in Heaven, paused briefly, staring over the crowd, appeared disappointed. Clint, not known for an unusual reluctance, studied the question on the faces of the many amused delegates before him, said:

"Let us hear from an Englishman, or a Frenchman, or a German. Let's hear from a good democrat. The chair is open to suggestions by members from the former 'darkest Africa,' perhaps Siberia or any Asian land which until just lately were in alienation behind their country's wall, somewhat in obscurity. Perhaps they are new to a ruler with conscience and compassion, who as a leader from among their countrymen who sees political office as offering only riches."

"If an Indian holy man alone can stop by petition to his god to scratch an anticipated invasion of his country or a neighboring countryman's nation by the Chinese communist red tide after being asked to do so, then think what another holy man, a powerful persuader of men from any nation, can do through a like appeal. This must have been true, since it was in all the papers."

From the left and the right, from east and west of the vast heavenly hall, came voices calling out: "Mister Chairman." "I say, mine host." "May a voice from one of the few great world's progressive third world nations, as they have placed us because we are small and have not been heard from before, accept recognition from the chair?" "I say, Herr Man Monsieur Senor Mister Chairman, allow me to speak. Yes?"

"The chair will recognize the beautiful lady from a seat in the eleventh row, or is it the one in front or behind her, since she is now on her way to the aisle?" A tall lady already was ambling toward the center aisle. Tall lady —- could this be? Someone else I have known before? They must all —- people I knew back there —- be here today. Yes, Clint remembered her or a twin sister as she stood proudly in her garden asking about his family, offering two red ripe tomatoes for him to give to his mother.

He recalled her hand which was soft and warm as she rolled the pride of her garden across his palm. He knew her, had always. Her garden, her church, her then lonely life, and did she once have something more than that? It was told that she waited days, months, years, 'they' said, "forever and a day;" It was a secret, widely noted after she died - by her few friends, members of her church.

In her loneliness 'she'd kept a candle burning in her window until she died.' Waiting all those many years in grief and short breaths for word from the front, the killing fields of Europe, until she died, they said . . . that was the 'first war,' what they called it in the opening months of Clint's World War II. Tall lady's man-friend in love kissed her, turned his back and stepped aboard the train ready to carry him to the trenches beneath the poisoned gas fields of World War I.

"Wait for me," he'd said. "I'll be back. Keep those bright eyes just for me." She had watched the train until it turned into oblivion steaming away into the long valley just a few miles east, deeper and forever into the mountain country, like to Heaven.

How many dreams of that parting day had she painted a man's face on the skies over her garden, the small house that bordered it? How many years had she endured alone and in prayer sitting on bare board pews of her church? How many others out there in the mass had waited out a war, in the centuries?

How near is someday, that every wish for a somehow to, would, caress his face, feel his tight muscles trained by his job and Army cadence and muscle-toning calisthenics? At times her reverie was as real as those sad moments of forever written about by a nation's scribes and its poets still eager and alive as he stepped from the train that bore him home, to fall into her arms again?

Clint looked for a man's face next to the empty chair where she'd sat before she moved to the aisle on her left. Yes, there he was. Surely that was her man, as sure as Clint was that this is the once sad lady of the garden. The dream the man from the blue skies above her garden —- it was, he knew, what This Place was about. They'd become man and his woman again.

Clint's reverie was now fading as it should from that life-long and anticipated place of infinity as he recalled today's task that awaited him. As he listened to the far-off voice that sang to the once respectful silence of the vast number of sympathetic souls, an audience that sensed her earthly pain and turned in sincere respect to the tall lady in the aisle; he was fitting the lady in the garden into two lifetimes ago; at least the one known to him and his mother.

In his earthly home he'd have been by her side if he'd been older, more sympathetic in her appeal that encouraged his thoughts. He had that dread feeling of hurt, a thing of his past, and hers'. This woman for sure could be the lady of the garden; a sojourn on Earth could have intervened (reincarnated?) in the journey between Earth and This Place, perhaps as a young girl who'd never known why her life was so full of sadness, even carried into another life. After her years of grief she had found some happiness in an earthly heavenly garden. This thing he would classify in a memory file as 'not his to know.' If he had even attempted to explain his feelings to anyone on Earth, just simple words would never do it. As a listener, would they be as understanding, as with a few?

"Mr. Chairman," said the tall lady, "I'm from a country I would say was just as huge or as habitable and earth-green as yours, just south of your own on the lower continent of the newer west, called 'South America,' Mister Chairman, which was my short but life-long home. As in yours, our people struggled to build a nation out of a jungle, but we did."

"Among our 'greats' are many men and women who in another time and another place would have been as industrious, unselfish, as creative as the 'greats' of the world, as history has reported in yours and other nations of the new west. I loved my country, and I suffered humiliation, many wounds, for a land I had loved since birth."

"At this time I would call the assembly's attention to a man who in my new nation's history which is called our second empire, is forgotten by other nations. With this man came for the first time in centuries an era of peace and progress, if not a newer order that would make any national people proud."

"He was known as Emperor Pedro II, son of Pedro I. He ruled my country wisely for forty-six years, selecting the best men and women from among our citizens as his aides who together unified the country. Like your Abraham Lincoln, Mister Chairman, he was a fighter, ending the practice of slavery but without a bloody war done without a horrific spilling of blood as it was in your America. We had no war; with us it was done by his accepted proclamation in a document signed by his daughter who was acting as regent while he was ill in a hospital in Europe."

"While he was away a military coup soon after took over the country's leadership and the good emperor was banished from my nation. History recalls his tenure in office as the 'Age of Pedro II.' It was during the second Pedro's rule that so much progress was made for and by the common people."

"Do you wish to place Pedro Two's name as a nominee in our search?" So spoke the chair, still thinking of her as the lady of the garden.

"Yes, by all means."

"Then so be it. No reason for a second. "

When the next speaker spoke for a famous Polish pianist, Ignace Jan Paderewski, Clint could hear for the moment and for the tune itself a Tin Pan Alley musician, in one version of a Tchaikovsky concerto played vigorously across a college stage in America away from the man's own occupied country, a musical creation that gave inspiration to other youth in the musical world.

It was after a concert pianist in Clint's home town that the Polish premier likely never knew that the Americanized version might have been shown to him, a printed music store sheet, and he was asked to play it, and he did. It was the tune the college students and younger kids of the day knew as 'Tonight We Love.' Clint was there, and he heard the kids' request by a sounding and ringing talent for a lifetime memory. He would later try to sing it for his buddies in the Marine barracks, but knew his song couldn't play as it rang in his head.

Clint attended the local college briefly before he'd left home the first time. Despite the ancient instrument so out of tune which had nevertheless started him on a lifetime appreciation for the classics' distinctive power; and had its effect upon his boyhood imagination that was to touch him forever in so many uncounted pleasurable ways.

The resident before him wasn't talking about the man as the pianist — not yet, but the chairman tonight (or in Heaven, where there is no day) as an American in appreciation for the man of the piano, knew the speaker would do so: Clint would recall that the speaker for the man's nomination as a musician, also as a politician who later returned to Poland and became its president and a noted statesman, was loved long for his music.

The resident stood as a proud Polish nationalist, who still loved his country, said:

"Even his talent for music created by his fingertips was not of enough strength to deter a devotion to his country, his adopted state of Poland. During the war he had left his music at home to wrap himself in fight at first for Polish freedom and earned money to help his country re-build following the German occupation. After the armistice, he returned to his country for a while after its independence. He also returned to his music."

"He was to represent Poland at the Versailles Peace Conference at the end of World War I, followed by his service to the League of Nations. He became the new/old country's premier and minister of foreign affairs. He earned better than a half million dollars by his music, big money then, from his tours, he sent home the greater part of it to help agencies to the poor and other activities in the country. He gave money to a number of promising students of the piano."

When the speaker mentioned young piano students who were among those that he supported, Clint recalled one particular young man so recognized, the talented son of a minister of a church in his hometown. He later was to hear of others.

The local boy, son of a local church minister, was the only person Clint ever met who had received gifts from the Polish concert pianist; he thought of it as an honor for his town as well as a man whose music had inspired him.

His thoughts had strayed again to his own past; he suddenly became aware again of his lapse from the business at hand, and forgot that he had heard the nominee's name. The chairman noted that the speaker from the floor, too, had hesitated. "Yes, please continue," said the chairman, and he did, but not before he spoke of the pianist.

"In World War II, a pianist-statesman who was Paderewski was named president of the new Polish Parliament in exile. He would return to the country that had received him so well in previous (war) years, where he later died. It was your country, Mister Chairman, which also had been a refuge to others from the war-devastated countries of Europe."

"I nominate my fellow countryman, Mister Chairman, although he was much more a musician and statesman than a politician. He performed, as expected, as well in government; was known throughout the world for his music; he was remarkable in all his endeavors."

In recognition, "The chair thanks the speaker for her excellent presentation, and for her nomination of Paderewski, a fellow countryman." No other comment was sought, and none was given.

"Before we proceed with further nominations, and to a new category, I would defer to my co-chair as presiding officer. She will carry on for as long as you would receive her. at a later hour, with your permission, perhaps as long in time as an earthly day, I will return and proceed as before."

"During the recess, which you have earned, many might wish to discuss contributors to men or women of note and admired to their own country and society by earthlings whom we will see nominated, and who may well recall others of equal stature." Clint nodded to his friend Karl, who had been standing at the edge of the platform since they arrived.

Just like that, he was sure, a snap of a knuckle and he'd struck a match to light a fire that could introduce a new era of thought back on Earth. He felt it but hoped not to recall it in boast, not among his verbalized thoughts. That would have been the boast of an earthling, but not here, not in This Place. Yet, weren't his actions here, his work, his little speeches back there in the coffee senate chamber the very thing he was seeking when he came in welcome to his back porch of what he knew right off was now 'Over Here?'

As they walked toward the river, Karl, looking straight ahead, said he had just had a fancied up thought. Clint didn't want to ask, yet he would do so.

"It's my thinking that your next category, hoping for group discussion, would have been by a newspaperman named as chairman of an important heavenly committee." said Karl. It would have been of a personal appeal to him. "What I've heard is that journalists often, until recently let's say, to the mid-Twentieth Century, lived up to their convictions.

I have appreciated, from our conversations and from my own reading of history that so many news folk were recognized as fighters for a neglected human population wherever it existed, or perhaps I should say 'as unrecognized by their society.'"

"I've in the past had very little thought of just such that might be coming on, which I easily pushed away from me," said Clint. "Let's forget it and get on with another afternoon of old buddy talk of once fishing on Earth and how we used to chase girls whom we eluded when we were boys," said Clint. He gave a deep sigh for a particular earthly recollection.

Yet he said, as the thought lingered, "In my latter days I suspected that many in my profession would have so quickly compromised their ideals, muscle and sinew, perhaps even betraying their legendary privilege, and his family's and his country's expectations, but they were good newsmen. I had suffered for them, yet I was embarrassed by so many of them."

Clint also showed concern, Karl realized, that among seekers of men or women who might be nominated from among their former newsrooms for a return to life on Earth via reincarnation was not for him or his fellow penmen.

Karl for a once upon a time was aware that Clint was not prepared to accept belief in reincarnation. He was named to the committee, sure. That's one reason he'd pledged to do the best job he could. The committee might find other ways to honor their charge as like the encouragement of births (all made in Heaven, which was a wide belief on Earth) among honest, idealistic families. Clint would have been comfortable with that.

Someone over there believed in him, Clint said. "Was it a conviction with many residents that the 'fact' of reincarnation does exist?" Clint was onto how Karl's subtlety, surprisingly, had led them to the low road for their walk back to their lodgings. That's odd, he thought; when we came in he said it was the high road, and maybe he said that we'd go back on the same road.

What was it that Karl wanted him to see as Clint was aware that they were returning 'home' by a different route along paths that Clint had not seen before? He was grateful to be shown scenes and stories of Over Here, like earlier today, and found verification of deeds that touched almost everyone in the wide heavenly theatre, just like earlier.

He suspected that Karl was intent on reassuring him that his proposal which involved the right man or woman for another Earth appointment was not unusual; he vividly recalled it in the moments of their stroll to the Senate chamber, which was via the upper road. I know now that stories on both roads, new and verifiably old as he'd read about This Place long ago abed after lights out downstairs, now in the New Place were justifiable.

Questions he'd asked of the learned told him of the many ways that were imagined and were recalled in all the different unanswered replies which had left them confused.

In three minutes, Earth time, they stopped before a rude stage, crude but quite fit for history's recording. Astonished by its breadth and activity, a middle ages open front theatre drawn for him in picture books that was so vast in size to accommodate a battle scene in the annals of the early days of the Roman Empire.

That's not entirely correct. It was larger that performance stages, about the size of e back yard of an historical estate of a rich man of the era, and for portraying mass warfare and staging of expected impressive sword play. But it did have depth. Clint had wondered earlier why the athletes and actors he now was viewing had an arena that he realized was needed.

He recalled from picture books he'd seen in his town library the Coliseum in Rome as it was during the middle era Caesars. The Roman amphitheatre, in what remains since its structural stones began to fall away, is a reminder of a Roman day of flowering civilization, Clint thought. Built as a promise that narrowed down to .bread and circuses, the only real purpose to sell a government to the people, here it was.

The design of the theatre Karl was describing came in words almost akin to a boast for a lost reason or other. Karl was proud of the edifice just as a landowner back in his own mountain country could wish for enough level land to build one just like it. He was almost shouting to break the tour's spell. The simplistic edifice open at the front had spent its best hypnotic thrust on a theater addict like himself that fascinated Clint, but they moved on.

They stood before a series of what appeared to be Earthly boxing rings, but he hoped for a return to the smaller theater. He'd been taking an inactive part in the conflict before him. "That man, the taller of the two boxers you will soon meet," said Karl, pointing to the first ring with a mat, "was born with no feet. His opponent lost both legs while still a young man, maybe a teenager, in one of Earth's wars. It's almost as if they're out there trying out their brand new limbs is the why of all that fancy footwork. When you next come by, you'll see them in a foot race, like that race over there which has engaged maybe a dozen runners, half of them women."

From the foot race, Clint's attention was given to women and men on high swings. Beyond, a game of soccer was in progress, and to the left an agile woman was practicing basketball foul shots at a hoop adorned with what he'd swear was a pair of sharp wings. He couldn't see much of the swimming pool in the distance because of the activity, although he knew it was there.

He could identify a young woman balancing herself but slowly on a tapered tip of a springboard. She was preparing for a high dive, likely the highest that he would ever see. This very well could have been her challenge — which was that someday she would dive from far above the madding crowd. She didn't need an audience — apparently she was diving simply to prove that she could do it.

A baseball game was underway near the wooded path. A familiar fellow was at bat. He was in a uniform that dated to the late Nineteenth Century so identified by his haircut you'd say, and his mustache, if you were back home looking at it in a picture book.. Clint imagined that the batter was the storied Casey; today, he knew, Mighty Casey (of storied long verse) would not strike out.

Two men of out-sized muscles were wrestling in a raised ring. Gesturing spectators jumped to the floor with closed punching fists against nothing but air as an encouragement from the floor. They appeared satisfied that they were beyond the ropes. They were yelling, many of them taking sides, apparent by their screams of the names of one or the other of the two fighters. The wrestlers twisted and moved excitedly, like two sparring boxers carrying on in a recalled Earth day. Both were heavily tanned not from the present sun but like beach lifeguards back on Earth.

Clint wondered how they'd managed to bring with them to This Place their all-body suntans when, as he recalled from experience, a suntan was a fleeting thing, fading with the autumn of a first and last leaf as the seasons changed. He saw no tattoos. Over Here, color of skin had no distinction.

Every sport he knew of was part of the wide scenario.

"Champions all," said Karl.

Just a long step above them and they were taken aback abruptly by a different and much more appointed arena of what was meant to portray or imitate a popular but ancient actors theatre. Clint said: "Looks quite much like London's old Globe Theatre from pictures that I have seen."

"That's exactly what it is," said Karl. They had returned to it, as Clint had wished. "Look closely and you might pick out Queen Elizabeth."

"Let me amend that. You won't have to look too close. She will stand out, highly appointed but isolated in her balcony stall, a loge it was called in later English. She was there every night if she was not out of town.'

"Notice the actors on stage, how they watch her as they go into their lines. In her presence, the play's a thing just for the queen. They all seek the queen's approval; their careers in the theatre may well depend on it. In your modern theatre a main rule is you never turn your back on the audience. I suspect the sacred admonition began right here. It was, 'You never turn your back on the queen' —- or the king, I'd just as well add."

Clint said: "I'm more interested in Shakespeare right now. Back on Earth it was a question that arose now and then, during the return to popularity of the plays by Willie the Shake himself. Inevitably, it was, 'Just who was Shakespeare?'"

"You're losing me," said Karl. "What do you mean by that, 'Who was?'"

"Willie was a stable-boy before he broke into theatre as author of those plays. The subjects of Elizabeth would have known who he was, because of his background."

"He never had access to the castles of the lords and ladies he wrote about in his scripts, or a near perfect layout of the land around the castle or battlefield, which all was 'unvisited' scenery. I doubt that the customs of the castle of early English lords and kings and the wars between them and other royals were the result of envy and greed, but evil and jealous minds did exist in quantity."

"They even said, 'they' being the critics of a later day: a boy from Avon would have been illiterate," said Clint. "All the same, they kept his secret, if it were a secret."

"I could go down there and ask to be introduced to good ole Willie. I could decide right away if this man were capable of what literary history said he did; of course I'd never know the man if I weren't told, not knowing the faces, London's social life of the day, or a defense by his peers, fellow actors, writers who might sense my motive."

"It has been debated for years in many different quarters, just what was the true identity of Shakespeare. Even so, other playwrights and poets of the era were more popular with artists and fans than Willie. I wouldn't want to embarrass the literary icon of the ages."

"How could I get the word, the identity of the author-poet to the teachers the writers and the critics who inhabit every corner of a world where his works are taught and staged?" Clint, the old newspaper editor who would have the biggest literary story of the age in his hand and he couldn't get it into print.

Karl smiled, agreeing to something he knew not what, said:

"I often said that the lofty phrases as well as the one-liners attributed to the 'greats' of your day and mine were frequently from other-written scribes. In my time in the halls of times' literary greats we would have hit on it like you, tongue-in-cheek or in some tutor's personal belief; hangers-on around the king or queen who were hired for the job as a public relations man or woman, to do the writing?"

"What we were told is what we were wont to believe: not that every public spoken word was written by someone else," said Karl. "I expect you won't run into many know-it-alls over here."

Clint said, partly in jest:

"There we are, like a writer pouring out words by command hoping to be judged for his writings which came to him in inspiration given by Heaven and so were acknowledged, instead judging whether a writer to the king had sold his intelligence or his soul to assure the royal favor. Apparently it mattered not in those early days of the theatre and in what would have been called pamphleteering."

"I used to believe that half the people in our business —- reporters or even editors, were frustrated actors or novelists or poets. They dreamed of some day standing before an intelligent audience anticipating their loud applause. She could see the tears on their faces because her words had touched their hidden nature."

"In my country at the time I left, more than 40,000 books were published every year. The great bulk of them, even then, never saw more than the dawn of day, that is, the shining light by good reviews and purchasers in the marketplace as the final mark of acceptance."

"As you know, Karl, I made my living as a newspaperman. My papers were small, but if I said something I knew was not so, which I allowed it to print, someone would make their day by calling me down. They knew details of the story even before I did. It's that way in a small American town. It affected all of us in the business."

"I went into the business I reckon with the idea I could influence others with my own thinking, my press's editorial opinions. I could have been a preacher and said the same thing from a church pulpit. I reckoned I could reach more people through my paper. Did I have a right to do that? I thought so. We were a democracy. My pages were open even to a rabble-rouser who could use me as a mouthpiece; often I'd remind folks that they had a sounding-off place in my newspaper's heart: no 'cussin,' though."

"I reckon I'm among those earth-bound and I hoped honest losers we've been running into all round here today; that's a reason I expect that I was detached to this place. The people generally knew the difference, though, between good and evil," he said; "how a king or ruler was good for his people, while another was good primarily for his or her personal treasury."

They passed the Globe Theatre and concession booths catering to Earth people who at least had a stump as a platform; they could use their voice -- Clint had no need to define it —- Karl was onto him. Clint once had been like the others; he knew that he was among those who more than once had sought the spotlight.

"Look," Karl said, "I know where the politicians are. If you wish, I'll show you where they still do political things. I didn't overlook them. I intentionally passed it up since you may have seen many of your friends, sitting nervously on the platform itching to stand up and hoping to say something remarkable."

"You are right, my friend. Many times I was in the press box shaking my head and 'wondering' if a fellow politician on the platform knew what he was doing to his followers, and to his country. I can't judge, but for Heaven's sake I thought they must have been doing something right."

"I want no politicians around today, thanks. It's time to go home," Clint said. "But before we get away from the sore places in our talk of Earth's society, so much beyond our recall, I still haven't come to a satisfactory answer to the question, out there, or Over Here."

"I'm talking about a much maligned plain old heartbreak. My mother's sisters would talk among themselves about their mother, 'who died of a broken heart;' they agreed in their earthly assessment of her. The preacher at my mother's funeral alluded to it: so often in mama's life I knew and at the moment was reminded of it, that she spoke often as if from a broken heart like her mother—- I had always suspected it, but there wasn't much I could do about it; I was grieved that others had become aware of it."

"The preacher's final remarks at the church that day were, 'she's happier now than she has ever been.' Of course he was talking about This Place. How did he and the others know? In my church, her church, and from my mother's apron strings, I was persuaded that there would be no argument or sadness in Heaven."

"If it had to be; surely in some way must be an evening up of things. It was said of my mother, living above the town, higher up on the mountain where my people eked out a living from what was left of the soil after most of it had been washed out by spring and summer rains, that down the road she would find happiness. The ground was disturbed by the hoe and the plow and winds by stealing its life to erosion."

"We knew little about conservation in my time. The way of life on the mountain, amidst all that forest beauty undisturbed as far as you could see over mountain and fading mountain in sight, yet somewhat made up for little else the family had to enrich their days. They had their share of disappointment, they were as certain as not to die of heartbreak, as so many did; I in my weak earthly judgment knew."

"I realized that my mother had her big share of let-downs in her life, much more than I recognized in my youthful years. She so wished for an education, passed that hope along to me. The GI Bill after the big war made it possible for me and a few million others from life out there in the hinterland among the high winds and blowing rains of nature and the cruelty it left with the families who were forced to stay where they were they were by circumstances beyond their control. The youngest fortunately were away from home after World War II as part of American campus life. She took a sort of pride as she talked to neighbors and friends about 'my boy up at university.'"

"It might be said that the hurts of heartbreak endured by so many of Earth's people could have been the source of the creation of a Heaven, where cares of the world would at last be forgotten. Heartbreak as a term and malady, as it was kicked around, generally was applied to a romantic situation. I'm not talking about the earthling who for one reason or another never married. Many of them would say, quietly, 'I never found anybody,' but certainly the lady I knew as my mother comes on a day of recollection; she shed many tears in her loneliness."

"I remember the poem from school called 'Maud Muller,' of a young woman who wished, as the tall gentleman from town rode away after a brief encounter, 'it might have been.' We could have multiplied that by some million or so."

"Or that person who endured a loveless, bad marriage, or who was abandoned by a lover; the mother who watched the road for a son or daughter home from the wars or career that took them far from home; or the mother or father who sat alone at home during one of Earth's holidays that until recently was devoted to family gathering; it was a custom they came to expect, in some cases actually hoped for without knowing why it was so big."

"Heartbreak, friend Karl, which was so dominant among our people that many had begun to believe that they and they alone were punished for some possible 'sin' they now must atone for. Heartbreak —- it hurts just to hear the term. I've seen it in the faces along crowded streets in the cities or towns; many, I was told, were born to loneliness as their 'destiny.' I used to encounter what I believed were many sad people who bore its dark ominous clouds in their chests (hearts, the preachers said) for their entire lives. It's a big shortcoming of the perfect society, which we created in the name of democracy —- in the shadow of Heaven, our fathers said."

"They had no pill or salve or lotion or potion that would remedy those with the old dread, or malady. The nearest you could come to for relieving the soul's drag on a hurting human being was to show him or her that they were not then nor would they ever be alone, but words meant to be soothing and sympathetic, even these, were never enough."

"I wonder if a specific place Over Here is reserved for earthlings of lonely hearts, even more so of heartbreak?" posed Clint.

"You're asking me, after all you've seen? They are all around you, Clint, here, there, everywhere, in the midst of the beauty and the playfulness you've seen this hour," said Karl.

"This Place as far as I am concerned was created for these people, to be as they had imagined it, first among them Earth's Jewish people. These people suffered like few others this side of slavery, generation after generation."

"It is recorded in the Bible that was adopted by other religions that thrived on Earth. It apparently had to be," said Clint. "One more thing, before we part: Let's talk about the potato famine, and the River Shannon. I've heard since I was a boy about how a million people starved to death and another million maybe more left Ireland to settle and help build my country; they also went to other countries, where they at first were welcomed."

Karl said: "I don't know what a potato is, and I never heard of the River Shannon."

"Okay, buddy, you'll hear now," said Clint.

"The potato is a vegetable, see. It was discovered in South America by the Spanish explorers in the mid-1500s, and potato seeds, which were cut from a potato surface called eyes, were planted just like any other seed. The potato plants were grown by the Indians since longer than anybody could remember; it fascinated the Europeans, except for some among them who at first believed the potato was a poison."

Clint felt a little silly talking about a plant with eyes that grew its fruit underground, but he continued: "A big grower of potatoes was Ireland, after the plant had been taken to Europe; pretty soon it graced fields and gardens planted all over the continent, feeding a lot of people."

"The Irish people came to it like an alfalfa field to a big herd of cows, so much so that they became practically dependent on it. Then, about 300 years to the sad day after it was discovered in the Americas, the potato blight (an airborne disease) did in Irish gardens, fields of that single crop. History records that about a million people were to die without names to be buried in mass graves in Ireland alone during the famine."

"The Irish farm folk who didn't starve to death left their beloved crude homes mostly recalled in sad songs of the day, and their beloved country, if they could find the right song to help recall their happiest days there. They settled in the United States, in South Africa and other countries. And right here's where the whole of history began to change. This was in 1845 and 1846 that the famine hit in all its power. Migration took a few more years."

"In my country they helped build railroads, especially the rails that would span the continent. Irish labor built bridges in time to open the industrial age in my country and wherever else they would settle. They also had an affinity for politics, helping our nation become the democracy it wanted to be ever since the country was founded."

"Most people recalled the Irish as yearning for a land that they were forced to leave, how their lament, sad songs for their native land changed the culture of America, just as the children of Israel yearned for the Promised Land. They sang of the River Shannon, especially the green grass that grew along its banks. We had St. Patrick's Day in my country; on that day everybody wanted to be

Irish, and they wore little lapel pins or something green as part of their clothing. The Lord works in strange ways, his miracles that were made to succeed. It was never a holiday, but the people acted like it was. I wonder if this place has its memory of the River Shannon, eh?"

"You've come to the right place, me lad." said Karl. "Come with me," he said. They didn't have far to walk. As they sat on a slight, green hillock (obviously), Karl waved toward the green valley below, the green of trees and crops, especially long waves of green grass (potato fields?), all right in the middle of what to them appeared to be a fairyland. (Was this Heaven?). Karl said: "Behold! The River Shannon! I'd known she was here, but didn't know her name until you defined it."

And there it was. Lovers strolled in the grass along its banks. Men and women and even little kids held long fishing poles along the river's broad shoulders, their string fish lines moving in rhythm to the slow moving waters, the clear waters of Heaven's river; a hope for the river's largess to relieve empty stomachs.

Girls and boys traditional Irish lovers as memories recorded them, lovers of all ages lolled in rowboats, dropping their hands into the healing waters to feel its coolness. In pairs or groups or singly, they are as dreamers along the banks. They watched the flow of the river from Heaven flow toward the Heaven across ocean waters on another part of Earth to help recreate their loved waters again in foreign lands.

Karl said: "You've given me more of an understanding of This Place. It's a beginning again for a saddened people, who found their green and their river right where they knew it would be. It's like you and your cabin above the Cumberland, which is their story too, a tale told by the Irishmen of Heaven."

They continued along the path toward home. Karl said: "Did you think about This Place back in your days on Earth?"

"I can't recall that I ever gave it much thought, certainly with much of an idea of what was Over Here," said Clint. "I recall reading about The Place, some mentions among the classics. A seven hundred year-old work by a fellow, a poet I think, who was named Dante Alighieri, called simply Dante, whose classic was about both Heaven and hell. I would say that in his description, he was as far off as anyone who touched on the subject. His view was medieval, and the thought processes and beliefs of the people were much different from my time. A modern person, even if she's steeped in academic authority on

Dante, would have a much different sense of Heaven. John Milton, one literary voice whose words followed Dante's, was swimming in light air as the devil flew away with his followers. A wide angry circle of the angry it must have been. Like I've said, everybody thinks of Heaven in different ways."

"Knowing what I've learned during my new, old home, from here I would expect that all things pleasurable I enjoyed back on Earth were gifts of Heaven. I recall going to class by the music of chimes in the campus bell tower. I recall thinking in those few musical moments of days of delight, scenes that might have reminded me of Heaven."

"When I was in the Pacific during the war, when we could, we had coffee with our meals, but spoonfuls of powdered milk, powdered eggs even powdered potatoes. When I got back to civilization, Honolulu, then onto the states as then defined, these were the first foods I ordered when I got liberty. Ah Heaven, I said. I drank so many milk shakes I thought I'd bought the dairy and all profits would be gone with the evening breeze."

He paused for a moment. "I'll give credit to the logistics people who did a job I'm still trying to figure out how: They could get all our needs at the very hour we needed it, in most cases. We were scattered all over the world. Except ammo, maybe, we used so much of in slaying the enemy we most always were running a bit short."

They neared the evening primrose bush where their paths took separate ways. Karl started up the hill. Clint called out: "Wait, I see the messenger is at my door, sitting in the swing on my front porch."

As Karl came closer, he said: "Likely already been to see me. Let us go and see what it's about. When the messenger comes it must be important, even if his message is only an invitation to an ice cream social."

The messenger saw them coming, as a practice at attention even stiff maybe, but in all ways reverent. He became more relaxed with his heavenly traditional Mona Lisa smile, where the painter could have gotten his inspiration.

Clint said to him, "Surely you aren't here with a committee report from the others not already since we just left there."

"You must remember," said the messenger, "that you are in a place where time does not exist. What may have occurred at the chambers during your 'short walk,' well could have been many days, in Earth time, of much debate and decision by the committee."

"Then what is so urgent?" asked Clint.

The messenger said: "I'm here to report to the chairman and to you, Karl. The sub-committee has made a choice. They took their time, as you used to say in your earthly home, and that polling was accomplished in the democratic spirit that you insisted upon."

"That's good," said Clint. "May I inquire who this one-time Earth resident might be who will be returned to Earth in its present dire need, oh our wise and provident bearer of good tidings?"

"You realize, dear Mr. Chairman, that neither you nor I nor any among committee members will ever know or recall," said the messenger.

"Those who made the final selection will soon forget what they did here. No one, not even the nominee will recall the special session or the committee's initial report. Your service is certainly appreciated; it is over. It is done. You too will soon forget all that has transpired."

"The nominee will be returned to Earth. He or she will be given a noted background, which is a resume of an education for the profession to which he will or she will be fitted. He or she will have an entourage, they will serve their chosen leader or as leader himself, in a position that will require many aides. You very likely will appreciate the choice, but you will not know how his or her selection has come about."

"From his past —- written in the records, perhaps in the runes —- all of this for that one possible future, inevitable researchers as well as the 'press' the news people, of your country. It also will include a parentage, a mother and father who would have loved him since he was born to them; all others, his cronies, coffee buddies, playmates, teachers, colleagues —- each will recall him from his youth, talk of his brilliance, his kindnesses and certainly his religion."

"Every small or memorable aspect of his life until the call to leadership despite the misunderstood awareness upon a suggested memory or an ambition known only to herself or himself you might say, of a summons to greatness. If this sounds like a salute to the divine right of kings —- a one-time earthly belief - I must admit it is close. I know much about your former world, especially its past."

"Tell me," asked Clint, "who were some of the nominees that came off the floor after Karl and I left? Am I entitled to know? If I'd been there I would have known."

"Oh my," said the messenger, "dozens, maybe even hundreds. Many you would never know, or ever heard of. It was such a variety from the heart that if each of them appeared on a printed ballot it would go on and on and on. One in particular who impressed members of the committee was Solon, a figure who is known to Earth people who work crossword puzzles. His name for a puzzle was familiar, I suppose."

"Solon was a compromise candidate to us. He was duly elected in the days of the world's first democracy - Athens, Greece, a city-state -- in 594 B.C. Solon initiated numerous reforms. One 'law' in particular succeeded in 're-voking' the practice of debt slavery. The wealthy or ruling class up to that time would lend money to a person and if it were not repaid the borrower would become the slave of the lender. He brought the poor people into the government by giving them a voice they'd never known before."

"Also among them was of Hadrian, Roman emperor who brought about better understanding of the Roman law. As expected was a wide assortment of generals and admirals; from your century was Dag Hammarskjold, the United Nations' secretary-general, a poet and a peace maker, among many others. Named were religions leaders, politicians, poets galore, and a host of early Romans and Greeks; and Alexander the Great, again. Not surprising, eh?"

"Britain had its sway, of course, swinging from the Celts to Alfred the Great, the only islander who was accorded the term 'Great' by his countrymen; he was followed from the floor by Arthur, even in the present century declared by many to be a myth, but held out as a possibility, and Henry Plantagenet (Henry the Second), who may have been and so cited as England's greatest ruler of the country's early history. Edward the First was of first rank.

William Wallace of Scotland made a name for his adopted state in fight against the English and Scots even though he was Welsh by birth. And of course there were Good Queen Bess, and Mary, queen of Scots. Across the way was the Maid of Orleans."

"I say, old chap, you're asking too much of me, as if I held names of the great and the good in my hand. You took advantage of me. I wasn't expected by my associates to talk of these people."

"You've been a real help," said Clint, nodding to Karl, who acknowledged the report of the messenger as of vital interest.

"All this, even in the details, will be a part of what will never be entered in the record, because it all ended here," said the messenger, which Karl later said had confused him.

Clint said he had a good idea of the listing of nominees from his country, from the Pilgrims to near the end of what is called Earth's 20th Century. He said there is a good deal of honor -- men and women, who've been cited among England's historical figures, as well as refined, reborn France, Germany and Russia since their recovery from the late world war. In many other countries are men and women who have earned the respect of their people.

"Citizens of the world's democracies as well as subjects of those still with kings will find confidence in this man, or this woman. From wherever he may rise, we believe they will listen and follow him or her into a new world," the messenger agreed. As he rose to leave, with a 'grin of Heaven' on his face, the messenger saluted both, and hesitated. They waited. The Messenger gave a stiff respectful bow, and was gone.

Clint said to Karl, "You won't believe it, but I'd like to take a nap, like on a Sunday afternoon back there. Even in winter, the sun would shine and the papers were read."

Karl appeared surprised. "Good rest, my friend," said Karl his neighbor.

Clint would admit that he too, was surprised. A wish for a nap was more than a simple wish back on Earth. It spoke of fatigue, of weariness from the job at hand, or from sleeplessness on Earth's days and nights.

Karl was secure in his thoughts of Clint's job, which he would declare was 'well done.' "Your generation would be proud. I'm in mind of the many in your country and throughout the world whose sober voices will arise with the man we're sending them even as politicians and plebes who will be angling for credit for a happenstance, a stroke of lightning that has been tossed into their laps and ambitions."

"We will not chance to be concerned with fools," said Clint.

"Already, the media as you may call it, although they will not know of its origin —- will hail the season of good will that has emerged and soon will be onto the new idea; it will be a big story to fill news columns," Karl said. "Again, I say rest well."

Over Here you never tire, never need that precious nap Clint wished for. It is, among other good things in Clint's life on Earth that he brought with him from there to here, even if there was no need for it. Yet he was actually getting sleepy.

He was in his back porch chaise lounge watching the birds as they flew over, with no destination, across the river and his sister mountain. The birds were casting shadows near the moving waters of the river as seen from your side. Below the cliffs on the other side, which he now could view like he'd never seen them before as they emerged from the fog below on his own Cumberland River, a bunch of town kids crowded into a small boat like they once had piled by heavy count into a phone booth, enjoying their freedom.

The river boys revved the engine of their river tiger to its highest speed that caused the boat's prow to lift by the power thrust from the stern. He should have asked Karl to stay and see all this activity mostly from your own century.

The wild wind on wilder hair of one of the boys provided one more pleasantly recalled memory to the boy on the porch of a cabin far above the river where he now lay, getting sleepy. To the boys as well as an appointed aerie viewer, it was a re-discovered thrill for all time to lift the boredom of Earth's generations as he recalled it from his boyhood post high above them.

On each side of him were recliners that he'd reserved from his first front porch, now idly awaiting the arrival of more of his heavenly friends to an hour of welcome comradeship and conversation. In a little while he would call Karl and together they'd go looking for Asa his Indian friend from the Marine Corps who left his outfit while in the Pacific for an unidentified assignment.

Asa was not heard from again (by him or by other warriors of his wartime outfit). His search for his Native American friend had yielded not a trace. He thought it wasn't fair that Asa had been transferred. He had never fouled out, was ever loyal and a good soldier, or in his 'politically correct' (ah, me) situation, a good Marine. Was it Naval and Corps policy because of his race? No. No. No. They must have needed him on the battlefield.

The Indian would come for his right to an eternal heavenly tour if he were not still alive, followed by Bonzai, his dog for yet too short a time. The South Seas canine friend was his on a short visit from the Japanese, and his name came from the possible enemy outfit.

Bonzai ably provided needed comfort to him since he'd left behind his own dog in Oklahoma. When Asa arrived, Clint would call up old Tom and they'd all have a spot of tea together or something equally stimulating.

It was on this (his) back porch overlooking his Cumberland River and the mountains all around him that an ancient poet had described for his generation on a usual Earth's day in the spring like today and penned a simple phrase , 'whence cometh my strength.'

Chapter Five

He'd never thought seriously of a promised land while at home in the mountains; he could not recall it, or perhaps not until he was older, much older. Why did he recall what any poet said of his mountain, his river? He'd heard men say: "Before I die I want to do this," or they might say, "When I get to Heaven." Perhaps it was, "I will have it like this in Heaven."

Wishes abounded among men, believers or simply just the usual round of skepticism yet hope. He'd never heard any man deny the existence of Heaven.

"I only wished that I'd return from the war hale and hardy, not boastful —- which is a Marine's right —- but I've been so favored; back home I used to say, it was because of my mother's prayers given on her knees that I come home safe and sound from the battlefield." He didn't try to finish the sentence or talk about a night with a native girl of the hidden ways of life who might leave him with a disease.

Another wish was to have a bed in a place like the attic, right under the rafters where he could hear the patter of rain on the tin roof; to have a good book to read in bed before he became sleepy and reached over to turn off the light, wishing that someday he'd write like the many authors who nourished his thirst for adventure.

Like all newspapermen, I would write books, but books are no longer being read as they once were. The whole world was now hooked it seemed to him to be universal on the personal computer that did their thinking for them.

Even newspapers are on their way out, following the paths of the doodle-bug. It had become a day of the quick and easy, soon quite an alternate satisfaction. Life had become a slogan. Politicians who hoped to be remembered as great orators were looking for fancy writers who could come up with one-liners that would say it all.

Every bone every muscle every sinew in his still body after the incident in jungle forests came to him in pain to where he lay in nobody's land, The battle was done, and quit. The silence of the dead hovered over the wet field that he could see in the corner of his eye, the left one. Yet he knew he was alive. Nobody came to tell him that it was so. He knew because he could feel the fly crawling across his cheek a survivor insect that was drinking from the tear on his face.

He thought of snails and puppy-dog tails that little boys are made of. His body bore the afflicted Job scourge of the Old Testament: hurt was in his back and his legs and his head; his eyes were open, he knew that for certain —- but why wasn't he seeing?

He'd banked the fire in the fireplace before going up to bed in the attic; still warm days but welcome cool at night, so he'd built a fire. He couldn't have forgotten that (it was his job). Its embers had provided him a night light for a while if he stayed on the couch too sleepy to get up and go to bed, leaving it as on most nights, but tonight it burned out early.

His eyes and his brain could not fathom this thing, this absolute complete darkness that had a scary way of reminding him of a deep pit, part of an open cave formation he'd fallen into on a day of exploration of a friend's family farm farther down the river when he was a boy. The cave was a refuge from a school day he'd rather not recall, but there it was.

He had forgotten it for a long time, but the cave brought up the memory he thought he had for a time forgotten from his early school days when he'd been Tiny Tim in the Dickens story about Christmas and the school kids out front all laughed at him because he had a sore throat and his words came out squeaky-like. Right then the big red curtain began falling and he was in front of it before a full house, hostile audience. The fellow who tended the curtain let it fall to help Clint in a way to accept or forget the laughs from the audience.

He later realized that the school audience and teachers weren't laughing at him at all, but sort of laughing with him.

It was in appreciation of his squeaky imitation of how Tiny Tim would talk as the story switched to the poor family, They were seated around the dinner table and Tiny Tim let his boyish voice come out that way as he got a chance to tell of an incident out on the sidewalk as he and his father were on their way home. He always got excited and talked too fast when it was his turn to tell about something that had happened to him that day.

The kids were showing how proud they were of Clint's acting on the school stage that day. Ah me, I had a talent and didn't recognize it at the time.

What was so puzzling right now was his memory of pain and hurts before he left the Earth and found his way into a new land. This thing is no longer possible. What, may I ask, is the reason for all this?

Wait, he thought he saw a dim light way off, and figures —- two people; two persons except that they weren't moving -- but wait again, the people were looking at him, out of the night into the light; they were smiling. Where had he seen those smiles before? What am I doing in here? What is this 'in here'? Are they trying to wake him up so he and they won't be late for the game or something?

Face on the left in particular -- with a smile as big as his whole face -- something behind the face the man's body blocked out the bright of day. The sun couldn't get into the room. Move over man and let the sun come in. He thought of the song of a long ago boy's day when he had heard the song by mountain singers with the words' native accent.

The man's eyes say he knows me. Whole face a big smile says he's pleased that he knows me. "He's awake," said the face, "call the nurse. Looks like the old story teller's come to."

Clint looked at the dangling glass bottle beside him, a tube running into his sore arm.

"That's what they been feeding you nigh onto a month now, with that sugar tit there putting that flowery sweet water into your veins," said friend Leo, a Russian talking like a hillbilly. Yeah, it's Uncle Leo for sure. Only this time his accent, which usually is distant, is more distinct. People with accents speak more like the old country but the longest words come out in polished English, usually unless when they're excited, like Tiny Tim.

(What fooled most people was his hang of the King's English like Appalachian people among whom he lived and who pretty much have held onto the pure Elizabethan language of the hills since their arrival here more than a couple hundred years ago, before radio and TV came in to straighten out their talk.) Uncle Leo he'd said often was a fast learner. The longer Clint knew him, the more he appeared in accent and the quite dress of an Englishman.

I'd say to anybody who asked that Leo is pretty good at English, for a foreigner. We talk our way mainly to the Yankee preacher to get him to speak our language instead of that uppity Harvard way they liked to use to impress us hill folk with their smarts whether it is real or not. How we talk at church generally is the way reconstructed cultivators of the land of way down south let it come out when they get overly excited.

(Clint was talking out loud allowing his thoughts make words that wander until he was able to learn why he was here and if something had gone wrong with him.)

What's Uncle Leo doing here?

"Where's Lily?" asked Clint.

"Who's Lily?" answered Uncle Leo with a question to a question. "Oh, you mean the wife, right? She's gone, Clint." "Gone where?" another Clint question. Likely, he was still attempting to find his place and reason in his own fog that straddled the room in which he was beginning to realize was full of people.

"Lily's . . . just gone, Clint; you said she died."

Clint was silent for several minutes. Then, he smiled. He knew they knew she'd been dead a long time. It didn't hurt to smile like now, the only place on his body it didn't hurt.

"Been sittin' out there in that chair tryin' t' keep warm, Leo? Sure beats that old stiff worn out chair on the hotel porch, though, I bet. What you guys doin' here, anyway? Better yet, what am I doing here?" asked Clint. "Better still yet, how long have I been here?"

The other man was the local editor, Oscar Blues. I gotta . . . must ask him if he has a middle name. He couldn't even guess it, knowing that it would be one of a thousand or more hackneyed (cliché) something or other to fill out the 'Blues' ending. Maybe it's 'Little Boy,' I won't ask, maybe I did once. Likely he gets that all the time.

Oscar got up from his chair, he said, to call the nurse. "Don't go away Clint," he said. "I'll be right back."

"You say I've been here flat on my back being fed through that 'sugar tit' you called it all that time, a whole month? What in the world happened to put me in here? Did I fall out of maybe a two story window? Did my chute fail to open?" asked Clint. "I don't remember even jumping. I thought the war was over."

"None of the above, me bonny clabbered pussy cat," said Uncle Leo. Leo got that kind of talk, those riddling of the words from the Scots. Clint knew even in his misty mind that it didn't mean a doggoned squat. "With your face all puffed-up like that you look like you done been poured out of a churn an' come out looking like clabbered milk bread spread my good mother used to save for cooking on our farm back in the Caucasus. So she could churn it into butter."

The Caucasus, you say? Then Clint remembered the window poster and the brief talk they might have had about it, but Leo put if off, like always. The poster said he was Jack? No, Leo, the Cossack. Do they churn for butter over on the Don River? What I recall from reading about it is that they used an animal called a bullock in their farm work. What's called butter from a bullock's milk?

The Caucasus? Wow! That is in Russia, but Leo talks more like a Scot, maybe with a bit of Irish thrown in. I thought he was a Scot. Looked like one when we first met. The Russians, he recalled, or those he'd run across during the recent big hostile days and in the few years after, before the iron curtain fell; this fellow for one, anyway, had easily spoken the Queen's English. It's even more pronounced than by people in countries he knew that talked in one of the Romance languages. He'd learned all that in an Army school of languages, and more.

They'd (soldiers he knew from Army service in Europe had told him) also fought in a war alongside battalions of soldiers loyal to the King's way, so it must be the Queen's English he'd listened to. This little thing always puzzled Clint. Did Leo's tribe go with the Allies against their own country like I'd heard? Why was that?

"Well now, before we go into detail about how I got here, let me say you got a story to tell the world how you came to be such a crack shot back when you were riding wild as a boy Cossack. So you finally decided to come clean, eh? Wow, my head hurts."

Clint would save what else he might hear about if ever his head stopped hurting and his eyes stopped blurring over. "What month is it?" he asked Leo (old Jack) as the editor returned with the nurse. The nurse was a woman he'd known as a girl in one of his classes, way back in high school. She was smiling.

"It's the middle of October," said Oscar. "A month ago, the day you drove your car off the side of the mountain and went into the long night, it was still September. It's still summer but edging gently into autumn, or fall, as you all call it here in Kentucky land. The leaves are falling."

"So that's what happened? My car slipped over the edge? Funny, I don't recall even a little bit about it —- what I was doing that day? Where was I going? Not a blamed thing do I recall of the 'over the side.'" Sounds like Navy swabby talk —- that is Navy talk for the sailor who does all the work on board a ship.

"Do ye reckon I've missed the fall? Always been my favorite time of year, the leaves turning every shade of brown and tan and yellow. I always liked to walk through the leaves and listen to the rustle and watch as the wind scatters them all the way to Kingdom Come. I remember how people of New York and even Ohio would drive all the way to New England just to see the fall of the year all dressed up in all those colors."

He felt like talking, about anything that jumped into his mind. Clint's never-softening talk surprised even the nurse. She said, "Well, I do declare, you lay right there not saying a word for a whole month. Now we can't get you to shut up."

"Let him talk," said Uncle Leo. "He's alive once again, and it's up to his friends to see that he enjoys every minute of it, at least until I get him into a chess game or a friendly little fight over a pool table."

"Did I tell you that when I was riding with the Cossacks —- I was the champion pool player east of the Don?"

"No," said Oscar, "but I'll bet we're going to hear a lot of brag about it now that you have decided to talk about yourself." Clint noticed a wild glint in Leo's eye, but he wouldn't betray what he thought was response to a Yankee insult on his face.

Clint started talking again: "I said I liked the fall time of year." He looked at Leo. "I'll bet that summer in the mountains beats anything you'll find anywhere else, even along the Don on maybe a day when you were a boy. When my girl came 'home' with me one weekend before I married her —- I say 'home' because it'll always be so even if I move far away —- she was amazed, delighted at the beauty that was green as far as you could see; it was undisturbed then."

"For some reason, I want to get out of here and walk, simply walk, right through the whole countryside. We don't have a lot of green any more since the tops of the mountains have been shaved off to get at the coal. If there's any green left at all, I'll find it and . . . "

Leo said: "Looks like our little boy has gone back to sleep," and to the nurse, "We'll skedaddle for now but we'll all be back soon, like always for the past month."

"Thanks for all you boys have done," said the nurse. "It's good that you've defined just what friendship is. Keep in touch. He'll sleep awhile and then, glory be praised, he'll start out talking again."

And he would. Leo the Cossack was smiling again, like a minute ago, and Clint was hoping with his eyes partly closed to mock sleep, recall where he had seen such a big smiley honest face before, probably left over from that early time in his life, a day when honesty ruled in his country.

Oscar was back at the shop getting the paper to bed, Uncle Leo said upon his return to the hospital. "He'll do a story about the homecoming of Clint Greene, I'll bet," said Leo.

"Now that you're here and without any interference from the editor or anyone else," said Clint. "You can at last tell me about your days riding and playing like a soldier with your Cossacks, and how in the world you came all the way to our little burg buried here in the mountains."

"In time," said Leo, "and even why I came here for some other reason and found out I wanted to live out the rest of my days here."

"The editor's not here to take notes, but I'll be ready when you are more fully awake, at least in the bye and bye." Clint noticed the smile on Leo's face beginning to ebb, to be replaced by a grim and serious mien.

"All right, soon," said Leo. "But if you write about it and about me I want you to promise me that you'll let me read every word of it and ask you to erase what I don't want the rest of the world to know. I know I don't have a right, because you are a newspaperman and even if you've heard all the excuses, I'm not sure even that you have the right to it, not to all of it, which neither of us have a right to."

"Thank you muchly," said Clint. "We in this business have long been jealous of that little prerogative. I'm surprised that you, with a background alien to our western hard-won freedoms, mainly freedom of the press, know so much about it. But okay, I'll be kicked out of the Journalism Hall of Fame, but I'll have to agree, since you still have a right to privacy through the Constitution."

Like always, as a newspaperman, Clint wanted to do some hard background research on the Cossacks before he put Leo's story to paper. He also wanted to line up some ideas for a column he would be doing, an arrangement in syndication that Oscar had helped him put together before the wreck. It will be syndicated by a New York newspaper features agency. That would start right away," which pleased him.

He didn't know why but he felt unusually pressured to get his first column on the way before winter set in. He would write almost regularly about any major incident, an opinion piece calling for action against causes of climate change by anybody or government anywhere in the world, especially his own that would help alert people to the threat to their world and future.

As for Leo's story as a Cossack he believed it necessary to print in his own country because they are a people we in the west know so little about. Also, the Cossacks were once a free and hard working and hard fighting people before the Soviets tried to pull their teeth. Americans must be aware that it was in an effort by Stalin to silence their opposing ideas as well as their swordplay and addiction to battle against anyone who would try to suppress them.

Clint's own country was built by a once passionate, intense, slow-to-anger corps of men and women, though often vehement even to this day in reaction to a threat to freedom anywhere. Clint's loyalty to the idea, as it was with other Americans, was confirmed by a study of his own country's founding.

We, my dear fellow minutemen, he thought, acting along with those who join us, might awaken the people in sleep-busted reveille in early morning when they would be more acceptable to the idea. His people, he knew, would fight once they had tasted blood.

He was eager to get his hand on the keys once more, and to experience again the typewriter power he knew he possessed. He laughed. He knew that news people didn't have all the power they believed they had. Danged arrogant dogmatic hotshot bunch, he thought.

He also knew it was possible - that in one wee stone's toss against the still waters he could witness a disturbance he'd made, watch it fan out to touch the body politic, rouse the cynics and the indolent and all who have been too satisfied with things that are. It would be the beat beat beat call to battle.

Oscar said he had phone calls to make. First was to a lady named Doris, who'd been by the hospital at least once a day every day. One day she brought along her daughter, with some others. She told them the younger folks were her family, except for another daughter who lived in Huntington. "These two are my grandkids," Doris said.

Oscar had promised he'd call her the minute Clint came awake. Both of Clint's sons came in; a daughter had been in about once a week, down from Indiana. All wished to be phoned as soon as Clint 'woke up.' Oscar came back, said he wasn't able to reach Doris.

After a couple days, Clint said to try phoning Doris again. Sue, over at the phone company, told Oscar that she was visiting her daughter for a few days. "She, the daughter, was going through a divorce like her mother did seven, eight years ago."

"You won't have to call me," said a voice at the door. Doris smiled her way into the hospital room, said: "It got all over town quickly, but I didn't hear of it until a few minutes ago when I got home." Doris appeared angry that she wasn't here for the reawakening.

Doris said: "I've made arrangements, Clint. This very day two strong men will come to carry you out to the sunshine, and on to my house where you'll be until you're ready to fly again." Doris did not smile; her determination, stiff upper lip and all that stated a case well.

No one -- not Leo or Oscar, or the nurse standing there with a long needle ready to penetrate the skin of you know what, for sure not Clint himself -- was prepared for this big surprising bit of charitable exclusiveness. It hit the hospital room like an edict from Heaven.

Clint couldn't argue. He'd just got hit with a fence rail.

Doris said: "I talked to Doc Lewis. He said it was fine with him and his staff that Clint would get as good care in my hands as in here. His wounds have about healed as he slept out the month. The leg brace along with the pins in his left arm are about to come off if he proves he has no pain and exercises both every day, his doctor said. I will have help and a way to make him mind. I taught school for a while, you remember," she added.

"The doctor said he'll be stiff for a time. I have a neighbor who is a nurse and she'll be by every day or on call even at night since she's retired. Call her anytime, she promised, and she'll be there right away, if we need her. She will help him exercise his sore muscles until he is able to get up, and could administer his medication for pain if he needs it. The doc said he could get up now long enough to go to the bathroom." He said he'd already been twice.

"He needs sunshine and a place to walk on the grass —- as soon as you say that I am ready for you. My front porch has a good lounge chair. He can sit out there with his mint julep and observe the reapers at work in the cane fields just like the old southern colonel home from the war. I know I'm talking like Clint, but I learned some time ago that when he says it, everybody else understands it best. The rest of you are free to visit him anytime you feel like you want to be insulted. I see the 'ayes' have it, so get ready to help him get going."

Clint was looking straight into Doris' eyes and that victory smile of hers that slightly bent to the left side of her mouth. He knew he could get used to her teasing smile, even with her sort of raw dealing, which under its heaven-sent edict is possibly more a smirk; even her bossiness might be gotten used to. He'd gone through the same ways of other women, from many girl reporters and especially his once and only woman, a dedicated wife, who was his lifetime partner until she died. Ah, good old sweet Lily. I'll remember her always.

So in the afternoon they came for him, lashing him to the pallet that bore him to a place that the Lord in his kindness was whispering in his ear that 'you are going to enjoy since you like having a woman to boss you around. She'll feed you with a big spoon, stroke your hair or what is left of it as she whispers that she is "prettying you up because you can't do it yourself.'

He knew they were carrying him up about three steps and crossing the porch and to the back of the house. Right off, as he was able to count all the pillows on the bed, turning his face from the ceiling to the lacy curtains at the window, he recognized it as a woman's bedroom.

"This was my mother's bedroom," said Doris. "My room is upstairs, but I'll be on call from over there behind that door, the other side of the bathroom.

It was mother's sewing room. I'll have a cot in there and will be able to detect your every move."

Clint thought, 'What a predicament I've gotten myself into; she caught me with my pants down, that's a fact. She didn't give me a chance to fight back. Just like that I've been kidnapped by the Amazons and brought here for a fate worse than death. That's what Webster's says it is.'

"Are you in pain?" she asked.

"Nothing to brag about," he said. He added that he needed to go to the bathroom. Doris called out to a kitchen hidden somebody, or at least she came from where the kitchen ought to be; he couldn't recall that he had ever been in Doris's kitchen, but he must have gone there for a piece of pie when her mother was alive.

A tall woman, without any make-up, looking retired and slim as horseweed stuck out a hand to the man on the bed. "I'm Mollie," she said. "You may call me Countess." The Countess was smiling. "He's everything you said he was," she said.

Mollie held his arm as she walked him to the near bathroom at the corner of the room, and stood alongside Doris waiting for the knock indicating that he was finished. She said, "You're letting me do all the work, and you're coming in for the prize."

"You're not getting any of the credit, no matter what she said," Doris managed to interrupt. "You'd better hush before he hears you. Besides, he's mine, and you'd better not forget it."

When Clint returned, Mollie help put him to bed and pulled the covers over him and sort of patted them as she pulled them around his neck.

"The chair says thank you for introducing yourself," said Doris. In a near whisper, Doris said to Mollie but loud enough for Clint to hear, said, "You have made a friend for life in this old belly-snapper once newsman and stand down circus comedian."

Mollie had reached for both arms of the man on the bed, tugging slightly and becomingly graceful like an actor person from a lifetime on the stage, just like his mother would have done, and he was on his feet. She didn't offer to take his arm, but stood about a foot to his left and behind him. "Looks like you are on your way," she said. She followed him to the door, touching him real gentle-like, closing the door behind him. "Knock when you're through," she said.

Doris said that he should rest until suppertime. She would go and fix something he'd like for supper. She turned and asked him what it would be, since he'd been on a liquid diet for a month. "Doc said to be careful, that your stomach might not be able to handle solid food for awhile."

For the next few days this woman who reminded him in several ways of Lily was as solicitous as a handmaiden to the queen, keeping a proper distance and saying little, just like a professional. She allowed Mollie to talk the curative talk, the gentle person that she was. She appreciated Mollie doing all of that, but Clint was aware that a little jealousy might have crept in on Doris' part, and he had begun to let it bother him through the night.

At times through the rest of the week, he was aware that Doris had something of a stand-offish manner that puzzled him. Doris was like a sister, a mother, a mother hen always on board but tight in the talk, her mouth closed firmly, like a professional, as a Chinese waiter in a high-priced restaurant in Hong Kong or New York.

Through the rest of that first afternoon and early evening he could hear good ol' Doris busying herself with whatever women do to make it their duty for whatever it is to fulfill a promise made like on the day when he married Lily and all he and she together had to say was, 'I do.' She hummed as she moved about, dusting the tabletops, but not looking directly at him on the bed, yet he had the feeling that she responded to his every move, if it were possible to say so, to go about her chores like he recalled the same thing about his busy-bother mother.

If he had to go to the bathroom in the middle of the night, after he said that he could handle it, and he did, he would hear her stir as he passed her door. One night he woke up to see her standing over there against the light all woman with her figure outlined this side of the nightlight from the hallway from a front room to the kitchen, just standing there. Her full figure was carved like a classic painting by the masters from the darkened room by the night light behind her. Her body through the flimsy gown was exposed in its fullness without its birthmarks. It excited him.

To a mountain boy long months without a woman, and because of his injuries from the accident still unhealed, he grieved over his incompatibility to partake of this gift of the gods. The room now seemed colder, encouraging him to draw his legs toward his chin; that helped and he went back to sleep.

In an hour or two he woke up again; he had felt cold, now warmer, but comfortable, reaching over the covers to welcome an extra blanket that had been thrown over him.

He reverted to his siege of several nights without an ability to fall asleep, or to wake up after an hour and paint the ceiling with all sorts of oddities he had known in his past. The primary oddity, the gift of a woman awaiting the master's touch, barred him from even seeking the wee light from another room. When he again put his head under the pillow his forced distraction brought the roar of a big newspaper press which went on until way past midnight an d his thoughts went to a baseball game on Aiea Field in Honolulu as he recalled it, which was mainly a receiving area next to Pearl Harbor, and a serious game was underway. Those people out there really loved their baseball, especially when a professional league player now a soldier during the war was on the field.

He'd been brought down from the Naval hospital on the mountain to a series of games which they called the Little World Series for the island's soldiers and sailors. It was immediately after the big bombs were dropped on Japan and the war was essentially over and he was on his way home. He wasn't supposed to stop at Pearl since the end of the war was eminent and the ship got its orders to turn around and go back down under.

It was real baseball with a lot of league stars of the game, now all in service. Why was he thinking of those games when he had thoughts much more important to occupy his nights? The war was just over; he and his men were hoping for a ship to pick up the others of his company and take them home. It had been the third leg of a long journey from the Far East. About every ship in the Pacific was going island to island picking up men who were out of a war. In the meantime it was baseball. On the field, the DiMaggio brothers, Joe and Dom, and Ted Williams and Peewee Reese, helping the men forget war incidents of the past three years —- to some it was four years or more.

To Clint it was the brag of seeing a young soldier boy by the name of Harold Henry Reese, called Pee Wee from the days when he also was a champion marbles player, and a fellow Kentuckian. Men still in hurt at Aiea Heights Naval hospital on the hill above Pearl in pajamas and kimonos were brought down with lawn chairs to fit their sore backs or they were on the grass. He thought how thankful they must have been for somebody's job of care, not being sent out in the sun in hospital gowns with exposed behinds.

He couldn't sleep so he tried recalling good times from his Pacific visit, disturbed for the first time in Doris' house by the hint of a perfume which wasn't a scent he didn't know yet reminding him of Lily. It was a scent of woman, which he so breathed deeply. Its sweet subtle scent quietly surrounded his bed and crossed his nose like the lure of the island of the Sirens that called to Ulysses who begged his men to cut the lines that held him to the mast and let him go.

No. No. No. Please Lord let this not be happening. Clint thought of Delilah wondering if the walls would be tumbling down. He thought of a young Asian girl —- far too young to know such wiles which he knew by heart, coming naturally to her sex in spite of her age in the mid-teens. She was begging him to take her to America.

Stories out of the Great Depression had men leaving town on the midnight train going out from home to a wonderland in the north of their country where they would find a job. They were looking for any kind of job, digging ditches or felling trees with an axe or even cleaning up after horses on a race track. They told stories of their adventures on the rails, here and yonder, generally never lost in the promise until the end of a ride. They never said what they were running from but he suspected at the time that they knew most of the time that the sun would shine when they got there.

His mind was hopping around like a man on his deathbed; the ancient a dying man recalling scenes from his past life, all mixed up and ever changing; sad faces yet their worn clothing and one-time active muscles drooping from non-use passing before his eyes on the ceiling, from his bed on a midnight. Don't tell me I'm on my way out and that Doris has brought me here to die, or for the proverbial call of the sirens to Ulysses on his way hone from Troy. If he lived she'd expect the Navy Cross since she'd healed him all by herself.

He wished he could fall into a deep sleep and stay there at least through a few more nights in a Paradise he couldn't fully appreciate as he imagined it. He suspected the unthinkable would come as a result of her kindness that would lie on his chest uneasily despite all he could do to fight against it.

Each new dawn he felt fewer stabs of pain from the over-the-hill accident that now appeared to have sent his life into a new dimension. He'd begun to look to the once Friday morning coffee folk in talk; he would listen to tales of ships at sea, women in short pants, of round ball and golf balls on the green of what these men would do once they had an hour or a day in which to conquer a nation, of how the town's business folk would cure the world's hurt. They all, one by one, told how they would relieve evildoers and war makers of their precious seats of power.

The occasional muscle twitch reminded him that it could be weeks before he might function as he once did, even as he recognized that he had to fight in an aging body. Only today Doris and the Countess led him out to the porch, where he could observe life, what little of it passed the house hidden back of the trees on a lonely court. Still, he could hear the engines of civilization on the boulevard just like he was lying in bed in Doris' house.

The reward of the porch had come the day before when Leo walked over on his first visit and handed Clint his keys from his wrecked car. Leo said after a warning from the city council (they had to threaten somebody, so they came to Leo) that Clint's auto visible on the hillside made it look like a junk yard to the townspeople who complained that it was an eyesore. Uncle Leo said he'd thought about the keys before that anyway.

He hired Bishop's Filling Station to get a long cable and pull the car through the weeds and rocks and park what was left of it at his garage where it would sit until Clint claimed it. Bishop said it was beyond fixing up so Clint could drive it. Now that he thought about it, Clint would need to find money so he could buy a new or late model car. "I'm just plain broke," he said to Leo.

Bishop, by the way, Leo said, owned the only tow truck in town. That's when Doris said now that they also had Clint's house keys she'd have Nurse Mollie also known as the Countess drive both of them —- Mollie and Leo -- up the mountain to pick up clothes for Clint "to wear out on the porch."

Clint was glad he'd made his bed, surely he did because that was part of getting up to face the new day. He wasn't sure about his clothes, though. His mother had taught him to "always hang up his wear," day or night, when he went to bed and before his shower and when he later would look for clean clothes whether he was going out or not The clothes likely were on the bed, like every which way where former servicemen without a woman had tossed them.

When they returned, Clint noticed how both of them acted a bit sheepishly like they might have been holding hands. Well, well, thought Clint, Leo has found a new friend. Why did 'holding hands' cause a little blush?

Clint tried to recall what he was thinking when he lost the road and went 'over the side,' if he could recall any of it at all from that day. ('Over the side,' that's Navy talk, my friends). The sight of all those rocks below that could have been a final salute to the Corps surely would have bled him into a troubled mind. It was . . . nothing really, only a scratch: He'd gotten that phrase from the movies. The protagonist was lying out there on the ground as his girl friend held his head in her lap and he had to say something a hero might say.

They used to say over in Barracks Two when they got a reprieve back in civilization from a little spat with the enemy and the platoon was still bleeding red from the battle, "It was just a little old bee sting."

It had happened just that way before, or he at least was conscious of it that other time. Then, he'd recalled or at least told it that way: He was flapping his arms apparently trying to fly to avoid the same rocks only five thousand miles or so out on another Pacific Island cliff road. Why couldn't this Marine on a familiar hilltop road recall anything at all of that day that sentenced him to a month in the hospital?

He'd come closer to the end as a younger man in the Pacific jungles; he also dreamed of that day, and other stormy incidents for a long time afterwards.

Safe (?) at home, nightmares at first came after midnight with screams that startled the household. Now, it was day into night, and he still didn't know how he'd managed to live even if it was like his friends told what they knew about it, long enough for him not to remember. As he'd aged into the old soldier that he'd so suddenly become the screams of out there in harm's way somewhat abated.

For this he was thankful, since a scream like days of long ago from him would create a fright to Doris. Her neighbors would wonder what she was doing to him. He remembered too much of his life as a loser as people who knew him only slightly would say about him. During his first hospital stay, in the Pacific alone at night with noises from far away, he vowed to do it all differently. He'd kept his promise to himself and with his friends and certainly today with Doris a woman with whom he could come alive again.

He recalled the time he'd spent on the limbs of a tree in a heated land. He'd been given a tree, up high, for his watch. He was sitting on brittle limbs not far from the top. He worried that if he went to sleep, his screams and the cracking of limbs would alert the enemy and they would be all over his Marines.

The Polls of Heaven

If he had dreamed of any other incident he thought he had forgotten during the short time he'd relaxed against his will abed in hospital, he didn't recall it. He'd been asked by Leo and Oscar, even by his doctors and the nurses, what he'd seen in a dream that evoked the scream, perhaps during a semi-conscious moment, and could talk about it. Now why does everyone, including the hospital staff, want to know about that?

He was surprised at how alert he had been upon wakening —- right out of the fog, how he'd been so talkative. It was almost as if he'd been born again, though he was facing an all too familiar world even as he'd said before the incident that he, in a low period —- he'd told someone that he'd had about all he wanted of this world. Later he said it was his thoughts on the misery and failures he had witnessed from hither and war and the many disappointments in his short life that squeezed him.

To give him a few bright recollections to hope for, smiles thankful for deliverance, Oscar and Leo back at the hospital began talking about the visits of a woman named Doris, who had been by the hospital every day, maybe more often when they were not there: what she told them, with apparent sincerity and remembrance, was that she was an old sweetheart. They were surprised at this new knowledge, the woman, the incident, and right away jumped on it, kidding him, asking about this 'sweetheart' business:

"You don't hear that term much any more; this here now 'sweetheart business' goes way back, we thought it belonged to grandfather and grandma," said Oscar.

Later they would seek a way to ask Clint about it. He said, not surprised at the way they'd handled it, that he liked cherry cobbler. "What a way to avoid the boy-girl thing," said Leo.

Doris said for them to ask Clint when he woke up about what happened out on her mother's front porch. Start by making the big lover talk about the cherry cobbler her mother made that he liked so much, and she hoped, 'still did.' She said she had her mother's recipe book.

His children had come by to see him in the hospital and to call them the minute he woke up, or call one of them and he would call the others. The whole town seemed to be interested; Oscar ran a weekly report in his paper, and said that between editions people would stop him on the street to question him.

Clint didn't feel any bedsores or other pain, otherwise as a movie player man said on the screen, "Only when I laugh." Leo said Clint was flat on his back the whole time. He'd slept again, and with any threat of pain, the doctor said that the patient would be 'fine' by daylight. He cornered Oscar when the editor came asking what they'd talked about at coffee time when they'd gotten together at the caffeine hour for a cup of the wake-up. All Oscar would say was, "the usual." Both Oscar and Leo said they didn't cross the street to coffee every day.

Something Clint couldn't scare up lurked, pushing far back in his mind. He'd try but couldn't bring it to life. His mother told him once that to recall anything that was hiding and that dwelt way back there in his mind was to try and forget it. That didn't work either.

He sought to turn over to try for sleep, giving up on whatever was bothering him, but he couldn't move over his sore muscles. Clint's dreams, like always in his adulthood, were forgotten the moment he was awake, not like it was when he was a boy.

He allowed in every odd moment to put himself and his mind out on his porch at the cabin; he wanted to get back to it. Most leaves had fallen in the woods across the river that he could see from his mountain as winter also had told him when he was a boy that she was coming with her cold winds. He said he wanted to savor all the warmth of sunny days.

From his porch side he would have seen a few hunters across the way as they moved out of the trees into a clearing; mostly they were for squirrels; in a later season it could be for the deer. He knew the deer, fat and unafraid, were over there, and waiting. Too few, he reckoned, to ask hunters to lessen the herd. Time would wait for the state to say so, and let the hunters renew their licenses.

He thought of his dog Tom and even wanted to ask one of his bedside visitors to go get him before he recalled where he'd gone to while he was away, after Clint said goodbye to him. His dad's long letter during his days in the South Pacific talked of Tom's death. He believed that his loyal companion might have died of a broken heart, if dogs are capable of what most of us often fear might not belong by right only to humans.

Maybe he should have asked Doris to take him to his cabin on the mountain, but even that was too soon. He had dodged her before, later asking himself why he did so when he nearly ran into her on the streets for his occasional visit while downtown on a weekday.

Was he really so lucky then? Maybe it was plain out denial, at least for that moment. Doris called him once or twice before his accident and hospital; he was sure his tone had turned her away from anything she might have had in mind. He hadn't really promised Lily on her deathbed that he would never marry again. He told people they had an agreement. She had hinted that it was her wish. He had just sort of nodded and leaned over to kiss her on the forehead.

Doris never called back (not until she came roaring in like a Navy air show boasting in its noisy public brags of its precision flyers), but we're getting ahead of ourselves; He'll be talking later more about her surprising invitation to come sleep in her bed in her house. When it first came up, or was suggested in the presence of others in the room, he wondered if Doris had expected to sleep with him.

Clint's strength was returning, more rapidly than he had thought possible; he told Doris that he wanted to go home the next morning or the day after. She said okay but that she wanted Mollie to check him out first. She had promised that much to Dr. Lewis. He wanted to thank her in his hillbilly fashion, best defined as close-mouthed. He'd have to show appreciation for her good cooking; otherwise hands off, as it showed in her aloofness.

Two days later, in Doris' car, the four of them drove up to the cabin on the hill. Leo and Mollie were in the back seat; it was a bit amusing to Clint not to be too observant. Clint wondered about how his old buddy Leo managed to sit so close to Mollie like he was trying to absorb a by now forgotten woman's warmth on this Indian Summer day with degrees in the eighties, when he didn't need the heat. He was pleased with Leo's interest in a woman, as he wondered about the ultimate outcome.

They all liked Clint's back porch. Mollie said she'd drive up with Leo more often since he'd depended on Oscar to bring him to Clint's house when it was time for another meeting of OMEN. Clint would talk to the porch family about what OMEN was. Mollie had asked Doris about it and Doris said she didn't drink beer; she didn't feel that she had to explain.

Clint wondered why Leo always referred to Mollie as 'the Countess,' since he'd never heard her called that before the day he met her; he later learned everybody in the village called her that. He was surprised, thought how you could take the royal family away from the Russian people, but to Leo you could never take the old Russians out of the palace children's room.

Later Clint sat alone on his back porch. Not a thing had changed. It was almost like he had been up to Heaven, and had said something like, "If its okay with you, Pete (that's St. Peter), why not send me back down to my porch overlooking the Cumberland River way down there where the green tree line never ends? It is Heaven to me," he said, yet he likely knew less about Heaven than any other man or woman alive; he recalled a dream he'd had, or was it a dream of a dream about Heaven?

Before the accident his few trips downtown since he'd come home as he recalled and numbered were so very few. The others reminded how he went over the mountainside after dropping downtown maybe twice a week especially for the drug store 'club' in the city. The talk there and out on the street left him with a yearning for something else. He didn't know what. He said that in the future he would stay away sometimes from his reclaimed friends, go to town to pick up just what was necessary. Soon he would return routinely for small talk with his caffeine buddies. First, though, he would have to find a used car.

Upon one trip in the previous week with Oscar's courtesy necessary to get some house repair hardware, he had run into a much younger woman he knew, the daughter of a friend. It wasn't the girl on the train. He wondered why he hadn't seen her again, maybe like the angel she was, she simply appeared only to those she knew.

This young lady who had stopped him on the street just to say hello was being flirty, in subtle ways, he knew. Perhaps she was teasing, even offering a mouthful of the apple that he realized he'd better run away from. He worried like always that some few pushy (ladies?) of the town might think that by his own cooking he might commit serious error, like maybe poisoning himself; to date, there had been no casseroles, therefore no casualties.

After he'd left Doris and her kindness and was back down town on an errand he'd run into a farmer he knew, a woodcutter. The man talked of the laborer he had hired to help with the chores: "Good man with an axe," he said.

(Clint asked about him, curious since the hired man had been the talk of the town for several weeks since his encounter with the man, Clint was sure the farmer wasn't so fond of this hired help of his, but kept him on since he needed him.)

"Funny thing," the farmer said, "one morning bright and early the worker knocked on my door, said he wanted his pay. That week's pay period was up.

He said he was leaving. He'd been called away due to the death of a sister. I had never asked this fellow where he was from, or where his sister lived."That was odd, since the farmer knew his tenant had no transportation.

"Since he had a Hispanic name and look I figured he was from Mexico, South America or somewhere down there where they all spoke Spanish. If his sister had died she might be on t'other side of the border. We have lots of Spanish working around here; he talked like a Mexican, had a Spanish name, but somehow I doubted him; he acted a little like he was scared of somethin'. I paid him off, an' he took off, musta been picked up by somebody and he left the county for good. Nobody else in the town heard or tell of 'im," the old man said. He also wondered how the man found out his sister had died. "He never got mail."

Clint reckoned the farmer had to talk to somebody about it. He just happened to be handy. The farmer did say the man had a slight accent, "an' he sure to heck looked to me like a foreigner."

That's when Clint decided to learn more about Leo's fellow Russians, since so many citizens in town were a little suspicious of Leo and what they didn't know about his past —- until the poster came out. He hoped to know about the Cossacks by the next time Leo got around to talking about his life before the communists, Here was another man with a funny accent; maybe he wasn't what he'd said he was, but no, this man Clint's friend is a true and honest person, even if he is a Russian. But curious, he thought.

As he'd lain awake at night, after the nights when be was 'living' with Doris, who was often 'hovering around,' but somewhat at a distance when she thought he was asleep; that's understating how Doris reacted to his being in her house and sleeping in her bed. He thought of a lot of things that were unusual about the situation. On his way to recovery from chaos, in his mind he began to form what he'd look for to put in his log's pages once he got started on his reading about the Cossacks.

From notes in his log (entered during the countdown, to recall people who visited him during the days following his lengthy post-hospital stay, which is not unusual since his life had taken on a new dimension); he believed he could talk to and better understand most men. He never could understand women. He'd use his experience to look for the good and the better that had led him to his friend Leo today. He recalled the night a gun fired on Main

Street must have been aimed at Leo (in his first days in town they called him Jack) since a bullet just about came close enough to end his life.

In his early blizzard-like days and nights in the news business, all those people who generally kept to themselves until he so often encountered while on duty, would shock him by acting outside their real movie-inspired selves. These vile (mean) men described or even implied in old Mother Goose stories as wicked, leaves you trying to tell which was which. Was this a 'foreigner' of threat? Does Jack (Leo) somehow fit the picture of hostility?)

Clint was once more thinking like days of his youth at the picture show. Old Walt Disney in his movies would always have the bad guy come on transformed into a good guy (if he didn't fall into a pit by the end of the show, 'unmasked?'). Somehow, he is made not actually beautiful but more appealing all of a sudden.

What did Clint know about the Russians, in particular the Cossacks? A picture show on a Depression era Sunday afternoon was recalled as a Nelson Eddy songfest:

On this snow-clad day as seen on the local screen as well as outdoors at the drive-in in Clint's town, 'the ten cent' picture show depicted the singer with his fellow horse soldiers in a scene far from the battle and into a rare situation that lonely soldiers since the beginning of time and its wars had often dreamed about. He wrote in his log, first, what he already knew.

Eddy was a 'singing' Cossack. Clint knew from his early boyhood; he learned about life at the movies, that the star would end up with the girl after winning the duel over the bad guy's threats. The Cossacks were the best of the country's warriors, horse soldiers from the steppes of Russia. In the movies' first scene, Nelson Eddy, along with a bunch of his horse soldiers were in song as they headed to town, or maybe a tavern way out there on the steppes.

Actually, it was a small café apparently standing alone somewhere mainly built for the soldiers' business way out in the wilderness. They were going in for a bit of drinking, some horseplay, and for sure a little womanizing. That's the way Clint reviewed it. Eddy was singing -- the café was The Balalaika, named for the guitar. Its haunting music, the movie's definition, never let up. The soldiers again would begin singing along with Eddy,

They were men of battle on holiday with a good dram or two of vodka urging the night along. Music gave the scene a mystical splendor and the strings of the instrument reflected the same mystic as Russia herself, unknown to many American audiences now learning about her for the first time. (This is our review.)

Clint recalled that afternoon's movie as a display of the same cryptic (how do you like that word?) defining moments of every movie with a Russian theme he would have access to for just a few years to follow; subsequently, Russia and her people were shut out from the screen by the moguls of Hollywood. Clint's log only recently would reflect little more of the Cossack scene: Russian movies, primarily those that called for sympathy for the Russians, got banned.

(Mellow music and candle shine in the song by the Cossacks on leave didn't help either. As a newspaperman that's as far as Clint would go with the lyrics since the law said it hadn't as yet arrived to the public domain.)

He would meet Cossacks later, here, there, in picture magazines, but not on the screen. They all were generally embodied in the person of Leo the Cossack.

The soldiers rode in on spirited horses from the leveled Ukrainian battlefield and an awkward mud fight. Cossacks or cowboys —- they were the same in the imagination of teen-age boys.

From that time on, Western heroes in Hollywood's big celluloid Saturday afternoons would be for every boy in town who had a dime. The boy was roped into the he-man he would dream to be.

Clint did grow up with the Cossacks mostly in books, along with cowboys of his own West on the screen fighting with the long blade but without multiple rounds of the hand gun, ever singing as they and Clint rode with them in the wind. Until he ran into this fellow named Jack (Leo, no last name or even first name, not yet) whom he learned had been a Cossack and could ride like his ancestors and fight like them.

In battle against the Turks, Poles or Crimean Tartars, they became known for their battle cry, 'Volnista,' or 'Liberty:' a cry of 'freedom,' it was.

In 1941, when the Germans invaded, many Russians would welcome them at first as liberators. (We take louder notice of this 'quality' in subsequent notes by this writer.)

The Cossacks didn't exactly look with favor toward the communists who came to roost after Russia's civil war. During World War Two several Cossack army units were formed; how friend (Leo) Jack figured in all this, coming up in the next episode. Cossacks often were in the forefront against the Germans during the war, especially during the early Nazi invasion of Mother Russia.

Many Cossacks later would transfer their allegiance for military purposes to the Allies for and against both Hitler's army and the Reds. This meant that they would bear arms against their Mother Russia and its newer rulers, summed up in the visage of one man, known to Americans through the Western press as Joseph Stalin.

Following Germany's surrender one (regiment of 35,000 Cossacks} would take their families along now that they had a way to cross the border. They had migrated across Allied lines so the soldier in the family could enlist in the fight against the communists who'd held them captive along with others of various regiments who were called out. These were the 'traitors' who were rounded up and returned to Russia most of course realizing they would be executed. Many hid in the bush to escape what the Stalinists called one of the biggest betrayals in history; some in authority in the West had agreed to return them upon Stalin's request.

Clint would hear from Leo about all this. Clint, Leo and Oscar of the OMEN triangle began to talk about the 'betrayal.' Some historians said Roosevelt agreed to help Stalin round up the Russian fighters for their return. Historians who studied the minutes of the Yalta conference of the big three denied that the U.S. president would; he did not agree with the communists that the wayward fighters be returned.

Leo said later that there's very little in history that's been lied about as much. He said Roosevelt was a friend to his people, shielded them from the communists; Leo had been one of those Cossacks, they knew from what he told them. They hopped onto the reality of that in a hurry, recalling to Leo that he had promised to talk to them about his life on the steppes. That will be, let's say, the other two said, much more 'stimulating.' As a former soldier himself, Clint said it would be famous to hear from another warrior from another country in the same war.

The other friend the editor was younger possibly by five or six years than Leo. These days it is as much as a generation apart in the surrender of once cherished ideas and ideals; however arrived at. Ideas and loyalties can change overnight, especially in the weak.

Oscar said to a friend of the friends, "Look back to what a few years difference meant to the youngsters of the fifties and sixties. The GIs came home from the war and hopped right into bed. Boomers, a result of a nationwide liaison, asked for amendments to society's customs so long cherished by their 'elders.'"

"Generations in the making, the older beliefs had become a bigger part of American tradition. Respect for those older 'ideals,' life's ways that built a nation —- is what some had called 'my father's wars;' the 'making up years' on their part became antiquated and gave you a feeling —- to we elders —- that these kids couldn't wait to grow up and take over the country 'and everything that's in it,' "that's me, or it was, and I was eager for it to happen," said Oscar.

"Since he'd come alone to this nation of the free and the brave, Leo is as American as the rest of his contemporaries more so maybe since he'd been told to study us citizens before he could be an American through adoption."

The three OMEN men had begun to think alike; all knew, by instinct built into genes after an untold number of generations of war and peace, that man in cooperation with his fellow man is the one and bigger answer to survival.

Oscar gave them a funny piece one rainy day in which much of their future dialogue would wrap around the other two once they came to know one another more intimately. He said, after a question, but he was not expecting an answer.

"If we were a book, how would we three talk about pumpkins, Paris and persimmons seriously without women? I'm willing to talk about my woman. Despite what she did to me and our daughter —- how much she hurt me -- I'd welcome her to my empty bed, her love such as it might have been again a hundred times again to my lonely household, without a tear, without another heartbeat. I'd be asking her, as gently as possible, 'just where in tarnation have you been?'"

It was good that Clint had a fire in the grate that day of soul-bearing by three men of three very different wars, the same but different battlefields. A fire helps men think clearly, to 'bare their souls,' is the local way of saying it.

(We now see Clint again fully awake at midnight in a bed that would under other circumstances find Doris sleeping in, but at the moment he was alone. Clint, a man of deep thought, while warming himself by a home fire, is allowed to lose his abused life's thoughts, in the leaping flames,' often defined just that way in literature that provided comfort to a man's night bed, lonely, hurt and abused as dreamers, the forgotten and passed over of the world.)

The dancing flames offer an earthly optimism with its warmth to blood and dreams of many people who've never known a world that wasn't cold and full of pain. The watched flames carry many a sad day right up the chimney. It also asks for understanding. Somebody back in time said it better: "I didn't know him as a man, until we were silent together." A poet, long out of copyright, said:

"He who has no dreams is a man without hope." Dreaming, said by many to be just a word, likely is the most quoted, a 'Maud Muller' sentiment in any language, however said or put to paper by the poet, "It might have been."

An open fire dances and preens like a teenager getting ready for a first date. To the young and especially to the old, it is an invitation to be silent, but in a mind of many colors.

Each man before the fire could be thinking of a one-time woman in love. Clint knew that if he began talking about Lily or maybe Doris (now how did she get into this?), maybe just nigh onto a half dozen or so other women that he wouldn't lie about, or admit (as he viewed from afar), but he'd have to say those don't count.

"You should have known her," he said. "Lily -- I knew I'd marry her that first day I saw her; we stayed together all my adult years, until she died; nigh onto two generations, as today's society defines it."

"Had a business head on her, too; people in our town up in Ohio would never think of going somewhere else for flowers. Like the Japanese, she was an artist in a flowerbed.

She could arrange a bunch of flowers -- if you were an artist you'd want to sit down and paint them, like that Frenchman who was good at painting a bowl of the dainties, it was so appealing; you could smell the sweetness of them a yard and a half away."

"She could out-think me by a quarter mile, often finishing my sentences, if I had hesitated. She had the best smeller you'd ever meet aside from that old hunting hound I talked to once in that neighbor's back forty, and the best thinker. If some woman young or old stopped by the office and got too close to my face, if she were wearing a real strong perfume it would hang on sweet until I hardly noticed it on my way home. That is, except when I got home I'd no more than hit that front door than Lily would ask about my 'new girl friend.'"

"We got a lot of invitations to dine, to attend a party of sorts somewhere, and it wasn't aimed at lobbying the old editor on the other side of the table. It was because of Lily. People just wanted to talk to her; with some men it was just to look at her, and maybe wish. Far as I know she never once let any man get close enough to sprinkle holy water on all that beautiful hair, or to try and pinch her in a sly way."

"I asked why she hung around my office or seized a way to be in the same place at the same time? I said why would a woman with so many talents, so much endowed with Heaven's gifts of body and fair of face, why she would seek a feel of my muscles? She'd kid me about those two freckles I used to have. Why would she ever want to marry an old country boy like me, eh? That's when she'd click that tongue of hers. Do the same thing with her heels on the hard floor, and wink. Nothing in particular she'd say if I asked her; usually I got no straight answer, but boy how she made a feller feel like he'd just got off the train in Paradise."

"I'd come in singing, 'She's th' Lily of th' Valley,' and she'd say 'bosh' and 'wash up for supper, or I'll feed it to the dog,' so sooner said I'd sit down to the feast of the gods.

Yeah, that's exactly what I'd do," he would relate all this to his friends, reading from his log, "It is a blessing of Heaven when you have friends like these beside me now who'd never laugh at me when I got serious about my woman or told them about a dream I had just recalled."

This would be a good time for Leo Jack to start mumbling in an embarrassed show of words which you knew would come from his soul, the depths of the honest warmth of the god-like human who like himself could never understand today's timid ways of his fellow creatures about his days of courtship out on the steppes of his homeland.

Clint wanted Leo to reveal even the slightest feelings he'd so recently allowed in the presence of his 'nurse,' Mollie, the lady of the castle called Countess. By the way, how did he ever adopt such a term for a woman he'd just met? Clint would for sure have to ask Doris about it. Maybe there is more to Doris than is showing, that she's also a match maker bumping the two heads together, two friends who apparently had no need for bumping.

Instead, Leo started recalling a recent visit to his home at the hotel by the sheriff.

It was a clear day. The sheriff came marching up on the porch all arrogant quiet and authoritative, pulled up a chair like he was digging into dirt like a prancing horse prepared to challenge the champion bull chess player of Cumberland County to a silent jumping bullfrog match.

In his hand, the sheriff held a wad of metal of some kind. "This slug was dug out of the front wall of the hotel, not much to tell us, all mashed up like that. It was easy to find, though, since it was almost like a hollow-point round, which is made to splatter everything around it like a rock that somebody threw out into the still waters," as he called it.

"Nobody 'round here would've seen a hollow-point shell from a rifle since we used to see a feller or two who would've sneaked one in at a turkey shoot." The sheriff carried on with a mountain man's tone he might've used in breaking in a new deputy to the law. He got to the point: "I was wondering what you might know who took a shot at you, especially someone you might know doesn't like you and sneaked around in the dark to take a shot at you."

Leo sort of laughed, said: "I could say, Mister Sheriff, that I might think of a lot of good folks hereabouts who might be disturbed about this foreigner who lives just like any other American citizen just like the rest of all these people, especially one that never bothers anybody except in peaceful way of friendship and smiles with what he has for everybody. Besides, you're the sheriff. You're the law around here except for the state police you have to call now and then. Now you tell me who might want to shoot me in the dark?"

Leo said the sheriff put the slug into his shirt pocket and looked right skeptical as he got up, grumbling all over with the "loudest old grunting harrumph I had ever heard and proceeded to leave." He never looked back, slapped his gun holster as he hit the street, just like an old gunfighter out West in triumph after his last kill.

"I've known a lot of mean men in my time. They all had that killer instinct that made them such fierce warriors, like some Cossacks such good fighters on the battlefield.

"This sheriff of ours' may appear like he teaches Sunday school but never takes his gun off because he says a criminal might show up any time to do his meanness. He talks too much about his 'Creator,' which is his gentle way to speak of God without irritating a lot of people who say God is dead and want to fight about it. Commies started it like that."

Leo said he was not intending to be overly critical about mountain lawmen, because back in his village the most timid man of the village could be given a little power by the communists, and he'd become a danged hot shot and stalk around like he would hang the first comrade who challenged his authority.

"The communists had a knack for choosing the meanest critter living, and gave him a gun, which may be loaded or not, probably not with the firing pin filed off. He'd proceed to threaten everybody in town who might challenge him. Nobody in the leastest manner ever suspected him until then, to be able to carry out his threats."

"I've always heard that, 'give a man a little authority.' Soon we'll talk about such a critter who once was my good friend. He turned out to be so full of hate so that you would never expect him to have, and went about causing thousands of deaths of his and my people in the war. I'm not ready to talk about him, not yet. But soon, you will hear an explosion, and that'll be me."

The sheriff's office is in an old storefront across from the courthouse. You most of the time would see him just inside the double display windows, his outsized red necktie and his brass-banded leather holster with a forty-five pearl handle. It was just like the twin guns worn by General George Patton his hero for fifty years past and polished badge pinned against his left suspender(s?) or see the sheriff's body plastered so close to the door's window glass at first you would think it was a big cardboard cutout left over catching dust from his last run for re-election.

Clint nodded to the image as he passed on the street and was no farther than the corner of the haberdashery next door when he heard the sheriff calling: "Greene, come here. Come step into my office; I have something I need to talk to you about!" It was a shout, almost shrill, more command than request. Just the same, Clint would figure he'd better not ignore it. The next word was, "Have a chair, Greene, put your feet on the desk if you have to."

The sheriff said he'd offer him a cup of coffee but the county judge said they had to cut expenses so he knew the court meant for him to cut his coffee allotment like they also said his staff car was using too much gas and to spend his time serving warrants if he had to walk to the city limits. Clint didn't believe the first syllable of it.

The sheriff said: "I'll get right to the point, Greene. You are about the only person in town who could put my mind at ease. I have just been visited, yesterday afternoon actually, by two men from the Federal Bureau of Investigation."

"The FBI, huh, you don't say?" It was more an agreement than a question from Clint.

"That's right," said the sheriff. "They come down here and try to push me around, ready to take over like we don't know how to run the law down here. Both of these fellers came onto me like gangbusters. Right off the first thing they wanted was what my investigation of the shooting over at the hotel turned up. I said it left me with a little less hair but no noticeable loss of blood."

"I told them what I knew which was nothing except that I dug the slug all beat up out of the old hotel's decaying front wall with a pen knife. They demanded to see it I said I'd examined it for prints, but they wasn't any to be found. Also, you couldn't no way tell by the markings which maybe a kind of model it was fired from. One of them took it and said it had markings that it probably had a story to tell, that they had ways to dig it out."

"Did you know the apparent target, the man you all down here call Leo maybe Jack or the old man?"

"That's what they asked me. I was so taken aback with my eyes wide open to so little 'why?' I said nobody knew much about him; he kept to himself and that we didn't stop him at the county line and ask to see his papers from anybody coming in like 'Dolf Hitler did in Germany."

"They sort of took affront at that suggestion, said I was making fun of the FBI and they weren't going to put up with it. I said once more that I didn't ask him what he the man was doing down here. Yet I was curious, that I kept an eye on him like everybody else."

"We got a lot of strangers comin' through here all th' time," I said. "I figger they got as much right as anybody already here to go about their business in a real legal an' peaceful way.

"Then I asked them if this was one of those FBI protected cases where they hide a man from the Mafia and give him a new identity, mostly because I'd read he'd witnessed a killing and the mob would kill a witness. You can bet the fur on their backs stood out like a dog that just got kicked. Why were they interested in a feller who came among us carrying a white flag and nothing else?"

Clint was getting a bit amused, and was trying to hide it. He had to ask: "Mr. Sheriff, why are you telling me all this, me of all people in this here town of ours?"

The sheriff said, obviously anticipating Clint's question: "He's your friend. Being a former newspaperman to boot, I figured you'd already got that out of him: who he was and where he came from and what was he doing coming to this here town to what looks like he's gonna make our town his home for the rest of his short and natural life. I got it from them that the FBI expected me to find out and report back to them. They already knew, I'm sure, so what has this man done that is so important? These two FBI men were taking me for some kind of dumb hillbilly."

Clint said, "I accepted him as a friend. It was my thinking that when he got ready to tell me the story of his life, I'd not interfere. So that's the end of story, take it or leave it."

"Well, as an old friend, you've got to find out and report back to me."

It was Clint's time to bristle. "Well, you know he was born in Russia. That big show you read about on the window poster said that much. Or at least that he was a Cossack, so what else can you want to know about 'im?"

The sheriff said: "Oh yes, the poster. It was tacked on the telephone poles around here. I've got three of 'em, stacked over there in the corner. Someday I'll tack one on my wall."

"Why, you old recalcitrant, first you're suspicious of him now you are so proud of him you are nailing his picture to the wall like an old piece of paper like a wanted poster after you said you did and then that you didn't trust him because he's a foreigner," said Clint.

"I don't know what that word recalcitrant means. It better be good or I'll arrest you for insulting a peace officer . . . recalls it what?"

Clint said the word didn't exactly fit here, but it was the best term he could think of to describe an old stubborn sheriff and how he viewed his authority in his role as a servant of the people. Clint said he'd accept the sheriff as his friend, but he had absolutely no intention of reporting back to the sheriff or to anyone else about the customs or doings of anyone whom he called a friend, maybe even if he knew they were breaking a law of no consequence as this one appears to be as the sheriff said he was.

"As an American citizen certainly he could not be expected to betray any such confidential matter, unless he saw it as being harmful to the community. That's your job, anyway," he said.

"Now, Clint, don't go and get your dander up, but I need your help. The FBI is about holding a forty-five to my head and they like threatened my job if I didn't cooperate in their wishes; no, I take that back —- to their orders."

Clint realized that the conversation meant nothing, just as the sheriff's version of why the Feds implied that what they had asked of the sheriff was of no or little importance. He was beginning to wonder why his government was so interested in Citizen Leo. Since their questions were so out of a cola bottle, their interest was not evidence that Leo was a criminal. All indications pointed to Leo as their ward, even that, nothing more.

Clint himself had been curious about Leo's background. He had met some inquiring minds in his time during the international Cold War, but it appeared that neither Leo nor anybody else wanted to talk to anybody else about what could be just another big secret, on the books, because everything these days appeared as just another conspiracy. "Even ol' Leo," Clint said, "wasn't ready to talk about himself."

He reckoned that Leo probably was one of the smartest men he'd ever known, except for that fellow he knew who was an electrician for a coal company that worked a mine not far from his home on a nearby mountain. That electric fellow explained to him exactly how an atomic bomb was made and Clint had read and heard from all sorts of studies, chalk board talk that didn't say much at all to the layman; even Einstein could never make a guy understand it like Clint's old mountain friend. This fellow didn't even have an eighth grade education, but he knew all about electricity, using his trade's rudiments as an analogy.

It was time to go before the sheriff decided to pound the desk with his pistol butt.

Now what was that really all about? Clint put his feet on the floor knowing or hoping he might have left a little manure on the sheriff's desk. In his mind, unspoken, he'd want to thank the city for keeping clean streets.

"See ya, Mister Sheriff, thanks for our little chat." He hit the street without looking back to see if the red-faced burr of a sheriff, the people protector, might be after him with a summons in hand all drawn up legal with the power of the courts behind him like he was bragging about.

It was a clear day and Clint was determined not to allow any more distraction from any other nincompoop of the city. Fortunately there came a bit of something to help him get it all out of his mind. Clint was stopped on the street just this side of the drug store by a one-time feminine classmate. She'd inquire of his health and that she was sorry to hear about his wife dying and she was glad he had decided to come home to his hometown where his intelligence was so much needed, She did ask (about the casserole syndrome) if maybe he was getting enough to eat, if he ate properly by living alone like that up on the mountain. Clint thanked her and said he was doing fine yes ma'am and I'm doing real good yep real good.

He stopped at the paper office to let Oscar know about his talk with the sheriff and to expect a call from the law any time soon and to be sure not to carry his pistol. Oscar said his daughter was coming down that afternoon after the paper was out. He wanted Clint to meet her. Oscar said he'd talked a lot about Clint to her and she said she was 'dying' to meet him. Curious, he thought, that anybody was willing to die just to shake his hand.

Leo wasn't at his chair on the hotel's porch. He had hoped to lure his friend to the café down the street for a bit of talk about life and circumstance.

Truly, he could never understand why humans had to create a conspiracy around a little, no, not little, but friendship built on nothing more than trust and the recognition that we as human beings no matter who or what or where we live it is necessary for survival and the completion of life and living among others. He met Leo on the street headed his way.

Clint followed Leo into the café down from the hotel, right at his heels, noting the military spit shine of his boots, the square of his shoulders. His hands slightly clenched, almost a fist, touched the pleats if his britches when he halted his walk. He was an old soldier, standing out in any crowd.

His two inches taller than Clint's six one which was set in stone for lifetime as it was measured by a ruler tacked to a wall back of him when he was photographed for his Marine Corps ID card that gave Clint a feeling of military respect toward Leo. When they were seated Clint as generally by now held as customary when talking to a veteran of his war looked straight into the pale once blue eyes across from him.

Warriors he had known from his own war would declare that they could tell by looking into a former soldier's eyes if he had seen action in battle. As such a man not far from a battle's aftermath, Clint and his mates often witnessed in return fire the fear that was in the sweat of the enemy who had triggered it. When the roar of the battle is over and the smoke has blown away, the noise the smell the tears the fear the pain the hate even the respect you gave, was made of a piece of similar soul; as you weep, you must say:

"Forgive me, Lord, for what I have made me do." As you sat silent together, as you watched the flames' music in the fireplace together you were aware that the man at table with you held a facial manner of knowledge of your kind; you were certain he prays to the same deity, dreams of family and kin back there somewhere as they were in the sunshine as well as the smell of battle in your day that forever will remain in his nostrils.

Leo's lightly lined neck and cheeks, up close now rather than as assayed from about six feet, a distance from street or sidewalk to Leo's perch on the hotel porch, were nearer the slight skin shade of an Arizona sunset as you had at first noted.

Clint had his own formulation of the man's skin coloring. You would expect a leathery tanned skin made by living months beneath a sun that could be cruel as sagebrush or cactus known by the cowboy working a Texas cattle ranch.

Leo was a man of the outdoors. The man's presence up close could be intimidating as it might be to a small boy upon his first excited encounter with a hero of a war, or when he was face to face with Santa Claus. As a boy Clint had noted the same peaches and cream face (not feminine-like, please) worn by a preacher like others he had known when he'd first begun interpreting people in manner and mien, men and women he met along life's way. Later, as a Marine at a Pacific Navy base, he had noted up close the face of an admiral as he entered a land vehicle when Clint on temporary duty as a headquarters aide had held the open car door for him. The Navy man had the same (soft slightly pink) face. Leo's was an assured manner. It was like that of many corporation presidents Clint had known or met as a newspaperman. Arrogance you might say like it appeared that way to a celebrity-struck seaman? Yes, Leo did have a commanding presence. Yes, until the day there was evidence, a sign, that he'd broken through to the inner man and his newsman's intuition had not failed him —- he'd beheld a glow of sunshine and country boy humor, sitting there on Leo's face.

It was like a scene from afar of a desert oasis rising from the ever-pregnant sand; Leo reminded him of a puppy looking into a butcher store's window. Despite other sobering distractions in the man's demeanor, Clint could well imagine Leo astride a steed bred for war on the steppes of a Russia he was just beginning to learn about.

Leo's wide shoulders, his apparently muscled arms, his torso hidden by modern street clothes, were revealing the man as among the world's well-disciplined soldiers. He pictured Leo riding top hoof speed into an old-fashioned battle, like the cavalryman of his own U.S. Civil War General Jeb Stuart, holding his sword in a frightening pose of battle readiness.

Leo hadn't any need to talk to Clint about his role as a Cossack from the outer edge of Russia. He'd already lived up to a Hollywood agent's dream. If the South had won the Civil War, Jeb Stuart or John Hunt Morgan or Nathan Bedford Forrest, all horse soldiers, might be listed among the nation's vice presidents, along with Robert E. Lee as president. In his country (re-united in the South's image, of course), he could imagine Leo as head of state.

"I had no children," Leo said, "wasn't even married, though I've gotten my share of women, all any soldier is entitled to. A warrior can never be assured of staying in one place long enough to share that part of his life with a woman."

"I could have gotten married though; came mighty close after the war and still in my Englander's uniform, which I got in exchange for that scratchy battle dress of my Red Army days. The British in return for my contributions to their army made it possible for me to enjoy their civilian luxuries, and later, even a girl."

"They first gave me the chance to attend university, where I met her. She was a coed you call it, a classmate, and we got snuggly. She wanted to get married but therein lies the rub, like a disgruntled somebody said in a drama, probably Shakespeare, that not little happenstance roused the biased feathers of the old goat of a father. They were not of the royal family, but they lived on an estate and likely at one time were titled."

"Marry that communist? You'd think that I had the blood of the Reds' Revolution, still on my hands. They tried to hide her from me, pulled her out of school and I saw her just one more secret time before I left her country for yours."

"Early one night I left the library for my dorm and she jumped from behind a tree, right into my path. Threw her arms around me, and started crying. The story quite much ended right there. She said she must say goodbye, that her family must be obeyed. They must be first in her life despite her deep love as she called it, for me."

"A bit more of just talk and she disappeared from my life. I never saw her again. Just as well, I could never be much of a husband to her, anyway." That is all Leo —- maybe he was Jack then —- had to say about it; Clint knew it best not to follow up.

He thought of Oscar who on this sad day might weep over the past. This wasn't at all expected. Clint started to say he was 'sorry' to Leo, but he didn't. They left the café.

Oscar Bell Blues . . . on the other hand . . .

You figured the local editor, friend to Leo and to Clint, who helped form their classical trio, like the Three Musketeers, must have a wife or at one time had a wife. You remember him saying once that he had been over to visit a daughter in that college town up the road even though it was forty miles on narrow highways as such, which this story told you about.

At Clint's cherished spot on the hilltop above the river, the former soldiers three talked of the Countess and Clint talked more about Lily. They wanted assurance that the others (each) had once experienced a love life. This was an invitation to Oscar, as Clint had hoped it would, to talk about his own great love and what happened to it.

"Met in college," Oscar said . . . (Where else?)

"Back in my early student days we were darn near a revolution -- I guess you could call it that; the establishment did. It really was a bit of historic note right here in America." Those kids, with one step more, could very well have taken over the country. Their leaders needed just one more boom, a stronger firecracker, to make it happen.

"As it was, our leadership stood a bit above," he said. Oscar and his ilk wanted to be the big cheese(s). If he had gotten behind one trusted little girl or boy rebel, "If we'd given up a bit more of our own ambition to follow him, or her, and they had lots, hundreds really in their menagerie of charismatic persons, all Hades couldn't have stopped us. We scared our elders half to death. We walked away together from it. She and I were hand in hand in accord with our philosophy.'

"My dear little woman, whom I later married, lived with me for some years, bearing a child for the future, until that bad sad unanticipated day when she looked back, smack into the face of the maelstrom, and turned into a pillar of salt."

Clint asked, "Was it a yearning for power that encouraged the students to protest? Tell us, Oscar, had democracy failed to that vast youth multitude? They had told us by way of the press that they thought of themselves as sisters and brothers, they were of one big family, as I recall, at the same time telling each other not to trust anyone over the age of thirty?"

Oscar hesitated, like he was thinking, said, "I'll agree with the first part of what you asked, which came in the form of a question. It wasn't students as crusaders bent on rebellion that suffered the rash on the body politic."

"Out of the far west came the lettuce pickers, largely made up of Mexican peasants who followed the seasonal ripening of the crops; moving with the sun, you may say."

"Men like Martin Luther King were heard in their moment on the stage; too long had the poor, the dispossessed the huddled masses struggled without a champion. Like bronzed natives the Indian, a magnificent people who gave much to our society only to have the best of their nation, the people and their land, abused and destroyed as the deluge riding in from the Eastern seaboard came swarming over them in avarice, greediness and covetousness."

"These folk who had been repressed sought an answer from the country's nobility, officialdom within the establishment and without, from the rulers of the comfortable, but offering only weak and hackneyed proposals as a solution. As expected it turned into one more repression through laws created by politicians who sold out and controlled the courts and a majority of the lawmakers."

"We said it was time our country's leaders looked at the new facts of life offered by the thinkers among us. A surprise came in the vast growth in population which called for an update in democracy's acceptance of the fact of their needs."

"The Vietnam War came as a thundering reminder of how life was cheapened by its unfairness, its daily reports of death in wholesale piles of body bags. Human dignity was the next to go."

"I realized how my dear wife had been caught up in the new electric. She was excited by 'evidence' she found that their ideals were being accepted, even beyond their peer group."

"I began to feel for my country. By the time I became an editor, I no longer sought to re-write the first ten amendments to the Constitution."

"My wife's first-born in her mind began dying almost from the sad day we left the hospital. We started fighting each other for no reason, and upon such rare occasion that we made love together, followed by blame on both our parts that the other had contributed to the death of our baby. Ridiculous, but the baby's death had in its own tangled way created a cause that grew until the marriage in love was down in the gutter, despite the day she became pregnant again."

"After our next child, a daughter, was born, I sensed even stronger hostile feelings in my woman's every attitude, and in attempts at even small talk -- until that day when she wasn't there anymore. She had vanished from the face of the Earth. Ever after -- call it a generation if you will -- my daughter grew into a beautiful compassionate woman and is now in college."

"I did, some long years ago, receive a letter from a lawyer in Hawaii telling me that I was now divorced. That sir was all; that's it."

Clint said, "Are you in any way, subtly perhaps, trying to change the world through your pen to paper, especially in your editorials?"

"I don't think so, though I try to recognize the dignity of the individual, a civil and heavenly right of every man, every woman and every child, allow me to say, to life, liberty and whatever that has come to us out of a true revolutionary past."

"If I were called an idealist -- it would be a compliment. My way is soul satisfying but much harder. I wouldn't give up what I do unless I was dragged out to the street feet first. Perhaps you would call it surrender, not even to a day of real success on the stock market. Not for anything else the devil might use to tempt me."

"My idealism has never changed from the day I followed my wife, my woman into the streets in protest. It's changed though from what I later came to realize what we were doing with it."

"Of course I miss my wife. For years, as I sat reading and a knock on the door tore me way, I had hoped it would be her, and I would have welcomed her without a word of 'where have you been?' or 'have you finally found yourself?' But these things were never to happen; I do believe I've finally found contentment. My daughter has never disappointed me. She's happy."

"I've found new friends here, in this town. It's really back of nowhere. If Abraham, the log cabin boy and once country boy president will forgive me, the world out there will little note what I write in my diary, if I kept one, nor what I say here."

"To a younger man coming into my newsroom, or my art, or simply to where I now live, it well could be today a frustrating thing to him or her; furthermore it would be heart breaking, if he could see into the future."

"Past doctrines have been buried by the age of technology, snaring us into its labyrinth of multiple persuasions. Since the Cross, so many 'new worlds' have opened to man; he has found that the varied roads bring him to many a fork where he must make a life decision."

"That is not something come upon me while my woman and I were on the road. We weren't into thinking in those days of our youth. We didn't realize it —- maybe it was with me, alone, and I just assumed my girl, my wife, was in agreement. She really gave me at the time to realize otherwise."

"In retrospect, I know that we were letting our leadership, as thin as it was, make the decisions and we simply fell in line with a million or so other little rebels. Many of our rebel brothers and sisters never recovered from it and even today will tell you that they have no respect for the flag, for anyone who'd surrendered, willingly or not. They bled themselves back into the overall society but they never forgot their days of ill-defined glory."

"I generally like what I do. Newspapers are pretty much doomed. The electric age is too deeply mired in the day's routine and we must either find a way to change with it or die, even though for most of us it already is too late."

"As for marrying again, I never really considered it. I did love my sick wife; you probably agree that I loved her too much not to consider another woman in my life. I've had a lot of one-night stands, some with much younger women who would make a man a good mate, a wonderful wife. Others, I was a little disgusted if anything soon after the affair when I felt lucky not to have gotten caught up in a new marriage that I knew would never have amounted to anything."

"My daughter never encouraged my getting a new life with a woman, but said not long ago that she be forgiven because she might have stood in the way of my happiness. I told her that as long as she was alive and healthy and satisfied with any decision concerning her own love life, that decision would be exactly the thing that would keep me happy."

"She likes this town and I believe she would want to come here to live when she graduates, if we could find something for her to do here, that is, a job that would help her grow and be of service to society."

"As for myself, I'll be run out of town maybe even tarred and feathered. That could be sooner than you'd think. In the newspaper business every time you write an editorial you lose a friend or a subscriber, even though some of the great American public out there will stick with you through the devil's curse."

"We are a strange breed, we writers and editors. We know we will never get rich, but we try to compensate by saying we are doing our part in helping keep the Republic intact for the next generation. Most of the time I say hogwash, because we realize that we could never make it anywhere else."

Clint said not long after 'pointing with alarm' (that's news family talk) to the decline in his countrymen's faith in the newspaper business and the men and women who went on believing in front porch delivery of the news to the two men on his cabin porch with him who have never given up."It's time we got down in some way to the business of saving the world," he said.

"That is what OMEN is all about, and we'd better do something with it or it's going to slip away while we sit here talking only about ourselves and hickory nuts and Kentucky bourbon and pretty girls and loving women and cabbages and kings and talking nonsense about men like Il Duce."

Yet he knew that somehow he could catch the moon and steal its midnight beam and run away with it to hide it in his cave. Then why was he so restless? Didn't he still have his allotted acres of the present world to conquer?

He said that when he retired he would make a big dent in books he had reserved for a someday. As he looked at the huge stack near his chair by the fireplace, if he managed to subdue three maybe four a week, the best-laid of reading plans would never happen; if he did little else in what he figured was not more than ten or twenty years that he had left —- his echo told him it was impossible.

His mind was way out there somewhere in never-never land. Is this frustration what the magazines' health pages call the onslaught of senility?

His friends decided to lay off friendly bother as much as they could, at least for the first few days, allowing the old man of the mountain to heal his body, as well as what was evident, to be a confused acceptance of the world around him, or against him.

They talked for hours about what they presumed to be simply parlor talk among their peers over coffee down at the occasional escape to the drug store, but the now few visits a month was as much as Clint wanted before he went back to his cabin.

He told Oscar the dreamer who owned a bench at the railroad station, where he would sit watching the trains come in, and Jack called Leo, who climbed up the beanstalk, that he needed the time to rest his mind and that he'd soon be in touch, especially since nobody got off the train. In the meantime, he would dispatch the weekly column he'd contracted for -- as they'd been in on the plan, he waited like the other two members of the blessed self-appointed celestial staff, the real thinkers of OMEN came on with new ideas.

Jack (Leo) asked him to stop by the hotel for an inspiring game of chess: "Takes your mind off your troubles. Yeah, and in just two minutes you'd have me checkmated. You'd sit there gloating in that Russian shut mouth grin of yours. That's okay for a little back rest, but for gosh sakes man, this is serious stuff. Which came in last, the chicken or the egg?"

The editor said: "Your column is due by noon next Monday. Keep the syndicate off my back. Our attempt to save the world is weighing too heavily on me at the moment as it is. You realize, old buddy, how much a deadline means in this business. This is the big guys we're dealing with; they will not accept any excuse however much you are in stress. Come on pal, forget everything else and get 'er done."

Clint could manage the semi-weekly surrender of his blood and tears to the corporate owners of his soul —- you have to type it out in tight little phrases that fit the current political fashion (some say 'the correct') as it is understood in the big press board rooms. By now he had begun to think, write like them. That means he is now into 'doublethink.' Biblically it is a conflict between God and mammon. He was prepared to resent board talk that his column was not doing its job, despite the recognized best approach to doing what OMEN is about.

Still, it is better than what came off the street in oily blandness that stole its way over the sidewalk into his working office above the printing plant up in Ohio during his last days in the business.

He often was tempted to do it the plebeian way, invent purple passages for his column, believing for the first time that a bit of high school journalism is what the people want. He'd always made an effort to avoid an attempt at prosody writing, even as the successful in his profession poured it on. Time after time he tore up his first thoughts and squeezed his mind to find his way again —- in street plain talk.

In the quiet of his cabin, the mountain formed an invisible arm to surround the writer at creation and shield him from gloom and frustration, defined as 'depression' in current street talk and mass diagnosis.

When you write about something you really truly (cliché) believe in, the brain comes alert and the discourse strikes the page like a fishing rod with line thrown across a moving trout stream.

Clint the former newspaperman knew by now that the average man or woman out there cared little for or depended on any woman or man or any other source as their opinion mentor. That is, he might already be in agreement with his ragged source, based on what the press in black type cited as the blue or red tinted dogma, the right or the left, liberal or the overused 'uneducated,' the eager or the nonchalant - whatever the nom de guerre.

Finishing his weekend column, he ran it downtown to Oscar's desk. The editor would be standing in the doorway to his office, arms crossed. Clint said he wanted to try out his 'new car,' a clunker if it could be called that, but Oscar said he hadn't time to listen, since he had a paper to get out.

Clint was breathing deeply as he walked up the blushing worn steps of the guillotine before turning to face the good citizens sitting in the front row, the arrogant the rich the sun dried faces the haughty revolutionists whose eyes were an embarrassing field of eager uncut yet sparkling live diamonds, each challenging him.

Clint knew as well as Oscar the editor, who in his silent sarcasm yet with a grin that this friend the former newsman who in his old age needed an extra shove to meet a deadline. Oscar would laugh just like you'd expect from him.

Clint needed a distraction like a high grandstand seat at the Kentucky Derby, or a swim in Lake Erie or Herman's Pond, the kiss of a mermaid, perhaps; maybe a long giggle over a good joke.

As well, he knew he was running down the railroad track just ahead of the afternoon train of pickup cars pushing for speed with a load from the last existing big coal mines in the hollow just behind him.

The column wasn't doing its intended job. He needed to tap the secret dynamics of nature, jazz it up, not the column but the idea. Others told him he needed a 'gimmick.' He'd never thought of it that way; sounded cheap.

Today's readers and viewers would see right through it and begin to distrust him. In the old days it was the chair by the fireplace that had so inspired his father.

He'd go out to the porch high above the river; sit in the big rocker. He would not think of anything if he could manage since a brain spell of nothing told him that simply attempting not to think was adoptive to the best thinking. He had been surprised in his earlier writing sweating heart-swelling moments when he needed a word or sentence to say it in a good old hillbilly way, it was already on paper laughing at him.

His non-thinking paid off. Right then he recalled the face of a girl, woman now who upon his first week's return to his old home and their 'accidental' meeting on a downtown street, had blushed, "Don't you remember an old sweetheart?"

That man-woman business as he recalled it one day to his friends brought on some big hee-haws, who even after Clint's stay in Doris' house had created a wee bewilderment about human kindness to an absurd level never before reached by anyone they knew.

His friends still kidded him about it. They had gotten to know her during her several routine visits to his bedside at the hospital.

(Sweetheart is a term that in the childhood of Clint's country summoned up a liaison or partnership between two people, preferably mixing up the sexes, boy and girl, man and his woman. The term largely left the American vocabulary after the fifties [of the Twentieth Century]; too bad, since he'd liked it better than new terms like 'lovers,' which for his gang had a tantalizing and comfortable meaning nevertheless to its drug store stool use.)

(In the earlier part of the same century its young couples during the Great Depression found their amusement at the picture show and dreamed along with the screen, especially a Sunday matinee when they'd come face to face [in a semi-light more conducive to romantic really its own reality] with Nelson Eddy, singing with Jeanette MacDonald: 'Sweetheart, Sweetheart, Sweetheart.')

After he'd left Doris and her hospitality for his home on the mountain, he felt she was avoiding him when he walked onto the town's main drag. He was to blame since he hadn't made an effort to call and thank her.

Was he prepared to offer some fanciful thoughts, called 'romantic' in his native language? He waited for the confident feelings he of late strove so hard to find, a landing place for it in himself; he tried especially to discover that undefined feeling it was that he earlier had for girls he knew in high school, who later turned into women whose bodies made his blood boil. He was sure these feelings still belonged to a new generation.

Since he was out of practice, throwing his hesitancy to the ebb tide, Clint would call the girl named simply Doris; she's more than a girl, yet all woman now, and he would suggest that they together go somewhere far away.

"Doris? This is an old sweetheart calling to ask you for a date," another term lost to history, the pseudo romantic history of his time. "I have two tickets to a stage play put on by students at that quaint little Baptist school over in Mountain City, Tennessee. I won't tell you the name of the play, mainly because it is only said of it that 'the play's the thing.' What's important is that you and I go there together and maybe just look longingly at each other afterwards."

Clint couldn't believe he'd actually said all that. Lily would be proud although she for sure might not approve of the competition.

"We could have a bite at that cozy Greek café just off the highway going in and get to the play by curtain time," continued Clint. Then it was an extended pause before she'd even acknowledged that she'd been listening.

"Sounds exciting," she said, "but I will need some time to wash my hair and get into something seductive. Suggest a time to pick me up. I'll be ready."

"Oh, and by the way. We will be breaking the law. Just be aware that I'll be taking you across the state line for 'immortal' purposes," he said. Oh boy, you can't say Clint Greene is out of practice, if he was ever 'in practice.'

Doris laughed then said, "I'm glad you said 'immortal' purposes. I will have to think long, even wistfully about that. With two M's and a T or without, I expect either way will give me a longer life."

Perhaps this is just the reprieve from the writer's block he needed. At its very best it would save him from the guillotine. He'd noticed a nervous bit of surprise in her voice yet he knew she was waiting for his call. She'd answered on the first ring. She acted surprised.

He dropped the phone onto its cradle, after telling her he'd bought a car, "Couple years old but runs good. Need one these days; Detroit has us by the petticoats." He stood for a moment looking through the porch window to the low afternoon sun.

Clint thought of the years his family had lived without a telephone. Now that the wires have been run up here, he thought how it was easier to talk to a woman without a first face-to-face encounter. All he could think about, examining the instrument upon which he had rested his hand, was the phrase "ah, shucks." Lily never left me alone with another woman; she, Lily my love, was still fighting from wherever she was.

He was forced to squeeze his eyes shut to clear a scene from never-never land, simply nowhere it was, could not be, that had briefly distracted him from the anticipated evening ahead.

What had passed like a theatre projection camera shot to the wall: people on a white sandy beach, a scene among tropic palms and a sun-blinding reflection created just for his Marine outfit and a few natives far out in the Pacific. It was so clear he felt as if he were among the people who were in fear of something they didn't quite understand. A man had taken a child in his arms and was running with her through the trees to a hill behind them. Great waters came in with a mysterious darkness, destroying buildings, everything.

Clint shook the vision from his mind. Or attempted to, but the scene was pasted over the vision of the woman he'd just left on the phone. It was so real he felt the pull of safety toward the hills back of the hotel where the man ran with the child.

His feet were moving like the people in a rhythm of panic. He tried to recall the movie that must have placed the scene so solidly in his memory. That must have been what he was viewing. Later he was to read in the papers of the incident, exactly as he'd seen it.

With difficulty he returned his thoughts to Doris, saying aloud that a face and body of a woman, which could block out the drama of all he'd seen, must mean something to an otherwise powerful invasion to his thinking.

Doris stood in a dark outline in the hallway behind her which came from a wee light from the adjoining room where she had been sleeping yet awake now to note that she was doing her job as say a nurse in a hospital somewhere looking toward Clint 'asleep' in her bed. The weak light nevertheless just strong enough to outline each curve and curse of a woman enticingly calling to him from a land of nevermore.

By the time he'd crossed the town bridge at the foot of his mountain and turned west toward the old residential area, he was sure the scene he'd partly created in his own mind was shown in the far-off ocean's wayward movement toward a people in like panic what he had just witnessed was by now fading from his conscious.

It was about dusk in the valley where the river flowed. All but the town's movie house was shut down for the end of day. The town was at home and dinner. In the west, the sun's few scattered rays lingered over darkening hills; in the mountains you didn't get the rays of a setting sun like the pictures in a church calendar. The sun just disappeared behind the tallest mountain or shorter hill then it was dark, well not entirely; he was recalling the sun from his year or two in the Pacific doing the same thing.

He wasn't surprised to recall Doris and her mother living together in the large frame house on the court he thought he'd remember for the rest of his life. He felt an unfamiliar warmth move over his body. He didn't need to ask why, except to say it was the return of an old itch, surprisingly almost forgotten.

Right off she volunteered the why of her little previous and mostly secretly kept story of marriage to another man that just didn't work out, beginning with why she had left her husband those many years ago. She said she felt she had to tell him. She could have talked of her life when he was abed in her house, but she hadn't, which puzzled him except that she accepted the fact that she had him there because nobody else would have helped him in his recovery.

She described the bitter aftermath —- like the usual bitterness of the dime novels and of late, modern paperback successors among adult romantics -- the divorce and the ill-chosen 'dilemma' of a divorcee.

Then came, with 'all consuming' hard luck —- how she'd fed her family, managed to keep body and soul together, and in school, and clean and safe.

Said her mother left a hefty mortgage; repairs were needed. She had lost her precious vitality. Alone and no promise of how she would build new bridges, she was by now drained completely of assurance of a future. Her mother was ill and needed her, so she came home.

That's all that could be said about coming back to a 'lost' town in a far valley. Her room had scarcely been touched since she went away. Her two teenage girls —- one of them later became ill and needed her mother's nursing skill. For a short while both she and the daughter thought she was going die -- they'd fought over her old room, as predicted like in the old movies. Doris won that battle, though, by creating a contest in which the winner took all, including the room.

After her mother died it was too late to rejoin a career. Besides, her daughter when she came home brought two grandkids and they all would be getting into new expensive ways. She didn't add any more to the history of her family, except for a fact here and there, and he never asked where they were now.

Clint didn't need to leave his car to open a door for her; she was out front and halfway down the sidewalk, her long legs in stride clinging and promising as the tight skirt made all that possible to a man who, like himself, was proud of it because it could be his. He noticed if he hadn't done so before, that she still had her figure, all-American.

On the road into Tennessee, little more than a slow short drive -- it doesn't take long to exchange life stories even after years away for each of them —- almost a quarter century; little talk during the first miles, then hemming, some haw. Each was full of himself, and herself, interrupting almost like a child listening to the mother in a fairy tale involving the child.

Clint punched in the dash radio hoping, he said, "to pick up some music, something soothing to the boy-girl senses," but he didn't add, 'with just a touch of smooth skin and darkened bedrooms,' like he started to. The music was coming in from the college's FM station: a little dinner music, maybe: really a little night music to dim bad thoughts of the day? It wasn't for a question; he'd asked, just talk.

Clint was trying to think of something amusing to ease a serious mood being created by the music:

"A little Bach might lead to a Bacchanalia; that's a one-time Roman festival in times ancient as an invitation to frenzied dancing and a lot of revelry, often it was an orgy that the Romans were famous for. Maybe that's why the empire fell."

He was not looking at her. He kept his eyes on the road and both hands on the wheel, seriously, nervously quiet. He was waiting for her to do some more of the talking.

"You don't say," she said. From the corner of his eye he knew she was watching him with a wide grin that gave away her thoughts, her reaction to his off-hand comments, which weren't as serious as all that, just small talk up from the belly, thought this old hillbilly.

As he had driven around the circle where her house sat at the end of a cul-de-sac, he saw the figure outlined at the glass door that opened to the soft lighting of the front room. He'd thought, but briefly, how eager she must be for male company. By the time he'd put on the brakes, she was here, outside on the walkway.

Her years, which were near his, demanded some dowdiness. He expected it would be so. As she came closer to his car at the end of the walk, he was surprised at what she was wearing —- it was a dress from an earlier time in America, of course, where dress changed in style so often; but on her it looked just right for a night on the Riviera. In many ways she was of the middle forties, suddenly she was of today.

He had remembered her in a dress back in time, which is how he wanted to recall all budding young women from his youth. He thought of a dress on a young girl was like boys' approach to puberty wearing silly hats and black white shoes called moccasins. He'd had a pair of those, the first shoes he'd ever bought for himself by doing little chores and real jobs for the Main Street apartment people. Beat those brogans his mother always bought for him, mainly as like his grandmother purchased in town for his grandfather.

She hadn't apologized for not asking him in first before they got on the road, but softly closed the car door and touched his arm. Her high heels, yes, had created a tantalizing tattoo on the concrete, a woman's way of saying I am feminine and 'here I am.' He felt its rampant wild throughout his old body as about twenty maybe just five more years than that before time had begun to drop away.

Silk stockings and high heels, designed to stir a man even of a new era, which she for sure knew would recall in him an earlier thrill. He was thinking, in tune to her thoughts, I'd have painted this face this body as it was, on the side of a World War Two bomber.

He hadn't a plane of his own out in the Pacific, but he saw the figures on the sides of the big airships as they began to join the men on the exotic islands now held by him and his buddies. He thought as he looked at the painted figures, a little touch of nostalgia but more fanciful than that, dream of women really, like they didn't already know what everybody was fighting for.

THE POLLS OF HEAVEN

Not far along the road, in his mind he was making love to this woman; he said, since he hadn't said it before (hey man, this woman like any woman I reckon sure can mix a man up), "I'll keep the music on low. I like to listen to good music as I keep rolling right along. Between those hills back there, I had hesitated to change the dial, since any radio signal would not be coming through enough to make any sense to us."

She said: "Oh, I love the music." He could feel her body moving in the seat to the music, adjusting to a soft silent dance in its rhythm, if you picture someone dancing even silently, to Bach. It was a lengthy pause before she was telling him the subject would right away take a different direction.

Then, "Clint," she said, "Have you ever thought at all about getting married again?" Oh-oh, he said to himself as he felt the kick in his stomach. He wasn't sure how to respond to that little bit of surprise (premeditated bombshell?).

"Not especially," he answered. "I said that after I lost Lily I would never re-marry. So far, I have never even considered it; how about you?"

"After my divorce, especially the misery and what I went through in its unexpected aftermath, I could very well have said the same thing. I enjoy the company of people that I like —- both men and women -- so let me say I've become comfortable with my life. But I do have more of my share of loneliness. Oh how much I missed in the silence of the night the company of a man. You won't believe it, but that's when I thought so much of you, and the little girl times I had with you."

The road had straightened out a bit. Despite the power jumps of the music's teasing promise of crescendo, then the calm, held by or like the music. Clint kept the vehicle below the road's invitation to rev the engine to a higher speed, surprisingly realizing that he wanted more time out here alone with this woman. "Is this a part of life that I've been missing and never knew there was a solution to my restlessness?" he said, but only to himself.

He thought, 'I really believe she is enjoying it, and likes my company.' He allowed his thoughts to roam, consider a likely performance in bed, and this bothered him as he thought of the nights with Lily. 'It's been many long months since Lily died, and I've never taken another woman.' He wasn't sure that he was still capable since his age like it was said to be with other men who were crossing that same barrier now included him as it was with many good men.

That latest step to time of no return would rule out a satisfying future with a woman and to him as well. So again it was a struggle to think of something else.

They both were surprised that no waiting line had formed at the café, an expectation based on its regional reputation. Their repast at the small country retreat was excellent. He felt that she enjoyed it. She said she did. When she ordered the cheapest item on the menu, he thought of his mother, in the few times she ever left the small house on the mountain and accompanied he and his father for dinner in town: always the less costly, when he knew she would have enjoyed a more expensive plate with a steak, maybe. Yet, this pleased him.

For a woman living alone and sentenced to her own cooking, he'd expected Doris to hit the table like a starving woods wolf. But, no, she was quite restrained. She treated the food with respect. He thought that little bit of manners always brings its own brand of satisfaction to a man. He wasn't surprised that she selected the lowest priced course on the menu.

As they waited for their food, Clint said, reaching across the table for her hand, "I'm staring at your face. I hope you aren't embarrassed as I study you, maybe playing with your emotions."

"You can play with me in any way you like. I'm receptive to any desire you might wish to display," she said.

"I'm looking into your soul," he said.

"Well, if you find it, take me with you."

She's got a terrific sense of humor, he thought. He liked that in anybody.

The play in spite of it's quite overmuch interpretation of the Muse that governed the amateur at work and on stage, added up surprisingly in its bruised emotions to three or more hours of pleasure of a sort, he wanted to say. Clint the rare critic had not experienced such aroused feelings since many seasons ago, really not since his college years.

As he searched her face, he was surprised at what he saw there, recalling the words of an art instructor from his college days who said that few artists could ever put on canvas what they saw certainly felt what they believed they had discovered in the subject.

The art prof said that in a time beginning in the lives of the great artists in western European culture, that artists, painters and interpreters of the human body, could not receive and create in a universal reception of their type of art from among the elite and educated, such an emotion interpreted on canvas. He said such talent was reserved for a few, such as Leonardo da Vinci, but even da Vinci had to employ another artist to paint the hands.

Nevertheless, Clint believed he found what he saw in the face of his wife, Lily, and here it was once again in the exposed character of Doris, his dinner partner:

He saw an inner beauty; it was with an unpretentious and chaste character of an evasive soul that placed a low interpretive estimate of herself to the outside observer. Here was that frontier woman who followed a husband to a new land to support him and their children in an effort to make a home in the wilderness.

Doris the woman was 'open' and graceful 'obedient and virtuous in interpretation of her welcomed century's standards. He had no intention of telling her any of this, not if or he decided that he might marry her. That very well might never occur. He'd have to talk it over with Lily.

He knew that after her divorce she had to raise two daughters with no support from her former husband (without alimony), that she didn't come from a money family.

He said to Doris, "A good time this night has been. We'll have to try it again right away, sometime." At one point back there he said he "felt like he was back in college and watching a bunch of amateurs in a play that spread their talents like gravy on ice cream."

A few miles out of town on the way home he extended his hand, feeling for her. She as quickly found it, and squeezed. The warmth, the softness, the giving and its promise, ah, a woman is all that. Of such, nations rise and a people and kingdoms fall.

A man's intentions and goals in life thus can change as fast as a politician's promise. A woman's touch, soft hands like all that is good in life gives something of a deep and sane feeling that nothing else in this life matters; just this. The only blessing he would dedicate it to, as is simply said and so it is written, has to be . . . fate. How surely it is appointed to be, since the days of Eden, a thing between man and woman.

Old Scratch sure did mess up in all but one important corner of that one.

They both had been silent for several minutes. They were out of the valley now nearing too soon and with undefined emotions, their home town.

The music and with its cymbals and symbols, horns and strings and drums came roaring through as the walls of the canyon yielded to it. Clint as soon touched the dial.

Music, now soft like the ripples of a wheat field in the wind, gave promise as to the Don Juan in all men, even this aging lover man. Ahead of them and the end of the road of a tremendous evening, was the town with its critics and sore tail townspeople. The moon at full was up. Its smile across the river provided intermittent soft sparkles to the waters in the night. Its reflection of moonlight encouraged sleep, like that of a tired child, innocent yet mysterious, dreams of always.

"Sleepy?" he asked.

"Some, but I don't want to give up the night."

He didn't respond in spite of its postscript invitation. He knew he wasn't ready for this, could feel his face reddening in embarrassment. Someday soon he'd talk to her about it. He walked her to the door, holding her head in both hands as he bent to kiss her good night. "Is that it?" she said. "We're right back to where we were with forty a hundred years to live. Is this how it ended with Caesar and Cleopatra down in Egypt land?

"Is this the movie moment when Rhett the he-man gathered up his sassy little rebel, carrying his little wife Scarlett O'Hara, up the wide stairs to bed? Was panic the ancients would call it? Oh, that old biblical time like this honored familiar black panic."

She's not giving me room to hide in retreat, he thought. He knew from long ago that a door to a woman's boudoir was a closed gate to man's dreams of becoming president of the United States, but to her, rather, queen of the Nile. Go. Go.

Go home. The words yelled and faded sliding toward the horizon. He turned to leave once more, pausing at the porch steps to face her in the semi-darkness. Without a word he hoped would have been an answer to all her woman's guile, deceitful creature whose lure directed to the male in creation was on that first day inborn.

If you spoke of it to a boy or girl of a newer, younger lovers club, who came of age too soon, it was of a truth. They are said to be so much more aware of what life was meant to be for future biographies — almost a hundred percent about their lives are put to diaries, to ink, on paper and in the newer age, the screen — you'd be the talk of every back yard grill and cola fountain.

Clint said in the presence of other men in a far off jungle, of the free sex era: 'I'd like to get in on it.' Yet he and most of his now older generation had survived and they'd tell each other how they had 'overcome,' which was a lame retort to the question, a lack of something or other for the other sex in a time of hands off like his mother said was a respect to the Commandment and to the opposite sex.

Before Doris was Lily; before Lily, a lot of kid stuff, games of post office at after dark parties in some home with fun time in a bedroom which after one clandestine kiss you asked another member of the party to come into the darkness to meet in an embrace a kissing cousin defined roughly as of the other sex and its limitations.

Shortly after these promising girls, these women really, because of how much they knew of the other sex, were the so soft tan girls of Indo China, one especially, he recalled.

So warm she was, with lips just like that girl to that boy that day in the garden, Adam and Eve the day when they gave it all up, all of it, for another . . . kiss. This Marine, away far from home, knew he was entitled. Loneliness, too long a big denial, months as a soldier when the last girl he had known was an eon ago.

It was a war-time scene (life-time?) eager to be viewed like somebody else's. After the war ended and a time of waiting for a ship home began, Clint's government set up a point system so sixteen million men and women of war, efficiently so they could be sent home, he was dropped off with a dozen or so other Marines in a country once run pretty much by the French before the war.

Just like that, with hostility all around them in Asia, his country's state department moved to set up a legation. It was in a Southeast Asian country, which would in time lead to an anticipated full diplomatic exchange. Of course they would need a few United States Marines to stand in full parade regalia, sharp and impressive as guards out front.

And impress, yah, they did, maybe to the wrong wayfarers. Way out here, so far far from home, he soon was to learn a bit more about men and women: that his uniform had attracted as many young girls as it did back home. He always sensed a big thrill at showing off his perfect body to any woman who passed. He'd just retrieved that coat of many colors shiny brass and its stripes and many medals.

One native girl —- said she was eighteen, a few months to legal age, but she looked more like sixteen maybe fifteen or even fourteen —- he took her word for it. She kept walking by the Marines who decorated their end of the street scene, even in a country where every other person you met was an artist, given to elaborate, colorful dress and even outdoors' decoration. Often, the guards were more at parade rest than attention.

The apparent relaxed Marines encouraged the locals, who wanted to try out their English lessons on Americans. Too long since they'd begun thinking only in defensive French.

The copper-skinned girl walked by, turned to retrace her steps, showing off her slim body with an inherited old-fashioned Eden-born tease. Nobody could 'tease' like one slender shapely black-haired Asian girl in a tight rose-figured skirt; sometimes she was barefooted, suggesting overall nudeness, er, lewdness.

Long black shiny hair hanging loosely down her back and you wanted to reach out, stroke it, this one in a not so tight skirt as you would expect but with a looseness that failed to hide the curves inviting all sorts of speculation. Her every girl-woman movement which was crowned at birth was her inheritance for just this moment.

This little tan wench with an ancient lure moved like a snake through the flower patch of Eden —- she was that all right —- came as close as her peers would accept before one of them ran home to tell the girl's mommy about her brazen ways; looked him right in the eye from just a few inches from his boot camp ordained frozen face. She was impudent, audacious and shameless, like it began in the Garden when Eve offered her soul mate (?) a bite from her apple. Oh Lord and the smell of homemade perfumed soap.

Clint's Marines were warned against fraternization as well as venereal disease which entangling alliances out here that would lead to the devil knew what —- think about the girl back home whom you promised once upon a time that you'd be back, and that she must keep her nose clean and her legs crossed. That warning mostly came from the lieutenant who knew the ways of soldiers far from home. So often you wanted to call him papa, even if he was more like a mother hen.

He'd thought of her often these days, like when he was back in the states and a passing tanned beauty looked his way where he relaxed on the grass with friends amid college halls in the sun and warmth of the spring.

The Polls of Heaven

Once, briefly, Clint way out there in a hot land with hot women (girls) briefly had considered not going home at all but remaining in this exotic land. It was the better nature he'd later say he knew he didn't possess that nevertheless at last had won out.

If this little native jezebel had done this thing for him as a reward, how often would she use her wiles to attract other men even as she might be his woman (that he brought home; sorry), there are no other words that would say what he envisioned would be their (possible union); besides, his kin and friends were expecting him home (and alone).

To get around military regulations, a shut tight and locked barracks door (a hotel it was), she had despite all that security and in some way managed a liaison. She moved through the night like a phantom. He'd wake up with her body next to him, writhing and touching every inch of his body.

How had she found his room, even though it was a limited and tiny hotel? Of course with just one roommate, one or the other of them would be on duty while the other slept.

This little detail bothered him for a long time. One wicked day out of nowhere came an answer. His roommate had purposely left the door unlocked as he left for his 'watch.' Had she bribed him, not with the usual 'filthy lucre,' but with the only thing she at the time possessed, with her body? He had overlooked that little possibility. He put it at first from his mind because his roommate in so doing would have broken the Marine honor code.

She whispered, close to his ear: "Take me back to United States of America, to be your wife and love forever. Show me off proud to family."

They were almost a curse, these hot-blooded sirens of the South Seas, exotic vixens, mostly island lands known to a Ulysses ear which happened to drift his way, like our Clint. Better to read about them, loving them in your lustful heart from afar than to become locked in their embrace forever, Clint at last in severe discontent concluded.

On an earlier night of panic, which as he recalled, it ended in feelings of remorse, even regret, Doris had invited him in for a cup of hot cocoa —- which would allow him to 'sleep better' when he got home. This was before his full recovery, which had been aided immensely by her hands.

He didn't know why, but he felt uneasy about tarrying so close to the lady's boudoir that he could not control his two feet which were urging him to run away as fast as a male rabbit. (It was a poor choice of analogy. No male rabbit ever ran from a female hare.)

He'd lifted his arms to ask forgiveness for the native girl in his bed out there and the later visit to the bed of an unmarried woman. He said, "Lily, please forgive me for taking these women without your consent." Forgive his right to brag. He afterwards denied all of it.

Clint's lieutenant was one of the wisest men he'd ever know. Two days after the tan girl's bedroom invasion by a most desirable woman —- also, as one he would ever know, his Marine officer found him at chow, a feed trough set up which on another day would be the hotel's lobby. His lieutenant invited him out to the hallway.

Speaking in a whisper, leaning close so that Clint's chow mates would not hear, the lieutenant told Corporal Greene, one of his better Marines, to pack his gear and stand ready at the door to his quarters, waiting for the summons which would be just minutes before twenty hundred hours that night.

A truck and Marine driver would be waiting at the rear door to the hotel to pick him up, and head for parts unknown. Others would be given the same orders, which Clint would be handed just before he boarded the ship. They would be driven to dockside. A Navy destroyer escort (a DE) would be waiting for them.

The ship would put into port at possibly three other sites before heading straight for San Francisco, after picking up a few strays like him. They would get to the states in little more than three weeks, unless they hit a storm. And home.

Clint wanted to know, why all the secrecy? "The war is over."

The lieutenant said, with a slightly bent smile taking up most of his face: "Let's say that someday you'll write to thank me. That, Sergeant Greene is 'Dismissed'." Clint smiled. What a time to be promoted to sergeant, and to be told about it on a night of low moonlight.

The lieutenant not only knew where his men were every minute or hour of a day but what they might be thinking.

Clint had never told anyone about the incident or the little tan (copper-colored) Asian girl at an ancient hotel in the semi-tropics soon after the end of the war so far away in a far country. Long after Indo China he would see a Southeast Asian girl on the street. The years dropped out of the present; he could almost feel his hand stroking the girl's black hair drop his hand onto the warm smooth skin alongside him. She would be an Asian girl of a latter day, so he could pretend then and today not to be distracted by a vision.

The tan girl on the street, one of many, had come home to America from a country now with a new name, pronounced Vietnam. Or maybe it was Thailand, now with an American GI on her arm who had claimed her as a wife, coming home to USA to make a family proud.

Out of Indo China was to come a long ugly war, which cost his country 50,000 lives and introduced to crowded streets and alleyways hundreds of others who had no home, only a comfort of the brotherhood to listen to them, to show the same world what a new Indo China war had done to them.

Many theories exist for the decline of values, which were left to his country by the founding fathers.

Clint and his generation believed their Constitution would stand forever against what time and mud would be thrown against it. They hadn't reckoned on a broad system of paved roads built to oblige a new god, the internal combustion engine: The highway monsters with an unwelcome exhaust contributed to an ill ecology.

He hadn't since Lily either dated a woman or felt driven to consider any one of them as possible sex partners despite the warm blood in his veins as he watched younger women and even some nearer his age, as he'd seen them on the street, in downtown stores, always in passing, some saying in sweet patronizing, 'you remind me so much of someone I knew,' or in sober thought for an old warrior, 'of my father.' Or even, of 'my grandfather'. They did not intend to rub in the old ugly wagon grease. That is salve for sick sheep. So he had begun calling them one by one, 'my daughter.'

He'd sloughed it all off, as a hand was stuck out and they said, 'thank you,' for his part in his war, even as new wars raged against his country and the hurting soldiers of a new generation.

Now, after a generation and restructure of the relationship between man and woman (did it really change all that much?) what should he say to this woman? Doris, sweetheart of long ago she'd called herself. She'd said she was lonely. She was too quick to react to what could be nothing but innuendoes, hoping he'd follow up with an invitation, perhaps with a male leer on his face.

Clint wasn't prepared for Doris, He had gone far toward a commitment as much as he wanted; yes, old-fashioned old Clint Greene, hearing his mother's voice as she warned him about some women who in this world would have many old ideas.

They had so many biblical ways even to lure him into her bedroom. As a younger man before Lily he'd have welcomed it.

He listened as today's younger generation fell into a great big laugh about this old man and his reaction to a real, innocent suggestion that he come into (her) parlor. He thought about the fable he had read when he was a lad growing up in a lonely mountain place. It was the spider saying to the fly, 'come into my parlor.'

Nevertheless, he thought it was time to retreat from a whisper of this so casual thing, enabling him to fight on another day, more on a familiar level. He'd simply smiled or thought he did, saying, "Upon a later time, perhaps. This old boy needs to get to the hill and to the old typewriter, as late as it is. Good night, Doris; my mama said to tell you I had a nice time."

He initially turned then to the street, not without a feeling that he was a fool. The common man and poets would have called him that. The fool in him would force his eyes to the second floor window where a lamp had just been lighted. He would stand in the street a few more minutes, wondering if he really was a fool. He would wait for a shape a shadow to cross against a lamp and shrug, also unsure what the shrug meant, whether for a lost love or a twittered-away life.

He knew what he would do, had planned it out, right down to the shadows. Instead, just before Doris turned the doorknob, he called out: "Would you happen to have any cherry cobbler left in your refrigerator?"

"Not yet, but come on in and we'll batter up some pans and I'll make coffee and we'll dine together by candlelight."

Where did you go my once upon a time Asian bronzed butterfly-clad midnight caller . . . who taught you to love so . . . who sent you out to greet the mighty Caesar who came to conquer . . . your country, my country . . . were you named to send love to a savage world as the conqueror has been conquered . . . by love . . . from a bench in Egypt land that was made from the sweetened leaves of a eucalyptus tree . . .

King David would see you at bath from his palace window . . . What did you hide in your bonnet to cause good King Edward to give up his throne . . . for the woman in love . . . so young you were and I was old . . . so warm . . . so eager . . . so wild . . . you were all woman and I was only one man . . .

The Polls of Heaven

Well, who ever said I as a young man ever aspired to be president of my country?

It was past three in the a.m. as Clint climbed the mountain to his castle on high. He'd left it once, no twice, for northern climes . . . riding the black, mightiest steed of the whole kingdom given to him by the Prince of Araby for service against the Turks.

He surveyed the hills to the east, where his people from a past of neglect, alienation and poverty settled with a primary goal as will be written in their history books, if anyone would be so inclined . . . to be left alone. They came as free men with like-minded women and sons, only to find more pain and poverty as the captains of industry came to take away their timber and their black gold (in future pageants called coal) as well as pride once prized as their extensive Elizabethan heritage.

They had seen the worst of society's scorn and contempt as their skills yes even their souls were bought first as products of their forests and then the riches that lay beneath their gardens. At last in the mopping up after the battle society with the greedy banner came for their dignity, known to posterity and to the world as the ultimate of grief and destruction.

Yet, out of the maelstrom of all that was present in the beginning, to a world that hailed their Scotch-Irish heritage, gifts of blood and brains and ambition departed to help nurse to recovery their new country, which by fate was meant to be.

This is how in a rousing spirit which rose to the heights of man's possibilities, Clint Greene would go home to write about, as the day's sun came to verify his inspiration.

Is this what happens when man is given a way to recover his worth after he'd thought his life was about to expire — with the recent feeling that he'd lived in vain?

The fool didn't touch the typing machine when he got home. He wanted to think a bit more about the night, and . . . Doris.

"You mean you just kissed her good night and walked away?" That was Oscar.

"Have you forgotten already that this is more than just a baseball game? Or in my country maybe a little joust? Don't we at least get in on just a tiny bit of something you're not telling us?" And that was Leo, the Russian.

"Even if it was, I'd never tell you guys. So you're both going to imagine the rest.

"Good friends or not, some events great or small in this world must be kept personal. That's all, that's a quit; as the bard would say, 'the rest is silence.' I don't want to hear any more from those curious little myna birds I see sitting on your shoulders;" Yet, Clint really believed that ended it.

Clint told them about his first 'vision,' then others, if you could call them that. He said he'd seen much on TV and in the papers of incidents and disturbing behavior in Earth's recent relations with itself. If it kept up, he'd be forced to give up hard drinking and soft women (the latter is a distraction). He was upset because of the 'visions,' he said.

"But I'm sure the ocean's roar in such a riot came from the east. That is the only pronounced memory of it that first vision, I can say for sure. The rest was too unreal."

Oscar suggested that Clint should write about the 'visuals' into his future columns, suggesting that it was his over-worked brain at work putting the different incidents together. He argued that it could be much more. Oscar could tell Clint was reluctant to use it in his column.

"You don't reckon you've all of a sudden become psychic," said Oscar. It was more of a statement than a question.

"Of course not;" Clint said. "As a newspaperman, I am not expected to see visions or believe in psychic phenomena. I would right off lose most of my readers.

"I need more people in my corner, not fewer," Clint said.

Yet stranger things have happened to a man or woman who was coming out of a coma following an accident; he recalled reading a story about such foreign awareness. He hoped that it was only something that he'd read about, "but not in fictional accounts." Near death injuries such as his did its mysterious work on the mind, the article told him.

"Has anything like this ever happened to you before, like when you were a boy, or on those days after you were wounded in the South Pacific?" That was Oscar again.

"Nope, it's the first time I've ever crossed over to where man is not supposed to tread, and it frightens me." He said he'd read of such things, but being busy looking for 'incidents' for his column he admitted that fatigue and desperation could lead to some invention.

The Polls of Heaven

Leo said it was not uncommon to believe in psychics in his primitive country.

"Among superstitious Cossacks primarily in the area of my village, there could be a hundred households with an icon of some sort. It sometimes made you think that something from another world had overtaken many of the old beliefs, recalling that whenever a 'seer' showed up in his neighborhood, the village people would "beat a path to his host's seminar." You're right, he said, most people believed that "if a resident began seeing things, he was thought of as pretty much a fraud, by our long-time neighbors." "A communist will believe anything," he added; it comes naturally to their little minds.

"All the reason to use it but to soften it up a bit," said Clint, hoping he'd posed it as a question. He waited while Oscar and Leo went on talking about it.

Just the same he first decided to accept an earlier decision of his and would not allow its use any other that way. He hesitated, said to Oscar and Leo, "well, go on," that they'd gauge public reaction to the column's format by composing it in another way. "The public will still call me a crumbled cookie anyway for believing that stuff about climate change."

He added that maybe the column was not the right approach to awaken the people to a threat to Earth by its warming up and to the country itself, about how they are dishonoring their moral heritage by giving it all up as has happened in every like nation in the past. At least we should dub in some gimmick you call it, so people can feel it —- so they better can understand it as a threat.

It's like a "threat of the month club," following decades of fear of atomic warfare, especially with the bomb in the hands of a hostile nation. They were told that it could destroy the Earth; dozens of other threats began to emerge.

Clint talked about wayward asteroids, and 'the big one' -- California's long awaited earthquake. He told his friends of another recent vision: The city's river waters stirred by a hurricane breaking through New Orleans levees, destroying hundreds of homes and lives.

"Those people spent whole lifetimes building their homes and life savings; they all vanished." Changes in the Earth ecology maybe causes —- scientists can't agree —- these odd things to happen out there," he said. "We were first warned twenty-five or so years ago about many of these disasters that could come. Anyway, let's put it aside for a moment. Let Leo tell us about his Cossacks. I have been waiting for this for a long time."

Leo swallowed, stuttering in his slight Russian accent, said: "All right, dang it, (this is an adopted American term), if you all really want to hear about it, but Oscar has to shut down tight his promise, not a word gets into the papers, or in Clint's column."

Oscar acknowledged: it will be so, "it hurts, but okay." Clint nodded, a 'no,' it was by his silence, meaning no, a loud 'NO.' He recalled taking an oath of a lifetime ago by way of the puncture (what's a pinprick?) in his lower back that caused him to wince. Clint wasn't smiling. He had never promised to keep something out of the paper.

Leo continued: "Right off I'd like to say that we are people with similar feelings and compassion as are you and most of the rest of the world — all walking upright on two legs, as thinking beings since leaving the water and acting like humans with developing brains."

"We are all, you and me, on this smallest of planets where man rules over all wild blooded animals. No better and no worse. My people have been kicked around a lot, called scapegoats of misrule, but we survived. Before Hitler was Napoleon's attempt, and by most of our czars.'

"It has been as written in Western literature that, in battle, the Cossacks gave no quarter. Under the same conditions, in the past we were and still are a fierce often a vengeful feared people. Men in face-to-face combat can be cruel; that's what war was about —- and before the new weapons, huge air fighters and bombers and triggers was a planned famine, scorched earth, ovens and the suffering of our families over mass graves."

"In the 'civilized war' (his emphasis), which we were ready to accept, we've seen no gentler way to kill a man. When the fight is over, the battle won, we can be tender, even kind. We've never impugned your history. As we accepted it as true, so you should not slander us for our love, for peace."

"The communists as soon as they came to power began to grind out derogatory and evil reports about our people, as well did they murder by the hundreds, even thousands."

"We always came back with ways to intimidate them, to harass their satraps. They selected from among us a sordid crowd bordering on stupidity, a 'pie in the sky' bunch, to rule our neighborhoods."

"They used our people to steal our crops and work animals, which they'd slaughter for the meat to be distributed among themselves.

"Historians have held that until the (Russian) civil war —- when the communists came in —- Cossacks were by history vital to the nation's safety."

"Perhaps the Czars Romanov felt indebted to us since we had been invited in on the selection of a seventeen-year-old boy back in 1613 as the first Romanov to be elected as emperor. We really held the cards in that election and the nose of the Romanovs to the grinder for the next three centuries."

"Communists killed my father and mother at the turn of the 1930s, only a few weeks after my birth. My uncles took me in, saw to my education. They taught me and so did the academy, to respect and handle weapons and ride like the old Cossacks."

"That little lesson was what a New York sports agent heard about and sent an emissary here to inquire about my skills, perhaps my availability for big outdoor shows, to make big money, mostly for them, by performing at fairs and other places where lots of people gather."

"That's turned out to be about my last war whoop by these old Cossack bones. They learned that I'd done the same thing in London, but under another name. Ah, I've had a lot of names."

"My uncles got me sent to the academy. That's where the Red Army found me. I did my duty during the Second World War, even as a teenager when I began —- I was just fourteen —- among others of like age of nearby Cossack villages."

"We most of us hated the communists and their evil regime. Many more did not, but we outnumbered them. Let's say they were — as you and many of us who are American —as we Yankees say, a 'bunch of suck-ups.' In battle our little outfit didn't provide much help to soldiers who were commies."

"Many of the resisters to the commies easily found their way to the Allied armies of the west across the lines after the Allies had gotten their foothold on the continent. The men were eagerly accepted into Allied army regiments.'

"Soon we were fighting against Mother Russia — her commie rulers. We hoped to gain for our people a release from the communists."

"Our boys as the British say were vastly admired by our people, who knew our soldiers were with British, French, Polish and the Americans —- close to a million of our men fought with the Nazi —- but with the same spirit of not fighting against the motherland."

"Instead, our loyalties were against the commies who with evil intent had taken over our country. I speak again of the commie bunch; they knew, I believe, someday we would see their demise.

"I'll have more to say about these soldiers, most every one a hero to our people, upon a later time. In telling it you will hear much of the story of my life, which took on an entire new dimension that has resulted in the day when I could sit here alongside you as an American in an American town living a dream that as boy and young idealist I'd never even in a space age imagination have believed possible."

"I won't tell you how soon I went over to the Allies; I did most of my service with the British. I must have performed worthy of high praise by the British. Winston Churchill gave me 'heart-felt' credit when he sent me a medal and a written commendation. Because of these actions I was taken to London at the end of the war."

"In the end, my service led to university. After that it was in service to my fellow Cossacks that brought me to the United States. In my subsidized (commanded) quest in this country I was given the full cooperation by your government."

"A peasant in my country -- I often think since the dawn of time -- lived under stern rule from Moscow and Petersburg, but in the Cossack corner of the country the people in spite of their patriotism and love of the motherland had I'd say a rebellious spirit that took form in resistance to the nation's later leaders that more often than not smacked of tyranny and despotism."

Leo appeared to be proud of his little recital. He leaned far back in his huge wicker chair near the edge of Clint's porch. A smile almost made it to his face, but it just as quickly disappeared as he gazed across the river valley to the thick woods and the hills beyond. Clint and Oscar were certain that Leo was looking deeply into the past.

Any other time and in any other place, Leo's countenance and presence, grim and sober, reminding of a commander of vast military forces above the field of battle moving toward its objective far and near, would have entered the history books of both countries, the old of his boyhood and youth, and the new.

It likely will never happen, but time and the commies in years of screwed-up command at last coming to naught, may try to make up for past evils —- to Leo. It is inevitable.

As far as Leo himself is concerned, his ties to the older as well as the new government of Russia do not exist. That's finis.

This, despite an attempt to escape the pain of his past, and his part in helping bring about the new day for his people, he has to endure the hate and barbs of many of his own Russians. It is time to allow the past be put to rest, at least for now.

Clint suggested tea, coffee or beer.

On this summer day, all opted for the cold one. "Next time you come up, I'll cook hot dogs, or rabbit if you prefer," he said, wishing he hadn't said that because his guests, in near harmony, would start bragging about rabbits in their home counties that are bigger than any wild animal found in Texas.

They didn't. It wasn't the moment to brag or make jokes.

Clint and his friends were silent. The trio that formed OMEN was deep in thought: The best of friends. Night came, with its coolness, a relief from the heat, of lightning bugs with their night love hope to attract the other sex.

Leo said he'd give them a more acceptable story of his Cossacks soon, at a later hour and of his own choosing when he could talk with a clearer recollection, whatever that meant. He added: "My mission in America has yet to be concluded."

Clint and Oscar eyed each other, confused. It wasn't the time to probe for report of events further.

It was Oscar's day with the single rocking chair, and he was making his own brand of field hay with it, back forward rocking, there was no reason for tension between them.

Clint knew his moments of respite from certain facts of the past that belonged strictly to Leo would not be his last.

To assure Leo they were not ignoring him, instead honoring him, Clint turned to the rocking chair. "It's your turn, Oscar, to tell us without brag of your 'flower power' days."

Without any hesitation Oscar grunted, cleared his throat gave the gang a half smile and hawed a little before he began and you felt he'd been waiting for weeks until someone asked him.

"'Wal,' said this crotchety old codger (if a simple profile is not redundant?).

Chapter Six

"We were way out on the plains. I smiled at my camping girl companions who were all around me: One especially; our young folks have at last proved what every one of us of the present and of allied generations said about our work: they've plumb gone to the woods canines. Those are 'dogs' in both of your languages."

"We his companions lying sleepily on the other side of the flames of an in-house fire to which we with no urging now had joined, reckoned in agreement. The dogs, one of us said, had at last finally come home to prove their worth." Clint thought it unusual for a newsman to be so wordy (loud, with no deadline.)

"It took thirty years for all the noise to die down. What the dogs once had so defiantly bellowed against —- lo these many years ago, had taken shape in our image while the rest of mankind was unaware of it."

"Not the bulk of it, but enough say in compromise to satisfy both we, and they."

Oscar was speaking in the voice of his youth, yet slowing it for a latter day audience, denying his own past, 'revealing' what most of us had long suspected. He had our attention, apparently uneasy trying to fit his own role into what others considered at the time had been a threat to democracy and the establishment.

Oscar had said that his companions in protest "were on the edge of revolution." We suspected that. You felt even more his reluctance to join himself to them. Yet he didn't attempt to hide the fact that he might have come to an acceptance of a revised order; for his country's sake he'd joined the enemy, which was the majority, the rest of us, and which was not a fact, since he'd once said he had joined for one reason, his undying love for a woman.

"Our angry boys and girls of free love and reason accused our elders of losing all their respect for the ideologues who had built a new nation among men for all men . . . and women. Yet, as time marched on and they grew up and took over the government and the corporations, it was an age-old story."

"They in the main wouldn't recognize an ideal if it jumped from the bushes hugging them around the neck. Yes, unto this day, prophets of the faith say, we have met the loss of our once so precious ideals," Clint said.

"Like James Joyce I think it was said, 'the loss of ideals became us.' That is slightly paraphrased, of course. This age will never know the full truth of it. You simply had to be there."

"They (we) believed then that our right to free speech had been taken from us, and in reality it had been. Our 'free-speech' scream became a rallying point. This one issue during the first days was an open invitation, an open door, which the students as revolutionaries walked through. Other 'causes' then came out of our raised fist demands," Oscar said.

"We were called cowards, even traitors, renegades, because we were looking for ways to avoid military service. The bloody rage had already begun in Vietnam. The cry continued, becoming universal. It now was, 'Hell no, we won't go.'"

"Our uniform was shagginess with holes in the knees and rips in our behinds —- the better in our nakedness to invite some sex, as if sex needed an invitation —- and the non-civilized said it was in sympathy with our elders who themselves were denied even the basics of culture and pressed pants because of the Great Depression. Even so, our elders never realized just how much we did it in imitation and in respect for them."

"We let our hair down, over our ears and as far down our backs as it would grow. Then there were the drugs. Let me tell you man it was an exciting time. You should thank us."

"The ecology movement, if we did not invent it, we gave it an emphasis that was needed. We honored our past, the founders, which were beginning to be forgotten, through folk songs and poetry and our creation of art that honored the one-time era of good feeling. We looked for ways to end the war. We called attention to injustice in our society which had brought about new Civil Rights laws."

"We helped the nation know its poor and recognize injustice to our black citizens. Women were encouraged into the political arena, into the seats of judges and board rooms.

"Did we really change much? Were reforms inevitable? Came an era of blandness to mock us; but our generation of protesters had muddled through. The nation, as we've since come to know it, is again sliding toward mediocrity. As citizens we are worse; nobody today pretty much gives a damn."

Clint said, without a smile or grimace: "I understand what you say. A story of my life would be described in the four words spoken over the tomb of one young girl in a poem from the past century, (it's like a stage direction) in that quaint little assessment: 'it might have been.' Like I've repeated it so often, I let it become my assessment of democracy."

"I reckon this old boy about always was in the wrong place at the wrong time. I was there, always ready and alert, for the call to greatness that never came. I reckon when you have the opportunity as you see it, you better take it."

"Aw bull and shucks," said Leo the Russian, "as you all, you folks down here in the Allegheny Mountains would say."

"If Oscar's own assessment of the beats as a genuine protest generation is correct," said Clint, "perhaps we should bring them back, if we could find enough troops to form a company, let alone a slim regiment of barking sergeants as drill instructors."

"Somehow I don't believe our little endeavor is getting through to people that matter; America is too bland, too comfortable, a generation avoiding the call to rally in protest of what we are doing to the planet, to ourselves."

"Even if we call it America's heritage, which much of the world says it is, it is our duty to find a way for them to come to us with 'we've come to support you.' Gibberbosh."

Clint said it was time their little committee went in a more subtle direction or gave it up as a hopeless venture. It's been years since both he and Oscar went into news as writers 'to save the world,' among other less grandiose reasons.

"A rallying cry has become a whimper, even a laugh among the new generation's aspiring journalists."

A few scattered readers' letters were still coming in, he said, "but that's all."

He said a phone call to one of the cooperating newspapers brought an answer. They all added up to an embarrassment. Letters to the papers might have come in —- not to be ignored, and right then they stopped coming at all, a situation of abandonment. Clint could proudly hail the honor with fighting emotions because more than a few of the editors 'liked his style;' they cited his country boy way of looking at life in the latter part of the century.

This is where the disappointment began. Their Speaker's Bureau also was flunking out and the trio wondered where all those zeroes were coming from.

Later, after such vast applause in elation became dark days of despair, they talked of giving it up. Clint's column, which was aimed at the common folk but also the educated reader and voter, yet were the same folk who apparently didn't give a damn about what is happening to the Earth -- let us say it was like oatmeal thrown into a fan. A show aimed at hot blood came from the same people who every day would call the voice on a radio talk show, over again and again with nonsense as expected.

Clint knew by now that the people were not behind him. Tomorrow is another day, and Americans would go in another direction, wonder if they thought of it at all.

Why they'd gotten excited in the beginning of their efforts and why it so quickly was yesterday's news and interest is understandable. Our people are faddists, what's hot today is in the trash heap tomorrow, he said. That's why garage sales are so popular. People go out looking for that cheap doodad throw-away because today's play pretty will be tomorrow's collectible; they buy for the future collector store it up and stand ready.

It was a heck of a way to run a railroad.

He'd written that radical changes in the atmosphere could be the result of a 'warming up' of the Earth as scientists had suggested. It might be a dire prediction of what's to come but everybody else in the business was doing the same thing. It's for sure the time we caught the midnight train, he said to Oscar and Leo.

They were out on the porch of Clint's cabin late on a spring day. "I mean to get so far out of town that reporters or anybody else will lose days trying to locate me, I might say in my present feeling of great worth, that I still hope they find me, then I'll speak to them in a different voice," said a despondent Clint.

"Man, talk about a big hullabaloo. What have we created?" Too many columnists were rallying to the same melody, he said.

Yet it appears that the situation is just getting worse.

The 'cheapness' of the use of 'disaster' stories without proof was that change in the weather was causing all the fear and doubt; well, this is not good journalism and we know it.

Clint, the country boy become writer, who believed what he wrote, felt the nervous power 'in these fingers' at the typewriter, which surged to his fingertips like water over the Hoover Dam. His thoughts he knew could condemn him to a cell for the insane by any court in the land. He had no right to believe he had any such power. Yet his editorials in the past had gotten results, but he had earned no more than filled potholes in the streets. Others of his craft had brought down presidents, started wars, crowned kings and launched ships to sea and rockets to the moon.

On what day did people no longer feel an urge to act other than by the harangue of a demagogue? Could they hear an honest editor or serious politician who was asking that they follow him to the seats of the mighty?

"It likely is well that most of us no longer can do that — but we of the dream should be speaking in memory of the times when a kid's head lay on his mother's lap and she told her wee son that she knew that 'God is not ready to give up on us.'"

Later, Oscar said that when he and his lady love once stood on the red-stained streets of America's cities, it became — now in memory — a moment when he was all-powerful, king of the day and of the night, They were God-chosen to take over the Earth and to condemn the past for its misdirection, he to take this woman for his queen, both to send to every corner of the land the word of peace and victory over all evil, with the promise of eternal sunshine. "But my love so soon already is living in a despairing moment that I yet have not recognized."

Clint said that when his generation first declared that God was dead, he'd mocked them - the raving of a modern day King Lear. "Scientists say 'evidence' points to a dead God. Among Earth's multitudes, many of faith, there must be an encouraging voice that is also demanding to be heard. I wanted to be that voice."

"Mayan star gazers and intellectual kin warned that Earth might die in an end-time; some modern interpreters said it was to come in this generation, which could be lo, before we pass on in a normal way as have all men before us. Must a possible survivor, beginning with a single seed, start over again just after a few million years out there?" Clint wished he knew more about how the Maya came to their interpretation.

"In their stargazing could they dare say it was by an alignment of all the planets that in our day could be setting itself up as the big one."

He hesitated, "They must have meant that the 'big one' was a big disappointment."

Tolstoy's Count Pierre Bezukhov, viewing Moscow society (in 'War and Peace'} said, "What's the use?" Oscar said he should have asked, "What is going on in the World?"

Right then, Citizen Leo of the U.S. interrupted. The Russian with the long Russian tribal name said: "My father, as a curious lad, yet was of an age to recall the day when Leo Tolstoy was pointed out to boys of his village as a man of nobility, my uncles told me." He said Tolstoy was quite respected in his village, and had hopes for the future."

Both Clint and Oscar felt relief in the pull away from what had become simply weary speculation: Likely, why Leo said what he did.

"The count had come to Cossack country where he would spend a few years on what he called the 'frontier,'" Leo of America continued.

"Tolstoy mainly wanted to hunt. Yet he wanted also to become a fighting soldier with the Cossacks."

"I learned later that the count who would become famous as a writer wrote his first stories about my people, how they lived, loved and fought. He lived in the village, which he would describe as a line of reed-thatched log cabins that faced the single village street."

(Tolstoy's visit to the village is from Morris Philipson's book, 'The Count Who Wished He Were a Peasant,' Pantheon Books, Random House, Inc., N.Y. pp 32-36 (1967).

"My father said the count boarded in the village with one Epishka Sekhin, then in his eighties. As recalled by villagers, Sekhin as a young man among them already was of great size. The big man's reputation was as a reprobate."

'Just the same,'(a phrase used here as a Tolstoy term but as often said in speech by Clint's people today), this huge Cossack was big in classic heroism to Tolstoy, as he was to the Cossacks who'd heard of him."

"Sekhin had a huge following among our admiring village boys —- he drank alcohol in flowing draughts, gambled day and night, and was favored by leagues of women —- of every age."

"I thought of him the day they came for me to send out against the German invaders —- as cannon fodder. This old boy was just twelve at the time. By 1942 I had seen more men active at war that any boy or man is entitled to."

"The German's guns destroyed what was left of my village and killed the last of my cousins still at home," said Kentucky's Leo. "The new government burned what could be found of my village's once stored food for existence, in an effort to deny anything that would provide warmth for the people."

"The Nazi army was not used to our Russian winters; we knew that they had been sent out in their summer uniforms. If the Nazi expected to live off the land, the 'scorched Earth' policy of the Russian command was a surprise to them."

"I was hiding in the hills when the Red Army found me. With my military training and discipline in the academy I thought they might even make me an officer, but I knew it was silly to put bars on the shoulders of a kid not yet pushing sixteen who hadn't even had his first shave."

"Yet I knew that a horseman with slingshot and maybe a rifle was frightening as a BB gun. We couldn't do much fighting against the German tanks."

"In this period of the war we barely teen-year-olds, maybe a few even younger —- were child soldiers like your American kids in 'cowboy' games with cap pistols, who were only playing at war."

"Just the same, we kids made up a big part of the army. We were fighting the German army for a second, even a third time in Hitler's so-called famous pincer moves to the east, toward the Don and the Volga —- their goal was Stalingrad. We studied how the Germans made war —- back and forth —- and we knew what to expect. Their tactics seldom varied."

"The Nazi quite much tore up my neighbors' farms. We all laughed and said that 'they at least got it plowed up' in time for spring planting. By the way, I had little chance to ride a horse, which might have been more effective against the enemy whose machinery we kept getting it mired down in all that mud which they also created with tanks on snow."

"How I survived that big war has always been seen by me and my buddies as a near miracle. I lost a lot of friends to battle. My wounds, strange as it may be, were superficial."

"It also was hard for a Cossack to receive a medal from the Red Army, which we'd laugh at anyway. Like you heard me say, we were just plain old cannon fodder."

"You won't find much in history, either, about all those hundreds even thousands of Cossacks who found the road to the west and fought against their (communist) country with the Nazi army against the Red Army."

"They weren't under any patriotic oath or other reason to fight Mother Russia —- or the Motherland. It was the communists who were the enemy to us."

An army friend of Leo's said it was easier to kill a communist than a once declared enemy in the west. "When German troops first crossed into Cossack country many people came out to greet them as liberators, but that feeling didn't last."

"Our people were, as individuals, lovers of their country as much as your Americans were loyal to yours when they were fighting for freedom. In spite of what the Red Army up to that time had done to them, they wanted to single out the recognized communist haters among our neighbors, who also were victims of the Red hate."

"The Nazi were pleased to receive our people into their ranks, but we learned that our people still were treated like the Red Army treated us, we Cossacks. They allowed few if any of our men to serve in any rank, even former high-ranking officers of the Red Army."

"And that, dear U. S. friends, leads to one of the old true Russians' target —- to my own Cossacks —- our greatest disappointment, since we supported the old Czars."

"This is that bit of history that is not taught in American schoolrooms. Russians, yes, Russians, we who fought on the other side against the Red Army, of course we knew what we were doing. The soldiers knew if they survived and returned to their homes inside the Motherland, that they'd be charged as traitors and would face death by firing squad."

"Rumors were that one of our Cossacks had pointed to Cossacks, who were arrested, along with others who had served in the ranks of the Allies or Axis armies."

"These were the men that Stalin in particular wanted. I was disappointed in this man who had been from my own village, and I knew him well. I never knew that even he could go as far in his 'suck-up' as it turned out. This man, not just two-faced in his treachery but four-faced, had become the biggest scoundrel of them all.'

"In past years our people watched as the commies would come and go directly to the home of the villager who by some means had hidden food he hoped to save for the harsh winter that was to come. The man was arrested, and the food was taken."

"We finally identified the traitor among us, the betrayer of his people. He and the Judas goat known to the armies in the west were one and the same."

"Many of our soldiers who'd gone to the west took their families along, most toward war's end and afterwards; they were put up in apartments in western cities, or nearby."

"These people and their wives would open their doors to the same soldiers who had been their friends. Entire families were put aboard trucks bound for Moscow."

"And who led the arresting soldiers to their homes? Why, our friend of the village food storage haunts which the communists considered a major sin against the collectives."

"Many of our people would take their families, so warned by the raids elsewhere, to a bridge where their children were thrown into the waters to be followed by their fathers and mothers," the men sometimes back in the uniform of the Red Army.

Oscar and Clint were reluctant to look directly into Leo's face. They knew by the change of tone in his voice that tears had formed on Leo's cheeks. It wasn't the best time to interrupt.

Leo came back to his story: "The war was over and after long months in the army I managed to stay in the west and was steered by friends toward England, to folks to whom I'll always be indebted. They took me in and helped me at last to finish my education, which by good luck led to university."

"It was at university when some 'old soldiers' of my former outfit visited me. They appealed to me to travel to America where they had heard that the Judas goat had somehow broken through the immigration wall to hole up nobody knew where, although they did give me some possible clues that might help find him. I set out as directed. You'd be surprised if I told you who financed me."

"I was years at the task with help from your government which had taken me in as a result of action by the British. I went hither and yonder ending up some years later sitting on the porch of an old hotel in a Kentucky town by the river. That's where you discovered me."

"As they say here on the hillside, I was just about plumb wore out. My man was a slick one and got away just days —- in one case, just hours before I stepped on his long tail."

"You men probably saw him around town, that is, before I got here. He got this far in his meandering escape path away from Cossack justice. I learned his alias, adopted name or one of his names since he'd taken several over the years just as I had, in my case new ones given to me by one of my sponsoring agencies. Of course I knew by then who he was and where. He had been working as a farm hand and by now was known by the name, Arturo Rodriquez, which it is said is a common Hispanic name. I also had learned about some of the places he'd been. By then I sought no more the idea of killing. I had known for some time where he was living which was real close and I vowed to leave him alone, but now his every move would be followed."

My helpers said, 'We have no proof about those other murders.'

"He has that Mongol look, more than me, which is a stock look with many Cossack people since the Mongols back in time had invaded my part of the country and left their mark, dominant features with many of our women whose women ancestors of the region had been raped by the Mongols."

"As you are aware by now, Arturo got away a few days before I got to town, or very soon after. Or did he? I dare ask, how did this fellow know I was in town, getting close?"

"It had to be somebody in the government to warn him, which also is of my new country, mine since I became one as you are, not many years ago through naturalization."

"My job at first was to find him and kill him. My sponsors meant, To Kill! Like on the battlefield, or off, wherever. It by now had become distasteful to me — as softly as I can say to you, mild."

Leo said his finances, including living expenses, all came from the British and American governments, and his Cossacks, who had dispatched him to the west. 'Kill him!' A lot of men back home said. "We won't rest until you do."

Clint commented on Leo's accent, which was so slight most would never be aware of it. He also mentioned his apparent knowledge of the English language. Leo said the printed language of Russia, even much of the Romance language accents of the west were not far different but so confusing by the 'odd' way so much of it appears on paper.

Leo played down 'my necessary movement across the continent' to ask Oscar about 'Oscar's retreat,' which was an old cabin only a few miles from town.

He said: "I'm not a poet, but I've read a good deal of your western literature, mostly British and American, in your poetry."

"Your cabin above the river on the hillside would be an ideal place for this here old Russian (and American hillbilly) poet, to create a living word, which as a gift in literature among my people even in intended prose, which so often comes across as poetry."

Oscar said for Clint's memory that it was the old falling-down cabin on the old Gelig family farm which was never lived in after the family practically gave it away or for a little traveling money and went north during the Great Depression.

"There's no water or electric. A fireplace with no wood left. But do not be alarmed, there's plenty of wood around; a lot of dead trees that can be cut down with a pocket knife. A mountain stream with fresh water is a couple hundred yards away, closer than it once was because of the stream's change in direction that could be piped to the cabin. The rest room as such, an old broken shack affair with just one hole, is close in."

Leo was smiling. He said to Oscar, and to Clint: "I will tell you what I have in mind after I restore the cabin; I pipe in the water and arrange for an electrical connection, which means stretching power lines across the river, if you'll allow me to go down there when I need a moment of solitude. Who knows, maybe I'll even try my hand at writing a bit of poetry that is in the heart of this old mountain codger."

Clint said. "I believe any man as reader and respectful of an ancient philosophy at a late time in his life hopes to end it in surrender to the beauty of the classics as he imagines his brand of Heaven to be. If anybody who has a resolution and sticks to it, it probably will be you." This was the lonely farm boy Clint Greene; apparent from the blood flow in his speech that he was envious.

Clint had listened intently to Leo's long biographical tale through his guest's third beer, which began with Leo at an early age (thirteen), and continued right up to the lip of the beer can with Clint's idea in mind that someday he, Clint the writer, might put it all into a book he would write.

Clint didn't want to tackle the task until after he had rid himself of the fluff in his own life, which had taken an unfamiliar turn just lately. Had it really? Clint could think that returning to the mountain of his boyhood to read books, drink coffee, hey hey hey . . . was retirement as it was meant to be in the late Twentieth Century.

A mountain man transplanted to Ohio once told Clint Greene: "For every moment of elation there is a moment of despair."

When he recalled that old mountaineer's proverb and its source from a man he knew as a neighbor and would meet every day, when he mentioned it to him on that later day, the Buckeye would refute 'such drivel' as of 'low caliber,' and not worthy of any better advice he'd gotten to know in the past from the current local editor of the county newspaper (before Oscar), even though he too called himself a hillbilly.

Nevertheless, it helped Clint accept his lot. He tried to reconcile the events of his dwindling time on Earth by recall of a good life with wife Lily and his children, and days of satisfaction, at first, with his career as a newspaperman, which he would say in his latter days (and that thought was some time ago).

Alas, of late, despair was winning out over elation. Clint thought of himself now as just one more among life's failures, years wasted at a typewriter and printing press. He could have done better for his fellow man.

In his contributions to society and his passing into another dimension he would like to take with him a respect for the words and works of the founders of his country. He also had been derelict in his time and duty to his family. He'd told Leo and Oscar just the day before that he had failed at everything he'd ever attempted.

Man, was he crawling along the cold, cold ground today. What I need, he said to himself, is the advice of a mentor, someone like myself who has been through the same dissatisfaction with his life's chosen work. He said to nobody, "I've never had a shoulder to cry on. Right now I need somewhere to turn for spiritual food, like maybe what you guys can give me. That is the only thing at this moment I can think of to bring me back to circulation with my fellow creatures on this Earth."

In his late night talk session with himself and his maker, he generally found enough release from his misery to find himself on the way to a good sleep. For the next hour as his thoughts turned to Doris with the words but the face of Lily trying to break through, the two became one person, or alike in his feelings for a life partner, even at his age. If asked, he'd say that he would have died for either of them.

He'd loved Lily and was devastated upon her sudden death. He'd had only his kids, now all pretty much adult and wise, to hold his heart and collect the tears from his face as he thought of their years together —- always with her counsel and comforting words.

Now here comes Doris, both she and he on the other side, down hill you could call it, briefly bringing back into his life the near side of happiness, reaching for his (heart?) with promises of collecting his tears which he would welcome and bottling them up and hiding away the whole shebang.

He hoped the kids would be needed again like they did when they were at home. He wished they depended on him more, as they'd once done so.

His feelings of failure were put into the same old bottle. He hoped his losses in life all his disappointments were not a human trait reserved just for him, admitting by now that he was dependant on his fellow creature. He'd looked for them in the faces of everyone he met on the street of his town and decided that loneliness is nigh onto a universal attribute of life of every man or every woman wherever he went. The faces of people like the reflected misery like his.

Yet, the dew came on like polished silver across the mountains, reflecting the return of the sun of day after the dark and despairing night, bringing budding springtime to Earth life in the hills for what was left of the poet in the bothered creative part of all he once was, Clint thought as he crossed his own piece of the Earth on the way to his carriage.

Back home as an ex-Marine he surveyed his old/new jalopy, a vehicle he figured he could afford with the insurance tidbit (not enough to cover his scrambled eggs) which he had received since he'd lost his other transport when it went over the side of the mountain five or six months ago, with him in it, of course. He hoped it would keep going for him during the planned journey to as yet unrevealed destination. He'd been planning this journey for the past several days.

Two days ago Clint had given an envelope to each of his OMEN friends. He said: "All that is in there is a slip of paper with a wireless number for a phone. Also, you'll find just one word, which is a password. The password will provide your contact permission to contact me. Shades of duh uh duh CIA and de FBI, oh wow —- memorize the password, tear it off and burn it, says my friend if I had one in the FBI. If you do not use it right away, your contact will ask for it."

He'd learned all that from his sergeant in boot camp, he said, and from the TV shows that involved any or all the investigative agencies of the federal government, which he'd had so much faith in because they were of his government, his democratic trust and loyalty to the people.

He thought it was silly, a big joke. Somebody else had asked the higher-up instructor if he'd been kidding, especially if he was an officer. All he got for a questionable answer was a little almost not-to be an educated retort.

"I won't tell you where I'm going, but if anybody in these days can disappear, I am going to try. Don't contact me, unless it is vital, absolutely dire, and necessary."

"Well if our old buddy has lost his way in the jungle, we should have him checked out." That was friend Leo.

Why all this big secret crap —- so the three of them laughed together over what might be a secret, not because he had a Russian friend who was expected to be used to it.

"Conspiracy is all around us," his friend said.

(His matter of the big secret and his estimate was not exactly as printed here. Back in his newspaper days up in Ohio, a man determined to have been killed by gunshot as said by the law, was found dead on the street. He wrote a story with the little information he could obtain from the coroner, the local sheriff and the funeral home, which was as far as he could go, taking without suspicion that more was not needed. It was a sort of thing that happened all the time, unless it was called for, which he would have looked into to satisfy his role as a newspaperman.)

A few days later a fellow who said he was FBI showed him his identification card at his office and Clint for the moment accepted his explanation. of it. The story might have had more to say and the FBI man asked if he knew more and to hide the fact that the case which called for security reasons be kept out of the press. Clint said that was all he knew.

(This aroused Clint's interest. Ever since he tried to study the man and who in his agency had given such authority. The agency man shut up, for no reason given. For sure Clint did not believe him and for years thought it over and simply left it in the past, except for losing all respect for the man and his actions, along with others in federal offices. He had encountered others and the way they did business did not change his mind. He began to criticize them, bringing a big laugh from the readers of his papers' humor column and the idea of OMEN, which he had written just this week).

No more columns, no more action on our little serious planning, he said to others in OMEN. No explanation. Call Doris and tell her I'll call in a few days, no more than a few weeks. She'll use her wiles to get you to talk, like batting those long lashes.

He felt guilty that he had resorted to a TV show script that called for such secrecy, since long ago he'd been taken in again and again by someone close to him in an unguarded moment who had betrayed him in what he'd believed was a 'don't tell anybody' pact. His friends were surprised, but accepted the OMEN idea with a hint of a grin. The unspoken agreement written on a grain of sand on a New Jersey shore lingered in raised eyebrows.

He should have alerted Doris to his plan. That last little situation with Doris he'd not anticipated. Until just lately it wouldn't have mattered, but he felt, surprisingly, that it did so belong with Leo, as a big part of his new unfolding citizenship back in his first hour before in his new home, which happened every few months, maybe a year or so, again and again. Yeah, in his new home in America, by now a sacred thing. Take that, ye, Thomas Wolfe, ye.

If anybody had said he should at least have told Doris he was going away for awhile to sort of think through all that was happening in his life lo these past several months, he'd have answered briskly that 'a woman can't keep a secret; even if he didn't mean it.' As he thought of it, he said he had allegiance to no man, only to the flag of his country, and to his God. Doris would wait, in silence, for 'her man' to come home.

An experienced newsman had to tell what he knew to somebody. (Today it is 'a newspaperman who isn't worthy of the title.' He can't keep a secret that belongs to the public, or he believes it does not belong out there.) His job meant relating to his readers or to somebody every word he knew. Since he was of late considered because of OMEN to be 'a public man,' otherwise, he would not be a shirt tail accepted journalist, a live working hot lead reporter.

(That society was the toughest to get into without establishment approval of his experience and acclaim, and worst to get out of. Such as it is, all that 'stuff' otherwise is junk nonsense; he would declare.)

(He'd thought how his native-born mountain stubbornness had gone toward the day when he'd lost his newspaper and come close to being ridden out of town on a narrow fence rail that would leave him with a bunch of splinters in his behind if there was still room back there —- like a sort of James Joyce discourse, the flow of subconscious thinking to fill out the pages of a novel based on the daily life of a journalist or citizen, as some writers have interpreted his writing; as some critics understood the Irish poet; maybe it was the flow of conscious thinking).

The sun was high into a blue and somewhat cloud-broken sky taking the fog that had covered his path for the past half hour through a forest along the long ridge, coming out in the glare that wouldn't be kind to his eyes as he headed east. He turned right onto the brief promise of a trail built for the use of the wider trucks for the first growth of trees after the original cut was built to get to market with logs for the speeded up demand by a growing building industry. The road needed a newly paved black top.

A constant changing of lanes for a moment evinced from him a gentle cuss because he thought he'd missed the last lap, as told to him by a phone at a filling station and country store by his host not far along the road. He now was on an ancient ridge highway much too narrow in a brief encounter that at first was two lanes then a single lane designed to confuse an invader by the graveled two lanes that became the interstate entrance he passed on his left that was at last the final lap's mountain approach to the magnificent high country of Carolina.

It was delicately told by his Indian friend, all of that approach to his home could have been designed more than a hundred years or so ago during the exile of his people to the recently called Indian territory of Oklahoma to confuse their pursuers to the salvation edict by the president of his country. Whew, said his friend at the end of the line.

Managing a living on this land would be hardscrabble even to the most energetic, but a lot of unbound folks settled here to live out their lives, and began to restore it.

Included were the Cherokee, the Creek, the Chickasaw and the Choctaw. From the deeper south in the western movement were the Seminole — the Five Civilized Tribes. All were targets of the white settlers.

Among early settlers on the Carolina lands were Scotch-Irish (sic), an industrious people of coastal Northern Ireland who were first 'invited' by King James to leave Scotland. They left for America in the mid-to-late Eighteenth and early Nineteenth centuries only to leave again eventually to set up homes in the valleys and the rocks of hill ground of the Appalachians that would be a real challenge to a soil breaker. It was hardpan ground but far from the lords of the manor.

Their neighbors right away were Germans and assorted Europeans, all suspicious of the different religious beliefs of each other. They were jealous of the Indians who had earlier settled the more fertile lands of the mountains and through their (U.S.) government later to exile; the Indians were expected to leave by force their Promised Land of the east. The white settlers early in the Nineteenth Century wanted the occupied Indian lands.

The Indians would be among the hundreds of their kind who in just a few cold winter months left on what was called the Trail of Tears to re-settle the hardened Earth of the mid-west, which the white man at the moment feared to tread. White men then had occupied the pre-historic eastern Indian lands until they conceived the plan to remove the Indians to the west by order of President Andrew Jackson.

About the only way European settlers in southern Appalachia could get their corn crop to market from here was to carry it in liquid form in their saddlebags, but to the new men on their new land, were of a new sort of government, a reminder that what they said about making their own whiskey for the market was not legal.

That is one more reason they became such good riflemen and cannon fodder as soldiers in service to the same (American now) European governors.

When the Europeans passed through on their way west they found the Melungeons, a people not knowing how they got here or where they came from but content to live and farm in isolation on the mountaintops and bother nobody. This, the Scotch Irish could understand.

These beautiful people known to the pioneers to their area as Melungeons, content in their former isolation, and perhaps Caucasian in profile, were determined by the newcomers to be neither Native Americans nor Blacks (who as slaves might have fled their masters or arrived by choice before and after the Civil War), were said by some historians had joined the people on the mountain and possibly were integrated into the community. Their dark hair, a slight Mediterranean skin color and manner were to cause speculation about their origin.

Native to these hills, slightly to the east and south, was Thomas Wolfe, who wrote: 'You Can't Go Home Again,' but he did. Wherever he went he carried his 'home' with him.

Controversial to this day the land and the people faced another challenge coming with each new generation.

Whatever fate came across the mountains to recall ancient ways the new settlers would cling as much as they were able to the land, their church, and many of the mores of their ancestors, like the Melungeons, whoever they were.

They still came, the Scotch-Irish, at first identified by clans and sects, many of them exiled from their European and Asian homes to the New World where others of their kin had found peace and a way to feed their families. Indians accepted them and many thrived, only to lose themselves later to the greedy from the outside.

Peace and contentment that helps to define it means dissimilar change and a shaded generational movement among a free people whatever their origin; it also is the story of the new nation and its culture from across the sea.

Gold! What this metal has done to the appetite of civilized man cannot be measured even by the educated and 'legal' yet unselfish mind of the times. Let's say it was a cry of 'gold' that purportedly arose in the southern mountains by the white man who said they had a 'right' to the land.

It worked, all the way to the White House then occupied by a southerner, arousing the covetous invaders who claimed the land occupied by the native farmers and other later residents who tilled the somewhat uneven lands of the upper Carolinas and adjacent estates.

Free land still was to be had in the west to anyone who would claim it. A far off land of much promise that was withdrawn almost on the day the disrupted and worn out caravans from the south arrived with what was left of their families and worldly goods.

The Europeans, the White-Eyes wanted southern Indian lands that had been plowed and cropped since an ancient, lost in time, beginning.

History tells how some stubborn men who with their families hid beneath cliffs, later to recover farmlands, at least bits and pieces of it among the rocks and rills. They lived on berries and wild game, as had their ancestors (men of the woods) for half the lives of their generation. Families left 'hidden behind,' emerged from rock shelters to rebuild on land the whites did not want.

Perhaps the white men who were attracted to the lands soon discovered some gold and other valuable metals. It is still John Swift's silver mine, waiting for the believer but not like what happened in California a few years later. In the upper South, it was a big piece of property that in not many years had become some of the most valuable land in America. Much of what you read here is to recognize an historic thriving Cherokee country.

Seminoles in Florida thrive in their welcome to the tourist invasion; Creek farmers expanded their holdings until many descendants live today in the shadow of the big Navy ships parked in Mobile Bay.

Clint wondered: had he missed the farm? He must be more aware. The road by now had become more a path than roadway.

It is not how he had remembered it, but it must be. He had not been distracted. Had he overshot his objective by what the biographers of James Joyce called 'the flow of thought into the consciousness?' Had his musings led him away from the dirt road by that 'interior monologue?' Man, what a definition had crept into his non-thinking.

Dead ahead where the road had found its end was a low-built but adequate to a large family ranch-style brick house which backed up to a white painted barn all proud, with its face to the morning sun. A Kentucky Blue Grass horseman would call it fit for his favorite steed obviously of blood going back a few thousand years to Arabia. At its back door next to the barn were three wide white-fenced paddocks, grassy plots for the finely-appointed horses dining on the Irish green, which could be called 'full bosomed' grass.

A man at the near paddock resting his chin in the palms of his hands on the top fence rail looked up as the stuttering of Clint's vehicle might have disturbed his deep thinking.

Clint had stopped a few feet from the fence and shut down the engine as his friend stuck his hand through the fence in greeting. The man had a mile wide grin, as more than a few European writers Clint had known might identify it, more than you'd expect from a stoic-like solemnity of the red man recalled for him from an early day of the Hollywood screen. His raised arm was a salute not accorded many men.

It was a recognized Indian trait of a movie-for-boys inside dark Saturday, which was carried over by the young fans from watching Indians at war on the prairie as depicted in a matinee battle thriller made in the infant years of the movie business.

An odd thing about early 'cowboys and Indians' films: many overseas viewers still think that is America today. Otherwise it is all tall buildings that disappear into the ether on a clouded day.

"Hail to my White Eyes friend, defender of the buffalo, lordly taker of beautiful Indian women. Welcome again to my humble tepee (tipi)," said the straight tanned man in a light-colored suede jacket with the fringe on top (and hem).

The jacket reminded Clint Greene of so many dangling icicles from a tree limb in mid-Winter. On a cool mountaintop at mid-day in late season a coat was a wise thing to depend on as he remembered he had forgotten to pack his own jacket. Then he thought, 'I might have a coat in the trunk,' hoping it was so. His friend would consider him to be wise in such a decision.

Dick's outer coat likely could be a subconscious imitation of society's typecast of the recently hailed and newspaper-touted oil-rich red man, and the white man in proper business wear in the west. Some white men would have been delighted to say that such red men of wealth and otherwise not of the western European race, were the same 'mocking' Indians whatever the source of their wealth. Clint thought of the 'red man' who only recently had begun to flourish in casino halls. Later, Clint's friend would say, "we try to get back something of the wampum the white man had often denied us, or was stolen from our honorable ancestors."

Another badge of 'arrival,' even by this man of the soil and breeder of fine horses and purebred cattle, was his grand polished and decorated high leather boots that in his late life 'emergence' were designed to set off the wide-brimmed western style Stetson hat and the moderate (deerskin or suede) jacket.

"Why you fat old firewater addicted reprobate," said Clint.

"How long have you been in the racing business? This here Kentucky boy knows a string of thoroughbreds and the care you've given them; beginning when you sent them into a field of oats to feast on as their reward for service to man in the last million years and in as many ways," he said.

It was an admirable gesture, words to greet friends who as warriors together, or college friends, like Clint and Chief Dick, which proved to be a genuine respect for each other.

Upon reminder, he also could be Soaring Baptist Eagle. The latter moniker would have been awarded by college campus hangers-on who were pleased to have a real 'live American Indian' living in their midst. Clint's friend, Richard Whitewater, had been called 'Baptist Eagle,' by many dormitory mates; later to become, in jest, of course, 'Barefoot Boy with Cheek.' Chief Dick had learned a long time ago that all these nicknames were given in sport. They came in friendship to an Indian, and he showed his pleasure in it.

'Barefoot Boy,' even then almost an insult, on this day had just said: "We'll talk about this place later, my wife's blessing from waiting tables so her man could be content later in retirement. Come on, dismount and we'll go on up to the house. Before dark we'll move your Kentucky steel steed to the far end of the driveway out back."

Pointing to a horse at grass, he said, there is the most valued thing identified by the 'white man' as a sign of wealth. "Right there old buddy mine is the one powerful way to bring a noble American Indian to parity with the white man."

Dick would say: "It is not our way to imitate the white man; in fact far far more white eyes make the generally weak and silly effort to break into our Indian style."

"It helps make them feel powerful, all-seeing, and even attractive to women if they are successful in imitation. We laugh and recall the treaty-making and treaty-breaking wily European white men traders. If you are not aware, it is money old filthy green stuff with big numbers on it, which is all they look for in their fellow human beings, and which brings the Native American to the hound dogs of a newfound equality."

"But we're out here killing precious time; to an Indian time's too rare to waste. Evelyn has gone to town to pick up a few steaks in our corner of the frozen-food locker there. We'll grill 'em out back on the patio as soon as she returns."

By the light of the disappearing day the two sat where they could watch the dying embers of the grill.

"Good steak," said Clint.

"We thank you," said Richard. "That beef came from my own herd. I kill a beef every fall; they cut it up for packaging down at the locker; they package it for me and stow it for the blowing snows of a hilltop winter. A long way, I reckon, from jerky made from a buffalo kill. That's how we did it before you White Eyes bought tickets to ride a tour train through the buffalo herd and kill them from the coach windows. Five, maybe more million buffalo reduced to a couple thousand in a puff of smoke from a railroad engine."

"Owners of the railroad paid Buffalo Bill a fortune to cut down the herds. The dead animals were piled up on the ground to rot away."

Clint asked if anyone ever speculated on how an Indian like him with all the walls built around him and against him managed to build this empire on a hill.

"You know the usual answer to that," said Chief Richard. "Every 'empire plank' of it began in a hidden-away place, and with that one calf, a farm project I was given as a start when I was in 4-H. The horse business grew through the years from profits from our cattle herds."

"It's a good thing I didn't have to drive my herd across sage grass country down in Texas up to Abilene every year, but I'll aver that those longhorn boys built that dried up country," and he added: "That's what I had hoped to do on this land that was first plowed by my people. I pretty much had to buy it back, foot by foot, acre by acre."

After dark as the cool of the evening began creeping in, they retreated to the kitchen for a while, then to the sitting room for coffee late into the pleasant spring night they talked of many things, mainly the girls they dated up at college.

They talked of Richard's bit of a problem he met at the admissions office when his race, his birthplace, and one or two other little ugly items concerning boyhood playmates and the girls he courted in high school were recalled; he thanked Clint once more for his action before the board.

"I didn't do all that, whatever you say," said Clint. "You had the big United States of America behind you. You'd helped win the war for our country despite the fact that we pale faces always managed to keep a war going. You were the fighting men in the right places; time would ever be grateful. In the Second World War, the U.S. government was on your side for a change, the whole bunch of soldiers and Marines were behind you. Your kind had been kicked around long enough. Almost sixteen million teen-agers, maybe a few more men and women from the big war were fighting for you this time."

Clint had defended this Indian against a few of the country boy hotshots on his first day on campus who wanted to play dirty because of what the history books had taught them.

Just one more fighter's sacrifices during the war that he'd remembered in particular had left one of his legs stiff and unbending like thirsty men of the thirties whose leg became near useless, stiffened from drinking a kind of rum (Jamaican Rum). Clint couldn't recall the rum by label. He knew it had been imported to the U.S. during Prohibition from Jamaica, to cash in on sealed alcohol sales -- enforced by law, for gosh sakes.

Clint's Marines talked about it on a dark night in the bush (in the jungle) by drinking the ooze of wanton heat-treated trees to cut out too many pained voices of suffering men of war across the jungle near the dividing lines of the two civilized nations at war.

As the sun was about to drop into night, Clint through silent pleasure a triumph once more proud of his friend yet as always seeking to define this dark, stately Native American. His friend was like many first Americans who had become distinguished in the world as its first resident citizens by aliens (outsiders?) on that long ago by now distant day. Clint had been surely blessed, for want of a better sorting out, to be in his presence and accepted.

On that near-forgotten day, Richard, with tongue in cheek, a bit of jollity on his face and without looking up from his book, accused Clint of trying to steal his girl friends. Clint retorted that soon as Richard learned Clint had found a "someone among the campus coeds newly-arrived and as soon wooed by this Kentuckian," as told by Dick who finished Clint's sentence, he would find a way to exercise his own continental charm, try to win her before he lost her to the savage white man.

Chief Dick quickly referred again to his earlier barb that it was in smart answer to the white men who were attracted to and sometimes took as wives, comely Indian women from one of the up-country civilized tribes.

"Remember that red haired girl who used to follow you around? Red headed she was, but a big part Indian. She only did that so she could be with you when I was nearby, to make me jealous."

"I don't believe a word of what you're telling me, but I admire you for not taking advantage of her interest in you. Besides, we broke up even before we ever got together."

Dick went on to say that soon as a white man took an Indian wife, she would start to remember how much happier she was among her Indians. First chance she got, she would go right back to her tribe.

This nonsense went on between them into the dimming of day, even as Dick's wife Evelyn sat over there intent on her knitting or reading but with lit-up amusement. Right then an opening was provided which allowed Dick to get serious, a first of the afternoon:

"As you'll be our guest for as long as you wish to stay —- and I say how fortunate we are that you came to visit and we sure look forward to many days of your presence —- so let's delay for a while the real reason for your coming to our mountain. You really sounded like it was a crucial thing on the telephone."

"I'd thought about coming down here for a short visit with friends for a long time, but I let it stay in the back of my mind because I thought I had too much to do in my little old newspaper business. I should have come on anyway, because I would have wanted you to meet Lily."

"You know I need you, always have. I planned to get to it soon enough."

"What I need from you is advice only an Indian can give, with the wisdom of an ancient people who have been honored in life and death by the Great Spirit. Yes, we will talk of it."

You might expect at this point that Chief Dick would look at Clint's face with the quizzical cynicism of a plainsman's narrowed eyes. In full trust these two friends vowed to speak no more about it until it was time. They'd know the hour when they could talk about women or of anything else. It would come with the respect each had for the other.

Clint would say that if you were not an Indian you'd never understand.

In days that followed, he was taken on a rifle shoot in woods just beyond Dick's green fields. They would fire at rocks and tree stumps in the woods, limbs big and small (the small in fierce competition). Dick declared that they would find no tin cans set up for targets in his woods, often placed opportunely on others' woods to give the sportsman noisy kickers to shoot at, as some might prefer. He expected, he said, always to have "a clean woods," as clean and green as his farmland.

One afternoon they went out with brushes and white paint to finish the replacement boards to his white fences. Richard said his people out west stretched barbed wire on their ranches, a disgraceful legacy of the white man, but he saw no need of mean barriers 'up here.' He said that Indians had no love at all for boundary wire. Barbed wire, in memory was an unwelcome intrusion. The white fences would separate the paddocks. It dented an Indian's idea of freedom. The land belonged to all, that is, until a white man took a liking to it.

Horses, Dick said on the way to the fields the next day, were born to serve men, all people, children, and girl friends. Too bad, he said, that muscles were replaced in so many instances by gasoline engines. Apart from their use in man's wars, and like today's betting track, the thoroughbred horse was a pleasurable thing just to have around. They rode out to survey once more the hidden (and secret) corners of the farm.

One night his Indian friend and Evelyn drove them into town, where it was like old-home week as the two hill Indians and their outlander friend entered a restaurant that was more dedicated to tourist business than just another fast food service to the locals. It was fancy, a dining palace, as Clint had not seen in a long time, surprised and proud to see the Whitewater family receiving a welcome like the king and queen of England. Dick either owned the place or they were among the regulars, the few among other townsfolk amid the tourists, easily identified. Clint thought that Dick and the other (local) diners acted as if Dick and Evelyn owned the place, deciding that was exactly the truth of it.

The town was in a valley about eight miles in the direction opposite from where Clint had entered Dick and Evelyn's place. The road down to town was rocky and narrow, most likely muddy in the winter.

Clint asked about it, wondering why he'd been given such complicated directions up to the farm when just a few miles or so along, it was just down the hill from them. Evelyn answered the query this time: "That's to keep tourists or curious other people with a yen to explore hoping to find Indians living in bearskin teepees and cooking on an outdoor fire,"

It sounded reasonable to Clint. On Sunday it was church in the tiny wooden recently painted building almost hidden in a bushy corner of the woods about a mile back of Dick's and Evelyn's place. It was to Clint an all-purpose building a school during the week with a wooden floor for square dancing like the church of America's first settlers. The wildwood church, not imitative of the towered bricks of coastal cities the grandchildren of the pioneers had known for much of their generation.

Dick bellowed out the familiar songs known by Clint from his own boyhood in the mountains of Kentucky. It felt good during his visit in the church with Dick's aging mother and father; he was comfortable as they sat and talked prior to the service with them at ease among their neighbors. He noted that differences in the church and his own on his mountain was the seating, cushions instead of the hard wooden benches of his home church he never exactly appreciated when he was growing up. He figured that for the added padded comfort Dick and Evelyn were responsible through a personal gift.

Along the rows, and the church was nearly packed, were as many men and women of paler faces as there were Indians. Country people, faithful to the church; he knew they were as loyal to their country. As they prepared to leave, the entire congregation formed lines to shake his hand to thank him for visiting their little Sunday gathering and reminding that he would always be welcome.

Late Sunday afternoon, sleepy, dozing as they watched one TV re-run after another in the family room, Clint began talking:

"I reckon you know what I've been doing since I came home after Lily died and I sold my paper, gave it away, really. My kids didn't want it after watching me count dimes to give them a good old-time Christmas or college money after those years of neglecting them and Lily, around-the-clock proofing type galleys with my eyes propped open with sucker sticks and printer's ink all over my shirt front."

"I no longer felt at home up in Ohio; reckon I never did. Our generation of 'news hounds' (yes, as in dogs) looked for a place in journalism history alongside William Allen White. In an effort to imitate him, many of us made fools of ourselves. I'd begun to realize that White, of an earlier generation, had set a pace that could not be reckoned with in a quiet but difficult time and citified place.'

"White, for your information, was publisher of the Emporia, Kansas, Gazette. He gained national fame after publication of his, 'What's the Matter with Kansas?' editorial. He had angered the 'powers that be' and was cited by his peers as an editor of courage. When I tried it, the dam broke."

"Imitation of White's newspaper venture by others never seemed to work any more. Newsmen of my era were no different from a sea commander's man with a deck swab. He or she is a narcissus, in vanity ever hoping to be noticed as he notices himself. I would declare that our little man hoped to be reckoned worth his meager wages mainly by news people for his writing."

"In our time, to the orators go most of the rare salutes, sometimes for poets as they read their lines before a literary bunch of bookstore habitués. We of the press believe, or it is so with many of us who like to read, that a literary talent is a gift of the gods, so in gratitude we feel that we must take advantage of it, perhaps in any publication we can find."

"This old hillbilly knows that he was never so endowed. He goes right on with his share of stupidity, writing of local doings to make people believe he really does have some little fire, especially on their behalf. Well, I did I in public. I made myself look stupid in the eyes of my people at a downtown chit chat over coffee and sweet stuff not so long after I retired and came home to Kentucky."

"What I did was suggest that someone from among us go to Heaven where we might encourage some great leader from the past to accept reincarnation and come back to tell us that we had 'nothing to fea-uh but fea-uh itself;' joking, of course, to so be taken. Well, by golly, that sunk it for me. As a normal or common man, I felt alone, so dang inadequate to a degree that I halfway believed I had to help deliver such a person, eat my words whole without sugar and cream, or run and hide for good. I kicked myself all the way out to the Groundhog Sinks (that's a Post Office back in my county)."

"It all began with that coffee gang talking about the shape the world was in because of a universal looseness of morals in government and bed-diving into old motels, or out in the woods or bedrooms where they didn't belong and loose with somebody else's money.

Many in society, especially scientists and much of the God-fearing population were laughed at for their belief that the big troubles apparent in the weather caused by man were leading to an eruption in the ecology and everything else all about, where we lived. Serious stuff, man, at least I thought so —- and I wanted to encourage collective attitudes." I began to write with the idea of urging readers and citizens throughout the land, expecting the majority of the people, to get serious.

"I've told you about how three of us organized OMEN, to alert the citizens. In their day-to-day business it was possible to stop this thing just outside the city walls, I wrote. My little but big stupidities kept right on happening but now right out on the porch of my cabin. Soon, I learned that nobody gave a dad-burned second thought to what I said. I knew I had failed. Here I am; for one thing I want to go home from here all fired up with new ideas from about the smartest feller I ever knew in my life."

"Mainly, though, I've sought the self-confidence that you've given me in the past that might still be rubbed off on me. I want you to assure me that I'm worth something. I'm a loser right now, sure do, I feel it, Dick, among my people, and if it mattered to anyone else in the rest of the world."

"Help me, Sir Richard, as I try to regain the faith I once might have had. Tell me, 'the Great Spirit is real,' that he lives in the souls of men and especially among Native Americans despite all the insults, the killings, the taking of their lands and dignity by the greedy Europeans, our ancestors, we my people certainly and embarrassingly to put it mildly well among them."

"Frankly, I've been more down-spirited and empty-hearted than I've ever been; I've lost my faith in both man and God. I'm looking for my soul. Once more, I need your help."

Clint figured he'd said all that could be said, and it was, he thought, evident by the too long pause before he received a response from Chief Dick or his wife Evelyn. Evelyn went right on with her book —- reading was easier than working with a needle. Dick gazed at the fire, which was doing tricks of its own and not at all concerned about applause.

In the corner of his eye he knew that Evelyn was watching him. He recalled that Dick had said once that Evelyn wrote a lot of poetry, had begun putting pretty words on paper when she was in grade school. One big reason he had married her was that she was smarter than was. Clint hadn't said that what he was doing in the years ever since a boyhood dream to someday through his writing make an attempt to 'save the world,' or do his part in that too large an endeavor for him, but he was sure that his friends understood.

Even now it was slightly edited to read: 'Save the Earth.' Dick the Indian looked across the brief space between the den chairs set facing the fireplace, right into the eye of a friend, his guest, without a grin or even a hint of reproach or rebuke. He said:

"Clint, my blood brother and since that day long past that the youths we encountered once on campus were not being exposed to the wisdom that was stored in the libraries and classroom shelves and books and rare brains of young American college people as well as in the hearts we can call it of a great number of new white Americans. I am aware that neither you nor I are any more prepared at this time to give advice or in any way or try to seek, or understand why a Caucasian would even hope to save the world."

"Let me think about this for a day or two. I'm not sure I can help you. Tomorrow will be a new day. Perhaps both of us can get some inspiration from the sun and the Earth. It's getting late. Let's go to bed."

Dick said: "You're going to be mighty disappointed when a lightning strike comes close enough to tell you —- in an electric moment and right soon —- that you've been seeking an impossibly perfect world. I think you are getting real close to persuading yourself that it has never been and never will be. The masked expectation may proffer only a dark cloud that has held so little promise."

"Melting icebergs, earthquakes, hurricanes and flowing lava from a volcanic eruption in a far land - all these things they'd seen. They became yesterday's headline, as soon forgotten. If they thought of them at all, perhaps with a sigh, they only knew that they themselves had survived."

"Yes, it's what's called optimism in the human psyche," said Clint. "In spite of all the warnings about not turning to look back at her world being consumed by fire, the mass destruction of her home town, Lot's wife, who thought hers was a perfect world, did so right after being warned to look straight ahead and was turned into a pillar of salt when she hesitated."

Dick said: "I've always wondered about that. I've looked for the lesson it's supposed to teach us. Except for keeping a memory alive, respecting the past through time heeding the advice of their elders and to always look to the next day, a next season, a next hunt; it is the optimistic nature of people."

"You have hinted at it, you've touched its edge, even wept for the loss of freedom by Americans despite war and economic depression, demagoguery, executive thievery, and just plain old stupidity and inefficiency of 'the great body of common men and women.' These you have with your faith in God, the Great Spirit, told you two thousand or more years ago."

"Somewhere, in history class or in one of the Great Books with which you've made acquaintance, you quote a source that says the Indian since prior to time has always known about themselves, their thirst for freedom, with many, or a sincere wish for or a desire for simply, war. They had to maintain a life based on the goals of others, who can be called 'warlike.'

"With us, it has always been a spiritual thing. That's why, in conquering my people with your gunpowder and destroying our villages and source of food, taking us down tribe by tribe, man for man, you've never killed our faith in the Great Spirit, call him or her, God, Supreme Being of the Universe, which is the soul itself in the Indian of antiquity, of today, and tomorrow, and always."

"You know of our respect for the Earth itself, and this, I believe, is what you want to understand so you can sell it, or try in some way to instill it in the minds and customs of the people as the only way they can save the possible destruction of the Earth. I have faith in what we can call 'your intentions.'"

"Now that I've made my little speech, bared my soul, let's get on with talk about how you, and we, the Indian as a partner, as fellow citizens, can go out once more in our weak attempt to save the Earth, without further discussion of the possible, or impossible."

Clint: "Whew, I'll say. It's been in front of us right from the start -- if we could get you elected to the U.S. Senate, maybe President. If those things happened we'd know we'd gotten much out of this life. We could greet our ancestors and report that all is well back here." Hee-haw from Dick's corner was heard miles away.

Chief Dick told Clint at breakfast that they would have an early supper:

"It will be the last meal you'll have until maybe Friday. This is just Tuesday. Think you can handle it? You ask, handle what?"

"It is an unknown experience to a one-time Marine. Your abstinence and 'ordeal,' as you may refer to it the future -- if you tell about it -- will take place into a third day in silence, beginning right after supper. On Friday, you may ask questions of me and any other Indian. I suggest that you go into that two-day separation from all men and society with an unclouded attitude."

"Obstruct any and all thoughts of revenge against all and everyone. Forgive anyone that you can recall who has ever intended you harm, insulted you, or kept you from achieving a desire or goal you might once have had."

"At some previous time in your life you might have encouraged within yourself to forget all that and get on with your life. Don't consider their words, their actions or those who caused them. Remember also that whatever you think in view of present circumstance, someone will be nearby to hear you when you have a need to be heard. This is an ancient Indian rite; it is amended little over many millennia for a purpose, which we will discuss with you after it is over, keeping the words of one of the men of outstanding ability among the Indians."

"Men in what you might call 'modern' Indian history above all else will be in your thoughts, put there we hope by the Great Spirit so you may better understand that all men suffer; they dream of what might or could be. Your past will be your present. It is to your purpose in what is left of your life here that you know this."

"In your thoughts will be Sitting Bull, a wise old prophet, one of a number of Indians of similar name. He was a 'Hunkpapa Teton Sioux,' and he received visions mostly in his dreams from the Great Spirit. As the 'chief' who was turned to in his role as medicine man prior to an anticipated battle, especially against the white man, he comes in history from a ground that is familiar to Americans. He had much to say to his fellow Indians concerning the Earth and its harsh treatment by whites."

"Sitting Bull, who is killed late in 1889, knew a seasonal renewal of the Earth that awakens every seed and all animal life that comes with each spring 'of course with the same right as ourselves to inhabit this land,' he said at a council meeting: 'We have to deal with another race.' He was referring to an overbearing white man whose love of possessions is a disease with them. They claim that this mother of ours, the Earth, 'is their own,'" he said: "They fence their neighbors away; they deface the Earth as a spring freshet that overruns its borders and 'destroys all growth, which is on its banks.'"

"Sitting Bull helped create the Ghost Dance, which we will talk about in the future. The American government believed the 'dance' was to encourage the renewal of the so-called Indian wars, and the word itself of unusual Indian practice which indirectly led to his murder. He never smiled, nor did he express concern."

Dick at this point apparently thought it best that he not answer any question Clint might have. Dick still talked of Sitting Bull: "Along with his son and the Indian policeman who'd been hired for this very thing were killed both in what you call cold blood."

The night came in without a sunset, as Clint later was to recall as he was driven soon in Dick's pick-up toward the twin peaks outlined against a near invisible sky. He'd soon be able to surrender to the night about the darkest night he'd ever known, believing his Indian friend and his two aides had selected it as the night of a dark moon for his 'vigil.' The other men were close behind, in their own truck. He hadn't been introduced but believed he'd seen the taller man because of his height that day at the church with Dick and Evelyn.

The men were just outside the door as Dick opened it, "Time to go, ready?" These were his last 'few' words. No more advice from anyone; physically they were the outlines of men under an almost quarter moon and the dark sky's dimmer stars.

It seemed they'd driven at least an hour before they parked among trees and started up the mountain, with Dick in the lead and his friends on either side of Clint, a step or two behind, as he stumbled on an unseen trail. In a misstep, he felt one of the Indians lightly touch his elbow. One of the men had reached out to part the limb of a bush that could have slapped his face. Even in the dark, he felt it more than viewed the action, marveling at the night vision of the Indians.

His thoughts briefly were of a child, maybe it was him, who believed the dark night brought all sorts of dragons and bad things from the devil's den coming to harm him. He was later to know it as nothing, amused that he'd pulled up the memory from his boyhood.

Nevertheless, did he detect some unearthly movement back there? Am I at the mouth of some animal's habitat? I can't let it frighten me. It's too early in the season for a bear to go into hibernation. As for cougars I've heard of living in these parts, don't they sleep in the trees? No, my friend Richard would never do this to me his old buddy. Would he? At this moment he managed a silent vow, to fear nothing. He decided to face the night in peace with himself, and that's exactly what happened.

Even at peace, he knew his mind was in a foot race, if that's possible, in war between hurtful thoughts that he had been warned against, and recollections of people who had been kind to him. Good deeds, huh? Like helping an old lady across the street, a good deed for the day the press (his press) enjoyed using as an example when they wrote on Boy Scout Day.

He'd been a Boy Scout, proud of his uniform on a day he'd gone into the downtown drug store for a milkshake and scooted to a stool next to the prettiest girl in town. Uh oh, he had a wrong thought, going in a wrong direction.

Richard said nothing about staying awake, or trying to. Clint lowered himself onto the flat stone. Right there was why Richard had not mentioned it. He vowed to stay awake. At the first dawn he would look for a soft bed for the rest of the day, for the next night.

Richard had asked for two blessings, two memories of instances in his life that asked to be recorded in the book kept by Saint Peter at the gates of Heaven, to be followed by two great perhaps soul wrenching disappointments that in their encounters with his belief in the idea of their philosophy that were designed to enlist him deep in the Earth in the halls of the enemies of the Great Spirit.

He could never reconcile these experiences with what he had learned at his mother's knee. Fortunately, his early boyhood years were filled with a trust of other people, and his lifelong dedication to the best, the good, to the praise of his fellow creatures on the Earth. So here he was and the test was to begin.

Alone on the top of the mountain, with no interference from the good or the evil, or both in a free fight or a hint of the sure winner, he thought up a kindness that he often had considered to be the truth. He was to put all other thoughts or memories from his mind.

He thought first of a quite sweet memory, recalling that in the beginning of it he'd thought of revenge against the man who had caused it. Of course, it was that lost day he'd hitchhiked the country miles up to Cincinnati to buy his first suit and tie. His graduation was coming up in a too soon month and he was still in his swaddling clothes, a pair of denims so washed out they were almost white.

Someone had left a Cincinnati paper on a table at a tiny café down town where his gang went for coffee or a bottle of pop and oatcake. At home that night he read of the U.S. headed toward war, an earthquake in Asia, Katmandu, and a job by the Cees (the three C's, a Rooseveltian attempt to create jobs), in the northern woods of his country or the Kentucky mountains, a job that at least in the still of the day was trying to fight the Great Depression. He turned the page. A men's store in Cincinnati was going out of business and men's suits were on sale for half price, or even better.

Early next morning he counted his cash, borrowed a five from his dad and shoved off for the far trading post across the river. Hitchhiking was good in those days, and as safe as a train or the bus. In no time he stood, being measured by a salesman by pulling a little here and there about his body. For his money, the store threw in a matching tie for free, delicately placing it in the box and covering it all with a thin purple piece of paper.

He carried the box under his arm; he had time before a bus. Clint the high school boy walked around downtown, looking in store windows. He shifted his cargo from arm to arm hoping he wouldn't crush it. He was secure in the realization that he had enough money left to buy a bus ticket home, if he didn't splurge on a hamburger. He could eat when he got home.

Darkness was setting in. It was almost time for the bus. He could see the lights of the station down the street. From out of nowhere came this big fellow with an ugly knife in his left hand, and his right hand with the open palm that said the same thing as his demand of "gimmee."

Clint slowly tendered the precious box toward the knife. The big crook then said: "Now, the billfold." Clint said: "My billfold was a gift to me from my grandmother, and what little money in it is all I have in the world."

"You don't say. Tell grandma 'thanks for me,'" and he was off, but not before he peeled Clint's watch off his wrist. The man walked into a dark alley that Clint hadn't noticed before. Clint just stood there, knowing his house had burned and he may as well go up in smoke with the rest of his world.

It was too late in the day to hit the road. No money and no place to sleep. The only possibility was the 'Y.' He asked a man on the street about its location, and after walking for several blocks he dragged his weakening body across its threshold, to be told the place was full up. Clint asked the clerk if he could sit in the small lobby until dawn. "No, I'm sorry. The city has an ordinance against that sort of thing," the attendant said.

Some time later -- Clint thought it was two, three hours later. He looked at his watch that wasn't there, and sat with his head in his arms on a bench at the bus station. Must not go to sleep, I'd say a city ordinance is against it down here, too. He looked up, into the face of a policeman who had touched his shoulder with his nightstick.

"Missed your bus, son?"

The officer sat down beside him as he heard Clint's story, adding to Clint's sad tale with a question about where he was from, how he got to town, more specifically about the holdup man with the knife. The officer patted him on the back and said to sit there as long as he needed to.

In a few more minutes the officer stood before him, handing him a ticket to his hometown, saying that another bus was going that way and would be leaving in about an hour. Clint looked at the man. The face of the police officer with its non-smile would always be remembered.

He said: "That's something. Give me your name so I can send you the money for the ticket."

The next word from the police officer moved gently across the good memory of this country boy who had lost everything, almost himself, in the big city. "You don't need to know my name," he said. "Just don't hold it against us because of some germ of a man who took advantage of a precious visitor." With that the policeman turned and left by the bus station door, as Clint, bewildered, said nothing, not even, 'thanks.'

Years later, when Clint became somewhat successful or thought he was, he sent a check of considerable amount to the city's police department, telling of the day of the event. For certain he wrote about a phantom, a looming officer of the law.

The officer's simple act of kindness was on his mind quite often after that. When he left for the Marine Corps and later he had to go up to Cincinnati to formalize his discharge and take in the city and buy a few doo-dads for some kin and friends back home, that is, a few young cousins.

It had been more than a 'simple' act of kindness by an officer of the law, since the cost of the ticket probably was at least a third of what the officer had earned for that day's civic duty. Clint saluted every officer he met on the streets of the city.

Back home that bad day of long ago, graduation day loomed. His mother with a sharp scissors and needle and thread had cut into one of his dad's two suits and even if it was out of style he got comments about his clothes as they stood in line to receive their diplomas.

Then the memory of a day back during the war kicked in, as Clint began to recall another kindness, then another. That other: his Marine outfit had arrived at a base on Oahu and after several days the men began to wonder when payday would catch up to them. They were out of everything needed for their persons: razor blades, tooth paste -- plain old soap - shaving cream, and most of all, cigarettes.

They couldn't even buy a newspaper or a late magazine at the Navy Ship Store or in Honolulu, their new liberty town until they were ready to be sent on to the Solomon Islands battle zone just down the road. How do you deny a bottle of beer to a Marine?

Logistics during World War II was a thing to be regarded with awe. Seldom if ever was any ship or unit without food or equipment at the hour it was needed to continue their assigned operation. On this day of Marine bodies become dirty because of a lack of plain old soap, the shortage of it was the depressive.

It was a Navy Seabee unit temporarily given a barracks for sleep next door at the Naval air station 'across an imaginary fence' that separated the two military bases, who heard about their dilemma. The Seabees first filled from their own stores, or lockers, a sea-bag with toiletries and all sorts of personal items needed for the morale of fighting men. They dumped it all on bunks at Marine quarters then tossed in a wad of cash contributed by the seamen themselves -- construction men and fighters, their slogan ran. ('We build and we fight.')

Such acts of kindness throughout the big hate between men of war became so routine that Clint was never surprised when during the following civilian years he often heard them referred to as 'Men of Eden,' or 'brothers and sisters of the hell.'

Now we can talk, he said, of three or four or half a dozen brothers of war home from the European theatre coming on to the Pacific who kept us in books out there. Every man of them each had discovered books in bookstores and at auctions during their stop at home first, that fitted into our Marine interests and they'd scoot them out to a private library at the edge of the jungle. No recompense or similar gift was expected in return.

During the war, especially in Chicago, it was difficult as a man in uniform to pay for anything, within reason. Businessmen of many U.S. cities had rented warehouses or large halls within reach of a military base where a soldier or sailor could bed down for the night.

They also were provided a good breakfast the next day.

USO clubs abounded all along U.S. railroad tracks between east and west, especially that celebrated kitchen out in Nebraska that 'I want to remember,' until the war itself was long gone. The whole town was in on that one.

After his father and mother died and he was at home on the hill where he grew up, it was never surprising to open his front door in the morning to find piles of garden produce, dropped anonymously prior to sunup.

Yes sir, my blood brother the Earthman whose people for many moons, and for many generations, held and carefully nourished the land that became the U.S.; it often is more difficult to recall acts of kindnesses even more than brief abuses because we have been selfish, an ungrateful people —- White Eyes, you once called us —- and I, we, as of the same blood and sinew ask for forgiveness.

Today we have watched the sun come in to warm the Earth, the night to reserve for contemplation and we've heard denizens of the forest act out their timeless imitations that invite us to share with them —- just as Sitting Bull reminded: They have the same right as ourselves to inhabit this land. When White Eyes killed the buffalo for sport, they destroyed part of themselves.

Shortly after the dawn of his second day as he had viewed all that was earthly and eternal around him, the rocks, the trees and the fallen leaves returning to nourish the Earth, perhaps it was in the sleepless hours of night in his efforts to return to life to full awareness, a feeling of renewal was beginning to take over his senses.

He awoke to the world of his boyhood. Stiff from his bed of stones, he could imagine his father was taking down the buckets from their pegs on the back porch.

The sound of the pinging of the metal pails rubbing together that he had waited for as they butted against one another was better than a rooster's crow to tell him he would have another day. His dad would be headed for the barn and the early milking.

Below, in the valley of the town by the river, the unique hard sound of automobiles of men and women on a sleepy way to their jobs, big trucks changing gears as the rise before them lifted them toward the hills over the river, another sound, a pleasant one, was creeping in. It was the college chimes assuring students on their way to class that all was well with their world.

Soon, in another hour, voices of school children at play during the day's first recess would isolate all else as joyous children's peals from teasing on the way to school or recess told the story of freedom better than in any other way.

These were the early morning merry songs that overpowered him on any spring day or summer's freedom wonder from his dad's and his mother's back porch. It was exactly what he was looking for when he came home from the north.

He wasn't sure he wanted to rise from his rock and head down the mountain again where a different sound of civilization awaited him. He wasn't sure whether it was better to stay here and to die here or greet his Indian friends as they arrived to take him home.

During the remainder of the day and into the evening of the third day he sat with his mind no longer in fear of escaping the past or even ready to acknowledge that time was of the presence or promise of a tomorrow. It was a contentment he could never describe to friends or to other people. He could not recall any evil instances of the past among the dawn light of another day.

The moment came as the second night settled itself on the land when he thought he'd become among the privileged few to look into the soul of an American Indian, which meant all the world's men and women of the same heart.

It was that simple thing which had evaded the philosophers and men of the cloth who'd spent lifetimes looking for this same heart and soul and fiber of man. To Clint Greene it was the race of a people who vowed that they would never be truly conquered and which had come to him as a gift of the Great Spirit:

The American Indian, fearless but warring night riders of the Cossack nation, his minutemen, all relentless in battle yet preferred to live in peace undisturbed by those wily outsiders with intent to do harm. The warriors rode their ponies across his mind.

He thought of men and women like his friend Oscar and his one-time bride who didn't know precisely what they were fighting for as they gave of themselves to bloodied streets and rebellion just forty or so years ago. They only knew or perhaps believed that something was wrong in their handed-down philosophy.

A slight morning breeze over his face and arms reminded him that his body was cold, a sudden conscious condition that he had been unaware of hours even minutes ago.

The sun peeping through the limbs promised a day of peace. The trees overhead gave him a little dance as the wind moved the branches. The sun's warmth would be received with gratitude soon, with a bird's song.

He examined his cave, wondering about its role in a forest an alien land maybe for a thousand two thousand years. Had tired hunters, Indian or European, found shelter in its mouth after a storm's approach as he might have been caught in a sudden threat from the skies? Had a mama bear given birth to her cubs within a rock's throw just behind him? Had a papa bear and a mama and baby bear looked at their dinner and asked: "Who has been sitting in my chair?" He wondered how come a cave atop a mountain with no water flow.

It could have been here. Yes sir, it might have been right here on this mountain.

At dawn the third day they came for Clint. The three tall Indians simply nodded, touched his arm and led him gently off the mountain.

Clint might have said, "I'm not ready to go," which he felt deeply in a sore body after using a rock for a pillow, the Earth for a bed, and looking through the three days to the whole of the forest and Earth before him in efforts to commune with the Great Spirit.

At coffee in Evelyn's kitchen, the Indians and Evelyn listened as Clint related some of his experiences and thoughts: "I never felt I was alone up there. In fact, by the second night, I was quite sure that someone was at the cave's mouth with me, beside me, touching me and speaking silently in my mind."

"That would be the Great Spirit," said Chief Dick.

He continued: "Before we go further, let us talk of some little item or two that may shield the Caucasian to Indian ways. We have no reason for need to speak in a moment of your recollection of experience with the Great Spirit. When you get home, put it on paper for us. But no one except we at this table will ever have reason to read it. Don't allow your newsman's soul crowd out a compulsion to publish."

"We talked of the Ghost Dance, called Wovoka's Ghost Dance. It might have been understood at this time -- which was sunset for the Indian nation —- that as a 'religion' it offered hope to the Indians' condition, which it was, but for the White Eyes, it was not. The 'Dance' to white men was prelude to war; to the Indian it was a war once more for a return to what was."

"That was an erasure or return of the white man to what it was for him before his invasion of our lands and his cruel intent to do us harm.

"In 1890, the dance by the Sioux went on and on for some days, arousing the Indians to arms at its climax. It also led to death for several of our best warriors at Wounded Knee Creek.'

"Indians had rallied around (the Ghost Dance) as a ritual of hope. They were told that it would give them a shield against the invader's bullets, and that the settlers would depart. At just this hour Indian Police moved in and fired their own bullets point-blank into the assembly. Among the deaths was Sitting Bull. Many other Indians were to die before the Ghost Dance (as part of a religion?) disappeared from history."

"Wovoka, by the way, was a Paiute. It is said that he alone created the 'Dance.' As a boy he was taken in by the family of a Nevada rancher, one David Wilson, following the death of Wovoka's father, and given the name Jack. While ill and with fever he had a vision. His dream was the Ghost Dance. Indians flocked to him; through the Great Spirit it soon became an appeal for a return to the way things were before the Europeans."

"I tell you this because Indians through misguided faith believed in its promise of an end to their troubles brought on by the white man -- just as they continued to express faith in the Great Spirit, just as later many men and women born of the faith of the Cross and the religion founded by Father Abraham, were prepared to ask, 'Where is their faith in the future of man, in the Earth itself?'"

Chief Dick hesitated, referring to the two Indians at his side, asking if either would consent to talk about 'the vigil.' Neither of the men left their silence.

Richard, as he'd promised, set out to explain the 'vigil.' Known as 'Vision Quest,' to most Indians, but as experienced by Clint and inverted by his Indian friends to be much modified, Chief Dick said:

"For a pup, the youth hoping for initiation as a brave prior to test in battle, it might have been more than the usual three-day regimen. The ordeal of the rock and hard place would still be the same with most tribes."

"With Indians of the Southwest, the Apache especially, a like initiation generally was more severe, with the youth lying on his back, held down by rocks placed around his body. He would not be able to move his arms or legs; his eyes would be on the sky by day and only the stars, the shape of the moon by night."

The two Indian friends of Richard stood to leave. Clint shook their hands. They both looked into his eyes, penetratingly, betraying something of a respect for this old White Eyes. Not a word was spoken between the three. Clint felt good about it. He stood to go, also.

Richard interrupted. "Stay for just a few more hours. It will still be daylight in the forest. Come with me on a little trip."

Clint had said it was time for him to go, also. Richard's reason for delay, he thought, must be important to him. It was something that Richard had intended to say or show him earlier and now the last thing he wanted was held for Clint until the last moment.

They took the pickup and headed down the rocky hillside to the township on the paved highway. After a turn to the right they drove for at least two miles, stopping by a construction project on the hillock before them, a few yards back from the highway.

"This is my little resort hotel that I'm building. It will be finished in another month, first thing is we'll have a Grand Opening, right at the beginning of the big tourist season, Yankees from the north mostly. The design and interior will be all-Indian. Slick, huh?"

"Awesome," said Clint. "It's bound to be a success. Is this your land?"

"It's close. My farm is over there on the other side of that hill. These few acres, six or seven acres, became available after a neighbor sad he was moving to a new town with a college so the kids could finish their schooling, big time."

"All I can say is 'wow,' said Clint.

"I've brought you down here for a reason, agree with me or not." said the Indian.

"My lawyer suggested we incorporate and offer stock. I'm giving you a quarter interest (in the stock plan) in the company. Now before you say anything, just let me finish," said Dick.

"It won't cost me or you a thing. You're one of the builders, like me. You can pay me back through the bank with cash from a quarterly dividend and do what you want with the rest. From what I've assumed from what you told me, you've come back from Ohio pretty much broke. You have no income and you want to marry that woman. How can you do that without a way to support her? Besides, you need a new car."

"Wow, again, what makes you want to do a thing like that?"

"Like I say, it won't cost you a thing. A little maybe, but I'm a rich man, believe it or not. And you are closer to me than any other living soul, except my wife, Evelyn, of course, and she's already agreed with me. For all you did for me, you white eyes you, and for what your friendship has meant for me, I will not expect another word from you. Tell Doris you all will be coming back for the Grand Opening. I'll be in touch."

"I I I I'm speechless for the first time my life. Goodbye. Tell Evelyn for me, I'm so hepped up from it all that I'll forget to go in the house."

"For all thou hast given me," he at last said to Evelyn. "To make my stay here so comfortable, I'm thankful. For your hospitality, and for Richard's, I will be eternally in your debt. Never have I felt so welcome, and certainly well fed. Call me when this old rascal of yours' decides to leave you —- come to Kentucky, where Doris and I will welcome you."

"How you ever consented to marry this old hillbilly, with all your good looks, your smiles, and certainly brains I will never understand, and by the way, your husband has given me the greatest gift. I asked for his help, and he gave me several blessed hours with the Great Spirit. I will be eternally grateful." To Richard, he said: "I'm out of words. This is simply a goodbye, for sure."

Clint's Indian friend followed him to his car, once more shaking his hand. The barefoot boy with cheek, of the mountains and plains, said: "Remember me in your next book, but don't say my name. I will know it's me."

Clint said, "You're doggoned right." He was gone, adjusting his car mirror to see Dick at ease at the fence rail watching him go until he was out of sight, or off the glass. He'd said he wanted to ride the Blue Ridge all the way into Virginia, but as he hit the high country he again decided to turn off above the Smokies toward his own high ground in Kentucky, his home, realizing he was a bit homesick.

He'd skirted the Qualla Boundary on the north. He had never visited or even seen an Indian Reservation, planning in his mind for a future return for a visit, one other thing he must do before he died. Recalling his earlier survey from the Parkway of the Carolina and Virginia valleys as he and Lily and the kids were returning from vacation in the Deep South, he laughed as he did then at the antics of his older boy in the back seat, with his brother and sister.

High above the green farmlands below, most edged by groves of fruit trees to set them off as he recalled the pastures of England and Ireland, he'd looked into the rear-view mirror at his oldest son, his arms tight on the joy stick of his own imaginary plane, banking to take in the wonder of one of God's greatest gifts: An Eden it was that stretched out almost forever for more green as viewed from the roof of the mountain —- to a far horizon.

Clint sighed, knowing he'd probably never travel by this way again. Far west, out of the way of his favorite route again, saying almost aloud to himself that life is plainly too short to have it all. Having it all was close, though, as he thought back to his visit in the home of his friends Richard and Evelyn. Never had such a treat as this been handed to him, so gracefully -- on a day when he'd needed it more than anything else in his life that he most would rather not recall. Never yes never, had he such a good friend.

Although he had been to Richard and Evelyn's place before, he was amazed to find a Kentucky-like thoroughbred farm deep in the hills of North Carolina. At a point in their talks, Clint asked Richard if other men —- especially horsemen and cattlemen of European descent —- in their devious ways of the late Twentieth Century, might have wondered at the possibility of Andrew Jackson's men ignoring the farm, intentionally overlooking it for no revealed reason when the Indians were dispossessed and sent on the trail to the west.

Richard repeated his earlier brag that when he'd bought it at auction back in his early manhood that the farm, which he had added to through further purchase, was only a rough hilltop rock and briar patch. He'd about all by himself returned it to life.

"Besides," he'd said, those characters that came knocking at his door wanted to develop it for townspeople as an escape from their crowded and impersonal neighborhoods. "They thought I'd grab at the wad of cash they had in their hands, but they're not doing to this old Indian what they did to me a hundred fifty years ago."

Clint thought of his country's sore past as he drove through the land beautiful. He recalled Chief Dick's grievous moments for the past that he knew might well come again. As we become even more crowded, there sits a piece of Paradise.

The Black man, neighbors of both Clint and Richard in both Kentucky and Carolina, believed he was safe by pitching his tent along the coasts of the great waters, since the white man feared the waves and hurricanes that routinely reshaped the beach and its sand dunes that protected them —- until the taxmen whose actions were directed by faceless men of greed and cupidity came through political connections to assess and get their taxes raised beyond an ability to pay by its inhabitants.

The coast became a retreat for richer builders who thought it would be 'nice to live on the ocean side.' That's the way it looked to him. Some time ago, but a change in the wild sea, because of climate change undoubtedly will change things around to what it once was.

Clint entered the interstate into Tennessee, pushing the gas pedal as he spied the chance to fit into the traffic flow. Within moments the big rigs were left of him, to the right of him, all roaring and thundering.

He immediately felt himself divided on the question of the worth of it all. Here was the menace and the bliss of the era to his civilization. As a positive; they were carrying goods and products of citizen farmers and workers to this nation's consumers and to the coasts for export, returning imports as a result of vital trade.

As a negative: by mining the nation's disappearing resources of oil and energy to fuel their movement, they made possible at the moment the gnawing positive. From his view of a truck's cab with its tailpipes straight up, as the cartoonists depict a scared cat with its tail pointing straight into the ozone, was an exhaust aimed at life's breath taken from the Earth's future, appearing to be the norm along the nation's commercial lanes.

As a big rig passed on his left, in what seemed an eternity, he thought: what a huge blessing the trailer would have been to western bound pioneers of just little more than a hundred or so years ago. Why, one trailer could carry the worldly goods and many of the settlers in just one load. How about circling the big trucks as the Indians attacked?

Think of today's battle tanks and big guns we would use against the Indians to take their lands in one big pounce. You can bet they'd have been fired wholesale if we'd had them at the time.

Against what people called the enemy were the Gatling guns first used? Chief Dick, me lad, count your blessings. We long ago sought your forgiveness.

After we destroyed the topsoil we tried to give the land back to you, that is, first the badlands and then the most productive, which we had called during the Indian wars 'the fields of glory,' later to find that you didn't want it back -- or most of it. Our later generations did not like the hard work it took to till the land we took, and moved away, back to the city to the good life, which meant less work.

The traffic on the interstate was pushy, as glaring drivers ready for today's kill passed that old man who was observing the speed limit and trying to protect a few lives, including his own. The same drivers, who for certain knew they owned the streets in town, also owned the roads in the hinterland. They told you so through an evil glare and a rear-view mirror.

Clint suddenly felt tired. On the road for two hours or better after three days in a hard place without sleep on a mountain-top in an exercise he was just beginning to know plus the tension of the crowded road, suggested to him that he was being taken under arrest on a dangerous ride.

Ahead was the flashing sign of a motel, its many colors looming from a remembered once upon a time. It was as if fate itself brought it like a one-time dream from a motel just a whisper off the highway, a quarter mile ahead. He was beginning to believe that somebody out there was looking after him. How could he have forgotten the smiling face of Mr. Abell Guthrie?

It was a pleasure recalling the welcome as Mr. Guthrie looked up from his high chair behind the desk. His grin was from here to yonder as Clint approached. "Well, well, by the beard of the saints, if it isn't Mr. Greene?" he said. "It's been a long time Mr. Greene sir, far too long since we've seen you." Clint was surprised that Guthrie recalled his name, said so.

He and Lily, before the kids became too sophisticated to be seen on the road with their parents, had stayed there many times. It dated to a long ago time, since their host opened up for business. "Been saving our best room for you, Mr. Greene; I knew you would be back for a night of 'Sleep Well,' which has been our only motto for lo these many years."

More conversation as Mr. Guthrie asked about the kids and Lily's health, "sorry to hear about your lady. I thought very much of her."

After he'd gotten to know them, Abell said one morning back then that the missus had fixed a warm breakfast and that the table was ready for them, back in the kitchen. Ah, for the good warm old days. That's a cliché, Clint knew, but it is as valuable today as any other piece of conversation from a past as he later would write a whole column about it for his newspaper.

Before he'd left Mr. Guthrie at his desk to rediscover his room, he had been told to 'sleep well,' rest a bit for the drive back to Kentucky and Ohio. He had said it just like that, probably for the first time since Lily's death. Before he'd gone to his room, he asked how long he could stay, that he had a lot to think about before he hit the mountain road into Kentucky.

They agreed on five nights. Guthrie said the tourist season didn't start for at least a month, and that Clint would have the run of the 'whole place.'

Clint didn't have to turn on the TV to get the news. He had lived it almost every hour by the TV which crept in on low while visiting Dick and Evelyn. Richard had handed him a newspaper as he started to leave, and all he wanted to read about was a couple of comic strips that gave him an insight to all the past he needed to know about on the last leg of his journey where all men might go at least once before they were called to way up yonder. He was the only man in the side road café with a newspaper. All others had their eyes on the TV attached to the wall behind the counter.

In his room, on his back without moving the spread, he went over the slight cracks in the ceiling then turned to the windows, behind closed drapes. He got up to open the folds, only to face the pool, which was empty of water and people who would have been in deck chairs on a day like this. The pool, center of a court, was focus of a dozen or more rooms, none showing signs of life.

Now what do I have to think about? His mind was wandering. He envisioned Doris walking out of the fog. He said aloud, "Git, you have no business in there." She wouldn't go away, kept walking toward him. "Git," he repeated. She kept coming, her arms outstretched like a mother receiving a child.

Then began his debate again, arguing with his thoughts. I don't want to get married again. I have too much to do, way too many bridges before I get to the other side. Heaven will not let me in, until I save the world. Don't make me quit when I've just found a way —-I hope. I'm a free man now, and I like it. He'd stopped counting the little lines in the plastered ceiling.

That was because the face of Doris kept looking out at him lying on the bed. She was smiling, like she'd won the battle.

He recalled the words to an old song, too long out of a mountain backwater. The tune long in the public domain, that went (to begin maybe) like thusly: 'old man, old man, I want your daughter....

.... 'I want your daughter, to bake my bread and carry my water.' It is a real old song? Likely nobody outside the mountains had ever heard it.

The song was a proposal. Was he getting too close to what his body was saying and his brain was denying? That's from days long gone, he knew. He was glad though for the moment of memory. A woman in his own youth's time came into partnership with him. The world since had begun to change and his own society was on its way once again to the fires of you know what.

Yet it was a gift of Heaven, a good relaxed feeling, as he left his bed in the morning and found Lily across from him at the breakfast table, his coffee hot and poured with eggs sizzling on the stove, and a warm kiss still on his cheek. Yet too, no matter how a woman fits into his life, married, not married, ex this and former, a woman sure can mix a man up.

As Lily lay dying, still young in most ways when she could eat anything she wanted, he'd carried breakfast up to her. The meal had been prepared for him and for her by the lady departing night sitter. He'd told the day lady that this was one thing he could do, especially for Lily.

They never talked about her illness. She would hold his hand and say 'thanks,' for all he had done to make her happy, and he had no way to respond to that except to say, 'and for all you've done to make all of us comfortable and glad to be alive.'

She would be glad to hear that Mr. Guthrie had remembered her and he was asking about her health. She'd say that those days when they had time to travel with the kids to exotic places were days to remember and to carry with her into Heaven where the best part of Heaven was recalling those days back on the Earth.

Now Doris, as he wondered what life would be like if he got on his knees and asked her to be his wife.

Lily had her arguments and most likely would stand by them, but by bedtime they both had forgotten what the difference had been about.

Now Doris, again, this woman sure has a way to stand by what she says, which is in the manner of the new society; asked to bake the bread and carry the water was not in the marriage vows.

Why did he leave the road and stop at Guthrie's motel? Was it because he would recall days when he would have been there with Lily?

No, he told himself, it was because he wanted to sort out all the mixed-up circuits in his mind, right? The matter with Doris, after he'd said to Lily that he'd never marry again. The marriage to Lily, his lifetime partner during all those years of struggle with the paper, and the children she had given him, were the little things for his biography.

His biggest concern was his one-time belief that he had a job to do in this world, and he was facing the last years of his life with too much left undone. Did he receive an answer during the past several weeks from his visit to his friend Richard and his wife Evelyn?

There had been moments when he was sure of the direction he wished to take in his remaining time on Earth. He had to be sure where he really wished to go to attain a dint of satisfaction.

It was the fifth night since he'd left Richard's ranch. Now in his home on his own mountain, he decided he wouldn't call his friends until the following morning. He tossed his sweat-soaked shirt onto the nearest chair and himself onto his own bed. Doris and his friends wouldn't forgive him for not calling as soon as he got home.

As he tried to avoid the tiring of his thoughts he decided his friends meant more. A twinge of pain recalled after a life-long marriage to good dear Lily, a long ago vow that the freedom he would face as a man living by himself would define a new kind of life, since it meant that he was alone. The promise he'd made had begun to elude him. He realized he was not free. He liked being told to hang his clothes in the closet before hitting the sack. Ho ho ho, said a voice from deep in the closet. Lily was speaking to him now more strident than ever.

He had never forgotten Lily's wagging finger of reproof, which became customary as they'd aged together. He got off the bed and hung his pants and shirt neatly arranged with his coat in the closet.

Hear me out, he said audibly, almost prepared to believe that he was talking to Lily. I'm pleased that I, Clint Greene, once and eternally a free and confirmed man of leisure now more than ever needs a woman around.

In the morning he'd find a month's pile of mail and papers (no mountain delivery), all bagged and placed against the hill door inside the screen. His neighbor who'd collected the lot also would know when he got home, which meant his place had been well guarded, verifying that an old-time neighbor was still around.

It was late but not too late to call Doris. He had planned to call after midnight, which would show a great interest in reminding her that he really was concerned about what might have been a bit of anxiety on her part. Naw, she'd likely given up several days ago expecting the phone to ring, and left her chair by the telephone for bed.

He was sleepy, but hunger roared in. He ignored the phone table and crossed over to the kitchen to fix a sandwich. He was glad that the peanut butter jar was at least half full. He took a frozen loaf of bread from the freezer. He reached for the jelly, stopped, said out loud, "Ah, the heck with it."

Doris picked up the phone on the first ring; she sounded real excited, not waiting for him to speak. "Hi, you old rascal," she said.

He said, "Yeah, you're right, it's the old rascal calling. Did I wake you up?" "At eleven-thirty in the middle of the night, are you demented or just plain crazy? Why did you leave without telling anybody where you were going? And you never called. Everybody thought you'd been kidnapped or taken aboard an alien space ship like maybe something."

"I'll tell you in the morning where I've been, maybe I will and maybe I won't, so get some sleep. It's real good to hear your voice. Good night."

"Now I know you are completely off your shelf. Keep your ear to the ground and the front light on. I'm coming up there."

Clint looked around the room; nothing that a man living alone had left undone. No empty bottles or coffee cups. He remembered the undone sandwich in the kitchen. Leave it.

Doris had stopped by the All-Nite Market and picked up a dozen eggs, bacon and sausage and everything nice, put them on the kitchen counter and turned to kiss him.

"It's a good thing I thought about breakfast. You're still hungry for that peanut butter jelly sandwich you didn't finish. You have to move your makings for the eggs."

"Kiss me again so I can tell my bridge friends."

"They'll be waiting to hear about it."

"Maybe I ought to put it in the paper," he said.

"Is this Oscar Blues? This here's the old Flintlock Kid, just in from Valley Forge. Doris brought up enough groceries for all of us. Call Mollie and tell her to pick up Leo, and we all will sup together . . . yeah, got in late last night."

"Won't have to, Leo's moved in with Mollie. She says they are going to be married. Welcome back," he said.

"Now that's a bit of astounding good news; when did all this happen?" he asked.

Clint didn't tell his other friends that Doris brought the eggs up the hill last night and stayed to fix most of them for breakfast. It was a jolly homecoming. Nobody asked where he'd been. At table, Oscar raised his coffee cup in salute. Before him sat Doris and Clint, Mollie and Leo, all coupled up.

"Boy/girl, man/woman, and here I sit among the ashes with no invitation to the ball, though maybe expecting my fairy godmother."

Mollie said she could understand living alone without a mate. "I imagine I've been waiting all those years for my Leo to come riding in on his white steed. I know you've got a daughter, Oscar, and she visits you often, even on a working day. The entire town knows about her. You must at one time have had a woman. I apologize for something that likely is not any of my business."

Oscar could've been embarrassed; attempting to avoid the fact that he was a loner, while his two male friends and their women faced him with expectations for you never knew what, especially from the founders three of OMEN. Instead, he invented someone right there by his side, telling the world that he at one time or another did have this woman. Again came the coffee cup at half mast, unexpected by the rest of them.

Oscar said, hesitating but gaining courage as he spoke. "I wrote a letter to my dear departed wife some months ago. I carry it with me all the time, in case I run into her maybe sometime, which I'm sure is never; I take it out and read it every now and then.

I want to read it to you, because it says it all, every bit of it tearing me apart every time. Stop me if it bores you. Don't hesitate to stop me. I want you to. I want somebody to sympathize with me, to help me forget a deep pain that I've endured lo these many years. If you are bored, please tell me."

"To my ex-wife," he read, "Wherever she is; ah,

"- Wherever you are —- as I take pencil to paper and report whether you want to hear from me or no, so many things have happened in my life in the past few years, about all of it weird I mean really really weird, so much so that even one of the Fates of Greece and Rome would assign the wild stomp encountered by your daughter and me to the realm of myth, or in your eyes to the realm of Hades.

"—- Yes, your daughter, Jenny; yes Jenny, named for you.

"—- In spite of years —- a generation, really -- since I knew you, I am compelled to put most of the unbelievable to paper and as soon into your hands since you, and you alone, might know the pain you left behind when you abandoned the two of us.

"—- That's because you, only you, never seemed to give a hoot —- that is, until fate treacherous as she often is, stepped from the dark to point an ugly finger at the part of your soul that is pure evil. There is no other definition; nevertheless, I had to tell someone, and I am thinking of you."

(Oscar continued):

"—- Allow me first to get some personal stuff out of the way.

"—- Since I heard from your lawyer telling me that I was divorced, Jenny and I have so often wondered about you, if you were still alive, if you might in some way discovered what much of your generation said that the 'thing' they were looking for was 'myself.'

"- I had hoped that by now you would have found 'who I am.' That seemed to be the battle cry of our generation, or an effort to hide our motives from our parents, a family, for running, hiding out from society in the open with raised fists against what you never told us about the corrupt and compromising world."

Oscar hesitated, before continuing. Doris, believing he was finished, said: "You mean you were one of those 'beats?'" "Sure was, the term wasn't ours' despite the fact that some accepted it and still didn't give a hoot dang. Beat? Yep, sure was. Face all street dirty, like our shoes or no shoes, denims with the knees out. That was our uniform."

"Yep, our hair was dirty from sleeping on wet grass and benches and in barns and wherever the longhorns with pistols couldn't find us. They delighted in beating us up. They spotted our long hair down on our shoulders almost hiding a beard that was our badge of 'rebellion' and a dead giveaway to the gendermenter."

"You would not believe what our brothers and sisters said was our [motive?], or purpose, without knowing in the least a direction we might take, which was to form a 'new' society, even though we wouldn't know what to do with it. Yet, we said it was."

Oscar picked up his letter, without further comment, pocketed it. He went on, 'ad lib'. "- Did you, my dear absent love of my life, my wife, actually believe that it was possible? What was life before that made us you and I, to first forget our purpose and try to live together among what you more so than I believed to be an impure society, a life into which we were born?

"—- Dear Jenny, our precious Jenny, our daughter, never even got a chance to know you —- you certainly saw to that —- yet she loved you, like any child would love the idea of mother, even in her absence.

"—- That's not to say that she didn't miss you.

"—- We grew up together, Jenny and I. We learned to cook. She fared well, in spite of her odd situation. We partook of loads of peanut butter and crackers, great cans of soup.

"—- We ate a lot of fast food from you know where. We learned from you not to eat while watching TV, since it had a threat of obesity. That admonition oddly came from you, before the rest of the world got onto it.

"Odd," interrupted Doris, "How men living alone try to exist on bread or crackers, and peanut butter. I know of one case sitting right here at this table."

"Yeah," said Clint. "I still do."

"With me, however," said Oscar, "I've been there; at some time I dared to put a roast in the oven. I reckon that day I was returned to civilization. It was a step up from grilling a cut of meat on the grill out back. We learned a lot."

"As a Boy Scout I'd roasted potatoes or field corn with the shucks still on and mud thrown into an open (camp) fire. It helped like Saint Reynolds day to discover foil wrap. I believe my wife would have preferred the open fire, say, a 'spit' among heated rocks on the prairie. The gods, she would have said, intended it that way."

"When she was in high school and beat me home, Jenny Number Two would have a spread (bowl) of spaghetti waiting, for supper. She learned to bake bread, too - French style. She read a lot of cookbook recipes to surprise me with what she could do with her hands and a dollar's worth of fixings."

"I managed to obtain suitable clothing for her to wear to school and I was always there to meet the school bus. She never gave me any sass and certainly never any trouble. Together, we solved any problem that came up. Nothing was ever insurmountable."

He stopped his letter, studied the faces of his new family and continued reading.

"—- My one my only Jenny baby, Jenny, daughter Jenny, easily learned about the newspaper business sitting at her own desk across from me in the front office. Even before I could buy the paper, she was getting her own by-lines and praise for what she wrote by the town's elite as well as the (sniff) social and exclusively burdened of our city.

"—- For that endowment I give credit to you and your native talent. Her poetry may never equal your passion and strength though, but it is poetry, and good; the drama of life's dreams and savagery of modern civilization comes through —- without being forced, with the same feeling of you and your peers of our day.

"—- I recall that cold night as you and I walked from a poetry reading at a friend's house, I in a heavy sweater and coat and you in a Pat Nixon cloth coat and you leaned close to me to take as much of my body heat as I could muster. As we left home I said you needed a sweater; you said no, you wanted to get much 'closer to Nature.'

"—- I always questioned your definition of Nature's gifts, but I tried my doggondest to understand it.

"—- After you became pregnant I thought the poetry readings, and I listened to a lot of bad poetry from your friends, would be replaced by something more apt to your theory of what life was about, or what it should be, but that didn't happen. I do recall saying that this human activity so seriously practiced by the new generation must be catching, since about all the young women also were pregnant. It seemed to kindle the fire of everyone there. No kidding.

"—- You were about always the center of it all, as your poet's words shouted in song, smooth and soft, moving like a mist over a long lost lake that was held sacred by the Indians right out of Longfellow by his man Hiawatha.

"—- You defined the blood flow, wakening the juices of creation of your so many peers, your fellow poets.

"—- Jenny my little girl and I looked in every closet, under the paper linings of all the shelves, even for a possible hidden compartment of your small desk for just a shred of something you might have written for us, especially in your poetry. All our efforts of course ended, obviously, with nothing.

"—- Much of it survived with just a memory, though, right in the forefront of those lobes of a brain that already was crowded with overmuch of life's folly and nonsense. The best that I could do was record our sacred songs (as together) I might have preserved them.

"—- Fragmented as they were at first, Jenny's poetry would never have disappointed you or your crowd. When it was time to go I let her make the decision.

"—= We sold out up there and I came here.

"—- I bought the small weekly paper in this town; as it turned out, even with its share of soreheads, it was a godsend for us. Jenny for weeks had been readying to leave, to go out on her own. I believe I came here because of the college's proximity, just a few corn rows away. The little college that welcomed Jenny from the moment of her visit and enrollment, kept us together, really selected as a place that fitted both our careers.

"—- You ought to read some of her byline best in the yearbook and school paper, which she also edited.

"—- On graduation day, as valedictorian, and as the lady of the lake, she stood on the platform ensnared by a beam of light that could only have come from Heaven itself.

"—- Her beauty and delicate form even before she spoke could have captured the hopes and desires of every young man, every boy in the audience, and a memory of anyone who was left."

" I'll finish my letter."

"—- You, Jenny One, may not have liked what she said at the end of her short talk. She said: "I never knew my mother; she lives only as a song in my heart. It is my father to whom in a wholeness of love and care that my heart belongs.

"—- He it was who encouraged me and guided me every step of the way, sometimes n loneliness for both of us."

Oscar halted his reading, looked away, obviously overcome.

He didn't apologize, knew the others understood. Then, ("To my pocket letter soon to Jenny, again"). I must halt it before I am overwhelmed by its comments by my daughter and by its hurt."

He said: "—- Jenny has no plans I know of for marriage, yet I must assume that she will have gotten many proposals.

"—- A time or two she brought home a young man; home, meaning down here. "

Doris in her kindness said to Oscar, "She is a beautiful girl. I hope some fine young man of our city will find her, and keep her here."

Oscar read, "—- It was never the same boy that she came home with. I don't know if that was good or otherwise. But I trust that she will find the right one of many she had met in the city she'd first adopted for a career after college and the several months she visited before she could make it permanent, at least until she became homesick again for the big town. I would hope that she came home looking for my approval, as she often visited me from Lexington. She found a good job up there."

"In my egocentric country boy self-educated manner I believe my wife was looking for perfection; I long suspected it was a hellish curse that contributed to a desire to hit the road. I have no reason why she left for another life. I could not fulfill her expectations."

"I had hoped that she'd finally found what it was that she sought. Just the same I am grateful for what she has given me —- a child of great price and legacy from someone in her mother's family even ancestry with such a great heart whose wholesome genes very well may have skipped a generation."

"I have looked to the little magazines and to the reviews of novels for my daughter's mother's name on the cover. It is to the world's loss that, alas, it has never come to pass. I believe that if she had continued to write, she would have discovered that tiny thing that had eluded her. If she read all of the above and in my next letter and know that she had suffered, which I am sharing with friends, she would know what follows may offer great satisfaction, since it is tide and tribulations of a life in a land so far away, as far as I would allow it in my heart, from memories of beauty and love that by the time of the final paragraph, I know that she ran from a common dream of one hopeful journalist who was out to save what was left of her world, pardon the cliché —- I just heard a sigh way out there in an alien land; you can still find it here through your daughter."

"—- Now to the weirdest part that I (not the journalist's 'we') promised you, primarily to put to paper what I say here, and for posterity, that I myself might better understand.

"—- My time here on my little newspaper, which I have so often thought was dying by the day, has begun to question all my talent and dedication. Larger papers, especially those of multi circulation in larger cities, also appear to be dying. Some already have, may they rest in peace and in the recorded history of the country.

"—- Often of late I would go to a place in the country that I bought for the purpose, to get time away from people, residents and readers, supporters and critics.

"—- Believe me, my fellow townsfolk were about to send me out to an isolated part of the world where I could scream and cuss and condemn until my soul and its being could settle down to a point that I might handle, and to begin life again, such as it is.

"—- At first, back in town, I expected to make a new friend in the person of a retired newspaperman, because I and he could find a common understanding. I did; as it turned out I likely found one of the strongest friendships I ever knew.

"—- This led to a third person, and this is the oddest thing, or the most weird that even you might have heard about. He is a Russian, a Cossack even, of all the people in the world that I have been privileged to know, the most honest, loyal, and the smartest.

"—- Together, we formed a trio in common cause like the 'Three Musketeers' of French literature, by Alexander Dumas, the elder, that is."

"—- The three of us were without social attachment, that is, without wives. We began to gather for conversation and for a bit perhaps of the fermented juice of the grape, and coffee, of course, primarily at the home of a member on the mountain overlooking the town. Whether we needed a cause and it was thrust upon us as the direst threat to the world we'd been born into, or was something else, it was a beginning.

"—- It would define what to me was the core of a needed friendship; we three found the biggest challenge of our times.

"—- In so many ways we arrived at a conclusion: Earth was in a heck of a bind as never seen before. Man has been accused of destroying an atmosphere that was taking the air we breathed and the Earth that fed us and sustained our civilization: Really big stuff, so we looked for a way to tell the world of the danger.

"—- The atomic bomb in the hands of inconsiderate people would kill us off en masse, or a realignment of the outer planets would cause the Earth to shift on its axis and we would freeze to death because the North Pole would relocate right in the middle of old Kentucky.

"—- That's a bit of mistaken analysis since the earth turns the other way from side by side, eh? The latter is due in our generation as predicted by the world's earlier societies, the Maya of central America a millennium even more ago, before the rest of the world knew what a 'mathematic' was, which is how they came to a conclusion. It's all in the pile-up pulled by the several planets against Earth at the bottom end. Don't ask me how."

He said, "Lordy lordy what's next? Lots of people have begun to ask, scientists asked. We knew the possibilities, events that might not be challenged. Therefore it has created a feeling of immunity among the world population. Right out of the past came to us the scare of ecological change, bringing a big heat or overheating of the Earth.

"Alas, it appears that no one pays attention. Gloom sits on our doorstep, and we wrestle with ideas to revive it. Nothing will awaken people to the danger sitting out there beside the road ready to toss rusty nails into the path of Earth's salvage."

Oscar stopped reading his letter, just kept talking. He said, "It was like teaching a monkey to read. Let's go our little fiendish ways in the face of a disaster that was to come even if it means that tomorrow we die."

"Just today Leo and I began a little clearing around the broken down log cabin on my little acreage east of town. Leo was so doggoned pleased that I had sold him that cabin out there, along with a couple or so acres, that he gave his eventual home a new name, calling it the Blues Place. He showed us how he'd pipe water in from that little stream that fed into the river."

"Talk about political art, Clint got the cooperation without tremendous charges from the power company. The electric folks said they'd string a new line across the river from the few acres, only with the cost of the connection from the main line to his cabin. Leo says because they expected our little hillside would someday be sold (sigh) for a subdivision."

"Leo says that his biggest job would be re-building the fireplace and its chimney. A strong woods growth on the back of our acres will give us firewood for many a day.'

"It looks like Leo the Russian, the new American, and we toast him, has found a place where he will eventually die if Mollie, with whom he now lives, doesn't kick him out before then."

"I say at the end of my letter: Yours always, Oscar, a once and to the end of time lover."

Oscar had said all of it: The whole book. The others suffered right along with him, showed it. There was something unusual about it all, but they accepted it from a friend.

"A dream of a retiring working man is the luxury of lying abed in the warmth created by his own body heat and from the warmth of a mate next to him, on a morning when the urgent command of duty will never come for most of us," said Clint.

"It is yet of a strong call to him to throw back the covers and put his aging feet flat on the floor, then to 'obey.'"

"I'm not planning to allow a feeling of guilt spoil this," Leo said, but not aloud.

Alas, it was not to be as he thought it might sound to the others.

"Well," said Doris, "Whoever said we aren't good friends of this man, to sit here quiet-like through every minute of what he called a 'letter' to someone who hasn't been around for a whole generation. What say I go to the kitchen and get us all a bottle of pop, or something?"

"Okay," said Mollie, "But don't forget the crackers and peanut butter."

Oscar tried to be the life of the party. His laugh was forced —- any attempt to scoot his friends toward the enjoyment of a bottle of pop, or a beer and a hot dog would be in vain. But they didn't say it was time to go and say good night, either. They hadn't left an empty chair at the table, and he was grateful. That meant that they were conscious of the non-act. He'd thought he would never tell anyone how it was with him and his woman, but did.

Whoever was pounding on the door at dawn's first hour and yelling like hell-fire to arouse him to the summons of a quite inconsiderate person who might be a messenger of God Almighty or the law west of the Cumberland or of the sleeping town below, in the civilized flatland, gave no name.

As he with partly closed eyelids and sore ankles tolerated from a collision with his living room furniture opened the door, Clint said, "You, Mr. Sheriff, and only you would be kind enough to expect immediate compliance to a demand of little consequence to one of the country's better citizens before everybody else is awake. What in dickens do you want from me at this hour of the night?"

"Let me in. Unlock the screen," said the sheriff.

"Might as well. You'll break down my door if I don't. Whatever happened to a right of house and home —- to privacy? You'll barge right in whatever I say. Oh, come on in."

The sheriff refused the offer of coffee if he'd give Clint a few minutes to make it. Said he had been up before sun-up and already he'd had more coffee than his system could tolerate.

"Sorry I don't have a desk you could rake your spurs across and scar up. Now tell us what this casual and friendly visit is all about," said Clint.

The twisted lips of the sheriff, his eyes at half mast, his hand near his holster on his right hip like he'd seen in the TV Westerns, his head thrown back like a latter-day Caesar as he estimated the number in the mass below him, preparing to address the former citizens of Rome now subjects of the 'emperor,' was arrogance at its most condescending.

Clint anticipated the official explanation, what might be his reaction, although he knew to a 'tee,' what the sheriff who climbed Clint's mountain before the sun took the dew from the grass had on his wee mind. The law that the man hoping he represented at the moment realized its advantage before a common citizen.

Clint hadn't the leisure of speculation, for right then the door opened and Leo and Mollie entered. For long moments, not a word was spoken by anyone among the four. Even the sheriff lost a bit of his haughtiness, if that were possible.

The sheriff said: "Well, well, if it isn't the guarded Russian himself and his uppity girl friend. Just in time, both of you, because my visit up here is about you, Leo. It's time to lay out the entire story on the table right in front of us; time to resolve some questions that have bothered me since the day hell froze over. Sit down, both of you; we'll get right to it."

The sheriff got up and offered his chair with its pillow to Mollie, who neither said thank you nor softened the glare of a disapproving face that turned into its souring worst the longer she stayed in the presence of the fat man.

She accepted the offer, crossed her legs, which revealed to Clint such pleasure as it would to any other denied male yet any hopeful man of the village.

Bless Leo, my friend. It could be said that Molly was an appealing good-looking woman, a little skinny, maybe.

"Now, Leo, right off I want to know where you were on the 14th of June that famous day, a couple or so years ago. Did you leave town then? Can you prove you sat in that chair at the hotel all day so the people could see a real live commie from Russia?" The sheriff was wiping his mouth with the back of his hand and pulled up his shoulders like he was getting in posture before reviewing the troops.

"You know dang well where I was all that day, mister sheriff. If I got up to go pee, forgive me Mollie, you or your deputy will have made a report for your files."

"Yes, I was born in Russia, but I am not a communist. For your investigative report I'm used to bother even from my one-time best friends since boyhood back there."

"Even my cousins were set by the commies to watch me every hour of every day. I didn't expect to find a similar custom here in my adopted country —- not until I came to your town."

"You asked me once before if I knew who among your American citizens might have shot at me that twilight time a year or many months ago. If that's the same question you put to me back then, the answer is the same. It didn't bother me then and it doesn't get to me today as something to be concerned about. A number of people have tried to kill me, but as far as I know not one of them has succeeded."

"Well," said the sheriff. "Let me tell you about a man who was killed in Memphis who was identified as having lived here, like you, and he turned out to be a Russian who disappeared a little after we suspected he learned you were in town. How about that? Two Russians at the same time who did not know each other came to this squat little burg to live in freedom and the home of the brave at the same time."

"Well," welled Leo, in the high-pitched imitation of the sheriff's 'welling,' "if this fellow lived here I must tell you for your good citizens' files that I won't declare that I even would have known him, or even the fact that he lived here. Are you saying this is that person who tried to kill me, or maybe that he simply wanted to scare me?"

"I'm not prepared to say," said the lawman. "All I'm saying is that some things about his death don't in any dang way add up. He died by walking too soon into fast traffic, and the suspicion is, real big suspicion, that he was pushed. We think other evidence, which the FBI has revealed to me —- about all they've told me of it —- is that you know more than you're revealing to us, we real Americans."

"May I ask, if I may, at this point in our conversation is why you are here with my friend Clint Greene when we walked in and found you sitting there like on the throne of the king? We were puzzled when we saw your car out front," said Leo.

"You're his friend, and you might have told him things you wouldn't have said to anybody else," said the sheriff.

"And do you think that a friend, like Clint Greene here, in all the character he has meant to everybody else around here, and to me, and to Mollie here and to her or our friend Doris, and to Oscar, a good and dedicated friend, would run to you and tell you for some godly reason or ungodly all they knew about me?"

Leo continued, "For the sake of goodness and mercy, get off your hind end, sheriff, and go get a book at the library that explains just what wearing a badge in this country really entails."

Leo was red of face, his hands prepared to rip to shreds the upholstered chair where he sat, looking to Mollie for 'approval.' He was prepared to leap at the sheriff's throat, thinking better of it, because such an attack on a law enforcement person would not hold up to his favor in a court of law.

"Memphis is a long way from here, lawman, and the horse I ride could not make it in a day. With another day or more, two maybe at the least thrown in, your deputy would still be left far behind. If as you implied that the FBI dismissed the case or interest in it, please shut up."

"Why don't you accept their kindness and judgment? That's what they're doing, and for your ego," said Leo.

"On the other hand, if you won't take their word for it, why don't you recognize your duty as sheriff and protect the people. Instead, you are beating a dead horse."

"You are expecting the horse to whisper in your ear trying to explain what it is you don't understand about something that's not real to you but it is to everybody else."

With a couple of weak attempts at evasion without some cussing because of Mollie's presence, the sheriff slowly with pain got up from the chair nodding to Mollie and sneering at the two men and walked out the door. He knew he'd been beaten.

Neither were the two friends nor Mollie acknowledged by way of a sigh or gesture of relief, as the sheriff closed the door behind him, not as a parting gesture by slamming it in emphasis required during Act One by the theatre society, as a stupid way to say goodbye.

Mollie said: "That man will not be satisfied until he dies with his boots on and the town builds a monument to his memory."

Clint said: "I believe it's about time to put the entire episode to rest. How about that, Citizen Leo, our cousin from Russia?"

Leo said: "I have a lot of apologizing to you. It's too large an explanation for just the three of us, so I'll tell you the heart of the case, or the 'situation,' saving the full story and facts until we have the five of us together, including certainly Oscar and Doris. At last I will no longer keep the secrets of my life as they may be, certainly not from my friends."

"I told the sheriff I didn't know the man, but it wasn't exactly a lie, or was it as well the truth. I once knew the man —- as friend and resident of my village. We grew up together. The man I knew, the boy, gave his soul to the communists the minute they began setting up their program among my friends and kinfolk in an effort to de-humanize us, as well as all the people of Russia. From that point to us he was a non-person, yes, I knew him once. He betrayed us twice. As a snitch, or informer, he was set to watch and report on our every activity that might have been construed as anti-communist or anti-government."

"Then, many of us Cossacks —- thousands really - went over to the Allies during my country's war against Hitler. They went with one purpose, to fight the communists who had taken over our country, hopefully not to fight against Mother Russia."

"This man identified us for Stalin and where we could be found. So very many of my Cossacks and my fellow Russians were rounded up by the Allies and returned under guard by train or prison truck to Moscow, where they knew they would be executed."

"I fought alongside the British and Americans against my own government. After the war I lived in Britain, where my Cossacks found me and through the Brits sent me to the USA to track down the man who had betrayed us. My instructions were to kill him. We sort of played our own brand of chess —- he evading me by moving from city to city, and I always just a day short of encountering him and doing the quite distasteful business of carrying out my assignment."

"Now that he has been erased not by my hand even as I might be given credit for it since the report of his demise will have called it an accident or suicide or whatever, which was unknown at the time. The report will say he could have been pushed. Oh, and by the way, the sheriff didn't surprise me with the news. I knew about it from my friends, let us say, who are in high places. I wouldn't have believed it if the news came from the sheriff."

Clint said: "My fellow American, and one of its outstanding citizens, it's time to tell us your name. We know who you are. We don't know the brand you were given at birth."

Leo said: "My name, sir, is Maxim Shovlevski. (It is Leo, also, in the U.S. of A)."

"Maxim is an All-American by name, as well is it a name we gave you," said Clint.

"May you consider both as an honor to be etched on your tombstone, a long time out there in the future, we are sure."

"Look at the 'Irish' of any Notre Dame team now by year after year a football team with which they in pride will forever be stuck with," said Clint. "We know they are 'Irish."

"I've got lots more names, changed obviously through the years —- and a rose by any other name says I am still alive," said Max.

"If anybody in our village remembers me at all, it's how fast I was as a learner, if it was with a little bit of knowledge that would assist me in staying alive, contrary even sappy in my ways. I so often changed my name, I came to question just who I really was."

"I have been in Appalachia seven years now. At last, even as a wanderer following a prey, I settled here where I felt the Cossack-like comfort among these outdoor people, who until recently, when others began to come, were primarily descendants of earlier migrations of Scotch-Irish, whom the Cossacks would recognize as neighbors, like they've known them all their lives."

Mollie asked Leo," how you, a Russian, could have been protected, by the power and aid of the United States government, which watched over you and kept you informed about the movement of your people's enemy? Why didn't they just arrest him, be done with it?"

"They knew why I was here," said Leo," and they kept us apart, even in what was a cat-and-mouse situation. My feeling was that in the event of a murder of one Russian by another Russian on American soil might lead to the press exposure of an agreement made at Teheran, or maybe it was at Yalta but that's Truman among the Big Three or Big Four—- whatever. Roosevelt was a party to the agreement, or he wasn't, voting with the two other powers to turn us over to Stalin. They were afraid of Stalin, I suppose, if that was true. Most of my friends and I do not believe that Roosevelt agreed with Stalin to our murder. Bless him. That theory, of Roosevelt's innocence, is also agreed to by the academicians."

"Fantastic," said Clint. "Those were difficult times."

"You'll have more questions, and we'll talk more about it at a time when we're all together," said Maxim.

"By the way," said Clint, "how come Doris didn't come here with you this morning? I was glad you all came in when you did. As it turned out, it was quite a good little party."

Mollie said, "Doris had to leave early for Knoxville. A friend there just had a heart attack. Doris went down there to help out, since the friend lost her husband some time ago and was living alone. We came up to take you out to breakfast. Still will, if you are still hungry."

Clint: "Doris, I have come to believe, is happiest when she is doing for someone else. She will have that friend up here as soon as the doctor says so. Have her in bed and will be cooking for her and watching, with Mollie, her friend and nurse, by her bedside day and night. That's why I could never marry her, even as I love her. It would never work with us, living together in a hospital."

Mollie appeared surprised. "She loves you too Clint, I know she has been thinking of you as her future husband."

"We'll get along just as well," said Clint.

"Come on, let's go down and find breakfast." Over grits and eggs, Max, or Leo, a 'different name,' which we have to get use to all over again," Clint thought, as he asked "how the Russian received the funds from simply whomever?"

He said he "knew he had to pay his rent at the hotel and to feed his body." Leo said "the money came to the bank to be deposited under a code name, a series of numbers; the bank delivered the cash to him in a sealed envelope, at the hotel, by their own messenger."

"Boy, talk about the intrigue you've been living in the middle of and the speculation you've created wherever you have made a temporary home," said Mollie. She asked "how Leo managed to get an education amidst all the different societies he'd lived among."

"Let's start with this hillbilly," said Max, uh, Leo. "People in the hills of Kentucky are surprised that I am an American once a native of Russia, since I capably use all the local aphorisms and can speak to them with a nigh onto an undetectable accent, I've been told. You all (how do you like that figure of speech?) say more in one sentence than most of the rest of the world. Yankees, hah, might take a whole page to make a point. That's why we have such good writers down here."

"As for the prey, you knew who he was, and why I'm here; with that Cossack fighter instinct of self-preservation I knew so well. He seemed to know just where I always could be found. He could speak English, 'British English,' if I may call it that, even better than I. His failing, I've been told, was that he was not well versed in the Spanish language, since he lived for a while here and maybe elsewhere under a Hispanic name."

"I was taught German in the Academy. With English which came to me quickly I felt that I could get along anywhere in the world. Let me tell you how far along I am toward becoming a real hillbilly:"

"First, I have bought a piece of land. It has been a dream of many of our Cossacks to some day own acreage in the U. S. of A. You may tell anybody you know who just might be interested that I now am a landed American. Add that I, at last, am free and often greeted as 'sir' and 'mister,' or whatever else, with the respect an American may be accorded. No more 'comrade,' or even 'citizen' by the curious who are surprised that I haven't been shot as yet.

"I've often had a feeling that you've known about me since I left (you Americans) next to the bridge in that little town in Austria when we were looking for ways to escape the Stalin net sweeping in the Russians who defected to the other side. Many friends died during that great war, not all of them by the powder horns of the motherland's foreign enemies."

"Through the same people who brought me to this corner of the world for a specific purpose, my friends have managed to keep me in mind. Of that, I have no doubt."

"I was pleased to learn that my closest friend has returned to the village that was our home since we were boys, watching the girls become young women and the Cossacks, the greatest warriors, rumbling through our village with their brass buttons and shiny swords daring us to grow up and ride the steppes together. It was the ambition of us all."

"As for girls, I became extremely aware of la difference, on the day my friend Alexander (at home spelled 're' and so pronounced) and I as unshaven boys once visited Chelyabinsk and all we in shyness could do was sit out on the front steps of the library and watch the girls walk by. Some of them noticed us and made teasing remarks. (Our sexual prowess was all in our heads, but it was there.)"

"Since my mother and father died at the bloodied hands of Joseph Stalin and our village was virtually destroyed, I could only wait for the opportunity to leave the motherland until such time as the communists were sent to fertilize the sacred ground of our ancestors. You may follow me through Austria and Switzerland to the British Isles, and thence to America. For a long time I hoped conditions changed enough that I might return to our home in the Caucasus, in spire of the fact that I met many of you Americans when I was called by your generals to instruct the U.S. army on the use of Russian weapons. I became quite fond of you. I was given an American uniform, and it fit in every way."

"I never gave up hope that I might return, but the longer I stayed away the more I knew I loved this country. I've made many friends here. Some of them I would die for. "

"I have never taken a wife —- came close, when I was in England going to college.

I haven't told you this, Mollie, I sort of 'fell in love." Ah, such a beauty she was, all the way through, cultured, quite the lady, and she told me she loved me. That is, if you can understand the phrase 'sort of,' since I'd really had little or no experience in 'love.' But I felt it, told her so, and it hurt me terribly when I had to leave."

"What a wonderful time that was for an ex-Russian of the dreary mud fields and zero days in houses of straw and mud and the few stones we could find. The situation with this young lady, a college classmate in England, didn't work out because of her family. I heard years later from my sponsors that she had come to America looking for me. She was older than me by maybe seven or eight years. She's a mite dead of old age by now. I'm half sure of that. I always hoped she would find a new love, one who wasn't a 'commie;' I was so called that by her suspicious family."

"She had nigh on but not quite escaped the prejudice and stern dictatorship of her parents. By this time as much as I could have loved her, I thought it was for the better, due to my mission at the time to avoid her. I have never heard anything more about her. I would have been almost impossible to find, anyway. Others were hiding me too."

"I want to tell you about my few acres. Right in the middle is an old pioneer's cabin, which I plan to restore. Oscar sold it to me while you were away, Clint. I got water piped in from a mountain stream; the electric company is running a line on the other side of the river. They will throw a wire my way without charging me. They said they will do it because a sub-division would be built out there sometime in the future. I don't believe that, but it doesn't matter since I got a step up to civilization in America."

"Actually, I've learned about local politics, and I have a friend, a coffee buddy, who manages the electric company. The rebuilding of the fireplace will be my biggest job. Gus is out there today working on it. When you get out there to inspect it, know that someday we will sit by the fire and talk of old times. That's what old people do. That is about all they can do. I can't talk much about my life because nobody would believe me."

Clint said: "Why not now, me, you and Mollie, we all can go out there if we promise not to say you're out of mind if you're thinking of restoring that old falling-down cabin, and even think of living out there. I know there's no road, but I'll get a Jeep in town and we can crawl over the rocks."

"No," said Mollie. "Not until we have Doris to go with us."

As for Doris, who at that moment was driving on a country road out of town with her youngest daughter, pointing out scenes from her long ago childhood. She'd called her home and daughter to be picked up at the bus station.

"I thought I'd better talk to you now rather than allow you to hear it from elsewhere about some of my plans for the future," Doris said to her daughter, later, hoping; the girl had arrived home from her school in another part of the state about the same time Doris arrived home after visiting her friend. It was quite on her mind. "It's been several years since your father and mother divorced and went in different directions. I thought at the time we might have to live in a place like that cabin."

"I am sure you knew how despondent I was, for a long time, and that I did the best for my children and their grandmother that I could manage on the small paycheck I received for the best job I could find considering my lack of college education, and experience.

"After my siblings grew up and got jobs and families of their own, I came back here to take over our family's house, to save money, and to save the old home place, which was beginning to age and deteriorate."

"Clint hasn't asked me yet, to marry him, but I believe he will. In fact, I'm pushing it as subtly as I can." These thoughts weren't told directly to Clint, but from a friend of Clint's with whom she had confided. Included were other facts of life, personal secrets that she had passed on.

She continued: "You may have heard of Clint Greene, since he was from our town and became famous among readers of his short stories in magazines that were big once. His editorials were picked up across the country. That's a reason he attracted the politicians. They thought of him as a kingmaker. He is more cultured than I, but it doesn't show."

"As for his love for me, I believe he is on his way. That's a woman's intuition.

His thoughtfulness is something that would be the envy of every woman who is married to an inconsiderate man."

"The fact that he disappeared for a month not long ago is of no matter to me, since he was troubling in his effort to find his head. When he returned he called me first thing. Even before his partners in their crusade to enlist the country's voters in the climate change threat, his trip was a mystery. He said that some day soon he would tell us all about it."

"I believe he would make me very happy. If you and the rest of the family agree, that would give me a great deal of happiness."

"I ought to mention that I knew him when we were in school together, and may have gotten close if he hadn't done a lot of after school work for different people around town to help out his mother and father, who had never had much money for him as he was growing up. We dated a little, mostly with others."

"He kissed me once, but that's as far as it went. He left soon for the Marines; after the war he went to college on the GI Bill. Then he went north to find a newspaper job. He finally had a small paper of his own in a small town north of Dayton. He married a girl up there and they had three children, all of them mostly grown now, with families of their own."

"He has two close friends who protect him like he was judge of the universe. The three of them formed a club, to sell the people on fighting the Earth's heating up. They call it OMEN or something like that. They'd better learn pretty soon, despite their protection of their chairman, that I intend to crawl over their unconscious bodies to get to my man. I need him, and he needs me. As well, I need you and the others for your blessing. I love you, all of you, very much, kith and kin."

She was still talking to her daughter,

"Up ahead, back of those trees -- my how they have grown —- is the old home place. You all came up here with me six or so years ago. Lately on another excursion I came back and wished I hadn't, because the house was badly in need of repair and a new paint job.

Well, what you know? Somebody's bought the place and fixed it up. Bless them."

"We sold out when I left eighth grade at that little school we passed when we were on a drive on a Sunday afternoon back during that last summer. The school was so close I could walk except on a snow and ice day. I loved that little schoolhouse. We moved to town so I could go to high school. Daddy wasn't too keen on my riding the school bus, which started out as an open bed farm truck with the kids standing up. My my, how things have changed and I'm sure for the better."

"As a freshman in high school, it wasn't long before I saw him, Clint Greene, I mean, popular like a football player, though he couldn't go out for the team, I was told, because he had to get back up the mountain before dark. He had chores to do. I also knew right off that I would have a lot of competition for him. I didn't believe he hadn't noticed me; he said later that he had, but that boy was about as shy as anybody I ever saw.'

"Right away I saw how the boys looked to him for leadership, and when I read in the paper about how he'd been made sergeant, first corporal then sergeant, I remembered how the other boys sort of followed him around. That made me proud even though I figured at the time that he'd never remember me. I thought of keeping a scrapbook on him, but I never did, wish I had.

He was in the senior class school play. That was after the teacher who directed the play said she would take him home after practice. His parents came down the night of the play. First time I ever saw them."

"His daddy was like I imagined; tall, tan, like the man who rode the white horse in Saturday matinees at the picture show. His mother was a beautiful woman, but looked like she was overworked."

"I kept myself pure for him, but after I read that he had married a girl up in Ohio, I suppose I opened up with big hurt at first and said okay to the first boy who asked me. Don't worry I loved him and I was glad he was your father."

"A thing that worries me about him is his moodiness I guess you could call it. You never know what he's thinking, like his mind is way out yonder, largely as a result by his action with the Marines during the war, somebody said about him."

"He loses himself in music, listening to the classics on the radio as he drives. I expect he does that at home, also. Never heard him talk much about a TV show he had watched, although he often mentions some ancient movie he'd seen way back there in the days of black and white."

"When we watched a play down at Baptist College on that one big date, he held my hand all through it, or I think he held on that long. He later said he didn't recall it that way."

"When he talks, every word stops at a comma or period, which you'd expect from a newspaperman. So often when he talks, too, it is like he's reading from his own news story, and that's odd. In his reporter's mind that's I bet is exactly what he does. I wished he would read one of those romance novels when he's talking with me."

Comment: "How many newspapermen like Clint one day began telling news stories to himself so he could escape what he'd chosen to make of himself was no different from everybody else, that he was born to point out man's shortcomings in his writings was not his alone, that he'd not been touched by the gods to be a divine king's interpreter, yet he was helping along the man or woman who read his stuff."

"He reiterated how his ordeal had led to his acceptance of the ancient thinking by some of his college mates in shooting the old bull with them or down on his cabin's shaded back porch perched above the river on the side of the mountain was simply natural."

"Then he talked about his home in Ohio, for which, even as its ink and air dirt from the press left his shirt front smeared black at day's end, just the same gave him appreciation at the time, He had raised his three children around the make-up stone, and left it all in the keeping of Aaron, his eldest. The others thought it was a good arrangement for the boy since he stayed in the hometown, even though the paper would soon after Clint left be sold, or given away. 'He got tired of it quicker than I did,' Clint said."

"His interests were in a different direction. Norman and Chris, the girl, live not too far apart, all of them in central Ohio. Chris married her friend Joe and they have the one daughter, named Lily for her grandmother. He said he couldn't stay in the house, or even in the same town."

"Once in our conversation he recalled the drug store on the corner like the one here where we had our first milk shake together, or up there the park where Lily played the sax with the town's small band, the little family church where they were married, all became to him as a sort of Little America, giving him many unforgettable memories, I suppose because they meant so much to a country boy."

"It would have been as sad to stay as it was to leave," he said. "He also said he'd found some new friends in his old hometown down South, to which he earlier had returned."

'An accident,' he said to me, kept him in a coma for a month."

"He has fully recovered, though he often has a twitch or two to remind him to keep his eyes on the road. Then he left town for nearly another month and visited an old friend, once a mentor and a college classmate, who helped bring him back to Earth. I didn't know where he went for a long time. I still haven't told him that I knew about his little excursion."

"The friend also somehow saved his faith. I only yesterday learned for sure where he had been during that late out-of-towner." You will hear me in the future talking of Chief Dick, or Barefoot Boy, he said after it all just came out. That happened as I was planning a big secret wedding and I'll have to talk to you about that."

"An Indian can be known by many titles, honors, deeds or the way he looks. Think of Sitting Bull," Clint said, recalling thinking of some things

Chief Dick said: "He's a rough-looking fellow, rough as an old corn ear that dropped off the wagon on the way to the barn," which all leads to a recollection of my (Clint said) Russian friend, rather than try to remember how he was called in the several roles in which he starred "and each name seemed to belong to him."

"We down here in the mountains simply called Clint's close friend, Leo, who was at first, Jack. We looked for a good old hillbilly name that fit him rightly," said Doris.

"That's how Leo still is known throughout our town and the valley, a country town which also fills up about all the level ground around here. The town is below our mountain and he loves every inch of it. An American GI would brag about being Leo's friend. His other partner in the 'saving of the world' project is named Oscar, but often is called Bill; yes, just plain old Bill, because his predecessor on the paper was named Bill."

"You can see that I'm wasting time telling you all this. 'It's a long way from my boyhood Journalism,' he said, or maybe that's what the old 'J' is, just that and about little else. I'm trying to give you as much as possible about how I feel, as quickly and fully as I can. Just remember that I will always love Lily, and will cherish each moment we were together."

Clint had written the following note in his mind, which he kept to himself: "Lily, my love, I must tell you that I've met a woman a, girl from the time of my teen years in school who has indicated an interest in me —- decrepit old man that I am. I feel I must seek your kind permission to continue a courtship."

"We still talk of a happenstance that I'm ever trying to understand," he said. "We three men of OMEN, as we call it, for a time later believed our work would be in vain, even as so many people sympathized with us. In the past, as the believer's attention or a more firm belief was called to the blazing fires of hell coming over the mountain, they wanted to run out and party it up just before they are consumed by the spreading of what they knew as 'divine retribution.' That seems to be what they are doing now. It doesn't seem to bother them." Following a visit to the Chief's mountain and the ritual in which the Chief and his two Indian friends had included him, Clint had come home with a strong feeling that man will go on living.

"A writer whose books I read said it, 'man will go on as their creator intended.' I agree with him. In the event of another Sodom and Gomorrah, I think there are enough good men on that mountain to let us get started again."

"I don't believe that the Lord is ready to give up on us, which the Lord would call the most grand of Heaven's great experiments."

"My Indian friend added that we should go right ahead and order seed for planting in the growing seasons to come."

Leo, formerly known as Jack, now Max as he finally broke down and told us was because he was back in civilization, said, "Now that we no longer have OMEN to keep us busy, I once in a while ask, 'how will we manage?'"

The Duchess said: "I wouldn't be too concerned, old buddy. I can think of a million things around the house that need doing, and of a few other little things to keep us together, and quite busy." Mollie, as a former nurse, still is, knows a lot about men, young and old.

Max said: "I was thinking about writing my friend who is back in our village now that it's safe to be home, even to move around and to come visit us here in the beautiful Kentucky mountains: Take a letter, Duchess, to Alexandre Kareninov."

"Maybe I'll ask him to come visit us in these mountains, which he will never believe, as he also might be surprised that I have a woman in my old life whom I might ask 'if she will marry me?'"

Oscar came in the house dragged by two women, only one of them was not familiar. He headed to the icebox and squeezed the top off a cold beer, taking a long draught before introducing either of the two females. They just stood with their mouths open, like they were offended by his rudeness.

Oscar said: "You people remember my daughter, Jenny." The four nodded, "and her friend, Evelyn," who bore a deep tan, and was somewhat older than Jenny. Doris only, offered a greeting. Oscar introduced the more tanned of the two as Jenny's new friend. In the custom of the time, not surprising, but there was something in her voice that hinted that Doris knew the strange woman. Oscar offered no last name. To Clint it was a surprise to know that Chief Dick, or Richard, was in town. Evelyn wouldn't have come by herself.

Oscar said that Evelyn was interested in writing for what she called the media, and she wanted to meet Jenny's father and his friends Clint and Leo (she must not have heard that Leo was now Max) who she thought with Oscar that they might give her some advice in her possible new interest in literature and writing within it as part of a new career.

"I couldn't do so," Oscar said, "not offer any advice to her even though she just might be the exception. A long-time, maybe, er, uh, I feel honored, though."

Clint said, "She just might even know about me, as a one-time writer."

The others all showed a little surprise at Clint's remark. "Why that's not the true Clint, not with that unaccustomed egotism."

He looked into the faces of the others, turned to Evelyn, Clint pausing briefly before asking her why she wanted to be a journalist.

"I like to write," said Evelyn, and besides, she said she believed she could reach a lot of people with her pen that she could not do so in any other way.

"And just why do you want to reach a lot of people?" she was asked as Clint continued his probing.

"I'm not sure I could answer that, at least not to your satisfaction," she said.

"Don't be concerned about satisfying me," said Clint. "It distracts from one of the main reasons you might become a journalist. My chosen career, wacky as I learned quite early would not have happened if I had listened to my elders."

"You're right," said Evelyn. "I think I sort of panicked and gave you a trite answer, but allow me to say that I've always had a great belief in the truth."

He continued: "Let's change the subject, if it's not a challenge to what I have just heard from a fellow human being. I have been waiting to tell of something I first heard about long ago. Just today, my fair lady, I was reminded of the tale, and it's a story that I once had written about —- in my younger years. I had learned that local democrats built a cross, made of wood or iron maybe, and wrapped it in thin gold —- gild -- to be placed out in front of party headquarters."

"It subsequently disappeared, a really wild occurrence that encouraged a long search by the townspeople. It contributed to a following odd sort of celebration with a different but to each of them because of its quite disturbing religious overtone."

"The cross really was made of iron that my family knew about and talked about at our supper table," someone said. "We at first believed that it might be real gold and that a thief stole it to sell and make life easier for himself."

"After it became lost, other folks have been looking for it all these many years.I believed it was a sign that we were falling away from God's hopes for his purpose. If it's possible for Him to be disappointed, that His people were pursuing false gods, He still had the power to remind us just who He was and that we all were His own and what we were to Him. The pursuit of gold is not what He'd really expected of us. It was an age-old story of mankind. It was for us: not again. Not again."

"Maybe," Clint continued. "Who am I to dare look into the mind of the Almighty?"

"Just today the word was back on the street. Most people will not recall a gold cross -- too long ago —- which was built to honor a one-time nominee for the U.S. presidency. The word was: 'they found the cross.' The word went forth to every alleyway and every shack and hovel. Most people of the village didn't know why but they felt the flow of the electricity that surged through every blood vessel and sinew of their bodies," said Clint.

"It's only a piece of iron, but covered with a man-made solvent of yellow paint," Clint emphasized. "It was added by someone among the more educated among us, the same someone on the porch who had said, 'It's a sign, like they said in the town. You have to recognize it for what you see, and declare a faith in what is before you.'"

"You'd think it was the second coming the Christians are always talking about. It's not like the climate change is going to be the end of the world, but it means at least to us here that it is the real beginning of a new world," said Oscar.

"Astounding," said Clint. "Yes, that, my dear Miss Evelyn, is the thing among all of the little inconsequential stuff of the times, is what makes a newsperson. Do you think you could live with that?" Evelyn simply smiled, like everybody else.

Oscar said he'd take the girls home and be right back. He said he sensed because of some things Clint said that a change of some sort was in the wind, but not because the 'gold cross' had been found. When Oscar returned, Clint headed into the same untried territory with a new set of remarks, causing the others to put down their knitting and pay attention.

He said: "Before we fold our tents and move on to the hills to chase the hounds let's do a bit of soul-searching."

Clint started the story about the cross to divert what surely must be a secret about why Evelyn and Richard were in town without telling Clint that they had been sworn to the secret about the why of their presence.

"Uh-oh," said the duchess, "When men talk of time for soul-searching, it's a strong hint to the women to find the path into the woods to a place of solitude and talk of war."

Clint ignored the remark by Mollie yet was surprised that Doris and the duchess threw open the outside door and slammed it, each pretending to have been insulted.

"I've been thinking about what I proposed to you earlier, that we close up our shop, forgetting what we were actively pursuing, because I and you agreed that it was of no avail," said the chairman.

Oscar went to the kitchen sink and emptied the half empty coffee cups, a symbolic mark of throwing out the older destitute (thinking) for a beginning of new (ideas), about amending the current stubborn environmental blessing, Clint thought.

"I have been on track along the same lines," said the Russian-American. "Let's hear more about your thinking on this. I've figured that the climate was changing too fast for our good and the future of the Earth to a point no longer within reach of our weak attempts."

Clint said: "For one thing we coupled our ideas about the need for help in fighting the causes of climate change, with the appeal to changing our ways because of America's hint of its going belly-up."

"Strong talk cross the country lately on both sides of the street is about the surrender of knowledge of a tradition that we'd built and that had sustained this country since the day of its founding to world envy, that misled us to the fact that we've suddenly become aware that it has all gone missing like always."

Oscar recalled what Machiavelli said about politics: "That was five hundred or so years ago; he put his philosophy into 'The Prince,' a book that has influenced politicians ever since, at least until the present generation. He said his advice to a politician in a run for office was 'not to be too idealistic or too moral.' You know too many politicos who base a campaign on the people's sin and chase jackrabbits and get a lot of press support. Nobody else apparently talks or pounds the table."

The Russian recalled the Civil War in his country, how the people had power for a brief moment. "They allowed by rote the communists led by Lenin to steal it from them. It had happened so many times in the lives of the Russians."

Doris and the duchess had returned. Since the men had talked in their presence about dissolving OMEN, they quickly looked for discussion of the committee's direction toward the old OMEN and its visits to the future. They both knew since they would be a part of any action in the future, they both would be by its nature a part of it. When the duchess had left the room, she and Doris were being talked about also.

They would probably he in on any future plans for it, and they were excited. Doris especially would be glad to learn that Clint might have loved her, as it earlier was tipped into the conversation.

Mollie had entered the room ahead of Doris. Her heart jumped as she heard Max ask Clint if there was any change in his feelings toward Doris, as is quite usual in talk among men who so often begin discussion at a higher level. That would be a feeling but as soon amended to talk about women in general.

Mollie heard Max ask if Clint had any plans about marrying that woman. Mollie, in an awkward attempt to return to the porch, nearly knocked Doris to the floor, hoping Doris might not hear Clint's response. She told Doris: "Let's wait a moment. I think they're going to get into a fight."

She later learned from Max that Clint had said, "I reckon so, even as I have been running from the situation these many months."

"It would be good for both of us, if she'll have me. I don't intend to say some romantic things about it just now, since people of our age don't marry for a lot o' kissin' and th' bedroom. But I could say that I love her and not be too far wrong about it."

Clint later would ask Max the same question about him and Mollie. In a short time Mollie would confirm the answer that Max gave Clint that other day.

Max said: "No, and we've agreed on it. It simply won't be necessary. We'll have her home and the cabin I'm building down on the river. I'll use the cabin mostly for doing some pouting and as a retreat when I need to be alone with thoughts of the past. The Lord knows I've come a long way, and my kinfolks back there would never believe a minute of it."

"I've never told anybody about my liaison with the English girl I left in her family's castle. I've been told that she came to America several years ago, looking for me. I was told also that she had a child by me, a boy."

"We are going to spend a lot of time looking for the boy; if he's in this country. It will be the greatest joy. I'll be out there under my true name looking for my son."

As Max sat talking to Clint, Doris came out and asked Clint to stay but she thought Max would like to walk down town and get a cup of tea and talk to some friends while the women stayed in the kitchen getting a lot of things done before the wedding tomorrow. It'll help everybody get things done, she said; a wedding tomorrow? Lot of things came roaring in and apparently he had little time to figure it all out.

As Max left the porch, Doris asked Clint to get a firm grip on the chair's side rests because she said they had something serious to talk about. Clint was as usual surprised as Doris and her apparent nervous eyes and hands held his full attention over what she had to say and what she said 'they' should talk about.

"You go over to my house and take a shower. Your best suit and other clothes, your socks, even your underwear, are on the bed in my bedroom. I found a good pair of shoes that are next to the bed."

"How come my clothes are down here at your house?"

"I went up to your cabin and brought them down. You showed me where the key was over the door, remember?"

"Let me ask what in a fine fur of a frog are you going to tell me the why about all this, or command, really, means?" he asked.

"For the grooms and brides' wedding dinner tonight for Max and Mollie's union tomorrow, and for us," she said.

"For us," asked Clint, "uh, why just us?"

He knew he appeared stupid, with his whole body dropping into the black pit that had just opened up ahead of him.

"Oh, didn't I tell you? It's a double wedding, for Max and Mollie, for you and me."

"A double —- what?" So, I'm about to learn just what all this evasive talk has been about. Everybody but me knew the pits of hellfire was about to come in with the next big earthquake and we were waiting for Doris to say something like he agrees or he's damning the lot of us for knowing and not telling him. So she did, "All right, he knows, so let's hear 'im, after he's had time to digest it." Holy, holy holy, the room was spinning.

"Yeas, Clint, I went up to your house to get your clothes for tomorrow, and you were about to ask where we had hidden your friend, Richard. Well, I'll tell you: as I closed the closet door, I saw your address book lying open on your desk. Right at the top was the address and phone number of Dick and Evelyn, in North Carolina. Right then I knew for sure where you had been all of last month."

"When a woman's voice answered, I said, 'Evelyn, this is Doris, I didn't have time to give my last name, before she said: 'yes, I know who you are, something's happened to Clint.' Don't tell me until I sit down over here. Is he all right? He didn't call to tell us that he got home okay, like I told him. Dick's up on the north forty. By now he's found his pocket phone. I said Doris is on the phone, Clint's okay, but she has some news.' For some reason or other they knew why I called, or at least somebody would, with news about Clint. They drove all night. That's why Richard is up at my house asleep in your bed."

"In my bed?" said Clint, startled, as all dickens. "Oh, dang it, Doris, we aren't even married yet. Do you mean the bed I slept in when I was at your house – doing my recuperating?"

There is no way to find a way into Clint's mind during this debate, no that's not the word; let's say, his dilemma; no that's not the word either, danged if there is any way to describe his frustration in this occurrence between a man and a woman. In the first place, a man has to ask the woman, not the woman to ask the man, and not only that, but who, what, where, when and whether and why. "If I wrote the story about this, I'd lose my reporter's license."

Right now let's follow Max as he is still on the road to Aunt Emma's Tea Room. It's a little past noon of a June day in the Year of Our Lord. Max passed up that little coffee café beyond Main Street and around the corner. He wanted just a little more class. It would be his last cup of tea here for a long time, but no friends were around at this time of day.

It was a pleasant feeling he would have had greeting and talking to the townsfolk who knew by now where he would be found the next morning at tea-time —- at ease in a bright home kitchen.

Max wasn't really prepared to leave for good his chair in the warm corner of the street loggia or porch of the town's only hotel, which in recent years came in recollection by many loafers or retirees of an hour when to such a guest as him was a mark of a lifelong dream, a blessing it was, and more, if drawn in memory of its proximity to people as they strolled past on the nearby sidewalk.

Ahead was the Max Chair of Fame. "Ah ha, what is this? They couldn't wait to rid the premises of its most famous and reliable tenant, good old Max, eh?"

He thought of a child's first story book in which he comes nigh, only just yesterday introduced to "The Three Bears."

Some big bear of a fellow said, aloud. "Somebody is sitting in my chair."

"He is a man I do not know, healthy and obviously tall like a cherished ancestor.

"He sits and smirks not unlike my countrymen" yet as —- father bear sir —- as a man and his right, now that I am gone, "who would smirk as any, a man might well do so in his latest possession a chair at table —- who considers himself to be without any feeling at all of embarrassment."

It was a description of a man well dressed, rare with the dictates of a Yankee dude in the South for the first time who considers himself privileged among a back-country people of the uneducated elite of grits and gravy diners; he of a celebrated street, well spoken as a well-educated person who should be accorded the rights of his station (as we'd discover to be of an educated man); a Northlander yet, a grown man in short pants.

"Oh fie and go ye on thy way. Begone ye, worthless scoundrel, ye scout of the dark night, no friend of man who walks among the righteous oh ye wicked self who dares say he can take advantage of a moon's dimness to challenge a smiley knight of the old order."

"It is a man who believes the devil himself would not dare challenge an old warrior like himself, who would do battle like an old Cossack who would fight for his chair. . . oh ye knave mocking him whose high brave talk is answered from the glory of Mother Russia to a presumptuous mocking of a highfalutin Yank who came to England takes to himself in love a beautiful woman, a lady of the Court of King George, who then disappears into the night, and settles on the shores of an alien land." (it is knowledge by the older man upon the realization of the identity of the intruder, who was a smarty britches without a response).

If ever in the annals of time's most fierce warrior as one of King Richard's men, one of his general's best fighters, a man who felt so helpless alone at that moment when his king offered his kingdom for only a horse, quite as elated yet stunned as a soldier of loyalty the most prideful of his country's flag felt once yah thrice lost as unrewarded for his loyalty to God, and to his fellow soldiers because he could not win his dream's reward in this sad hour because of the lameness of his own mount ah but that is not so, he is life's winner.

Maxim Shovlevski was tall as the highest mountain that reached right into Heaven. He was Leo and Jack and Benjamin and Max by necessity by those others of himself who'd chased him through the better and bitter and the saddest times of his life: he who had been pinned by tin badges on his chest for his service to armies of men. He found for him the good life dedicated to all men as he wished for a good woman like his own and who he had thanked her his mother through him to his God for such a small thing, such a wise and forever loving being.

Great he became, what she had made of him, had done for her son, after first giving him that most precious thing that is life. Once he had found a moment from the roar of guns to say thank you to his mother and their God for bringing him home intact or almost a man (in part) or what was left of him from the battlefield. He had written: "Thank you mother —- and for I knew that you were on your knees last night, for safety in the battle that would come at first light."

This man's pen had spoken about the other women in his life, before he was blessed by the Heavens and had learned to breathe again, he'd found her, in an unexpected palace. A woman, warm and tiny enough to be lifted by his sergeants of trained muscles high above his head like an offering to the gods who on a bright day had sent her to him to be his own and pet like a puppy.

Maxim they called him Leo, but no more. Again I am Maxim, father of the man. His wish words came in stuttered invaders of his speech and his attempt to catch up with what he was trying to convey in his thoughts and excitement; Maxim strained and tugged at his dry tongue to say what he had rehearsed again (oh) a hundred times at least what he would say when the time such as this came he knew that it would, right out of the family wish book thrown like it was mankind's last hope, again and again.

"My son my son, I have found you, dropping right out of the sky like the first day of manna for the children of Israel. Rather you have found me and you have brought me food for my heart." His son was standing, walking toward him. And so was Maxim walking to his son. The two men were hugging each the other. "And you have found me," said Maxim.

"How did you find me?" Maxim, certain the elder the father, and the other, asked.

They stood as that, as close as time, together Leo he as Maxim again and forever pushed his son gentry away from him so they could stare deeply into the eyes and heart of the other man, whom he had encountered here and yonder in his dream whose resemblance reached into his stuttered stunned words of wise, and with no explanation.

Maxim said, "and that your mother had come to America looking for me I was told, and that she'd borne a son to me, I'd often wondered how we could find each other. Tell me, what is your name?"

"My name is Neil Cuthwaite. Mother knew you as Maxim, you told her it would be changed because of your next assignment, but that she never had a chance to tell anybody about you and the child in her belly or anything different because you were up and gone.

After that her whole world blew up because you were either dead or swallowed up in your new job, which was to be kept in its military type secrecy and after a time, a long time, she believed the family had watched the mail, which they did."

"I don't know how she found out that you were in America. The rest, except for me, she knew that you had changed into a new name for a new man. She'd been here all that time. I was born here. She could tell anyone who asked about me, that her husband was killed in the war, and that she still was in bereavement."

At tea across from his son, Maxim asked how his son had found him, even under a false name as they sat facing each other at the café around the corner.

His son said: "I had been working with a close friend who lately had given me a lot of help. He was with one of the U.S. government investigating agencies that were created during the Cold War; I won't say which one —- he could not-in-truth say so himself. Even as he said of everybody in Washington, all were in an agency that had some of investigative power that was a mimic of a Russian agency, I suppose you could say."

"He said they found in the pocket of the man killed in Memphis a list of names and other data in Russian. My friend learned from a colleague that the man and you had been chasing the other for several years. The worry, a big suspicion was that one or the other of your big chase was about to discover the other and had been bound to be part of a murder. Despite the many times you had to change your name again —- man, you and he sure did keep changing your names."

"I feared I'd find you at last in jail on a charge of murder. Or maybe read how you were the murdered man. Also, that not all names on that list were not once former Russian nationals. In my reasoning without knowing any details of the story was that you both were innocent in the public mind, my friend discovered."

"It didn't take long to learn when you came to town, and about the story of that somebody who had taken a shot at you which aroused local suspicion and that you were a Russian and with a lot of nonsense about both of you Russians that created a story of the money that regularly came to you and a lot of other nonsense, that helped create suspicions like an independent income and who you were associating with, calling friends among the locals and right off there you were, as big as life."

"Well, I be danged," said Maxim. "That dang computer has taken over our lives, and I've spent my whole life doing what that danged machine would have done for us and has robbed me of what happiness I could have had in just a few minutes if I had one of them. No, I can say that a need existed to keep all about me and my assignment as secret as a necessity, until that man, the other Russian, was killed and identified. I was released from a lot of fear and trust. I was in danger as long as he was alive. The computer will eventually kill this magnificent democracy we're in."

Maxim had lots more questions of his son as well as answers to questions that would be asked of him as their familiarity with each other increased. He asked where the younger man would be staying how long he would be in the city.

His answer startled him, and he laughed: "Well, I left that room a week ago. I'm with Mollie now, and we are being married tomorrow. You'll be my best man. After your long drive from New York, you will be tired. Meet me right here at six for supper at this little café which is about the best we have. It's where I had been when you saw me coming. I'll have two male friends with me. I think you will like them."

"One woman maybe two, will join us a little later. My woman may come over, if she's not too busy getting ready for tomorrow. The fiancée of one of the men who will be at supper with us is the other, his woman. I will introduce you to all these people at that time. By the way, where did you park your car?"

"The hotel owner said there was a parking lot behind the hotel, and that one of the four places would be vacant. It's exactly what I would expect the situation would be in your big little town. Is there a shower in your hotel?"

"Yeah, but you may have to wait your turn," Maxim said. "By the way, if you find any of my stuff in the room, save it for me."

After a lot of small talk around the supper table with the weddings' crown and other 'romantic' stuff hanging over them was the expected query that followed after introduction to each of the others at table anticipated and right soon again: "Where are you from?" Leo's boy had to repeat to everyone his answer to the same old buddy boy question, "I didn't know Leo had a boy," which came easily, except to the two men of OMEN, who both answered with a smile, one with a big wink. The third man said, "Right off after I'd arrived in town, they asked me," Neil learned quickly how a wink in the South worked.

He said to one man, "Yes I know you from Dad. He mentioned you during our first talk." This pleased the Yankee who'd changed out of his short britches, just to hear them talk. Neil thought how much he liked these people. "They sure are Dad's people all right."

"And what do you do?"

"I'm on the Street."

"You mean you're homeless?"

"No, I work on Wall Street."

"Hmmm, I reckon that means that you count the money?"

"Yeah, I suppose you can say that."

Doris arrived with a younger woman, whom Clint recognized right off from an early morning trip by train with two other overdressed women all bound for Lexington and a day of shopping in those fancy women's stores up there. Doris was out of breath, and Clint rose to greet her and stuttered even more as Doris said,

"This is my daughter Peewee. We've called her that since she was a child. She'd rather not be called that. She never liked it, and by the time she told us, it had gone on too long so we never tried to stop it and it appears she was stuck with it for life. She'd never cared much for her first or birth name, either. We won't speak of it right now."

What Clint didn't say were the thoughts he'd had since that day on the train about this much younger woman, and better yet for sure kept his silent vow never to repeat such thoughts again if he was going to marry her mother, praying that the younger woman would never be left in the house alone with him.

Clint reached out to shake her hand and was going to say that he'd met her one dark dawn or rather just before dawn and while it was still dark, but she said it, using about the same words, although the others heard it with suspicious looks on about all the faces.

The Russian said it, "This is one escapade that Clint never told us about."

Clint started to say something, but didn't, obviously trying to avoid any suspicion.

He'd never nursed any such hidden covetous feelings about the young woman or any doubt about himself that he'd be forced to live with.

"This is a lady's honor I had best defend right off before it gets out of hand. There were two others like her, and they were on a train across the aisle from me. It was Number Twenty-Four bound for the big city and they got off at the Sinks. I went on to Mt. Vernon and got a bus later on to Lexington so I could have breakfast with friends from our one-time newspaper days' relationship."

When Doris and her daughter were introduced to the Russian's son, Clint saw the far glint of the sun in the folding half mast eyes of the daughter. Clint hoped she'd soon meet a younger man and go to live with him far away from his possible prohibited and yet expected proximity.

The wedding went off without major incident through the sweat from an otherwise moderate day's guest nervousness and obvious soldiery stiffness of the military bearing of the Russian bridegroom on official governmental duty, yet with hints of being watched by his superior officers, with little or no attention paid to Clint's and Doris' presence among an amused entourage in the wedding of the year in Kentucky's small city in the old and sacred historic mountains around them.

With Mollie, the bride, it was as if she'd spent the past twenty years rehearsing for the big event like she'd had loads of maiden experience at this sort of dream.

Neil Cuthwaite was the most popular fellow you ever saw, and the older and used women, newly arrived to just another such great event in their otherwise dull and small town lives, at once recalling their waiting wafting for a personal ownership or ride in the coveted black English convertible parked out front all secretly planning parties in their own homes to introduce the present owner of the automobile to the community. They quickly formed a protective circle around him.

Neil dominated the back yard event, as tall as the old trees that offered relief from the late spring event. His Caucasian (Cossack) black hair and almost Mongolian origin touch to his face was a contrast to this bunch of Irish-American hillbillies. Their first question after writing their names as large as allowed on the 'register,' or bridal book, which called for comments mainly about the bride which was to tell of their association in their life story on lines as narrow as a small city's streets, that once were a pole cats' walkway. Here too, was space left for the added family trees or family origin of both bride and groom, of Mollie's set and Doris' family, as known to each of the guests, both ignoring where the men might have come from.

Tables for the reception were set up in the back yard under the shade trees. Clint and Oscar mainly Oscar had the job of tugging out of town guests around to shake hands with the men and hug the women. That was before and again after the double wedding.

Many appeared surprised when Gus and his wife walked over to greet Leo's boy with so much enthusiasm that Neil thought he was being set up as a joke. "I'm Gustavus Angus McNew of McNew Plantations. This is my wife, Drusilla," said Gus.

"Yes, Mr. McNew, I sat behind you, mostly stood, during the wedding," said Neil. "I assumed that it was you, the man who in art history was the pictured man with the hoe, who was building dad's cabin out there. You're the best, dad said, and he was sure lucky to find that you were available."

"I appreciate his recommendation," said Gus.

"Like everybody else around here, I didn't know Leo had a son," said Gus.

He didn't either for a long time.

"He was mighty proud of you, and you would have been the first among his friends to be told about me," said Neil. They talked on and on about this 'great event.' of Max and Mollie's lives, and their possible future together.

"All of a sudden Dad had a whole big family." Max is his first name, he was forced eventually to declare. That's really how we'll know him from now on.

"Well, I'd say that my father was just as proud of a good citizen like you and as pleased of you as the best of your wide trade and all that brag, and that the locals also were all eager to endorse you as the man who could do anything. Now that we've gotten all that out of the way, let's go to the tables and get something to eat. Drusilla, which of these fine foods did you fix for the bounty before us on this table?"

Gus was shaking his head. "Just like his pappy," he said. Later, Neil would say that meeting Gus and talking to him was one of the highlights of his visit.

It was exactly what he'd heard about the South, and proud that every bit of the day's activities appeared to honor his father, Leo, or Maxim, who said that as soon as this was over if there was any daylight left, he'd take Gus and Neil up the river and look at the land that Neil would have as his inheritance, "the only thing I could leave to my son, if I could ever find him, I'd said not long ago, of course with some kind of house well appointed on it," Max said. He added, "As I think more of it, I believe that is something your Mama would want me to do," Gus said to Neil.

"I reckon —- that's a word you can see what part of the local lingo I've already picked up —- that you might have wished to talk about to me, as a boy and his daddy," Neil said, recalling Maxim's remarks.

Neil said to his father: "The part of my life you probably are interested in most is my having been married and divorced. You might need to recognize that it is first priority in our talking about my life with my mother and your love for her. After our talk about my brief life with a wife is out of the way then there is no need to ever mention it again."

"Yes, I married her on a day filled with bad judgment. You should have met her for me and advised me before I did that really foolish thing. Your respected good judgment would have saved me a lot of grief, even as you could have been blinded as I was in her presence."

"You could very well have been taken in as I was. Her beauty her soft words like a baby's coos its first speech like the bells of a holy temple could have blinded all your senses as it did mine and like so many men I've known in New York. It is a city of much glamour, which was ruled despite all the care given you by a good mother from the time you were becoming aware of that side of yourself. Satan had timed his introduction of such women for his evil plans, just as a man of my age had arrived at an acceptable time to receive it. I was sorely awakened and became a victim of the most beautiful woman this side of Hades."

"I say that because Satan brought her to me straight out of hell. She was raised on a farm some miles down country from New York City, and she had come to the big town looking for a man with money and knew how to spend it and she thought I was it."

"I was a playboy on Wall Street driving that British made car out there, or one like it —- I've had three —- and spent money like I'd sold my soul to the devil at the devil's highest price. That car is an evil thing. She soon learned the truth about me and that car. By then, she'd bedded half the young and maybe a few men a little older in tailor-mades and in convertibles like mine for miles around, all while I was at work. Her plans were to have fun in spite of that little old marriage ensuring her future at the same time."

"I had a good lawyer, right off Wall Street. You'll agree that they are the best in the world. He still cost me most of the money I had in the bank but it paid for my big mistake. The devil got the hindmost and I had learned a big lesson. Since I've buried the perfume of her the sweet soft oh so soft skin with it I pray that you will never have need to mention her to me again."

"I need to hear you tell about my mother, what you two together had sensed in the traditional relationship to one another and the intrinsic nature of each other that blessed both of you in a clandestine hour I know to have been love what both of you would have known as love and not as two ships that passed in the night."

"I was held to her bosom and not sent to a home for the misdirected or called by some as lost souls, for which I have held as grateful for her always and for you even as your absence from one another turned into a near tragedy."

"Please always remember her as you were forced to leave her at a time in our history that brought the two of you together for an instant and very well tossed the ship that left you in time's waters for a meeting once again on a future's unknown isle of an afterlife. I am pleased that the gods that govern this sort of thing were so kind and understanding."

"Sir, my father, I'm thankful that it was you who was so loved by my mother and I'm so fortunate that it was you that I have found for my soul satisfaction and the few years that we will be together as father and son for what is left for us on this Earth. I want you to know now that I have made up my mind to spend the rest of my life perhaps as near your side that I had aimed to spend it at all near my good mother's grave and I will love my stepmother and will be ever by her side as long as she might survive you if that comes to pass and as she will allow me."

"I may not find a job here in your town and as soon mine, but maybe in Knoxville; even Lexington which also is not far away, off the Interstate in both places and I'm sure that either or the other might provide a home nearby for me —- and a job," said Neil.

Maxim told his brilliant son who talks in the language of a poet how thankful he was of him to have made such decision. "Let me talk to my friend Frank at the bank before you settle down for a bed in either town, like a good Cossack, who would be at home anywhere, you'd be maybe a bit surprised to find with so much going on in your present working world soon to be so widely known and accepted in a hillbilly town like this one."

Their conversation on Neil's future was carried on —- in of all places, the restful area within the wide loose confines of one major back porch on the closer mountain where Clint lived that was ever appreciated by any limited coterie of friends of man and their women or for the friends of women and their men —- both sexes among the small group left in this hemisphere who could be trusted. Neil thought it was the one place in the world with the porch and its mountain and the mountain opposite built by the world's architect for kings and their queens.

Clint's friend Frank was there and the talk for Neil was how to make money in the hinterland and the simple and easy way to get to New York and return home before supper the next day.

Clint and Doris as man and wife were living in Doris' mother's house and talking about building a back porch 'that overlooked the beautiful town creek.'

Oscar was telling Doris how Peewee was getting along as a staff writer on his little newspaper and hoping that his own daughter might join the gang when she graduated from college, next year. They both said they could easily have found jobs in larger places but as in chorus they said they hoped to make their homes back in the old hometown.

Richard and Evelyn had stayed around a couple days after the wedding and he and Neil had become good friends and went off together in Neil's car to explore the town and countryside especially what was left of the old mining enterprise. They'd been the only two outlanders, or strangers at the wedding and a good deal of speculation grew up around them. Neil's car still opened a lot of eyes and wishes.

Dick told Clint how surprised he'd been when he learned that Evelyn had talked about how she'd often wished she could write for a newspaper. He'd been asleep at the time and said you learn something new every day when married to an educated and talented woman. He recalled the afternoon in their home on the ranch when Clint had opened up about why he'd wanted as a young man to get into the newspaper business, and there sat Evelyn absorbed in her knitting but apparently being fully interested in Clint's every word.

Clint said he'd never realized how easy it was to persuade someone in his audience who might be influenced by what he was talking about. So why hadn't this worked with the efforts of the members of OMEN to make the people aware of the dangers of the change in the climate and threats of changes in the ecology.

Of course facing a live audience was different from holding a written invitation in their leisure moments under a night time reading lamp, which may as well have been a work of fiction.

Dick and Neil quickly learned how the hill people had taken to the simple foods that were offered them from words scribbled on a piece of cardboard nailed to the wall behind the counter at Lucy's Place and Country Store and they talked about how much they'd enjoyed a baloney on white bread sandwich without the condiments as well as did the local field workers and truck drivers who had stopped at Lucy's for the same thing.

Man, how those country boys stood around that convertible parked outside a country store, rubbing the upholstery and wondering about how the car looked under the hood.

Clint thought of this as a different twist to ambitions hopes of young men compared by their elders of a former day. He thought it was a questionable omen for the future of the country, since the automobile was reason enough to arouse a feeling that came with making money, an ambition considered above all other dreams the greater of the times.

As for what lay ahead when changes in the heavens had begun making the Earth's climate itself felt in the lives of many Earthlings, so few disruptions to their daily comfort occurred that citizens of the queen, no, her subjects in the colonies, were easily learning to live with what had been left to their young lives by their parents.

The city got state help building a road out to Max and Oscar's two model homes the first to be built in their new subdivision on the other side of the river.

Too many spectators had attempted to drive along the gravel road out that way to see just what two citizens had created, that so many of them, mostly in attempts to avoid the traffic going the other way on that muddy trail originally created to haul building supplies had also recalled their ancestors' deep deep mud, so the governor and his influence with the General Assembly got a real 'nice' road built, which consisted of one little spray of tar or blacktop over a bed of six inches of tamped down gravel.

You could see what would happen before the end of summer after a tide of locals drove out to check on the progress of the development of their first real subdivision.

Mollie hoped before the summer was over that she'd like to go for a wide open spin in the British convertible that her stepson Neil brought to town some months ago, the day before her wedding to Max. The car had been parked on the street since that day with the top down unless it looked like rain so the locals could examine it and its red leather interior.

Neil watched the blue sky as close as a country boy watched the clock on a working day in the field of corn or tobacco on a hot summer's day.

Clint was helping put together plans for a drive 'to somewhere just any old way.' He mainly wanted to take the whole bunch down to the Chief's and Evelyn's country to view progress on that motel of which he now was part owner, but that was a longer expedition.

One beautiful .day not long after he and Doris would be in the back seat of Neil's car with Neil. Mollie would drive with Max beside her and they would scoot over into Virginia to show Neil the magnificent countryside in the southern part of the state. It was a workday, a normal Wednesday, a fifth wheel for Oscar or no seat for a sixth person. It was his press day which meant he had to stay in town, which solved the question.

Neil was held —- you'd say, nature bound —- you were far above on a mountain road looking upon some of the most beautiful long valley of green grass and farmland that you'd find anywhere in the world.

He was experiencing, obviously, "All that love and care of the Earth that any citizen of the world, especially in Europe, could imagine and envy," he said.

They found a small town with a restaurant on Main Street which had an interesting menu that summoned ahs and smiles and other surprises.

As they'd ordered, and while they waited for their food, Neil brought up the subject of OMEN and why they'd decided to give up the idea of trying to save the world from all the evident threats in the skies and changes in the ecology of the Earth.

That left Clint or Max to take the floor. Both men of OMEN hesitated, so Clint's silence left it up to Max to answer. Clint believed that Max needed this moment to impress his son. Max readily did so with the headlined press reports of discussion that he could draw from, reams of speculation and such little Congressional debate and their reports to the people for the previous five years. Some said hot and cold activities of outer and inner space for decades of human life and from the Earth itself, was the cause.

"All right," said Maxim, "I reckon it's me. Where I came from, on the steppes of Russia it's all sky, so we've always been conscious of the sun and the rain and the seasons for all of our needs; which is the seed and the animals and wood to heat our homes."

"This has been the key to man's survival since the beginning of our place on Earth. Blessed with these elements for life, and for our daily existence, we've organized societies, first by tribes and then our towns and cities and our government, and places where we can thank our gods for all that comes from Heaven and the Earth."

"If I were giving a class lecture the school would allot me forty minutes to talk of how it came about. I hope to do it in far less time, before the sun sets," spoke Maxim.

"Let's look at where we are and where we were, and our possible survival. We know that the land where we sit once was beneath the sea because of the beds of limestone which came from the bones of living creatures, and the coal that was formed beneath us came from what was once forest. We find imprints of ferns and other vegetation in the coal, as it is mined. The sea moved out and the people such as they were moved in and settled."

"This speaks of changes in the ecology of the Earth as nothing new. This happened before according to the story of Adam and Eve that people who had learned to read in their Bible and became their history. The only other source of people origin was the one about the fish that came from the sea and grew arms and legs. Of late is the tale of explorers from outer space."

"Now we have people, and they've been fighting each other ever since they came.

So began myths and religious arguments about how the gods attempted to keep the people in line when it appeared that evil, wickedness, vice and destruction had come about, so the good, the respect of God in the Christian religion and other gods would remind them of their sins and invite them back to the fold, or the church, or Heaven's dictates."

"Many of Earth's people believe that all that current business out there is Heaven's reminder that we must change our ways or we'll have another Sodom and Gomorrah."

Max continued, sure of himself: "Let me say that extreme weather conditions in the recent past intermittently halted a proud routine of our country's commerce and the schools and almost all free everything else for several days at a time, often setting records. The long spells of cold with new snow on snow made you think that the Earth had turned on its axis."

"There was evidence that much of the people's suffering and their government and even public concern for them were inept or ignorant or without passion. No one appeared to know what they could do about it, so they each blamed someone else. This bothered them but not enough about society's place on Earth. As a result there was no serious belief or hope for a solution. So we in OMEN did the unpopular thing and tried to get people at least aware of what was happening."

"We again asked for people's feedback, for one thing. What we got were just about all chicken scratches in the cold ground, trying to persuade us to believe that no one cared, so we considered the fact that our efforts were fruitless. We almost decided that if the people were not interested, why then our little contribution to the effort was in vain. At least we for the moment should just live it up like everybody else, including feasts and Saturday night celebrations of TV games and parties, like the rest of them."

"It would mean no action by us but for only a little while, we said. That was not why we had formed our little organization. We couldn't and should not quit entirely because that was not the good old American Way. Pretty soon we will start up with new hopes and new ideas, when we see that time and the people again are ready. That is only for the moment. That is not the end of our story — we'll be back. We knew that in the past extraordinary events that appeared important at the time soon moved to a lower level and such omen were as soon forgotten. Even so, we must stay alert." Maxim said that was all he had to say.

Clint, among a larger and public group a day or two later, believed it was time to suggest Neil's latest opportunity for a local job and his perhaps decision to stay in town maybe even until hell freezes over or we were prepared to kick him out.

"My friend Frank said his bank board had voted even without Neil's permission or knowledge to offer him a vice presidency at the bank whenever he's ready. The presidency will follow not far in the future upon Frank's retirement that is, considering Frank's, ahem, advanced age. We'd have the only city in Kentucky, as far as we knew, with a bank being run by a recent graduate of Wall Street," a knowledgeable somebody on the street said.

Clint was asked by one of the others in the little group, "Who says?" Included were several investors in the bank, many of them on its board. "We won't dare say who."

"Wouldn't the state board have something to say about that?" He was told, we won't say who. "Not without an embarrassment or two, which would be called 'an interference' in the bank's legal authority to do so," added Frank.

It seemed that every business, every commercial entity that was ever thought of in the new democracy except the blacksmith whose shop was hidden away from the lower town scope and it wouldn't be long before even he would be required to have a federal license, began to open where the spots could be found on Main or nearby streets. Clint began to think his town would soon have too many stores for good business.

Clint and his new wife Doris had set a new societal identity to the local leadership of the social scene. They were accompanied in crowned identity by Leo, rapidly becoming known as Maxim, and his wife, Mollie. It was said at first in local social folklore that this was a greater attainment in small town life in America than in the greater cities of the land in the latter part of the Twentieth Century. Small town girl marries Russian count.

Gus with all his knowledge about his country, America, and his apparently greater faith than most people in a sense of man's destiny on the Earth, of man and his God, finally agreed to come aboard and to attend most sessions of whatever it might be called. These were held on Clint's back porch or in Doris' and his living room, maybe down the street with Maxim and Mollie.

Gus said that before, when the others sought his presence, that Drusilla felt 'ill at ease' (there's no better way to describe it and we ask forgiveness for the use of a cliché) socializing with white people for whom she'd once done their washing.

As it turned out Drusilla fit in like the first day of spring. So, on the club floor we had politics and books and fashions and new preachers and teachers. Also a little weather and too much rain and new foods and the cost of living and the difficulty of getting the kids into college and keeping them there and what they were supposed to do there.

That subdivision out on the old Gelig farm was rapidly losing its identity that was in the houses being erected. They were a variety of modern designs, yet of a forward look that was the new standard American fashion and size, a whole new lot of social centers, or you might say a movement of an entertainment variety. Everybody liked to party.

It wasn't long before Gus was no longer the only builder. The success of the site and local up state demand for the standard homes movement that had begun to attract all those outsiders especially the larger and successful corporations and their imported workers with mostly manufactured and pretty architectural panel designs from the bigger towns around the small burg in Southern Kentucky. New faces were on the streets, louder voices at PTA meetings said to having been more in favor of less traditional teaching methods.

The town was being dragged kicking and resistant to criticism into the narrow edge of the Twenty-first Century, the new people said. Oscar's editorials more often catered to an educated people and Oscar boasted of just that in his now several sections keyed to a Post Office uniform weight with larger circulation. He had a page with more national news and fewer lines throughout the paper of local gossip, which was being promoted by the new neighbors as quaint, such that had no place among a sophisticated people.

They were only concerned with today; the 'future', what is that? You had to get your paper most places with a coin in a street machine.

Oscar became president of the Chamber of Commerce. He'd still talk now and then of his 'beat' associates, but he never said any of them would be proud of him. He said he knew they were waiting out there, the few who knew about him and his past, to see if he saluted the flag of the United States.

Doris babied Clint like the baby boy she never had. He came to appreciate Peewee, and not be suspicions of her intentions like maybe she had grown up under Clint's tutelage with 'daddy' and the expected requests for money for this or for that, and he usually would say, 'ask your mother.' When she returned home from Richmond where she was working in a dental office she brought along a girl friend or two for a weekend. So far, there were few men, never the same one, who might have been a possibility as a marriage partner.

Doris said it was time to rid her of 'Peewee', and encourage use of her birth name, Kathleen Marie. That meant she'd hence be called, by her newer friends as the now accepted Katie Marie. The name Peewee, uh, Katie Marie, fits as a mountain identity. Everywhere it is or was like in the old days; now comes Lucy Mae, Dolly Seal or Delva June or Ella Sue. Her new hillbilly neighbors generally cite both names when referring to her or introducing any of them to outsiders; enough of that.

Doris and Clint's home in the flat country below the mountain became. or Clint said it was the social center of the whole town. Sometimes even the cabin got crowded. Girls, young and old, appeared to be everywhere. The entire population or at least Maxim said it was, all waited for Neil to find a wife. And they too were everywhere. The bigger papers and the AP sent reporters to interview Neil when he went to work for the bank. The press still hadn't finished with Maxim. His identity as a former Cossack fascinated a spoiled, national and bored people. Mollie wanted him on her arm almost every time she left the house, generally for a walk along the city's streets where she could show him off just like Neil's foreign car with its red leather seats.

Clint at first still had his moments of 'other' or outside smart aleck critics. To those people he dared not call his 'moments' anything but daydreams, like 'visions,' but they continued and disturbed him and he'd begun to keep them buried inside his head. Ever since the day he came out of his month-long coma, here they came, sometimes disguised as TV commercials. These big pictures, so real, let's say 'revelations' shoot out every week or two sometimes more often. He had no idea of the scene of the happenings, only that they might be identified as 'Acts of God.'

A few days later or sooner, what he had witnessed were spread across the news in the papers or TV. He could tell no one about them, even members of OMEN. As far as he knew or was concerned there was no reason why he, humble human being or even a citizen of a wee entity or just another country on the earth, should suddenly be blessed by the heavens or dispatches from elsewhere.

(He'd received scenes of earthquakes in which hundreds or even thousands would die, or it would be a terrorist act in a populous place that resulted in many deaths, or even a school boy with a gun found in a drawer at home that was used to avenge what the press called a stream of insults, that is, for no other known or suspected motive.)

(Many hints of changes in the ecology could or would be traced by the courage of a few editors to the change in the heavenly elements that controlled the winds and the storms and earthly phenomena. No one believed that any more, so Clint and members of OMEN continued to sit on it, refusing to offer any comment on any theory that might be suggested.)

Clint thought how his OMEN gang might reach the people or even expected them to become aware of any outside threats to their lives. His society already was splintered into so many sides of egotism. The politicians had divided the voters and the American people into women voters, which was one bloc. Then came the unions, ethnic groups, which meant what each believed was vital to their interest. And it didn't stop there. Gun owners wanted special laws that protected them; school teachers were an entity apart, and it never stopped.

He thought the thunder that brought about World War II encouraged the people at once to provide so many aspects of their uneducated selves to its need and they were many that would demand their talents and participation.

As war clouds accumulated his people found jobs in the north welcomed since they had been jobless so long; they found pride in their work. Clint's hill neighbors by tradition long had gone to Ohio and Michigan for jobs now would build tanks and other armament. They bought used cars and came home it looked like to Clint every weekend.

Clint especially was proud to be among Marine Corpsmen who tented with him on islands of the Southwest Pacific in the war against the two enemy nations. They were prepared to hit another beach where the Japanese were waiting for them with a firepower that was surprising to American soldiers who had been trained for battle in conventional warfare. Of course they experienced an apprehension by all those men of battle through the ages and by previous American warriors before their time, unashamedly but with the courage expected of them in battle.

This was apparent as they crouched in the landing boats scratching their bodies like they'd been attacked by a flight of mosquitoes, wiping the cold sweat from their brows. They ran their hands up and down their rifles as if they were cleaning them, rechecking the magazines and the live ammunition on their belts. Clint recognized, felt the expected pangs of fear traveling through his bloodstream. They re-checked their belts for their cartridge cases; the men carried their canteens, and most or all had smaller blades for use in hand-to-hand fighting. They were taught about the machete, carried into battle by the Japanese, had learned in boot camp that the weapon began in South America for cutting cane in the fields. It too was carried on their belts.

Many had replaced watches they'd received as gifts on birthdays or upon graduation and left behind, keeping cheap watches they did not care to lose. Clint knew that most of the men, the religious men, who were praying that they would survive the battle and return home when it was over. He knew that most were religious. They were intent on their mission which they had anticipated since they'd left home. Some even looked forward to battle, or pretended to.

In the early days of the Southwest Pacific war the survivors of one battle or even a second invasion were asked to fall out for the next expedition. The country was training replacements, but the raw fighters were still in boot camp. The U.S. was learning how to fight another sort of warfare.

In the meantime you cultivate in a reserved sort of way a bunch of new friends, like Asa the big Indian from Oklahoma; like men whose college years were spent at MIT or Yale or Penn State who otherwise thought Clint could have sought commissioned ranks, but preferred to be privates in the Marine Corps.

They had time to show pictures of the girls back home. Clint warned against the practice. In movies, men in battle the photo displayer soon would be shone in a bloodied scene. It was movie practice or custom to arouse sympathy, so "Beware the movie scene of the man pulling the photo from his wallet, since he is the next man to die." Even the music of a battle scene in the movies was like the 'volley and thunder' that accompanied the horse soldiers of the men in a cavalry charge.

About always he believed that the music of the times, and from what they'd become addicted to in school, by radio and by choice, echoed often along their minds' sound tracts.

They would be thinking of girls they knew, their moms and dads, all back there.

They could be thinking of the day they got home and walked downtown in full uniform, their coat of many colors, and the girls would be in awe of their uniforms and the men who wore them. Everybody would for sure be impressed by a Marine.

At rest following the battle, they didn't boast of their valor, their bravery beneath a roaring tattoo of machine gun fire. They would ask who died and if they had suffered.

Clint as a young man was a people watcher. He had no right to judge other men or women; it is a human trait, a fellow Marine said, and he'd grown up in agreement, or it was a method of adaptation to friendship, likely an aspect of the human psyche.

He'd said often that "I would not or could not share a foxhole with that man." As he watched these men, he recalled others, in those days mostly fellow Marines or Seabees.

As it had become a civilian trait for him through the years, it dwelt more today in his mind than ever. Just lately he'd become concerned since he'd run into a few, often he thought more than expected, with courage among men and women he encountered. What did this portend for the future of his country, which he had always considered to be a light to individual residents of countries in the rest of the world? Why were there so few men or women of courage out there?

It was upon his personal judgment, call it relationship to a fellow citizen, schoolmate or soldier, that he had been encouraged to the formation of OMEN. He would always look for men and women of courage.

It was so with his country; at first, after shedding his uniform and meeting himself, that is, fellow former warriors in every classroom, in cafeteria lines, at book stores, even movie lines. He learned not to talk about the war since the other fellow could easily top your own with their dodging of bullets and outshooting the enemy.

And then appeared to him another split it seemed in American society. You lived in a blue state, meaning the vast number of citizens voted the liberal ticket in politics, or you came from a red state. The latter (red) on their map, was not acceptable by the blues because they did not show the proper respect for their countrymen by vote in the belief that they believed that the country was better off as it was re-designed by the politicians of the post-World War Two era. The blues were better educated, made more money.

His own state was printed red since they were full of ignorant hillbillies. The blue state was the dragon and the red people hoped for the golden knight to come out and make battle not with the state itself, but the arrogance it represented. The founding fathers, you learned from the columnists, even after two hundred years or so, were wrong. The politicians called for uniting America even after supporting their popular views over the red state and blue state division.

What all this did for education in the schools of his hill country was set back right where they were before they were re-defined meant that the old challenge was back. The students there realize what will happen when they graduate and leave to find jobs in blue country.

It was a matter of the individual and his place in the great scheme of things. Clint thought that society had largely returned to an era of lack of respect for his country's flag and most of its two hundred-plus year cultivated institutions. Too many ideas of the kids' revolution of the fifties remained in his opinion, waiting for the 'right leadership' to get its better ideas going again. People of the blue states it was believed apparently had little respect for the country's institutions and considered the flag as just 'an old rag.'

The man of faith in the Constitution walks alone. His God had disappeared in the halls of academe. His people had watched the other society's favor of money and its accumulation and his people knew where it had come from, much of it from them.

So, to ask a simple question, what is there about the Blue State and the Red State that is of some consequence? Little, you say, because this, too, will pass. Tomorrow it will be the top hat and the tam. It will be the high-stepping thoroughbred show horse and the dray. It will be the Cadillac and the Chevy. It will be the cigar and the chaw.

What matters are pride, honesty, and dignity. Pride, one of the deadly sins, but without arrogance or haughtiness; honesty, with truth not capable of falsehood or lack of trust as in dignity and dignity itself with a salute to the other two and its education in manners like the castle's knights of old, all or many stood out in anyone's estimation.

Chapter Seven

"My name is Oscar Bell Blues." (Upon his introduction as president of the Chamber of Commerce).

"When I landed in your town my first day as new owner of your little weekly newspaper, I had to ask myself, 'what in carnation have I gotten myself into?' Which was a quite mild picture of my life before I even got to your city; I even thought of what I encountered as 'lost city,' really, believe it or not."

"It was a low point in my life. The paper had nothing to show for itself, a small and unpaid circulation, almost invisible business support, and a pile of ancient and neglected abused equipment that took all my time and ingenuity to restore it."

"Even then it took all my resources, every penny I could borrow or round up down at the poor farm to come up with the purchase price, which you could say was what I was looking for in my dreams and that I might be able to swing it. It had to be."

"And your town: the sun was shining thank the powers that be, which helped maybe just a little. The buildings were dark and shabby like a pair of overalls that needed washing. The streets needed much repair, and the people on the streets appeared sad and without any confidence like the Children of Israel in the wilderness who had given up on the Promised Land."

"Yet, in the struggling years that followed for both this person and your city things just happened. I owe what appeared to be much improvement in the paper to my honest sweat and many sleepless nights and a good deal of help from some of your merchants."

"As for the city. you yourself did it all. You've made it into a smiling city, clean overall and beautiful and efficient in its operation and government, a town that could boast its deserved pride among any municipality as near its size in the state."

"It shows why an honor such as this to me generally erupts into a universal animated streetwise discussion why you elected me to be your president. Of course I am proud of the honor you've shown me, and it is, you'll never know how much. I hope to be the initiator of a new day in our little city, even as our country is being led in a new direction by a new President, one being compared to the likes of Abraham Lincoln."

"It is now time to list my goals for our city:

First, it is to find jobs for the mountain citizens that surround us and who have fed us whether we advertise it or not, who lost their coal mining jobs.

Then there is the little college that is an offshoot of the state university. Too many of its graduates leave for the big time the minute they receive their diplomas. Too, we should underwrite scholarships for those who can't afford the nearly invisible tuition, and for the several students who need part-time jobs for living expenses. For talented art students, the kids who produce acceptable art, we could buy and hang their creations in our homes.

We could better welcome the outside educators to the college who come here partly because they have evinced a somewhat missionary feeling for living and serving in a poor mountain community such as ours. There is no question that the little community college has certainly found its place in its contribution to the local economy, The college's visiting celebrated citizens with talents in many areas, and outstanding musicians and lecturers ask for some ticket help from the community that they might come with more anticipation. I see needs that are many and we should strive to meet them, to offer it for no other reason than to prove that the college is a great additional asset to our little town.

That's all I have to say. So let me hear once more how I can better serve you. I will certainly need and appreciate all the help and suggestions from every one of you as we enter the new century that is almost upon us."

Clint and Maxim, who had been seated at the rear of the court house big legal room, smiled broadly as Oscar left the platform with its homemade church lectern and walked down the center aisle to greet them. The room was utilized by everybody in town for larger than routine small gatherings.

"You've come a long way, Oscar," said Clint, "that is, from those rebel days when you were looking for your country, as well as for your soul. Your mother and father would have been proud."

"Yeah," said Oscar, "if they had lived to be here today. They both died in a car head-on highway collision the first months after I was born. I'll never know how I survived the accident that killed both of them and left me an orphan."

"Does that mean you grew up in an orphan's home?" asked Maxim. "You never told us about that."

"I was taken in by my father's brother Tom. He and his wife, my new mother and aunt, Peggy raised me. I reckon I loved them both for what they did for me, but my new papa lost all his money gambling, and he also was an alcoholic. They really were good to me but I could see that I was a burden to them. Nevertheless I left Aunt Peggy as soon as I was old enough, trying as best as I could to stay in touch and remember her birthday. They'd also given me a sister and a brother."

"So here ye be, in a new life and all full of good will and for God's sake president of an establishment outfit that would amaze your hippie buddies," Clint continued, with not even a little sincerity. He also was somewhat embarrassed that he had encouraged Oscar to reveal an aspect of his boyhood which so far he had kept 'hidden' from his friends. Yet he was assured that nothing in it made any difference.

Just the same Oscar's reminiscence came crashing into his memory. His own boyhood was all-American, but when he got into the city high school he was conscious of an inadequacy; his hillbilly status was his undoing. The city girls ignored him, despite his Hollywood groomed blond hair and his he-man good looks.

The gloom that settled on his brow came and went, sometimes more than he could bear, and he wished he could find someone other than his mom and dad he could discuss it with. On cloudy days one after the other it returned, even in college and in the corps.

On occasions lately Oscar had offered an excuse as to why he couldn't join them, in some activity or other. He would say that the paper needed him, especially on press day which meant late into the night. Also, Mollie who knew a lot of medical people, said he was having bladder trouble and had to visit the bathroom every hour on the hour. This bothered Clint because he loved the little guy like a brother. It was a stormy day which contributed to his groping for daylight, and now this.

So Clint and his other friends went ahead with their plans to drive over to Carolina for the weekend. Richard wanted them there for the grand opening of his new motel and Neil in particular was anxious to see Chief Dick again. From the moment they met they had sort of taken to each other, like blood brothers, maybe it was because both men were business minded.

Neil said that it was something new to him to have an Indian friend. In New York he said, you meet faces from just about everywhere, red and yellow and black and white, He had likely met American Indians, or Native Americans on the street but had thought of them as Mexicans or South Americans.

Mollie knew the route at least through the Smoky Mountains, about half way there.

She suggested they stop for lunch. Neil said he didn't need to look at a menu. He for sure knew just what he wanted: "Southern fried chicken and corn bread, and of course blackberry cobbler. All the restaurants down here will have it on the menu, since that's what the people want, and I can see why. I expect that means I've at last become a native mountaineer."

They dined outdoors beneath the mountains of Virginia and Carolina on local foods, mainly country ham and sandwiches which Neil ordered on the advice of the natives. He averred also that country ham added to his choice of southern foods. Their talk was of Evelyn and Richard Whitewater and how fortunate they were to live under pure air and blue skies.

In the open car and the sun on his face, Clint was challenged by recent dialogue with earth's citizens and subjects of the Queen that apparent changes in the weather were already beginning to show up.

When they reached Virginia, they were high on the mountain road that took in the green valley that rolled toward a sister mountain, and gave them a view that could be matched only in Heaven, as he imagined it must be.

He could see why the citizens were not prepared to believe that changes in the weather pattern were upon us, now just mentioned with a small warning that more is to come and that it would be as the ecologists had been trying to warn us about.

It already had settled on the brow with which he and his friends in OMEN had decided to postpone their current activities until a time in the future when they felt it would again be upon them with its own huge slap in their face with a greater force. The people had endured but ignored nature's serious rampages before and they would accept them in the future.

At the moment Clint was prepared to accept it all. He was ready to accept life with the woman he had married and decided to live it up with her, as she hoped to find it in him to make her happy.

His Heaven would rearm the elements he knew and warnings would become the usual thing, at least twice more. He was glad to be with all his new family today and celebrate the success of their new friend which would be a pleasant change in their lives.

He recalled the day in the parlor of Chief Dick with Evelyn in their ranch home. Clint understood that the Indian had made his business a success before choosing from his many women, one ot them to join him in his home and life and future.

By now, time and history was acting in his favor and even though he was years older than his new bride, they were extremely happy together. "It had been worth it," Richard said, "I couldn't have found a better woman", and he was proud of her native American heritage. "She's smarter than me, and already being recognized for her writing, and even I can understand her poetry." "I thought she was the best, most beautiful woman I ever met, and still do."

Clint realized as he was talking that day in their home, trying to explain why he had come to visit, that Chief Dick was the smartest man he had ever known. He recalled the day he chose journalism as his life work and the newspaper which he owned and gave up. He had said that day that his hope was to help save the world. He noticed that Evelyn appeared not to be aware of their conversation but instead was wrapped up in a book she held in her lap.

His Cossack friend also had welcomed his life change since he had found his son. He watched the old soldier seated in the front seat with his back to him and was aware of the beauty of life, which was obvious.

The third member of OMEN would never find happiness until his wife gave up her wondering and what she would describe as finding herself. That's what she and her fellow protestors said was the only motive for what they were doing. His newspaper friend was never involved in any other romantic situation of which Clint was aware, his life only centering around two things, his newspaper and his daughter.

Clint thought again of Evelyn and realized a great hope for the future of the earth lay in the hands of her and her kind. In this hope lay his full confidence that the earth would continue to feed and sustain the future of its people.

He recalled the poems of John Milton, which even after satan rebelled and left the sight of God with thousands of his followers, he was sure that his Lord, God himself had never doubted the end of His creation. There would be a place in the future for man in His Hall of Angels.

The Indian met them as they drove up to the front of a magnificent structure the likes of which they had never seen. It was an elaborate wigwam with the frontal imprint of a Western teepee you could tell also by the poles reaching for the sky above it all, crossed as if they jutted from the roof. The edifice itself was of a tanned mountain stone, like the rocks that appeared in the land around the countryside.

Dick told them their rooms were ready. "Rest up and I will be back in a couple of days. Neil is going home with me. We will be back in time for the dedication."

After another excellent meal in the motel restaurant, Clint said he wanted to look at the kiosk he noticed on the way in. The four of them gathered around the small slender building.

Beneath its slightly gabled roof or overhang sat what was obviously an American infantryman's boot, glistening in its bronze finish against the bright noonday sun. Below was the legend: "Dedicated to the men and women of the world who died in their fight for freedom." And then the words . . .

The bodies are not here. They lie in the sands of Omaha Beach, of Iwo Jima and Tarawa and at Guadalcanal. They are in the dust of the roads to Paris and Berlin, the sacred fields of old Russia and the land of the Cossacks along the Don River where they fought against Communism."

"You can see who wrote those words," said Mollie. "Yes," said Clint, "they are from the pen of a young Indian woman named Evelyn who wanted to write. Her words now are on the laps of the gods and the appeal is in the hands of the Great Spirit."

Printed in the USA
CPSIA information can be obtained
at www.ICGtesting.com
LVHW011516211023
761548LV00002B/45